Praise for

"Marie Sutro's debut novel, Dark Associations, may just be this generation's Silence of the Lambs. Erotic and frightening, it keeps the reader guessing until the last pages."

—STEVE ALTEN, *New York Times* Best-Selling Author of *Meg* & *Domain*

"Dark Associations is a crime thriller extraordinaire that offers a deviously devilish mix of madness, murder, and mayhem. Marie Sutro's finely tuned and polished debut effort channels the best of Thomas Harris, while serving up a serial killer who'd make even Hannibal Lecter blush, and in rookie detective Kate Barnes, has come up with a heroine every bit the equal of Clarice Starling. Grisly without being gratuitous, Dark Associations is like a literary battering ram, as relentless as it is riveting."

—JON LAND, *USA Today* Best-Selling Author of *Strong Cold Dead*

"Dark Associations is a wickedly compelling debut by Marie Sutro, who presents us with a great cast of characters and a villain who's as sadistic as they come. This one will keep you guessing right up till the end."

—SPENCER KOPE, Author of *Collecting the Dead*

"There is nothing I love more on a dark night than sitting with a book and trying to work out 'who-done-it' before the truth is revealed. I love watching and reading murder mysteries, be it the more widely enjoyed CSI or the old classics first penned by Agatha Christie or Sir Arthur Conan Doyle. When I read a book of this genre it has a lot of expectations to meet in order to receive a five star and Dark Associations ticked all the boxes for me. It is dark, gripping, tense, and filled with deep and interesting characters. From the onset I knew this book had promise, but I did not expect to be so blown away by the author's skill at creating tension and a complex plot to keep the reader guessing right until the end. If time had allowed there would have been no prying this book from my hand, and I always wanted to read just a little longer. I will certainly be on the look out for more books from Marie Sutro, and would not find myself surprised, in the future, to find myself watching it on TV. A great book, deserving of five stars and my highest praise."

—K.J. SIMMELL, Author of *Darrienia: The Forgotten Legacy Series* & Blogger

DARK ASSOCIATIONS

A Kate Barnes Thriller

DARK ASSOCIATIONS

Marie Sutro

VIPER PRESS
AN IMPRINT OF A&M PUBLISHING
FLORIDA

DARK ASSOCIATIONS
Published by Viper Press
An imprint of A&M Publishing, L.L.C.
West Palm Beach, FL. 33411
www.AMPublishers.com

ISBN: 978-1-943957-03-3

Printed in the United States of America

10 9 8 7 6 5 4 3 2 1

For Dad & Little:

Thanks for the love, laughter and smiles.

ACKNOWLEDGMENTS

Years ago, I came upon one of those books which merged the best of science fiction with the transformative magic of good storytelling. For days after reading *The Loch*, I sang the book's praises to anyone who would listen—extolling the virtues of the author who had spun such a thrilling adventure tale about that lovely Scottish lake.

Little did I know that years later I would have the opportunity to work with that same author. Steve Alten's contribution to this book has been invaluable. He has been an incredible mentor who has challenged me to become a better storyteller. I will be forever grateful for his advice and support.

There are also those to whom I owe my gratitude for leading me through the ins and outs of disciplines which are not in my normal wheelhouse. Dena Webster was kind enough to start me on the right path into the world of psychology and the study of psychopaths in particular. Joy Viray generously shared her wisdom, as well as her crime lab with me, and was a great sport about fielding a few fevered text messages regarding potential plot twists. Joe Amaral had the patience to impart his preeminent knowledge of software and high tech devices in spoon size increments.

My editing and production team has been stellar. Editing maven, Barbara Becker, has been an unwavering partner in this process, who has kept me on the straight and narrow when my artist's heart tried to fly too close to the sun. Tim Schulte's dedication to the editing and publishing process has surpassed expectation. Jim Ruetenik kindly helped bring life to many of my imaginings, creating some of the wonderful graphics contained herein.

And then there are those who helped spark the flame of my passion for writing and those who have tended to it. I get my love of reading from my Mom who always had a book on her nightstand—I will always cherish our shared love of good stories. My brother Dennis has been a stalwart supporter, whose infectious passion for art and dedication to the big picture has helped to smooth the twists and turns of this roller coaster ride. Annette Ragona's fearless spirit and her ease in giving have been a lighthouse.

Writing a crime thriller set in San Francisco was a foregone conclusion. Growing up, I raptly listened to the sometimes harrowing, and often times hilarious, stories of my Dad's early experiences as an undercover cop with the SFPD. I was lucky enough to consult with my Dad on this book before he moved on to a world where raccoons frolic freely in every park and where smiles and laughter come as easily to those around him, as they do to him.

Lastly, I owe so much to my best friend and husband, Dave, for every big thing and all the little things.

THE THORN CAUSES ANGUISH TO WOMEN, MISFORTUNE MAKES FEW CHEERFUL.

*(Ancient poem describing the Norse Thorn—
a rune believed to have magical properties.)*

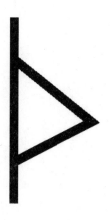

Chapter 1

THE BIG BAD WOLF eyed the beautiful young blonde woman. Innocence brimmed beneath the surface of her lustrous blue eyes.

The wolf paused, momentarily gripped by a twinge of conscience. Perhaps it was wrong to take advantage of this girl. It seemed as egregious as pulling a new bud from a perfect rose, or slaughtering a day-old calf.

But there was something else in the young woman's eyes—a persistence born of drive and ambition. The wolf knew the combination well. It was a combination that burned in the dark black depths of her own eyes.

"So you were saying?" The blonde perched on the edge of her seat, disconcerted by the long pause.

Kate Barnes flashed the young woman a quick smile, much like the wolf to whom she had mentally equated herself moments before. "I was saying that dealing with sexually deviant predators is not an easy occupation."

"But, I mean, it's got to feel good, right? Catching the bad guys and bringing them to justice?" Maggie watched as her mentor's lips compressed into a straight line.

1

"Justice is a relative term, Maggie." Kate regarded the younger woman, deciding the girl was indeed innocent. With her golden locks, sun-kissed complexion, and cornflower blue eyes, Maggie was an all-American girl. She'd been raised in Nebraska on the glowing ideals of truth, justice, and the American way.

After graduating high school two years before, Maggie had moved to San Francisco, intent on earning a criminal justice degree from San Francisco State. Her ultimate goal was to enter law enforcement. That's when the dream would fade. Another bright young being would wither in the iron grasp of the system. Glowing ideals were great for school children, but in the wrong hands they could be manipulated into weapons of mass destruction. She would learn, and it would cost her.

But Kate had not been asked to deflower the student's idealism, merely to provide basic intel on what it meant to be a detective in the San Francisco Police Department's Special Victims Unit. That was easy enough. Or so she'd hoped.

She had been paired with Maggie as part of the department's latest attempt at community outreach. The expectation was that she'd mentor an SFSU criminal justice student for three weeks.

Originally she had tried to duck the assignment, insisting she didn't have time. But the captain had been dead set on pairing Maggie with a female detective. Only two of the SVU detectives were equipped with the requisite ovary/uterus combo. One was out on maternity leave. Kate had won by default. The captain had even reassigned one of her cases so she could make time for Maggie.

Pulling the case had helped, but not much. After all, time hadn't really been the main issue—it was the very idea of being a mentor. Mentors could have ever-lasting impacts on their protégés. It was a role she was completely wrong for. There were dark things inside Kate, bad things she could not risk spreading to anyone else—especially a twenty year old who couldn't even buy herself a beer.

But here she was, sitting on the edge of the tired old couch in Maggie's apartment, feeling lupine and predatory in the presence of the radiant young woman. Kate glanced around, aware the apartment itself was a billboard for how different the two women were.

Unlike her own immaculate and sparsely decorated Victorian unit, this place was cramped and cluttered. A dated, oak entertainment center squatted across from the couch, struggling to support the ancient, box-style television set jammed into its belly. Like the old piece of oak, the rest of the furniture screamed starving student.

A panorama of smiling faces beamed at Kate from a variety of photos, which had been joyously tucked into every conceivable corner of the room. Besides Maggie, two other college coeds dominated the exhibition—probably the roommates she had mentioned earlier.

For all the tackiness and apparent overcrowding in the tiny apartment, there was an undercurrent of warmth and excitement. It wasn't just the heat radiating up from the tiny pizza parlor downstairs. It was something coming from the girls who lived here, an electric type of heat—fed by the anticipation of adulthood and the promise of a brilliant future.

Conversely, an arctic front chilled Kate's apartment year round. The only photos adorning her home were landscape prints she'd picked up some-where along the way.

The next question caught her off guard.

"Have you ever come across a psychopathic serial killer? I mean, by the real definition."

Kate was glad to hear Maggie's qualifier. The student had obviously paid attention in class. She knew to differentiate between the clinical definition of psychopath and the misapplied definition bandied about in popular culture.

"No, I haven't. You should have learned by now that serial killers are extremely rare. As I've told you before, this job isn't like what you see on TV or in the movies. It's about normal people who do horrible things." Kate's voice trailed off as her gaze turned inward.

"But aren't psychopaths normal people too? You know, like what friends and neighbors always say after they're caught."

Kate exhaled slowly. "Normal? No. Psychopaths are not normal. Clinically speaking, they are sociopaths —which means they are incapable of empathy, guilt, or conscience. They are missing the most crucial elements that make us human."

"So they're like, less than human?" Perfect blonde eyebrows pulled into a troubled frown. "But, what about all the other perps you go after?" Maggie swiped her finger across the iPad in her lap and read aloud. "Child molesters, rapists, murderers. Aren't they horrible too?"

"Of course they are. But their motivations are as varied as their opportunities for rehabilitation. Psychopaths, on the other hand, do what they do because they want to, not because something traumatic forced them to. And they never feel any guilt or remorse for what they've done." Kate paused, wanting to drive her point home. "Psychopaths cannot be rehabilitated because they are incapable of understanding that what they've done is wrong."

"Then what should we do with them? Just stick them in jail for the rest of their lives?"

Kate's thoughts returned to the justice system she served—a system that rarely lived up to its name. "I guess so."

"Come on, Kate. Don't guess, tell me what you really think." Maggie leaned over and playfully slapped her mentor's knee.

The detective drew back from the contact. Aware she'd gone too far, the student settled awkwardly back into her seat.

The girl was nothing if not direct. Kate figured she deserved an honest answer. "Kill them."

▷▷▷

The items on the shelves appeared to have been pulled fresh from the set of a horror movie. Disgusted, Maggie turned away, letting the door slam shut behind her. Her roommates were pigs, but she'd be damned if she would clean the fridge for them again.

Grumbling to no one in particular, she fished a granola bar from the box on the counter. Heading to her bedroom, her thoughts strayed to her younger brothers. Growing up, males had been the sole generators of the gross factor in her home. Mistakenly, she'd assumed all girls were naturally good housekeepers.

But gender roles were not set in stone. Just look at her mentor. Kate had been blessed with beautiful dark hair, smoldering eyes, and an awesome body. Yet, she was also a gun-toting, total badass who tried to contain her sexuality by primly binding her pretty tresses into a ponytail and wearing very little makeup.

Someday, Maggie wanted to be just like her. Well, maybe not exactly. From the little personal stuff she could wheedle out of Kate, Maggie guessed she was pretty lonely. Other than her job, she really didn't have much to talk about. She rarely dated, and had no social life at all. The woman didn't even have a pet, for cripes sake!

Settling in at the little secondhand desk tucked under the window, she decided to opt for the detective version of Kate, without the miserly old hermit thing.

Thank God she hadn't wanted anything to eat when she was here earlier. Kate would have puked if she'd seen all that nasty crap in the fridge.

Opening her laptop, Maggie pulled up the video she had been editing before hunger had lured her to the kitchen. A few minutes later, she scarfed down the last of the granola bar and opened her Facebook page. With a few swift clicks of her mouse, the video began to upload.

There was no question Katherine Barnes was the most awesome chick-detective ever. Now all Maggie's friends were going to know it too. Of course, she wouldn't bother telling them about Kate's personal life—or lack thereof. That was no one's business but hers.

Within fifteen minutes, responses came pouring in. As she'd assumed, everyone thought her mentor was super cool. Pleased, she hopped up from the desk and hurried down the hall to the bathroom. She was supposed to meet Troy in an hour.

Too bad Kate didn't have someone like Troy. Fleetingly, Maggie considered how awesome it would be if she could set her up with a guy. But the detective was at least fifteen years older than her. Guys that old didn't travel in Maggie's circle. Besides, she had never been a great matchmaker. In high school, a botched attempt at matchmaking had cost Maggie her best friend.

The perfect guy was probably out there right now, just waiting to meet Kate. Peeling off her skinny jeans, she figured it was best to leave everything in the hands of fate. Her involvement might only bring Kate misery.

ᚦᚦᚦ

January 24

Not that song again. The stupid beat had been stuck in her head all day. Maggie struggled to open her eyes. She was so tired. Maybe she'd skip her first class today. Maybe... An intense pressure in her head violently derailed that train of thought.

Opening her eyes, she fought to raise her head from the pillow. A full minute passed before her brain could make sense of the world to which she had just awakened. It was another few minutes before she understood what it all meant. A mere split second passed before terror spread throughout her body.

The beat playing in her head had not been a song at all. It had been the pounding of her pulse, driven to a maddening level by the volume of blood forced into her skull. She had been hung upside down from the ceiling in a black canvas harness with shiny metal clasps.

Like a bat in a cave, she was dangling a good three feet off the floor. Except where bats wrapped their wings protectively around their bodies, Maggie's arms had been bound behind her back. Looking upward toward the ceiling, she could see her feet had been secured separately, leaving a two-foot gap open between her legs. And, holy crap, she was naked!

As her brain processed the information, nerve receptors in her vagina telegraphed an added horror. The dry air in the room had settled over the gap between her legs, penetrating her with its icy touch.

A primitive roar tore through her throat, but she could not release it. Someone had affixed tape over her mouth to absorb her screams. God! She was going to suffocate!

Bucking wildly in the harness, Maggie struggled to free herself. Hot tears welled up from the corners of her eyes, searing her skin as they cut an unnatural trail down her forehead on their way to the floor. It was something about those tears, and the odd feeling of them running manically the wrong way across her face that destroyed what was left of her capacity for reason. Her mind spun out of control as she sucked desperately against the tape for air.

Almost six minutes passed before she began to breathe normally again. By then, the hyperventilation had pushed her to the brink of unconsciousness. With her mind momentarily stalled, her body responded instinctively, resuming respiration through her nose. As more oxygen fed her brain, the haze lifted and the wild panic returned.

Somewhere deep inside, a familiar voice commanded her to relax. It was the same voice that had helped her navigate her way out of the flooded irrigation ditch she'd fallen into as a child in Nebraska.

Fighting to control the panic, Maggie closed her eyes. If she were going to get out of this, she would have to use her brains. It was an almost impossible goal, with her body and mind screaming for escape. To quiet the chaotic cacophony in her head, she inhaled again—this time more deeply.

Who could have done this to her? The last thing she remembered was studying for her psych exam at the school library. Had she ever made it home? She looked around, searching for some clue as to how she got there.

Above her, two fluorescent lights burned brightly. The floor below was tiled, giving the large room the sterile appearance of a care facility. Directly across from where she hung, a bank of steel cabinets stood upright along the wall. There were no windows, but a full-length mirror ran along the wall on her left. She carefully avoided her reflection—it could easily return her to a writhing mess.

Somewhere behind her, a door opened. Straining every muscle in her body, she tried to turn toward the sound. The effort was fruitless. Another sound—the door closing. Despite the duct tape, she tried to cry out for help.

"So, you're awake." It was the sound of a man's voice. She turned her head toward the mirror. In the reflection, she could see him standing back near the wall, far from the glare of the harsh fluorescent bulbs shining overhead.

He held no weapons, but something in his stance conveyed a dark malice. Maggie watched as the man began setting up a video camera on a tripod. He went about the task with brisk efficiency—as if everyone walked into rooms with naked women dangling upside down in their center.

Unable to control her fear, Maggie began to whimper against the duct tape. Saliva pooled in her mouth while the fiery tears resumed their twisted trek across her forehead.

When satisfied the task was complete, the man

turned and faced the mirror. His features were barely discernable through the dark shadows. Though she couldn't see his eyes, she felt their dead caress. The cold scrutiny stifled her cries.

In the boring tone her psych professor often used, he launched into a dispassionate lecture on medieval torture. Unable to cover her ears against the disturbing rant, she squeezed her eyes shut instead, trying to keep from losing it again. She was rewarded with a slight lessening of the pressure on her bulging eyeballs.

Unfortunately, the gesture hadn't gone unnoticed. He abruptly stopped speaking. The ensuing silence was almost more disturbing than the sound of his voice.

Her eyelids snapped open. Pleased to have regained her attention, he resumed the lecture. A few moments later, he segued into a brief overview of one particular form of medieval torture—torture by saw.

"The problem with that form, of course, was that it was a two-man job. The victim would be hung upside down, like you are now. But to get through the human body, you'd need a large saw with handles on either end."

Cocking his head to the side, he considered her carefully, then walked past her, and opened one of the cabinets. Reverently, he extracted a chainsaw.

"But you've gotta love the human penchant for technological innovations."

Recognizing the object, she tried to plead with him through the tape. Unmoved, he strode back toward her, balancing the heavy tool between her legs. The cold weight of the implement bore down, pinching her labia as the harness tightened its relentless bite into her shoulders. Squatting down to her eye level, he regarded her appraisingly, then reached up and tore the tape from her face.

A small smile teased the corners of his mouth as she cried out in agony. The tape had removed multiple layers of skin. Blood dripped from her lips, joining her tears on their unusual journey downward. Eventually, the pain subsided enough for her to speak.

"P-p-please don't do this! I'll do whatever you want, just please, please…"

He snatched a wad of her long blonde hair, pulling her face within inches of his. "Why so sad?"

"W-w-why are you d-d-doing this?"

"One: Because it's so much fun. Two: Because I want you to tell me about Kate." Straightening, he returned to the camera—verifying every detail of their time together would be caught on film.

Moments later her shrieks rent the air, only to be drowned out by the roar of the chainsaw.

Chapter 2

IT WAS ALL ABOUT FAITH. Not the Bible-thumping, obnoxious type of faith doled out by wily political groups, but a quiet belief living deep inside your soul. Without it, running across the wooden bridge spanning the lake would be impossible. Well, maybe not in the middle of September. It was one of the few months of the year San Francisco lived up to the sunny expectations of its California address.

But on this cold January morning, the ever-present fog had enveloped the far side of the bridge completely. On either side of the wooden rails, the tranquil waters of Lake Merced appeared as liquid mercury, reflecting the silvery, wet blanket nestled tightly around them.

As Warren Benthe ran, his circle of visibility moved with him—as if some stagehand was following his progress with a giant fog-proof spotlight. He thundered across the weathered wooden planks, accompanied by resounding staccato foot-falls.

The previous night had been such a mess. The ever so sexy personal trainer he'd been dating for the past two months had finally brought up the dreaded M word. The M word wasn't in Warren's vocabulary —at least not now. He was committed to making a

12

name for himself at the advertising agency he'd called home for the last four years.

After grad school, he had landed a sweet position creating advertising campaigns for local tech companies. Starting as a lowly intern, he'd fought to impress the partners. His hustling soon paid off, earning him a corner office and the promise that if he brought in a few more large accounts, he might be up for a junior partnership.

It was all about keeping his clients sold on the importance of social media, and avoiding the M word. The M word led to kids, mortgages, Little League, and various equally nauseating anchors. He might as well just tie a real anchor around his throat and jump into the lake.

No. The M word was a fast track to nowhere, and Warren was definitely going somewhere. So last night, he'd opted for honesty and had been repaid with a crying jag that roared full throttle until he had unceremoniously dropped that pretty tight ass back on her doorstep.

Shaking his head to banish the memory of her piercing wail, Warren made it to the far side of the bridge, then followed the path to the left. Normally, he would have bypassed the bridge shortcut and conquered the entire lake trail. But he had an early conference call this morning and couldn't spare the time.

Instead of following the winding path back around the east side of the lake, he planned to make up more time by running along Lake Merced Boulevard. Earlier, he'd left his car in the lot near Skyline Boulevard. As long as he stuck to the route and kept a good pace, he'd be there in plenty of time to return to his condo for a quick shower before heading into the office.

Rounding the next curve in the path, something hit him. Not physically, but instinctively—and it packed a wallop. First he tried ignoring the feeling, but it grew so insistent he was forced to slow to a walk.

As a kid, he'd often played comic book super-heroes with his friends, always calling early dibs on the beloved wall crawler, Spider-Man. Back then, he'd spent countless hours trying to imagine what it would be like to have a real spider sense. With the lake at his back and the path lost in the fog ahead, Warren finally knew.

Hands on his hips, he walked in a slow circle, trying to identify what had set his internal fear-o-meter on high. He'd jogged this trail almost every morning for the last two years. Nothing seemed out of place, except...

He spun back around to his right and faced the De Anza statue. Perched on its concrete pedestal, the statue itself looked pretty much the way it did every day. But this morning, Don Juan Bautista de Anza, founder of the City of San Francisco, was not alone as he sat in regal bronze cast above his horse. Today, he appeared to have a companion.

Warren took a few steps toward the statue and stopped abruptly. A naked female dummy was sitting astride the horse, right in front of De Anza. What a stupid prank—the things some people thought were funny!

Warren was about to turn back and finish his run when he noticed the blood. It flowed generously in thick wet rivulets down the side of the horse. Staring at the blood made him aware of the almost impossible way the body had been positioned.

He walked around the front of the statue, never taking his eyes from the body. It was there, facing old De Anza himself, when Warren realized it wasn't just the legs that hung astride the horse—a good portion of the body itself did too. Someone had cut the torso upward through the crotch, tearing open the abdomen.

Then Warren, up-and-coming advertising guru extraordinaire, ran to the bushes and launched the most explosive campaign of his career.

▷▷▷

Parking wasn't a problem, but the cold could be. Bracing for the drop in temperature, Kate reached for the door handle. Believing all things were best resolved by immediate action, she pulled the handle and emerged from her car like a swimmer plunging headlong into the icy depths of the North Pacific.

She slammed the door shut behind her, barely registering the chill. Her mind had already shifted into detective mode, rendering it impervious to minor irritations such as temperature.

Straight ahead, a landscaped peninsula protruded into the parking lot, encircled by a pathway. A small group had assembled beneath the statue in the middle of the peninsula. Kate's partner, Detective Tyler Harding, was standing with two crime scene techs, staring up at De Anza and his macabre riding companion.

Half an hour before, Harding had interrupted Kate's morning Starbucks visit with the news a body had been discovered by the lake. She'd immediately abandoned her place in line and rushed over.

Kate stepped onto the path and joined the three men. Her attention riveted on the statue and the naked body splayed upon it. Her sharp eyes fixed on the damaged torso.

"Jesus!" The word escaped her lips before she could stop it. Unleashing random exclamations at crime scenes was rookie stuff.

"You can say that again." Prior to moving to San Francisco, Harding had been a detective with the Boston PD. Eight years older than Kate, with a below-average sense for fashion, he was a hardened investigator who had won her respect and loyalty. Yet, in the eighteen months they'd been partnered together, she had never heard a tone like the one he had just used to respond to her. A pragmatic straight shooter, he had never been one for drama.

Kate tore her eyes from the body and addressed the men. "How far have you gotten?"

One of the technicians lifted his camera. "We've taken all the *in situ* pics and processed the area immediately around the statue. The medical examiner's on the way. We warned them to bring a ladder."

Stepping off the path, Kate picked her way through the ground cover until she stood nose to nose with De Anza's horse. Above her, the woman's body was slumped forward, making it difficult to see its face. Long strands of blood-stained blonde hair hung limply around the head, further obscuring the features.

Kate began walking around the statue, noticing the deep bruising along the legs, arms, and torso. She finally made her way full circle, rejoining Harding on the path.

"So, what do you think?"

He regarded her quietly for a moment before responding—the pause almost as disquieting as the tone he'd used before. "I think this one is going to be different. How about you?" Something flashed in his hazel eyes as he asked the question—something Kate decided not to pursue.

"Come with me." She stepped off the path, walking briskly across the parking lot with Harding in tow. To their left, two police cruisers blocked the entrance to the lot. Two more cruisers had been positioned at the entrance further up Lake Merced Boulevard.

As they neared the street, the far side of the broad, multi-laned boulevard materialized through the fog. A squat row of tightly packed, two-story houses extended in either direction.

Kate stopped at the sidewalk and turned in the direction of the statue. It had disappeared from view behind the white, cloudy wall. She cast another glance over her shoulder. Behind her, intersection lights appeared blurry in the moist air. Beyond the lights, the four lanes of Sunset Boulevard shared the statue's fate.

She turned to Harding. "If the fog wasn't so thick, the houses on the east side would have a perfect view of the statue. The De Anza statue faces Sunset Boulevard, so anyone heading south would normally see it as well. Added bonus—the lake is a popular place for early morning runners and bikers. There could have been many witnesses."

"Could have been—if not for the fog."

"Exactly. Who called this in?"

"A jogger."

Kate's brow pulled into a frown. "A jogger, this morning? Visibility is less than fifteen feet. Doesn't sound very safe. I take it he's quite the adventurer."

"See what you think." Harding strode back across the parking lot, cutting a diagonal path away from the statue. He consulted his iPad as he walked. "Warren Benthe. Twenty-nine-year-old advertising exec. Claims

17

he's a die-hard jogger; insists he had an early call today."

They made their way over to another police cruiser parked in the interior corner of the lot. An exasperated uniformed officer met them. "Please let me know what to do with this guy. He's driving me fuckin' nuts! Bitchin' about how he needs to get to the office, yada, yada, yada."

Harding smiled wryly. "Stop complaining, Juarez. Otherwise, you might just have to babysit him all day."

Juarez retorted with a quick slew of Spanish expletives. Before Harding could respond, the door of the cruiser suddenly flew open. A trim, average-looking guy decked out in a designer jogging suit scrambled out and confronted them.

"Look, I gotta go! I'm sorry this happened to that woman. I mean, that's some fucking sick shit! But I've got to go—*now*."

He turned to head off, but Harding snared the man's small biceps in a vice-like hold. Warren whirled, trying to swat the detective away. Harding wasn't budging.

"Sir, as I explained, you're a material witness in a homicide. We need your help."

"I've already helped you as much as I can." His arrogant tone had melted into a whine within Harding's grip. Finally, he exhaled loudly.

Kate recognized the sound. The man's bravado was fading. Her partner had that affect on people. The man's shoulders slumped in defeat, earning him his release.

With the pissing contest settled, Kate stepped forward. "Sir, I'm Detective Barnes. I'd like to hear how you found the body.

She listened as Warren recounted his morning

adventure. During the story, she struggled to ignore the ceaseless buzzing from the vibrating cell phone in his pocket.

"And that's when the officers showed up. So, can I go now?" He flashed a hateful, yet cautious look at Harding. Then a sly expression lit up his features. "You guys can't make me stay here any longer!" He fished his phone from his pocket and held it up triumphantly. "I'll call my attorney!"

The sound of an approaching car drew Kate's attention. The medical examiner had arrived and was pulling into a spot near the statue. Harding had noted the new arrival as well. With a slight nod to her, Harding turned back to Warren. She headed back to the statue, confident Harding could handle the witness.

Tim Chau had been working with the San Francisco Medical Examiner's office for more than twenty years. From the way he stood staring at the statue, it was clear there were still things that could shock him after all this time.

Kate stood next to the examiner and waited until he pulled his eyes from the body to look at her. "Pretty different, huh?"

He flashed another look at the body and nodded his head. "Never found one like this before. And the bifurcating cut into the torso... Yeah, I'd say it's pretty different, Kate."

Chau's assistant set up an aluminum ladder at the base of the statue, then looked back at his boss. With a brief gesture, the younger man quickly climbed upward. Kate watched while the two men gingerly removed the woman and placed her into an open body bag on the path.

"Shall we see who we got?" Harding had silently taken up a position beside her.

"Done with Warren?"

"Yeah, he'll be at the station at eleven this morning to make a formal statement."

Kate addressed the older man. "Okay for us to take a look, Tim?"

"Sure." He waved them over impatiently.

As they neared the body, an odd sensation settled over Kate. Something seemed to be begging her not to get any closer to the black bag and its grisly contents. Steeling herself, she strode forward and peered inside.

Her eyes were immediately drawn to the unnatural separation running upward from the victim's crotch to the bottom of her rib cage. The damage was unimaginable. She could not fathom what had been used to make the cruel opening. Eventually, her eyes trailed upward over the bruised and battered torso, to the victim's face. Hidden from view while slumped forward on horseback, it was now clearly visible.

Recognition tore through Kate's mind like a hot steel poker. It wasn't just a dead young woman lying in the bag—it was her Maggie. The girl who had been so diligent in her studies and had been so committed to the mentoring program. The same girl who had insisted Kate join her in buying the kids' meal at a fast food restaurant, just because she thought the toys were cute.

Kate's stomach churned and her head spun. She didn't have time for this now. Tightening her hands into fists, she dug her fingernails viciously into her palms, allowing the physical pain to block out the sudden press of emotion.

It was not the first time she had recognized the face of a victim in a body bag. More times than she'd cared to remember, a domestic violence victim had returned to her abusive boyfriend or husband, heedless of Kate's warning that things would only get worse. In each of those instances, Kate had slipped easily into guilt mode—a seemingly age-old pain she bore for situations she couldn't control, and those she could not save.

Normally she kept the guilt tightly contained in a solid steel vault in her heart, allowing it only moments of acknowledgment during such losses. Yet despite her best efforts to annihilate it completely, it remained there—just under the surface. Its true origins were the reason Kate hadn't wanted to get involved in the mentor program.

But now her worst fears had been realized. Bright and beautiful Maggie, who had just had a ride-along with Kate three days earlier, was lying in a vile state before her. Had Kate's darkness somehow rubbed off on the innocent girl, inviting horror into her life?

"Fuck." The sympathetic expletive fell softly from Harding's lips. He must have recognized the girl from the tour of the precinct she gave Maggie last week.

The rational side of Kate's brain attempted to regain control. After all, she hadn't had anything to do with Maggie's death. It wasn't her fault at all—just a sad coincidence. At least that is what she tried to tell herself.

Chau regarded Harding carefully. "You know her?"

Harding flashed a wary look at Kate. "Yeah, we both do."

"Sorry to hear that. I…" Chau had glanced back down at Maggie, but broke off midsentence. With the movements of a much younger man, he dropped onto his knees and reached for Maggie's left thigh. Gingerly, his gloved fingers turned the thigh outward, exposing the inner skin.

Harding inhaled sharply.

"Looks like this is recent." The examiner glanced back at the detectives. Kate, who was known for her stoicism at crime scenes, looked shaken. But Harding looked downright ashen.

Still holding the thigh outward for inspection, Chau asked, "Recognize this?"

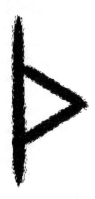

Harding stared at the symbol that had been branded into the young girl's thigh. It resembled a rudimentary rendition of a stem with a thorn sticking out of its side. Of course he recognized it. It was a Norse thorn—an ancient Viking symbol. Harding had seen it branded into human flesh before.

Back in Boston, he'd been on the task force assigned to hunt down the infamous serial killer who'd left the families of seven young women tragically bereft. After the death of the last victim six years before, the murders had suddenly stopped. The killer had never been caught.

Gazing down at the ravaged body, Tyler Harding knew the time had come. The Tower Torturer had reemerged in San Francisco. Kate's young friend would be the first of many to die.

22

Chapter 3

IT HAD BEEN A twenty-minute drive from San Francisco to the charming little 1960s ranch-style home in Millbrae. Like its neighbors, the immaculate blue house was perched along the hillside, offering sweeping views from San Francisco in the north to San Jose in the south. Across the steel-gray waters of the bay, Oakland and the rest of the East Bay cities sprawled across the lowlands and up through the hills.

During the drive from San Francisco, Kate had fought unsuccessfully to avoid thinking about the phone call she'd made an hour earlier. Normally she would have made the notification in person, but with the decedent's parents living in Nebraska, calling had been the best option.

When she'd first answered the phone, Maggie's mother had seemed pleasant and upbeat. Following the news of her daughter's death, the woman devolved into a wailing wraith. To Kate's relief, Maggie's father had remained composed enough to take the phone from his wife.

Unfortunately, he had not been able to offer any clues as to who might have killed his daughter. He'd insisted she was a wonderful young woman who had never had any real enemies. Kate hadn't pushed too hard, knowing from first-hand experience how wonderful Maggie had been.

23

Mr. Stevenson had told her they would be flying out to make funeral arrangements. He'd promised to contact Kate when they arrived, wanting to help with the investigation in any manner possible. He'd also been able to provide this address in Millbrae where Maggie's boyfriend lived with his parents.

Kate glanced at Harding as they approached the front door of the house. Since she had taken the parental notification, this one was all his. Harding hesitated momentarily before pressing the doorbell. No matter how many you had under your belt, homicide notifications were never easy.

A handsome young man with long brown hair answered the door. His earlobes had been stretched to amazing proportions to accommodate large black earrings, which nestled securely within them. He greeted them with a dimpled smile.

The smile disappeared when Harding identified himself as a detective with the SFPD. The sight of their badges, mingled with the murmur of his girlfriend's name, were enough to suck the strength from his bones. He took a weak step backward, allowing both detectives to enter the house.

Harding recommended they all take a seat in the living room. Troy sat on command, looking back and forth between the two detectives—clearly afraid to hear what they were about to tell him. The words slipped compassionately from Harding's mouth.

Troy's twenty-year-old brain seemed to misfire a few times initially, refusing to accept the truth. Harding laid a gentle hand on the young man's shoulder. Something about the gesture and its kindness penetrated Troy's weak defenses. The reality of Maggie's death had hit home. The young man broke.

Sitting across from Troy, Kate and Harding

exchanged a brief glance. They had been at this long enough to realize true grief when they witnessed it. The deep sobs struck a familiar note—one Kate had heard while talking to Maggie's parents.

"Troy, I know this is really hard right now, but I need you to try to focus. We're gonna need your help to find whoever did this to Maggie." Harding's words came out slow, steady, and sincere.

In addition to his experience, Kate often envied Harding's ability to connect with people. Like Kate, he had suffered his own profound loss. Unlike his partner, Harding had learned to channel that loss to better relate to others.

Eventually, his words wove their way through the deluge of grief. Troy's sobs slowly quieted and then ceased. The tears did not. They continued to flow as he dropped his hands from his face and raised his eyes to Harding's.

"What can I do?" The words escaped Troy's mouth in the barest of whispers, bearing no resemblance to the vivacious baritone that had greeted them when they'd arrived. They did, however, hold a note of resolve that had not been there before.

"We need to know more about Maggie so we can figure out who might have done this to her."

So far, Troy only knew his girlfriend had been murdered. They had not shared any of the details and they did not intend to.

"Nobody would ever hurt Maggie. You don't understand; she's super sweet. I…" Troy glanced around the living room of his parent's house, looking like a lost child. "I was going to ask her to marry me."

"Troy, someone *has* hurt Maggie. Unless we stop them soon, there's a good chance they'll kill again. We need you to focus."

Troy thrust his hands through his hair and fell back against the couch. Kate worried they were about to lose him again when he pursed his lips and dropped his hands to his knees.

"I'm just saying she doesn't...didn't...have any enemies."

"Okay. Was there anyone who had expressed a particular interest in her?"

"Try every guy in the Bay Area—she's gorgeous."

"Was there anyone she mentioned who stood out? Someone who wouldn't take no for an answer? Someone who she complained about?"

"No. Maggie's not a drama magnet. The only thing she ever complained about was schoolwork. And even that was rare. For the most part she was totally psyched about her major, and of course, you." The last part was directed at Kate.

"Me?"

"Yeah, she thought you were the greatest thing in the world. She's always joking that you're the big sister she never had." He smiled softly at the memory.

Kate's hands clenched into tight fists in her lap. Maggie thought of her as a big sister? How the hell had that happened? She knew the girl had thought her job was cool, maybe even looked up to her a little. That was normal—she had the career Maggie had aspired to have.

Yet, Kate had never tried to befriend the girl. The mentoring program had been part of the job. She hadn't wanted to be anyone's mentor, let alone their big sister.

Through the veil of grief, Troy noted the change in Kate's demeanor. His brows furrowed, and he regarded her with wonder. "Didn't you know?"

"No, I'm sure you must have misunderstood. I

was merely working with Maggie. We didn't get that close…"

Troy hopped from the couch and scrambled over to the dining table near the window. He opened a silver laptop, then typed in a series of short bursts. Harding was about to speak when the younger man placed the laptop on the large wooden coffee table facing the detectives.

Kate stared at the screen in surprise, recognizing herself in multiple photos. She leaned forward and swiped the touchpad, scrolling down the page. To her amazement, Maggie's Facebook page had been converted into a Kate Barnes fan club.

"Maggie would have made a great detective after all." Kate mused aloud. "I never posed for any of those pictures. She must have taken them with her phone when I wasn't looking."

Emotions welled up inside Kate. She wasn't sure whether to be annoyed or flattered. Harding reached over and tapped the touchpad, launching a video clip of Kate discussing psychopathic serial killers.

An odd sense of unease stole over Kate as she watched herself decree that extermination was the best way to deal with such deviants.

▷▷▷

Returning from their meeting with Troy in Millbrae, Kate and Harding had been summoned directly to Captain Singh's office. They took up their usual positions—Kate in the seat directly across from her boss, Harding leaning against the credenza to her left. They waited while the captain settled into his chair.

A slender man with a razor-sharp mind and single-minded professionalism, Singh had spent his entire career with the SFPD. During those two decades, he had only worked with the FBI on one case—it had not been a particularly good experience. But he did like the resources they offered, and his team needed those resources now.

Anxious to get started, Harding plunged in. "Who are they sending?"

Singh's eyes fixed on Harding. "Someone you know." He consulted the notes on the legal pad before him. "One of the FBI's superstar profilers, Ben Fraye. Big-time guy. When he's not working cases, he's on the lecture circuit. You remember him from the original investigation?"

"Yes." Harding straightened slightly.

Singh leaned back in his chair. "Yes? That's all? You worked with the guy on one of the worst serial killer investigations in modern times, and all you've got to say is yes?"

Harding's eyes quickly scanned the room, as if the answers he sought were concealed somewhere in its drab decor. Kate watched his jaw muscle clench tightly beneath his skin.

"Fraye knows his stuff. He's got a lot of ego, but then again, most of those guys always do."

The right corner of Singh's mouth twitched upward. Harding had scored a direct hit. Everyone knew about the captain's history with the FBI. One of the agents he'd worked with on that child-trafficking case had filed a formal complaint against Singh.

Of course, Singh had done nothing to warrant it. The agent had just been an asshole who'd become territorial and wanted Singh to back off. The complaint had been dismissed, but type-A that the captain was, he'd never gotten over it.

"Well, he'll be here tomorrow. You two better

watch yourselves. This is our case. Don't let Fraye edge you out."

Kate and Harding nodded. Satisfied, Singh continued. "You two sure the boyfriend isn't involved? And what about that jogger who found the body?"

"The boyfriend is clean. Immaculate record. He's genuinely broken up over all this." Harding looked over at Kate—her cue to take on the second part of Singh's question.

"Our jogger is a grade-A jackass. If this was corporate espionage or embezzlement, I'd be looking hard at him, but I don't think the guy's capable of something like this. This is…" Kate paused as the memory of Maggie's defiled form appeared in her mind.

Harding finished for her. "This is too hardcore for Warren Benthe."

Kate glanced at her partner. "The degree of torture Maggie, I mean the victim, endured. It's certainly the worst I've ever seen. And the Norse thorn branded on the body—that was the Tower Torturer's signature."

Singh sighed heavily. "If the Tower Torturer has resurfaced, things are going to get ugly quick."

The shrill ring of the desk phone cut off Harding's response. With a glance at the two detectives, Singh picked up the handset. As he listened, his grip on the receiver tightened. Moments later, he hung up. Without a word, he reached for the keyboard mounted under his desk.

Kate leaned forward. "What is it, Captain?"

"Hold on…" Seconds later, the typing ceased. Singh's mouth went slack and his eyes opened wide in disbelief.

"Holy shit!"

"What?" Kate demanded.

29

The captain stared at Kate, and in a volume as close to yelling as Kate had ever heard from her boss, he replied, "That jogger posted photos of our body on the fucking web!"

ᚦᚦᚦ

Kate leaned back in her chair, tilting her head from left to right. The pain was too much. It stole up between her shoulders and marched mercilessly up through the right side of her neck.

"Want me to get that for you?"

Turning, she found Harding standing over her. His proximity was unsettling. She scooted her chair closer to her desk. "No, I'm fine."

She glanced around quickly to see if anyone had heard the offer. The six desks in the drafty open area that housed the Special Victims Unit were empty.

Kate turned and checked the time on her computer monitor. It was five minutes past eleven—less than an hour before midnight. Crap! The day was gone, and she'd made no real progress on Maggie's murder. She closed her eyes, hoping to restore some of the moisture stolen from them by the building's temperamental heater.

She felt Harding move beside her. Opening her eyes, she discovered him leaning against her desk—far too close for comfort. "Do you have to lean on my desk? There's plenty of room around here. You don't need to be right on top of me."

One side of his mouth quirked upward in amusement while his eyes sparkled with keen interest. Kate had seen that look before. She had felt just what his mouth was capable of. But that had been an isolated mistake, which she'd vowed not to make again.

"Cut the crap, Harding. You know I didn't mean it like that."

"Hey, I can always hope, can't I?" Reluctantly, he moved a few feet away. The withdrawal calmed her heart rate, but did nothing for the inappropriate thoughts that had started to race through her head.

"All kidding aside, I never got a chance to tell you how sorry I am about Maggie." His hands plummeted deep into his pants pockets—as if they might be safer there.

The mention of her former protégée halted Kate's wayward thoughts. "Thanks. But, it's not as if Maggie and I ever got that close."

Harding nodded, recognizing his partner had retreated into self-defense mode. Kate had constructed some pretty thick walls to protect her heart. He had no idea what lay at their foundation, but he respected her need for them.

"Well, maybe you didn't feel that way, but Maggie obviously did. Troy was right. According to her Facebook page, Maggie thought the sun rose and set for you."

Kate exhaled loudly. "This day has been surreal. First Maggie, then the Tower Torturer, then that damn Warren! I'd love to wring his scrawny neck! What kind of a freak would take a picture of something like that, let alone post it on the web?"

"That is easy. Warren's an advertising exec—a glorified media whore. At least the district attorney got an emergency order to have it removed."

"Yeah, lucky us. Thanks to Warren, the media is already breathing down our necks. Now all we have to do is figure out whether we're really dealing with a notorious serial killer."

"Don't say it like that."

Kate bristled at his tone. "Like what?"

"Like this perp is some kind of mythic monster. If it is the Tower Torturer, he's no different than any of the other crazies we've gone up against."

"I know, but you guys couldn't catch him back in Boston. You told me you never had any viable leads. You never even got close."

"Well, we didn't have the mighty Kate Barnes on our side." He looked at her intensely for a moment. "Wait a minute. You're not intimidated by all this, are you?"

Kate broke eye contact, unable to admit it to herself, let alone her partner.

"Come on, Kate. This is just a case, like all the rest."

Straightening in her chair, Kate replied. "No, it's not. You saw Maggie this morning. Don't tell me we see victims like that every day. And in case you haven't been keeping track, I've only been assigned to Special Victims for eighteen months. I'd only been a detective about a year and a half before the transfer."

Uncomfortable with the turn in the conversation, Kate suddenly recalled Harding's evasiveness in Singh's office. She'd been so caught up in the drama created by the leaked photo, she'd completely forgotten about it. Still fighting the nagging pain in her neck, she laid her right elbow onto the desk, slipped her chin into her hand, and leveled her partner with her best penetrating stare.

"So, you and Ben Fraye. What's the story?"

He shrugged his shoulders dismissively, but Kate would be not be deterred. "You sidetracked Singh intentionally with the 'hate the FBI' smoke screen. Doesn't work with me. Try again."

Harding pulled his hands from his pocket and

settled into the chair on the other side of Kate's desk. "Little escapes the keen Barnes' powers of observation. It's nothing insidious. Just a general dislike. Fraye is a smart guy, like I said. Also has a hell of an ego."

"So what did you keep from the captain?"

"Just my personal feelings."

"Such as?"

"I don't always agree with the way he does things."

"And?"

"And nothing. Fraye will be here tomorrow. I'll let you draw your own conclusions. Come on, it's time to get out of here." He stood and gestured to the empty room. "Everyone else has."

"You go ahead. I've got a few more things to finish up before I go."

"Need any help?"

"No, I'm good—thanks."

"All right, see you tomorrow."

"Sure." She watched him walk to the elevator, glad he hadn't insisted on staying.

She spent the next few hours glued to her computer, researching serial killer cases. Ever since Harding had told her of the possible significance of the Norse thorn, Kate had been worried. She'd never come up against a serial killer before. Other than a brief overview in a criminal justice class years ago, she had no real idea how to handle a case like this.

By the time she shut down her computer and headed home, her trepidation had increased tenfold. She couldn't screw up in the meeting with Ben Fraye. According to Harding the guy had an attitude and an ego. Guys like that didn't typically have a lot of patience. The last thing she wanted was for Fraye to realize how inexperienced she was for this type of case and cut her from the team.

As much as she refused to admit it, Maggie's sunshiny personality had permeated her defenses. She had come to care for the girl, despite her intentions to the contrary. Kate had to stay on this case—to find justice for Maggie.

Chapter 4

IT WAS A LONG WALK to the conference room at the end of the hall. When she'd arrived home the night before, Kate had found sleep nearly impossible. Images of Maggie's brutalized body and apprehension over this morning's meeting with Ben Fraye had plagued her throughout the night.

Not long before rising, she had finally slipped into a deep sleep. Instead of offering a respite from her worries, her subconscious had merely provided a substitution. An old memory, triggered by grief over Maggie, had escaped from the rigid restraints with which she struggled daily to keep it confined.

She was a young teen again, waiting quietly in the front aisle seat of a church pew. A gap of only a few feet separated her from her parents, but it felt as wide and unforgiving as the Arctic Ocean.

The moment she heard the squeaky wheels, her stomach clenched and her eyes welled up with tears. Kate didn't need to turn around to identify the source of the sound.

The church was filled almost to capacity with those who were there to share in the family's mourning. At least that is what the people who had ventured up to talk to Kate's parents had said before the service started. But Kate knew they were lying. She had seen the awkward looks they had exchanged with her mother. She'd felt the sting of accusation in their gazes. It was palpable in the press of a hand, or the brief hug that was all too insincere.

Shame and guilt ravaged Kate's heart as the grating metal sound crawled slowly toward the altar from the back of the church. Eventually the source of the sound pulled even with her. Atop the utilitarian cart was the item she had most dreaded seeing—her sister's casket.

As the light blue coffin rolled into view, it stopped suddenly. The priest approached and began flicking drops of holy water across the top of it.

Kate clamped her eyes shut, trying to block out everything—especially her thoughts. She was certain everyone in attendance believed she should have been the one in the coffin, not her younger sister. It was a truth her mother had warned her about incessantly in the days leading to the funeral.

After all, Candace's death was her fault. Like Maggie, her sister had idolized her. Kate had repaid that love and dedication with sloth. Her laziness had caused the tragic and violent death that had wrenched the sweet girl's soul from its moorings.

A few drops of holy water missed their mark, and splattered across the side of Kate's face. The same thing had happened at the real funeral years ago. Back then the water had been a minor distraction. But in the dream, the drops of water turned to acid. Transformed by the darkness of her sin, they quickly burned through her skin and into her bone. Screaming, she raised her hands to her face and shot up from the pew.

Kate had snapped awake in her bed, her screams echoing off the walls of her bedroom. She had spent the next half-hour trying to coax the memories back into a mental vault. Yet, the weight of her guilt coated them in slick oil, making them impossible to control. By the time she had finally corralled them, the alarm on her nightstand had started chirping.

Taking a deep breath, Kate entered the large chamber. Three men stood at the front of the room, staring at an array of computer screens along the wall. Even from behind, she recognized Captain Singh standing on the right. She also recognized the extremely slender form of Kevin Nguyen, the department's head of IT, on the left. The unknown dark-haired man in the middle wore an expensive suit—one well beyond the pay grade of SFPD detectives.

Harding was seated at the table near the front of the room, engrossed in his iPad. He had abandoned his usual mismatched blazer and chinos for a navy blue suit. Kate made her way over to the vacant chair next to him.

Without looking up from the device, Harding murmured, "Mornin'. Ready for the show?"

She placed her iPad on the table in front of her and took her seat. Without glancing in his direction, she quietly responded. "Show? What are you talking about?"

He tapped on the screen of his device a couple of times and regarded her stoically. "You'll see. Just wait." Placing the iPad on the table, he leaned back casually in his chair.

The enigmatic response did nothing to relieve her apprehension. Luckily, she did not have to wait much longer. A few minutes later, the other three detectives in their unit filed in. Detectives Wallace and Felts were discussing a molestation case with Detective Karinsky, whose partner, Ella Hough, was still out on maternity leave.

As if prompted by an internal alarm, Captain Singh ended his conversation at exactly seven-thirty. Kevin hurried into his seat across from Harding and began quietly typing on his laptop.

The stranger did not move. He continued to stare at the monitors with his back to the room.

Singh glanced sharply at Kate and Harding before addressing the rest of his team. "Yesterday, the brutally tortured body of a young woman was found posed atop the De Anza statue at Lake Merced. Key forensics at the crime scene match those found during the Tower Torturer murders six years ago.

"The Tower Torturer murdered seven young women in Massachusetts during a twenty-three-month period. We do not know why the killings stopped abruptly, or if they actually did. We only know that no more bodies were ever found.

"Detective Harding had been part of the task force that investigated the case back in Boston. Benjamin Fraye of the FBI's Behavioral Analysis Unit headed that task force."

As if it were scripted for a Broadway show rather than a homicide investigation meeting, the stranger now turned and faced the team.

"We are lucky enough to have Special Agent Fraye here on loan from Quantico. He will be leading this investigation. Barnes and Harding will be running lead from our side. The rest of you will provide whatever extra manpower they need."

Singh looked at Fraye who stood impassive, silently regarding the rest of the room's occupants. "Special Agent Fraye, you already know Detective Harding. Next to him is Detective Barnes. Then we have Detectives Wallace, Felts, and Karinsky."

Fraye's eyes skimmed across each face in turn with

a detached efficiency. As the silence stretched into a full awkward minute, Singh stiffly took a step backward.

"Go ahead; they're all yours."

Fraye's gaze snapped in the captain's direction, then slowly swung back toward the detectives. Behind his silver-framed glasses, incredibly dark eyes flashed amid handsome, aristocratic features. The warm tones of his olive complexion hinted at a Mediterranean ancestry. A light scar was the only element that slightly marred his appearance. It trailed through his left eyebrow, ending just above his eye.

Special Agent Fraye was certainly a sight to behold. Kate's right hand flew unconsciously to the side of her head, desperate to secure a few stray hairs that had come loose from her ponytail.

"I'm pleased to have this team at my disposal." His voice was smooth and authoritative.

"Your captain has assured me you are all very capable law enforcement officers. Over the coming days, we are going to test that opinion." Fraye took a few steps to the right, allowing everyone an unobstructed view of the large screens he had been studying earlier. He nodded at Kevin, then turned back toward the monitors.

A photo of Maggie's corpse straddling the statue appeared on multiple screens. "Maggie Stevenson. Twenty-year-old student, criminal justice major at SFSU. Found yesterday morning at Lake Merced. Medical examiner's report is pending, but..." He flashed another glance at Kevin.

On the screens the original photo of Maggie was replaced by a series of close-ups of the nightmarish cut through her torso as well as numerous abrasions and bruises. They were the same photos that appeared in the reports each of the detectives had on their iPads, but Fraye paused a moment, allowing the detectives a few minutes to study the enlarged images.

"It is evident the victim endured extensive torture." His dark eyes darted back to Kevin. The photos on the screens disappeared, replaced by a single close-up of the brand Chau had discovered on Maggie's inner thigh.

"This is what brought me here—a brand of the Norse thorn on the inner thigh of the victim. It was the Tower Torturer's signature, found branded into each of the seven East Coast victims.

"Known as Thurisaz, the thorn is an ancient Norse rune. It represents the Frost Giants, who were considered the enemy of the gods. It also represents male power and conflict.

"The Tower Torturer was so named because he tortured his victims using methods made popular in the Middle Ages. The *Boston Globe* came up with the name after the third victim was discovered, linking the idea of medieval torture with perhaps the most infamous place where it was used—the Tower of London."

Another glance at Kevin yielded a new series of macabre crime scene photos. Next to each photo was a black-and-white, hand-drawn sketch. Each depicted a different form of medieval torture. The oddly linear shape of the figures reminded Kate of artwork she'd seen from the Middle Ages.

"There were seven original victims." Fraye gestured to the first photo in the series. "Shirley Jamison's limbs had been torn from her body, as if she had been stretched on the rack." He continued down the line, describing each photo and the corresponding form of torture.

"Michelle Steere had literally been boiled in hot water—the cauldron. Layla Obowitz had been bound and whipped—the pillory. Jennifer Swanstrom was burned over and over again with a hot iron in the shape of the Norse thorn—branding. Wendy Meyers was bound and set on fire—burning at the stake. Paula Rollins was dunked repeatedly in water until she finally drowned—water torture. And Gayle Nivens had been flayed alive with a curved iron comb—the cat's paw. Each victim had been held for a period of days during which these tortures were performed. All eventually succumbed to death."

Anticipating another glance from Fraye, Kevin cued up the next photo—a close-up of Maggie and the horrible opening in her torso.

"The Norse thorn found on Maggie's thigh isn't the only reason I'm here. I'm also here because of the way she was killed. Maggie Stevenson was hung upside down and cut open vertically though her torso." A final etching appeared on the screen showing the horrors Maggie might have endured. "The saw."

Kate glanced away from the screen. Fraye silently noted her reaction, then turned to Captain Singh. "I understand the victim's parents will be arriving from Nebraska tomorrow. I want them brought here so that I may speak with them. I will also want to interview the boyfriend."

Harding straightened in his chair. "We've already questioned the boyfriend. There's no way he was involved." His voice was slightly louder than it needed to be in the quiet room.

As if placating a frustrated child, Fraye's tone softened to an almost comical level. "Detective Harding, I appreciate your opinion, but I would like to form my own. We are not yet certain if this UNSUB is the Tower Torturer. We must remain as open-minded as possible."

Kate could almost feel Harding bristle at the implied insult. She was relieved at the lack of animosity in his reply. "Sure, Special Agent. It's your show. I'm just offering my opinion." Harding settled back into his seat, glancing poignantly at her as he did so.

Fraye watched the silent exchange and then addressed Kate. "Do you agree, Detective Barnes?"

Taken aback by the intensity of his dark stare, she suddenly felt like a student who had come to class without reading the assignment. She stared at Fraye blankly.

"Detective Barnes. I asked whether you concur with your partner's opinion? Do you think I shouldn't interview the boyfriend?"

Kate's pulse began to pound in her veins. A heated flush rose from her chest and into her cheeks. She prayed the thin layer of foundation she'd applied earlier that morning would be enough to hide her embarrassment.

"No, I… I don't."

"And why not?" The power behind his unflinching stare grew, as if feeding off her anxiety.

"Because we need you for your knowledge and expertise. If we had experience with this kind of thing, we wouldn't have asked for help."

To placate Harding, she added, "But I do agree with Detective Harding's analysis of the boyfriend. There's no way he was involved with this."

"If it turns out this murder was committed by the Tower Torturer, you will not have a choice in accepting my help, as the case will be under FBI jurisdiction. In either event, your captain has assured me of your capabilities. Yet, I am a man who deals in facts. And the fact is that this team has already allowed a photo of the crime scene to be leaked to the Internet. So I'm sure you can understand why I want to form my own opinions."

An awkward silence ensued, until Kevin finally broke it, piping up from behind his laptop. He informed them Fraye had been added as a limited user to their intranet to streamline file sharing and communications. As soon as Kevin finished reviewing communication protocols, the special agent jumped in, succinctly informing them there would be no further leaks in the investigation.

"Anyone who feels they cannot fully comply with that expectation can leave now." He waited for the statement to sink in, then informed the team that daily briefings would be held at seven-thirty each morning until the case was solved.

Kate caught Karinsky's eye as she glanced around the room. The look on the older man's face spoke volumes. A deep frown had taken root between his eyebrows. She guessed Felts and Wallace had similar reactions to their new team leader.

"Now for the interview assignments." Fraye glanced at Kevin again.

Kevin replaced the photo of the Norse thorn brand with a spreadsheet list of names.

The federal agent glanced briefly at the list. "Who compiled these?"

Dreading Fraye's response, Kate spoke up. "It's a list I put together based on feedback from Maggie's roommates, the boyfriend, and her Facebook contacts."

"Good."

Kate settled back into her chair. At least she'd done something right.

þþþ

The meeting ended thirty minutes later. Eager to

get back to work, but still smarting from Fraye's barb about the leaked photo, Kate stood and hurried toward the door. Everything would be fine. She was a capable detective. So she had some things to learn. So...

"Detective Barnes."

Kate stopped cold inside the doorway. Turning around, she spied Fraye standing with Harding. She reluctantly made her way back toward the two men.

Fraye waited until Kevin and the other three detectives left before addressing her. "I understand you knew the victim."

She flashed a look at Harding, unsure where this was going. "Yes. Captain Singh asked me to participate in a mentoring program with the criminal justice department at SFSU."

"Why was she killed?"

Had the man pulled a baby unicorn out from beneath the table, she could not have been taken more off guard. "I... I don't know." The words sounded useless and juvenile coming from the lips of an SVU detective.

Disappointment flashed in his eyes. He turned to Harding as if suddenly dismissing Kate. "Had you ever met the girl?"

Harding nodded and then added, "Yeah, when Kate brought her in for a tour. Their relationship was..."

"Was what?" Fraye demanded.

He grabbed his iPad. "Give me a second, and I'll show you." Kate clenched her teeth together so tightly her molars hurt. She knew what her partner was searching for on the web—Maggie's Facebook page.

"Here." He laid the iPad on the table in front of

Fraye, who sat down and began studying it with keen interest.

The gums under Kate's molars began to ache. She should have been the one to mention Maggie's Facebook page, not Harding. But she'd been struck mute by her own insecurities. She'd succeeded in making her worst fears a reality—Fraye must think she was totally incompetent.

Suddenly, Kate's voice rang out from the small speakers in the iPad. The agent had launched the video Maggie had taken of Kate discussing psychopathic serial killers. When it was over, Fraye sat staring silently at the screen for a few moments. Finally, he pushed his chair back and crossed his arms over his chest.

He looked at Harding meaningfully, then turned toward Kate.

"Well, I think we now have a good indication of why Maggie was killed."

Kate looked to Harding for help. He would not meet her eyes. Feeling as if she were drowning, she turned back to Fraye. "You can't think that I had anything to do with…"

"Detective Barnes, assuming our UNSUB saw this video, how do you think he might have responded to it? Hmm? Someone fixated on power and control, who prizes opportunities to exercise dominance over others."

"I really don't think…"

He snatched off his glasses, the intensity of his glare seeming to penetrate her soul. "Apparently you didn't, because that little diatribe of yours was an open invitation."

"Now wait a minute, we were just talking. I had no idea Maggie was taping me, let alone that she'd post our private conversation on Facebook."

"You really don't understand what you're dealing with, do you detective?"

Shooting a derisive glance at Kate, Fraye pushed the iPad across the table toward Harding. "This investigation just became infinitely more complicated."

Chapter 5

January 27

THE TEMPERATURE IN the elevator seemed as cold as the morgue Kate and Harding were about to visit. The medical examiner's office had just called to let them know the autopsy was complete. Dr. Chau had invited them to review his findings.

They were heading down from their department on the fourth floor of the Hall of Justice, to Chau's office on the ground floor. With all the architectural flair of a Cold War-era communist building, the seven-story, L-shaped Hall of Justice squatted on Bryant Street, surrounded by bail bonds offices and cheap fast food restaurants. Various city and county law enforcement departments had been crammed within the confines of its concrete walls.

On the same block, nestled within the gap left by the building's odd shape, was the jailhouse. With sleek, frosted glass and a modern curvilinear design, the jailhouse seemed to imply to the outside world that San Francisco cared more about its criminals than those who risked their lives to catch them.

When Harding had first transferred to the SFPD, he'd laughed at the name of the building. The only Hall of Justice he'd ever heard of was the one where the superheroes hung out in the campy 1970s cartoon series, Super Friends. He'd made a joke about it to Captain Singh on his first day, asking whether he should expect to find Superman or Batman traversing the halls. The joke had fallen flat with Singh, but it had proven a good icebreaker with Kate Barnes, the gorgeous brunette assigned to be his new partner.

The ice he'd broken that day had returned in glacial proportions. Harding glanced at Kate over the heads of their fellow passengers. She stared straight ahead, appearing transfixed by the dull surface of the elevator doors.

An electronic chime announced their arrival at the ground floor. The moment the doors opened, Kate was out like a shot. Harding hurried behind her as she practically flew down the crowded corridor toward the medical examiner's office.

"Kate, stop."

He grabbed her arm—the physical contact momentarily stunning her. Memories of a late night two months ago flashed in her mind and her heart. But that one night of passion had been an isolated mistake, just like her belief that Harding was a loyal partner.

She whirled on him, her dark ponytail slashing through the air. "What?"

"You've been pissy with me ever since the meeting yesterday morning."

She glanced at the throngs of people milling about, biting her lip briefly as if considering how to respond.

He was relieved when she chose honesty.

She leaned toward him slightly to ensure he could hear her as she whispered. "You didn't have my back with Fraye. You didn't stick up for me when he tried to blame me for Maggie's death."

Before he could respond, she pulled her arm from

his grasp and strode toward the door to the medical examiner's office. Pulling up short as she entered the reception area, Kate was surprised to find Fraye waiting for them. She regarded him warily as Harding came in behind her. Flashing her partner a cautionary look, she addressed the team leader.

"Special Agent, what are you doing here? I thought you were interviewing Maggie's boyfriend this morning."

"That was the plan, but then I heard the autopsy results were in. I would like to see the condition of the corpse for myself and talk to the medical examiner."

Another implied dig at her competency. She glanced back at Harding, nonplussed by her partner's passive demeanor. Turning on her heel, she headed to the reception window to check in. After signing in, she handed Harding his visitor's badge. It was identical to the one Fraye was already wearing. She affixed her badge to the lapel of her blazer, relieved when Chau appeared moments later.

The older man eyed the special agent speculatively.

Thrusting his hand forward, Fraye introduced himself. "Dr. Chau, I'm Special Agent Ben Fraye. We spoke on the phone."

Recognition flashed across Chau's features. He flashed a meaningful look at Kate and Harding. "Yes, we did." He clasped her partner's hand briefly before showing them back to his lab.

Maggie's naked body was lying on a stainless steel table. One of Chau's lab assistants, Raisa, was busy at a computer on the opposite side of the room.

The examiner led them to the table, and they gathered around it. He regarded the corpse dolefully over the rims of his glasses.

"The older I get, the sicker society becomes."

Sighing loudly, he continued. "But, you're not here to listen to me prattle on." He pushed his glasses further up on his nose and picked up a small pointer from a nearby counter.

"Contusions and abrasions are numerous and varied." He gestured to a long line of dark bruises snaking over Maggie's shoulders and across her chest in a large letter H pattern. "Lateral and horizontal bruising along the shoulders and torso indicate she was restrained in a harness. Based on the imprints and chaffing of the skin, it was probably made of canvas or a similar material."

Chau moved the pointer to Maggie's eyes. At the crime scene, they had been closed. With her lids now open, Maggie's pretty blue pupils seemed to be floating in a hellish red pool. "Subconjunctival hemorrhaging in the eyes. Coupled with pulmonary edema in the chest and excessive blood pooled in the brain, I'd say she was hung upside down for an extended period of time."

Fraye gazed up and down the length of the corpse. His eyes flickered over every inch of the body, as if performing a visual inventory. His gaze lingered momentarily on Maggie's scalp, which sat oddly on her brow.

To conduct the autopsy, Chau had needed access to Maggie's brain. Kate was thankful Chau had taken the time to reposition the scalp, even if it was a little haphazard.

Having finished his inspection, Fraye's head snapped up in Chau's direction. "Cause of death?"

"Surprisingly, it wasn't exsanguination—she didn't bleed to death from her wounds. She had suffered a massive stroke before the cutting began."

"A stroke?" Harding sounded unsure if he'd heard

correctly.

Chau turned to his assistant. "Raisa, please bring up the cerebrovascular shots."

Gesturing for them to follow, he walked over to a large monitor mounted to the wall behind Maggie. A photo appeared on the screen.

"Maggie's brain?" Kate murmured. Something in her tone prompted Harding to risk taking a step closer to her. Fraye's eyes flew from Kate to Harding and back again, then settled on the image before them.

"This is a cross-section of Maggie's brain." Here he indicated a dark area in the upper left portion of the organ. "Cause of death was a massive stroke."

"A massive stroke, at twenty years old?" Harding stared at the screen with incredulity.

"Not a common affliction in one so young, I'll grant you. But human beings are not designed to hang upside down for extended periods."

"Just hanging upside down too long can cause a stroke? What about bats—don't they do it all the time?"

"Yes, they do. But bats have evolved to contend with the engineering challenges of inversion. Humans have not. Because we spend the majority of our time right-side up, our bodies adapted to survive in that orientation. The key to circulatory system evolution is a dependence on the force of gravity. It is the force that helps propel blood downward into our legs. In order to send it back up into our bodies, we have evolved special muscles in the legs. They serve as a pumping station—effectively combating the force of gravity.

"The brain and lungs, on the other hand, have no such muscles. Thus, when upside down, blood pumps to the brain and lungs with no way to vacate. Not only is it pumped there, but without having to combat the drag of gravity, it pumps harder. Blood pools in both the lungs and the brain, causing pulmonary edema and strokes. The same principal applies to the blood you observed in Maggie's eyes."

An uncharacteristically soft voice came from Kate. "Does that mean she was dead before the cutting began?"

"Unfortunately, no."

Fraye cut in. "So, do we have any leads on our UNSUB?"

"No. This guy was meticulous. There was nothing at the scene or here." He gestured back toward the corpse. "Nothing that would allow us to test for DNA. But there was something else you might find of interest…"

He donned a pair of gloves and walked back to the table. Lifting Maggie's left arm, he held it up for inspection. A concentration of deep bruises and abrasions encircled her wrists like wicked jewelry. Gently, he bent her hand downward, causing the abrasions in her wrist to part slightly, revealing a small glimpse into the tissue below.

Harding piped up. "Her hands were bound, and she fought against her restraints." In the Special Victims Unit, the detectives had seen this kind of damage more times than they cared to remember. It was an especially awful sight when it marred the purity of a child's wrists.

"Correct. But unlike the canvas harness, I believe her wrists were bound in metal restraints. In the tissue, we found bits of ferrous oxide."

Fraye's sharp gaze fixed on Chau's face. "You found rust. Can you tell us what it came from?"

Chau sighed softly. "No. We can only say that it was rust."

"What about the tox screen? Did she test positive for anything?"

"Traces of scopolamine, a South American drug commonly referred to as the 'Devil's Breath.' It would have allowed her to remain conscious, but would have made her extremely compliant."

"The killer probably used it when he abducted her."

"I agree. It had worn off by the time the torture started, otherwise she would not have been able to struggle."

"How much longer will we have to wait for the report?"

Still holding Fraye's gaze, Chau called out to his assistant. "Raisa?"

A sweet voice chirped from the small woman at the computer. "I just emailed it to the team, Doctor." Chau smiled slightly.

"Good. Now, I'd like to know what did that." Fraye pointed to the cut through Maggie's torso.

"My best guess—a chain saw. The damage is too extensive for a meat saw—they cut with greater accuracy and less mess."

"A meat saw?" Kate's level gaze contrasted with the slight quiver in her voice.

"Yes, they're used in butchering cattle, and unlike the saws we use here, they are much easier to come by."

"Maybe he just doesn't know much about saws." Harding speculated.

Fraye cut in. "Or maybe he chose a more easily recognizable tool to maximize the victim's terror and cause the most carnage possible."

His words were delivered with the same detached professionalism he had used throughout the meeting. And though the federal agent had not even been looking in her direction when he said them, Kate remembered his accusation yesterday. Inside, guilt seared her stomach as she imagined how Maggie had spent her last moments of life.

ᛈᛈᛈ

Kate hung up the phone, relieved that the call was over. Maggie's father had called from his hotel room out by the airport. He and Maggie's mother had arrived that morning and were anxious to help with the investigation. Feeling as if she were Fraye's secretary, Kate had checked his schedule to confirm he'd be free to meet with them at two o'clock the following afternoon.

She glanced over at Harding's desk, where he sat with his phone wedged between his shoulder and his ear. From what she could hear, her partner was scheduling an interview with Maggie's advisor at SFSU.

Craving another caffeine fix, she grabbed her empty mug and made her way over to the kitchen. She'd just filled her mug and was ready to head back to her desk when Fraye poked his head in the doorway.

"Get Harding and meet me in the conference room in five minutes."

He was gone before she could reply. Pursing her lips, she strode back to her desk. Harding ended his call as she dropped into her chair.

Attempting to compose herself, Kate took a swig of the acrid brew, then turned to her partner.

"We've got a meeting with Fraye in the conference room in five minutes." She checked her clock. "Make that four minutes and twelve seconds."

"What about?"

"He didn't say."

Harding walked over to her desk and glanced around furtively. "Kate, I know you think I didn't have your back, but…"

She held up a hand. "But nothing. We have a meeting with our team leader. Let's go." She grabbed her coffee cup and iPad.

"Shit, Kate!"

Her face tipped upward abruptly, drawn by the singular vehemence in his tone. Shooting him a warning glare, she stood and headed for the conference room.

Harding stared after her for a few moments, his hands balling into fists. Finally, he took a deep breath, loosened his fists, and started off after his partner.

When he arrived in the conference room, Kate and Fraye were seated across from each other. He closed the door and purposely took a seat next to the agent. He watched Kate's face for a response—her expression was unreadable.

Fraye leaned back in his seat. "I met with the boyfriend."

Silence dragged on. Kate wasn't going to give him the satisfaction of jumping in and asking for his opinion. Apparently her partner wasn't going to either.

Fraye's glance pivoted from Kate to Harding. "I agree with both of you. I don't see the boyfriend as the type to commit a crime like this. According to your interviews with her roommates, the guy seemed to really care about our victim. Furthermore, the level of sophistication in the torture and killing is far beyond his capabilities."

He plunged ahead without waiting for a response. "So, let's discuss the autopsy results. I found this morning's meeting with Dr. Chau intriguing."

Kate kept quiet, but Harding nodded in agreement. "Yeah, especially that bit about the metal wrist restraints."

She looked from Harding to Fraye for an explanation. The federal agent jumped in. "All of the prior victims had been restrained with canvas bonds. Anything else, Detective?" He raised one eyebrow as if challenging Harding's powers of observation.

Harding stared steadily back at Fraye, replying in an even tone. "No, nothing else that stood out."

"I found the evidence of scopolamine intriguing as well. None of the East Coast victims had ever tested positive for that substance."

Eager to contribute, Kate piped up. "Maybe he's experimenting."

"Maybe, but there is something else that concerns me. Our best estimate puts the time of abduction between nine o'clock and ten o'clock on the evening of the twenty-third. The jogger found Maggie's body on the morning of the twenty-fifth."

He paused, as if waiting for Kate to connect the dots.

Harding spoke up. "All of the prior victims were held and tortured over a period of five to seven days."

Fraye turned to Kate. "If you are going to be a meaningful member of this investigation, you will need to be up to speed on the East Coast case files."

She sat up a little higher in her chair. "I'll be happy to, when they are made available to me."

Fraye's voice sounded doubtful. "Do you mean you haven't received copies of the original case files yet?"

"Yes, that is exactly what I mean."

"Hold on a minute." The agent pulled his cell phone from his suit jacket pocket and called his office in Quantico. After firing off a quick series of instructions, he ended the call. He stared at Kate as he slipped his phone back into his pocket. An expression she'd never expected to see appeared on the FBI agent's face.

Appearing contrite, Fraye assured Kate the files had just been sent to Kevin for upload into the team's shared drive. "See, as much as we hate to admit it, the FBI makes mistakes too."

The hint of a smile softened his features for a moment, making them appear almost boyish. Something inside Kate stirred, but she disregarded it with a mechanical efficiency. "Thank you. I'll do whatever it takes to get up to speed on the prior murders as soon as possible."

"Good. Now, back to those autopsy results and the shortened hold period. These are material changes in procedure. Changes like that don't just happen overnight."

Harding sniffed. "It hasn't exactly been overnight. I mean, the last time this guy killed anyone was more than six years ago."

Fraye's mouth set in a thin line. "That we know of. The truth is we have no idea why we stopped finding victims. Did the UNSUB move? Was he incarcerated for some other reason? Kevin is already cross-checking arrest and release dates for criminals in the Northeast."

Harding titled his head slightly to the left. "It could be that the UNSUB was jailed and spent the last six years fantasizing about how he might change things up. Or, maybe he's been killing all along, evolving his process."

"That would make sense, except for the posing of the body. He enjoys public recognition of his work. If he'd been killing all along, he would not have been able to give up that element. If he were in jail, prohibited from appeasing his compulsion, the first thing he would do upon his release would be to return to his pattern."

Following the logic behind his argument, Kate couldn't help but ask, "Then who do you think is behind this?"

He turned back to Kate. "I think there are too many variations from the original MO—including your involvement. Clearly, the video Maggie posted on her Facebook page caused the UNSUB to fixate on you, Kate."

She recoiled into her seat, but Fraye was not finished.

"The Tower Torturer that Harding and I investigated in Boston never chose his victims to send a message to anyone. He operated independent of society, its rules, or the relationships that form its foundations. We profiled him as a true psychopath—a veritable killing machine devoid of guilt or remorse."

He paused as if preparing for a concussive response to his words. "There is a chance we may be dealing with a copycat, and if we want to solve this case, we'll have to start looking at why the UNSUB chose to fixate on you, Kate."

Watching the exchange, Harding had grown increasingly uncomfortable in his seat. "Come on! A copycat! Are you fucking kidding me? Who the hell is going to copy that sick son of a bitch's crimes? Besides, no one ever knew about the Norse thorn. We kept it out of the papers. It's got to be the Tower Torturer, and for whatever reason, he chose Maggie as his next victim."

Fraye pushed his chair back from the table and crossed one ankle over the opposite knee. Responding to Harding's outburst with casual aplomb, he glanced back and forth between the partners. "Detectives, I understand you are both uncomfortable with the idea that Kate was the trigger for this crime, but that doesn't stop it from being true."

Harding sucked in a deep breath, prepared to defend his position further. But the agent continued. "The Norse thorn information did come out in the papers—after you moved out here. One of the victim's family members leaked it."

Harding sat back, partially deflated by the news.

Fraye continued, unaffected by the response. "At this point, I am keeping my mind open to the copycat option. If evidence surfaces to the contrary, I will alter my opinion. We do not have enough evidence to issue a profile yet, but we do need to employ some level of logic to this investigation. If your personal feelings are impeding your ability to remain impartial in this case, please let me know so I can make alternate arrangements."

Kate leaned forward. "That will not be necessary." She struggled to retain her straight posture, trying to support the weight of the guilt pressing down upon her shoulders. Guilt not just over Maggie, but over unforgivable things she'd done in the past.

A knock at the door provided a well-needed distraction.

Harding called out, "Come in."

Captain Singh entered and addressed Fraye. The chief of police was waiting in Singh's office for an update. The special agent excused himself and followed the captain out of the room.

"See what I mean? Guy puts on quite a show, doesn't he?"

Kate pinched her lips into a sad parody of a smile.

"Guess so." Keeping her eyes averted from his gaze, she stood. "I've got to check to see if Maggie's phone records are in yet."

She was out of the room before Harding could respond. He stared at the empty doorway, knowing they would have to talk at some point. He just hoped it didn't get too ugly when they did.

Chapter 6

THE WORDS ON THE SCREEN were starting to blur. Kate blinked her eyes a couple of times, trying to force them to focus.

"Sometimes our bodies just can't keep up."

Kate turned her attention from the screen. Fraye was standing on the other side of her desk. She glanced around. The department was empty, which was not surprising. According to her watch, it was well past midnight.

She'd been busy analyzing the old case files sent over from Quantico. The hours had slipped away.

In response to her blank look, the left side of his mouth quirked upward. "Your eyes—it looks like they've had it."

Flashing him a terse smile, Kate began shutting down her computer. "I guess they're letting me know I'm done for the day."

To her surprise, he didn't leave. Instead, he watched as she returned her desk to its normal state —a clean surface devoid of any personal effects or clutter. As she put her iPad into her bag, he spoke again.

"Were you able to make any headway with the old files?"

"Yes, I did. Now I understand the points you made during today's meeting."

61

"Good."

She pulled her bag onto her shoulder and bid him good night.

"Good night, Kate. Oh, and by the way, do you happen to know any place to get a late dinner at this hour?"

Great. He was relegating her to the secretary role again. She had already been booking meetings for him. Was she supposed to arrange his meals as well?

She walked around her desk and headed to the elevators, calling out over her shoulder. "There are a couple of tolerable fast food places nearby."

The sound of hurried footsteps made her want to cringe. She steeled herself as he appeared beside her. "What about you? Have you eaten?"

She pulled up in front of the elevator and turned to face him. "No, I haven't. But I don't think a meal at this hour will do anything for my waistline."

Fraye's eyes scanned her body with the same clinical detachment he'd used to examine Maggie's corpse earlier that morning. She hadn't intended for the comment to be leading, and she regretted it as soon as it slipped from her lips.

"I mean, I'm just not very hungry."

She'd been about to press the elevator button when his words caught her off guard. "Kate, I'm not propositioning you. I'm asking if you want to grab a bite to eat."

It was a completely reasonable invitation from one team member to another. But he'd misunderstood her response. Couldn't she ever do anything right around this man?

"I'm sorry, I didn't mean…"

"It's fine; never mind." He turned and began walking away.

Despite his contention that she had been the cause of Maggie's death—and all of the other remarks, both stated and implied, that he'd made about her competency—Kate found herself feeling guilty over the exchange.

Knowing she would regret it, she called out to him. "Wait."

He stopped walking.

"A late dinner sounds great." With his back to her, he could not see the adolescent way her eyes rolled upward as she spoke.

A moment or two ticked by. Finally, he turned around but did not take any steps toward her.

She decided to toss an apology into the silent void. "Look, I'm sorry about that weirdness. I'm just really tired."

"Is it that, or does it also have to do with the fact that you think I've been busting your balls the last few days?"

Taking her off guard seemed to be his favorite pastime. Too tired to search for the right response, Kate chose the honest one. "I almost wish I had a set for you to bust. As it is, I've had a heck of a time bobbing and weaving. I don't really enjoy having any of my parts busted."

Fraye pulled his hands to his hips and began to laugh. The throaty chuckle surprised Kate. Whether it was the actual sound or the very fact that Fraye was capable of laughing, Kate only knew that she found it pleasing.

Sobering, he looked up at her with a smile. "All right, then. Where do we eat at this hour?"

Fifteen minutes later, they were ordering Chinese food from a hole in the wall on the next block. With plates of steaming rice and Kung Pao chicken in hand, they made their way to an empty plastic booth near the windows.

Fraye sat watching her as she took her first bite. "Has it really been that bad?"

Kate paused, her chopsticks poised inches from her lips. "No." She lowered the utensil and sat back. "Most of what you've said has truth to it—especially the part about Maggie's Facebook page. Honestly, it's been a hard pill to swallow."

He said nothing, but the expression in his eyes urged her to continue.

"I didn't even want to get involved in this mentoring program in the first place. I knew it would be dangerous to pair me with a kid like that."

He'd just taken a bite of his food. Clearly taken aback by her statement, he pulled a napkin to his mouth and swallowed hard. "Dangerous?"

Kate glanced away. "Maybe dangerous is the wrong word. Let's just say it wasn't a good idea."

Fraye leaned back, his expensive suit pressed against the tacky booth. "Look, Maggie chose to put that stuff on her Facebook page. You didn't."

Kate's eyes flashed and she raised her chin—daring him to defy the truth of her words. "But, she did it because she liked me."

"Then, I'd say you should be glad you connected with the kid. What happened after that wasn't within your control. All you can do now is try to catch the person responsible for her death."

Kate looked at him wryly. "Right—as if I've been doing such a great job of that. For all that crap I said about serial killers on the video, I've never actually gone after one. If you haven't noticed, I'm way out of my depth here."

Fraye's clinical demeanor returned. "You are

inexperienced with this type of a case. But that doesn't mean you can't learn. Obviously, you have a strong work ethic. And from what I hear, you're one damn good cop. You're going to have to get up to speed fast if you want to make a better contribution on this team."

"Believe it or not, I have been trying to get up to speed."

"How?"

"Internet research, going through old SFPD files..."

"That will only get you so far."

He reached into his coat pocket and retrieved his cell phone. "I wrote a case study on the original Tower Torturer investigation." He swiped his finger a couple of times across the small screen, then began typing.

When he was done, he put the phone on the table. "I just emailed my assistant back in Quantico. She'll send you a copy of the case study along with some other materials. You'll want to start with the serial killer publication first—it provides a great over-view of how multiple agencies can come together to solve these types of crimes."

Picking up his chopsticks, he pinched some chicken and rice from his plate. He was about to deposit the bite into his mouth, when he artfully pointed the utensil toward Kate. "I also recommend you start reading Robert Hare's book, *Without Conscience*. He's still considered to be one of the foremost authorities on psychopaths."

Kate pulled her iPad from her purse, quickly typing the author's name and the book's title into the memo section. She smiled at him for the first time since they'd met. "Thank you very much."

"You're welcome. Now eat up. I don't know if it's

possible, but this stuff might actually taste worse when it's cold."

> ▷▷▷

January 28

Kate and Harding followed Professor Eileen Reddick into the tiny space that served as her office. Reaching the guest chairs across from the professor's desk required both detectives to side-step around a stack of boxes piled six feet high. Kate made it safely through, but Harding's shoulders were too broad. He clipped the edge of the top box as he passed by, causing the stack to wobble precariously. With the agility that had won him a starting spot as a linebacker in high school, Harding turned and righted the tower before it toppled.

"Good save!" The professor regarded him warmly as he settled in his seat. Her face was deeply lined with wrinkles. Fashionably styled, her silver hair framed an attractive face lit by a pair of lovely green eyes.

"Thanks. We're glad you were able to make time for us today." Harding guessed that in her heyday, Professor Reddick must have sent the hearts of many male students aflutter.

The older woman's expression changed dramatically. "I'm just so sorry about Maggie. She was a very bright young woman with a promising future. Do you know who killed her?"

"No, but we're investigating all aspects of Maggie's life. Since you were one of her teachers, as well as her academic counselor, we were hoping you might be able to give us some insights into Maggie's time here at San Francisco State."

"Well, as I said, Maggie was an incredibly bright

young woman. She earned an A in my Governments and Policies course last semester."

The professor leaned back into her chair, which loudly bemoaned its decades of service. "She was also an incredibly pleasant young woman who was driven and well respected by her peers." Sadness drew her mouth downward. "I understand she was very much in love with her boyfriend. I believe his name was… Trent, Travis…"

"Troy," Kate offered.

The professor smiled kindly at Kate. "Yes, Troy. And, of course, she was very pleased to have been accepted in the SFPD's mentoring program."

Her brows furrowed as she watched Kate's lips compress into a tight line at the mention of the program. "I'm sorry, my dear. I know how much Maggie idolized you. This must be horribly trying for you."

Kate held the professor's gaze, but didn't respond. Aware of his partner's discomfort, Harding stepped in.

"Professor Reddick, we would like to know whether…"

The door suddenly swung open. "Professor, I…"

Kate and Harding turned in their seats to find a balding man in his late thirties standing in the doorway. He glanced at the professor apologetically. "I'm sorry, I didn't realize you had company."

Professor Reddick stood. "That's all right, Jonas. This is Detective Harding and Detective Barnes. They're here about Maggie."

The man's chin drew backward as if it were a drawer that had just been slammed shut. "Oh. Well, I just need to know whether you wanted me to take your Power Struggles lecture on Thursday. I heard you were headed out of town."

Professor Reddick shut her eyes, pained by the

reminder. When they opened again, she beamed at him with gratitude. "Thank you, Jonas." She looked at Kate and Harding wistfully. "I don't know where my mind is these days."

Returning her attention to Jonas, she agreed. "Yes, please take that class for me. As soon as I finish up here, I'll let you know what I'll need for Thursday."

"Okay, Professor." His gaze flickered briefly in the direction of the detectives, and then he began pulling the door behind him. "Nice meeting you both." The door shut before he issued the last few words, rendering them barely discernable through the old oak.

Apologizing for the interruption, Professor Reddick dropped back into her seat, explaining that Jonas was a graduate student who also served as a teacher's assistant. Segueing into a diatribe about the challenges presented by ever-increasing budget cuts and increasing enrollment, she told them how she was lucky to have such a dedicated TA to keep her on point.

Harding kindly steered the conversation back to the investigation, asking her the same series of questions he and Kate had been asking each of Maggie's friends over the past few days. Twenty minutes later, Kate and Harding bid the professor good-bye and headed out. As they made their way down the worn steps of the political science building, Harding turned to Kate.

"More of the same stuff we've already heard."

"Unfortunately."

Harding flashed a sidelong look at his partner. When he'd left for home the night before, she'd been deeply immersed in reviewing old case files. Not eager for another cold brush off, he'd left without saying good-bye. This morning, Kate had seemed a little more like her old self.

She was still all business, but without the bitchy edge which had sharpened her words and facial expressions over the last few days. Glad she'd gotten over whatever she'd been pissed about, Harding strode confidently alongside her as they crossed the massive quad on their way to the parking lot.

They were forced to stop abruptly when a gaggle of giggling coeds obliviously cut across their path. Harding stared intently at the young women who were decked out in teeny shorts, despite the cold winter weather.

Smiling wryly at her partner's fascination with the pretty girls, Kate offered, "I've got a stop to make on the way back to the office. I can come back and pick you up later if you want."

"What?" Harding tore his eyes from the women and followed Kate as she continued down the path.

"I said I can pick you up later, if you're not done enjoying the view." Kate inclined her head in the direction of the long legs and spritely giggles retreating across the quad.

"Oh, cut the crap, Barnes. I just don't understand how they can walk around in shorts like that in this weather. I'm freezing my ass off!"

Kate laughed—a clear sound that the frost between them had melted.

"So, where do you need to go?"

"To the bookstore."

"The bookstore?"

"Yes. The bookstore. You know, the place where you can buy those square shapes filled with pages that have words printed on them."

Harding smiled—Kate was back and in rare form.

"I know what a bookstore is, Einstein. Why do you want to go now? Can't you wait 'til after work?"

"No, because the book I'm getting is for work. Fraye recommended it to me. I put it on hold this morning."

They crossed the quad and entered the parking lot.

"Fraye? He's giving you reading assignments now?"

"No, it's not like that."

Arriving at their car, Harding hurried inside. Kate was just about to shut her door when the heater almost blasted her out of her seat. "Geez! You want to turn that down a bit?"

Harding thrust his hands in front of the small round vents. "Too bad. I told you I'm freezing." After a few minutes he relaxed into his seat and put the car in gear.

"So what bookstore are we going to?"

"The Barnes & Noble right here in Stonestown." Kate hoped Harding wouldn't be a pain in the ass and correct her. Technically, the Stonestown Mall was not part of the SFSU campus. It abutted the campus on the north end, a mere minute or two away by car.

"Okay. What are you buyin'?"

"*Without Conscience*. It's an in-depth study of psychopaths."

"A good starting point, if our UNSUB is a real psychopath. He may just be someone who's fucked-up in the head just like all the rest of the perps we deal with."

"True, but I'd like to know a little more about them."

Harding sniffed loudly. "I'd like to know a little more about our UNSUB, like why he killed Maggie."

Kate regarded him critically. "You still think it

was the same guy who killed those women in Boston?"

"Hell yes. Fraye's full of shit. There's no way this could be a copycat."

Piqued by the arrogance in her partner's tone, Kate turned away, addressing her response to the front windshield. "He didn't say he was convinced this was a copycat. He only said that certain deviations between this crime and those on the East Coast led him to consider the possibility."

Harding tore his eyes from the road. "Are you saying you agree with him? The guy who's accusing you of being the cause of Maggie's murder?"

Kate swallowed the jagged barb. "I'm saying that I'm open to his theories."

A brooding silence descended as Harding pulled into the mall's driveway and found a spot in front of the bookstore. Turning off the car, he snapped his head in Kate's direction, demanding her attention.

"So Fraye knows everything, huh?"

Remembering Harding's unwillingness to stand up for her in their previous meetings with the special agent, Kate's temper flared. "He may not know everything, but he is a famous FBI profiler. I think he knows a lot more than an SFPD detective!"

Fury smoldered in Harding's eyes. He reached for the door handle and was out of the car without a word. Frustrated, Kate clambered out of the car and slammed the door shut behind her.

Chapter 7

LOCATED AT THE SOUTHERN TIP of the San Francisco Bay, the city of San Jose spread across the valley created between the Santa Cruz mountain range to the west and the Diablo mountain range to the east.

Over the last forty years, the city had transformed radically from its agricultural roots, becoming a world leader in technology and innovation. The development had been achieved with a suburban sprawl similar to that of Los Angeles—creating a population dependent upon their cars.

Twenty-two-year-old Becky Hammonds, full-time waitress and part-time student, walked toward the rusted 1994 gray Honda Civic parked at the curb. Worn down by more than two hundred and fifty thousand miles of service, the vehicle looked as tired as Becky felt.

When she'd left for work that morning, her lustrous blonde hair had been teased into beautiful waves. Ten hours later, her hair hung limply onto the shoulders of a snug, black t-shirt—the name of the tacky burger joint where she worked displayed in bold letters across her breasts.

She had parked in front of the daycare center with the cute little blue-and-white awning. Usually she had to wait in bumper-to-bumper traffic with other frenzied working parents willing to violate any parking statute in order to retrieve their child and get home for dinner. Forced to cover part of another waitress's shift at the restaurant, Becky had arrived long after the crowds had gone. Luckily, the daycare had agreed to watch her son, Hayden, for the additional two hours—provided she paid extra.

"Mommy, what're we gonna have for dinner t'night?"

Looking down at the big blue eyes and soft blonde curls, Becky's heart melted. Grasping her son's warm, little hand tighter, she hurried toward the car.

"Honey, you know Mommy has school tonight. Nana's going to make you dinner."

Hayden's legs suddenly turned to lead. He refused to take another step. In the orange glow of a nearby streetlight, Becky could see Hayden's eyes filling with tears. Bracing herself, she knelt down in front of him.

"Hayden, what's wrong?"

"Don't wanna go to Nana's. Wanna be with you, Mommy."

"It's okay, Honey." Standing, she lifted him onto her hip.

"You won't go?"

Becky reached the Honda and opened the back passenger door. Placing Hayden into his seat, she covered his hands with hers and looked him in the eye. "Honey, I have to go, and you know why, right?"

Hayden looked away. Petulantly he replied, "Cuz its your 'sponsibility."

"That's right. Mommy has responsibilities, and so do you. You go to your school to learn, and Mommy goes to hers."

It was true, but what four-year-old boy should be worried about responsibility? The next words flew out of Becky's mouth before she could stop herself. "I'll tell you what—you go to Nana's tonight and we'll go to Funland on Saturday."

Hayden's head snapped back in her direction. "Can we go all day?"

Becky didn't want to spend one minute in the nasty, super-loud indoor play center, let alone all day. Confident he wouldn't last more than an hour or two, she gave in. Her reward was a huge hug, and a big wet kiss on her cheek.

Crisis avoided, she secured Hayden's seat belt, then closed and locked the passenger door. Hurrying over to the driver's side, she dropped into her seat. The Honda grumbled to life, and Becky set off for her mother's house.

During the fifteen-minute drive, Hayden chatted happily about Funland, regaling her with disjointed stories of his past visits. Humoring her son, Becky kept a smile on her face, all the while struggling to remember the stuff she'd need to spit out for tonight's history exam at San Jose State University.

Silently reciting the major causes of the Bolshevik Revolution, she pulled into her mother's driveway and turned off the engine. A few minutes later, with Hayden safely locked in his grandmother's warm embrace, Becky hurried back to the Honda and headed off toward SJSU. Lost in concentration, she never noticed the white SUV that had been following her at a safe distance ever since Becky had left work earlier.

ᛈᛈᛈ

Staring at the question typed on the page wasn't helping. Becky checked the clock mounted to the wall at the front of the classroom. Six minutes had passed.

She still couldn't remember who the hell Julius Martov was, and what impact he'd had on the Russian Revolution of 1917.

Giving in, Becky glanced over the answers she'd written to the rest of the test questions, gathered her answer sheets, and walked to the professor's desk. Without making eye contact, she dropped the papers on the table. Turning on her heel, she walked back to her desk where she quietly gathered her things.

Careful not to disturb her fellow classmates, she walked out the door and headed across campus. The vibration of her phone provided a happy distraction from thinking about the exam.

Without breaking stride, Becky checked the display. It was a Facebook post from one of her girlfriends announcing she'd just broken up with her boyfriend. Reading the post, Becky stepped off the curb and crossed into the nearby residential neighborhood where she'd parked her car.

Bad breakups were something Becky knew a lot about. Burying her own dark experiences deep beneath the surface, she began typing a long-winded message of support and understanding.

Immersed in her response, Becky was oblivious to the increasing squalor of the neighborhood. Chainlink fencing separated the ramshackle residences from passersby. Behind the fences, front yards were dotted with old furniture and appliances that had been left to the elements and long forgotten.

When she'd arrived earlier, she had not been happy about parking in the freaky looking neighborhood. But money was tight and she'd been unable to come up with the extra two hundred bucks for a campus parking permit this semester.

Finishing her message, she glanced up, realizing

she still had two blocks to go. She stuffed her phone in her purse and hurried ahead.

"Hey, where're you goin'?" The ominous voice called out from across the street.

Startled, Becky turned and spotted two Hispanic men in their early twenties hanging out on the steps of a dilapidated porch. One was overweight, wearing a baseball cap and an oversized jacket. The other wore a large black hoodie over his lanky frame.

Encouraged, the guy in the baseball cap stood and called out again.

"I said, where're you goin'?"

As Becky struggled for a response, the second man rose. He plunged his hands deep into the low-slung pockets of his jeans. Tapping his elbow against his companion's arm, he growled in a thick Hispanic accent. "C'mon, *ese*."

Both of them started toward the sidewalk, their shoulders dipping and rolling like rap video thugs as they crossed the yard. Glaring at her intently, they stepped onto the street and started toward her.

She glanced around the block looking for help. No one else was in sight.

"Hey, *chica*! *Mi amigo* asked you a question!" Menace dripped from beneath the dark hood.

They were halfway across the street. The proximity made her want to run. She started casually toward her car, calling out a lie, "To my boyfriend's house."

"Boyfriend? I'll be your boyfriend, *chica*."

This time Becky didn't look in their direction. Pulse pounding, she kept walking toward her car.

From the corner of her eye, she watched as they began to jog toward her. Terrified, she reached into her purse. She had just freed her phone in time for the thug in the hoodie to seize her right arm and wrench the device from her grasp.

"What you gonna do with this, *chica*?" He held the lifeline high out of her reach.

Frantically, her eyes flew from one threatening face to the other. The guy in the cap suffered from severe acne. His partner had the hint of a mustache above his snarling upper lip. Elaborate tattoos made up of interconnected names were scrawled across their necks. She'd been wrong about their ages. Up close, they looked to be no more than teenagers.

Desperate, Becky forced an authoritative tone into her voice. "Give me back my phone."

Leering at her, the chubby one grabbed a handful of her hair, pulling her toward him. She lashed out, her left fist glancing weakly against his chin.

"You stupid bitch!" He yanked harder on her hair, pulling her tight against his body.

His partner pulled back his hand to hit her. Shaking from head to toe, Becky squeezed her eyes shut, and begged them to let her go.

Suddenly a new male voice rang out over her pleas. "Stop!"

Becky opened her eyes to find a fist frozen in midair in front of her. Her gaze moved from her assailant's hand to his face. To her surprise, the fury in his expression had changed to wariness. She could see why.

His hoodie had been tightly compressed against his left temple by the muzzle of a handgun. The blonde man holding it was at least ten to fifteen years older than her. Dressed in a sport coat and jeans, with thick black-rimmed glasses, he reminded her of one of her teachers at SJSU.

His eyes flashed to the jerk holding her hair. "Let her go … *NOW*!"

"Hey, man, relax. We was just talkin'." Despite the bravado in his tone, the tightness in her scalp dissipated. He shoved Becky roughly toward the stranger.

Steadying her with his free hand, her rescuer pushed the muzzle harder against the black hood. "Give me the phone and disappear. Unless you want one helluva headache."

"Easy, man. We was just messin'." The teenager thrust the phone toward Becky with a trembling hand. She snatched it back.

Scowling once more at Becky, the youths lumbered across the street to a lowered red Toyota and climbed inside. With a loud peel of rubber, they shot down the street—not bothering to slow for the stop sign at the corner.

The stranger turned toward Becky as he tucked his gun into the back waistband of his pants. "Are you okay?"

Becky's hand flew to her mouth. "I-I think so… I…"

"You're shaking pretty badly—probably in shock."

"I can't thank you enough. I wish I'd had a gun."

He scanned the street, then settled his gaze on her. "It's not a safe neighborhood. Come on; let's get you out of here."

"My car is two blocks down."

"My car's closer; I'll drive you. What's your name?"

"Becky… Becky Hammonds. I'm a student at SJSU."

"Then you should be parking in the campus lots —not out here."

"Just trying to save money. Hey, you look familiar. Do you teach there?"

"I'd like to think so." He gently took hold of her elbow and guided her a few feet down the sidewalk to a large white SUV with a rental car sticker on the back bumper.

Flashing her a quick smile, he pulled open the passenger door. She climbed inside and waited while he shut the door soundly behind her. Inhaling deeply, she pressed her hands against her thighs, trying to stop their erratic shaking.

He climbed into the driver's seat and smiled at her warmly. "Don't forget to fasten your seat belt."

Becky smiled back. "Right. You can't be too careful."

Turning in her seat, she had just reached up to grab the seat belt when a strong hand clamped down over her mouth. In the same moment, there was a vicious stinging in her throat. Lifting her hand in the direction of the pain, she felt the familiar shape of a needle protruding from her neck.

Panicked, she clawed at the hand holding the needle. But her efforts were short lived. Whatever the needle had delivered into her system seemed to be leeching away her energy at an amazing rate. In seconds she collapsed into her seat.

"You're right, Becky. You can't be too careful." He tossed his glasses into an open compartment in the dashboard, then reached up and tugged on his hair. The blonde wig came off easily and was tossed alongside the glasses.

With her willpower fading, Becky thought about Hayden and wished fervently that she could wake up in Funland.

Chapter 8

KATE WALKED INTO KEVIN NGUYEN'S immaculate office. The thirty-two-year-old IT director was sitting at his desk, hunched over the small laptop, dressed in a faded t-shirt and jeans.

Harding had taken the only guest chair and pulled it up next to Kevin's. Fraye stood behind the two men, peering over their shoulders at the tiny screen.

A large sticker had been affixed to the back panel of the computer. "Go Golden Gators!" was printed in block lettering next to a comical purple-and-orange alligator with a toothy smile. Kate recognized the San Francisco State sticker on Maggie's laptop immediately. Guilt clutched at her throat as she made her way around the desk and stood next to Fraye.

"Hey, Kate."

"Hey, Kevin. What've you got?"

Since Maggie's murder, Kevin had been combing through her laptop, phone, email, and social media accounts, trying to find any leads on her killer. He'd called them to his office a few minutes before to report his findings.

"Like I just told these guys, I got nothing on the laptop or phone. Zero from the email too." The words were issued in a slightly clipped cadence, the last remnants of Kevin's early childhood in Vietnam. "But we learned a little more from Facebook."

"Anyone with any priors hiding in Maggie's contacts?" Harding stared at the screen.

"No. We also cross-checked them against the list of suspects Fraye gave us from the East Coast investigations and Kate's prior collars. Double zero. But there was something interesting."

"Interesting?" Fraye stepped closer.

Kevin nodded to the laptop screen upon which Maggie's Facebook page was displayed, then pointed to a much larger screen behind it. "The victim had a few hundred contacts. Nine percent of those were bots."

"Bots?" Harding inquired.

"Yeah—short for robots. They're programs that move around on social media like real people."

"What do you mean, like real people?"

Fraye stepped in. "Spammers copy someone's profile information, then create a new profile under a new name using the same photos, likes, everything. These programs operate as the false identity—making friends, posting likes, et cetera. Think of it as identity theft in the social networking realm."

Kevin turned slowly to face Fraye. "True. But it's not just spammers that use the technology, is it?" He waited for Fraye to respond, then looked to Kate and Harding. "The FBI uses it too—to compile information on people. They're one of the largest creators of fake profiles out there."

Harding raised an eyebrow at Fraye. "One of the largest?"

"I wouldn't say we're the largest, but we do use the technology. It is a valuable tool with a variety of applications."

Kate crossed her arms. "No big deal. We create fake profiles to get intel on perps too. Maybe not en masse, but the FBI has broader responsibilities." From the corner of her eye, she watched Harding flinch. "Maggie was friends with some imaginary people. How does that help?"

"It tells us that like most people on Facebook, Maggie wasn't too cautious about who she chose to be friends with. I identified the bots using Google image search to find duplicate profile photos."

"So?" Harding was clearly losing patience.

"So, Maggie friended people she didn't know. It's a bonehead move—like sex without a condom."

Harding dragged a hand down his face. "Did you find anything besides spammers?"

"I found bots. Fraye's friends at Quantico identified an actual person who had friended Maggie under a fake profile." Kevin moved the cursor over the picture of an attractive, fit black man in his early twenties. A new Facebook profile appeared on the screen.

"Janeel Johnson. Twenty-three, employee at a local fitness club. Recently bought a brand new, silver Toyota pickup." He gestured to another photo on the page.

Kevin held a hand up before Harding could speak. "Yeah, Janeel is misrepresenting himself, but I doubt he's your suspect."

Harding glared at Kevin. "How the hell can you say that?"

Kevin smiled placidly. "Because when the FBI ran a search on Janeel Johnson living in Hayward, California, and cross-checked it against the license plate number shown in the picture, they confirmed that Janeel used to be Janelle. He had the surgery, just hasn't legally changed his name yet."

"Why'd you bother to call us down if you didn't find anything?" Harding cast a jaded glance at Kevin.

The IT guru was leaning back in his chair, his arms raised, his fingers threaded behind his head. "Well, we're assuming this guy went after Maggie because he was pissed about the video she posted on Facebook." He glanced quickly at Kate, then back at Harding. "Looking at the Facebook contacts should give us everyone—real or imaginary—that may have had access to that video. But it doesn't."

"What do you mean?"

"I mean that those people," he gestured back to the larger screen, "are the ones that had access to the video on Facebook. That doesn't account for the people they might have showed it to by simply running it on their phone or computer."

"Good point—thanks." Fraye looked meaning-fully at Kate, then started toward the door.

Before Fraye had exited, Harding resumed his lament about arriving at another dead end. Uninterested in her partner's complaints, Kate hurried after Fraye. She caught up to him in the hall.

"So what did you think of Kevin's findings?"

She pursed her lips. "Disappointing."

"So quick with the emotion, Detective Barnes." He smiled slightly.

She pulled her gaze from his lips, forcing it to his eyes—which were no less unsettling. "Should I be happy that we're no closer to catching this monster?"

He shook his head slowly and started briskly down the hall with Kate hurrying alongside. "I'd say you should be pleased. You have information you didn't possess fifteen minutes ago."

"But it's nothing new."

"That depends on your perspective. Do we have a name for our UNSUB? No. But we do know we need to expand our search." He stopped in front of the elevator and stared at her. "And that is valuable. You still have a lot to learn, Detective."

She opened her mouth to respond, but he interrupted. "If you're up for it, I've got a helpful little exercise in mind. It should assist you in expanding your perspective."

"Of course. What is it?"

He paused and studied her, as if reconsidering his offer.

She eagerly stepped forward, jutting her chin upward. "I told you I want to do whatever it takes to stop this guy."

"Then you're going to have to understand him first."

"I've been reading through the materials you recommended and…"

"There's a difference between knowing something and understanding it." His phone rang. Pulling it from his pocket, he paused to look at her. "Conference room. Eleven-thirty tonight."

He answered the phone and hurried off down the hall before she could respond.

"What's that about?" Harding had left Kevin's office and was now standing beside her with a sour expression on his face.

"Nothing."

He looked at her dubiously, then turned to watch Fraye disappear into an office. "Yeah. That's what we've got. A whole lotta nothing."

ᚦᚦᚦ

Kate backed her car carefully into the small parking space outside the Mark Hopkins Hotel. The vehicle clung to the incredibly steep section of Taylor Street as she stood on the brake and inched the car backward. She was mere feet from the top of San Francisco's famed Nob Hill, or as some locals called it—Snob Hill. Spared from the devastation of the 1906 earthquake and ensuing fire, the area consisted of lavish historic buildings housing world-class hotels, opulent churches, and premier residences.

Besides areas of Hyde Street and a few others, this stretch of Taylor required motorists to make one of the most vertical climbs in the city. A few harrowing moments later, Kate slid her sedan snugly into the spot and set the parking brake. Grabbing her purse, she opened the door and stared at the daunting angle of the street.

Three hours prior, she'd run into Fraye in the lunchroom. He'd cryptically recommended she stop at home for "more stylish attire" before their meeting. She'd taken his advice and gone home to change into a black pencil skirt, white blouse, and black patent leather stilettos. Pulling the ponytail holder from her hair, she'd brushed it out, allowing the dark tresses to spill freely over her shoulders. She had also taken time to apply a fresh coat of makeup and some jewelry.

When she'd met Fraye in the conference room, he had run his eyes over her briefly before affirming her fashion choice. Then he'd escorted her out of the building and instructed her to meet him at an address on Nob Hill.

After driving around for ten minutes, this had been the only spot she could find. Sighing loudly, she kicked off her shoes and stepped out of the car. It took a moment to get used to the pitch of the street. Once steady, she carefully reached back inside the car and retrieved her heels. The address Fraye had given her was two blocks away. There was no way she'd make it up the hill in these shoes.

She locked the car and headed upward barefoot. Mentally kicking herself for forgetting a jacket, she practically jogged across the blocks of freezing concrete and asphalt.

Arriving at her destination, she paused on the sidewalk, taking in the grandeur of the three-story, nineteenth-century stone house nestled shoulder to shoulder with its neighbors. Separating the house from the sidewalk was a small strip of lawn. A low iron fence encased the diminutive yard, matched by iron railings that climbed up the front steps and extended into an ornate porch.

Fraye was waiting for her on the stairs. Bemused, he watched while she stepped into her heels and joined him. "Feet hurt?"

"No—just cautious. These heels aren't ideal for climbing hills." She stuck out her right leg, giving him a good view of the side of her shoes from the glow of the antique porch light.

He studied her leg for a long moment before responding. "Ah, the unique challenges of womanhood."

Kate's lips pulled into a thin line as she shot him a dagger-laden glare.

"If it's any consolation, I feel for you. Not quite empathy perhaps, but I can offer sympathy. Remember, you won't need either to be a good profiler. You'll just need to be able to put yourself in another person's mindset—no matter how foreign it may be to your particular likes."

Kate nodded and looked at the large, wooden front doors. "So, what kind of exercise is this?"

"You'll see." He turned and rang the doorbell.

It took a good minute before one of the doors opened.

"Benjamin! I'm so glad you made it!" A gorgeous redhead in her mid-forties burst from the house, enveloping Fraye in a slender-armed hug. Her red hair had been shorn closely into a masculine cut. A strapless emerald dress clung to her amazing body, matching the shade of her teardrop earrings and slingback heels.

Kate stood quietly in the awkward silence as the embrace lingered.

Finally, Fraye broke away. "Genevieve, you look more beautiful than ever."

"Do you really think so?" Genevieve batted her long fake eyelashes coquettishly.

"You know I do."

Kate was enjoying the show. Though she'd caught a few glimpses behind Fraye's no-nonsense FBI persona, watching him flirt like a schoolboy was a rare treat. She glanced at Genevieve, silently agreeing with Fraye. The woman was exceptional.

A pale, manicured hand deftly snaked its way around Fraye's right arm, pulling him closely against ample cleavage. "Come on. We were about to start. I'm so glad you got here before…"

Fraye interrupted in a smooth tone. "Genevieve, I'd like to introduce you to my guest." He turned and gestured to Kate, who suddenly felt like an uncouth eleven-year-old boy standing next to the perfectly styled goddess.

Kate smiled tightly and extended her hand. "Hi, I'm Kate Barnes."

Genevieve reached for the detective's hand, her eyes sliding inquisitively toward Fraye's. Not finding an answer, she looked at her new guest and smiled warmly. "Welcome, Kate. I'm so glad you could join us tonight."

Tugging gently on Fraye's arm, Genevieve led him inside, leaving Kate to follow along behind. Frowning to herself, the detective stepped over the threshold into an ornate marble foyer with a spectacular chandelier at its center. Genevieve closed the front door, then breezed across the floor to a large set of double doors.

"And now my hostess duties require that we must briefly part ways." With a dazzling smile, Genevieve pulled open one of the doors and glided into the next room.

Fraye turned and slid an arm around Kate's waist, leading her toward the doors. She walked stiffly alongside him, disconcerted by the intimate proximity.

They stepped into a murky darkness, which intensified as Fraye closed the door behind them. Cop reflexes kicked in. Kate's body tensed.

Fraye leaned toward her and spoke quietly. "Relax, Detective."

His breath was warm against her ear, sparking an irrational urge to get closer to him. Shaking off the sensation, she concentrated on the haunting sound of Celtic music that was softly playing in the background.

Fraye guided Kate into the room, while her eyes adjusted to the dim light. The large chamber with its high ceilings might have once served as a ballroom in the house's heyday. Low-backed, slim leather couches had been set up in groups here and there. Small votive candles burned on little white tables positioned near each of the seating areas. There had to be at least thirty other guests in attendance.

Her escort led her through the maze of settees to the remaining vacant one that stood against the wall. Kate sat down. Fraye settled in next to her, leaving a discreet distance between them.

Toward the back of the room, two young women clad in sexy black mini dresses lit massive candelabras while Genevieve climbed three steps to what appeared to be a small stage with a tall red-velvet curtain.

Kate stole a sidelong glance at Fraye, whose eyes were fixed on their hostess.

"I want to thank you all for coming tonight. I hope I've brought enough here to captivate your heart and your imagination." She clasped her hands together theatrically and bowed slightly before stepping down to take a seat on the couch in front of the stage.

"Would you care for a cosmopolitan?" The silky words poured out in the barest whisper.

Kate turned to find a pretty Latino woman in another black mini dress leaning over the side of the couch with a tray of cosmos. Noting Kate's uncertainty, Fraye deftly plucked two drinks from the tray and handed one to her.

The rim of the glass had just met her lips when Fraye whispered in her ear. "Remember, Detective, you're here to learn to understand your UNSUB."

Kate paused as he spoke, the warmth of his breath having an almost hypnotic effect in the intimate setting. She sipped her drink primly and fixed her eyes on the stage.

The melodic Celtic tune ended, replaced by a deep gothic chant. The velvet curtains parted, and a beautiful raven-haired woman in her mid-twenties stalked out on stage. Thankfully, Kate had already put her glass down on the little table. Had she been drinking when the woman appeared, the cocktail may have spewed from her mouth like water from a broken fire hydrant.

The young beauty stood center stage in black thigh-high patent-leather boots and very little else.

Her arms were tucked flirtatiously behind her back, thrusting her full, round breasts forward.

Shiny metal nipple clamps had been fastened to the ends of her breasts, leaving only the swollen, red tips visible in the midst of the reflective steel. A stiff black patent-leather collar enveloped her neck from jawbone to collarbones, held in place by an overabundance of belts and buckles.

A large metal ring at the lowest part of the collar tethered it to another piece of patent leather, which ran down between her breasts into the cleft between her legs. The material had been bound so taut that the woman's labia swelled out on either side of it. Kate shifted slightly in her seat.

The only hair on the pale body could be found on her head. Trimmed in a style similar to Genevieve's, the tips had been dyed a deep purple. Bright blue eyes shone from beneath a whimsical mask made of black and blue feathers.

Speechless, Kate stared out at the rest of the guests who were all as chic and as well dressed as their hostess. Some wore smiles, while others titled their heads critically, as if appraising a frock on a runway fashion model. No one mirrored the open-mouthed astonishment on Kate's face.

Working in sex crimes, there wasn't much Kate hadn't seen or heard before. She had witnessed the pain and bloodshed that accompanied the reality of the S&M world often enough in abandoned warehouses, hotel rooms and underground clubs, but to see this—here, with these people—was a surprise.

Oddly, there was a little side of her that had toyed with the fantasy of experimenting with some of the rough stuff, assuming she ever found the right partner. (One who embraced the fantasy concept and stopped short of actual pain or degradation.)

Every day she was expected to be commanding and responsible—a role she'd been forced to take on long before her career as a police officer. There was a definite allure to the idea of ceding complete control to someone else.

Turning, she found Fraye smiling back at her broadly. Eyes blazing, he leaned forward until his lips were mere inches from hers. "Mind on the exercise, Detective."

Leaning back into the couch, he took another sip of his drink and watched the stage impassively. Embarrassed at being taken by surprise, Kate forced an unreadable expression onto her face and reached for her cocktail.

On the stage, the patent leather princess, her arms still tucked neatly behind her, took a step forward, then turned her back to the audience. Rigid leather tubes encircled her arms. Starting just below the shoulder, they terminated in a fitted leather sack that encased her hands. Buckles and locks were spaced every few inches along the tubes, an excessive measure of protection against her freedom.

Hushed murmurs of approval rang out from the guests. Kate took another sip of her cosmopolitan. The sight of the arm restraints was a bit disquieting, but as the woman turned around again, Kate admitted there was a certain appeal in the tightly constricted form. Certainly the little leather straps were sexy. And the nipple clamps, if not fastened too harshly, were definitely intriguing.

She settled back against the couch as the woman exited the stage. The song ended. Tribal drums filled the air. A young dark-haired man in his late twenties stepped onto the stage. Kate shot forward in her seat.

The man looked soullessly down at the floor. Like the woman, he was naked except for a series of straps and restraints. His face caught Kate's attention first.

A black latex mask fit snugly over his head. It covered his nose and mouth, causing something in Kate's stomach to move uncomfortably.

Tearing her eyes from the muzzle, she looked down at his chest where a large leather belt was bound across his nipples. Matching leather cuffs were affixed to his wrists. Small chains fettered his wrists to his chest. A studded leather ring encircled his engorged penis.

Despite the fact she hadn't had sex since that one night with Harding, Kate felt nothing as she looked at the well-endowed hunk. Her eyes kept returning to the muzzle and the downcast eyes. She tightened her grip on the martini glass, fighting the compulsion to leap onto the stage and pull the mask from his mouth.

The model turned his back to the audience. From the band around his chest, two additional straps fell in a V pattern, joined by a ring positioned just above his buttocks. A long metal hook hung from the ring, its tip disappearing into his anus.

Kate was suddenly aware her companion was watching her intently. Fraye had said she needed to understand the killer—not that she needed to agree with him. Looking back out into the room, she scanned the faces of the other guests. Many were clearly turned on by what they saw, whispering excitedly amongst themselves.

She leaned toward Fraye, her lips almost touching his ear. "The Tower Torturer revels in causing his victims extreme pain and humiliation. To some degree this crowd is no different."

Without taking his eyes from the stage Fraye asked

quietly. "No different. Really?"

"No, I... I mean yes. The Torturer's victims are unwilling participants. This," she nodded to the stage, "is based on consent."

Fraye nodded and took another sip of his drink. On stage, the young man exited gingerly. Two men in black rolled a small bed out onto the stage, then quickly disappeared behind the curtain. A petite Japanese woman had been chained to the bed spread eagle.

As the bed began to spin slowly, the audience was afforded an unobstructed view of her vagina. A large iron circle stood between the woman's legs; four small clips hung from the rim of the circle. Each clip held a section of the model's labia, allowing the audience to look right up inside her.

Fraye leaned toward Kate, his body pressing warmly against hers. "Do you understand?"

She turned and regarded him with half-lidded eyes. Her lips parted slightly as she looked at him. The artery at the base of her neck stood out, throbbing wildly.

She seemed to lean into him for a moment, then pinned her gaze back on the stage. "He wants to hurt and dehumanize them. But..."

"But?"

"But he doesn't think there's anything wrong with what he's doing. For him, it's just as natural as it is for everyone here."

Fraye returned his gaze to the stage but remained settled against her. "Good."

After a while, the bed was removed and replaced by another model. The tall blonde woman was bent over, her wrists shackled to the same long bar to which her ankles had been bound. Clad in a razor-thin thong and a studded bra, she balanced atop four-and-a-half-inch spiked heels.

Kate was aware of Fraye crossing his legs beside her. She wondered silently whether the show had affected the implacable special agent. Smiling slowly, she languidly crossed her own legs.

As the woman rotated on the spinning stage, the large plastic bit in her mouth stood out like a section of rot on a peach. A narrow piece of leather plunged down between her eyebrows. At its ends, two large metal hooks sunk deeply into her nostrils, pulling them vulgarly toward her eyes.

Kate's smile faded. The corners of her mouth pulled downward in disgust.

Another young man eventually replaced the blonde in the bondage bar. Like the first, he also walked out naked and erect. Instead of a ring around his penis, he wore a metal ring around his testicles. Threatening his reproductive future was a square metal weight that dangled precariously by a chain from the ring, stretching his testicles painfully downward.

Unlike the other models, his entire head was covered in a huge metal ball secured by large locks at his neck. His hands disappeared into similar metal globes, which were tethered to his head by long metal chains.

Kate inhaled deeply, fighting a sudden sense of claustrophobia.

Fraye's mouth was at her ear again, his lips barely brushing against her skin. "Sensory deprivation."

When she looked back at the stage, Genevieve had replaced the man. Smiling graciously, she begged the indulgence of her guests. "We're about to present our final item of the evening. Our models will be coming around shortly so you can get a better look at the products. As some of you recall, our last session ended with the Scavenger's Daughter. Tonight, we have something a little more special. Please enjoy!"

She bowed again and discreetly walked off stage. The music changed again. Discordant notes from a sitar filled the air.

This time it was Kate's lips at Fraye's ear. "The Scavenger's Daughter? I read about it—another medieval torture device, right?"

Fraye nodded, but remained silent.

"I knew the Rack is popular in the S&M crowd but had no idea they recreated other medieval devices. I guess the Torturer isn't the only one trying to bring back the good ol' days."

Fraye laughed softly at the quip.

"That's why we're here, isn't it?"

Fraye turned to her with one eyebrow raised.

Kate took a breath. "The Torturer is just doing what he enjoys. He doesn't consider himself a monster —just a regular guy who's not hung up on consent."

"We may just make a profiler of you yet." He glanced back at the stage where the red drapes parted to reveal a black table upon which a miniature scaffold-like structure had been erected.

Suspended from the steel frame face downward was yet another model, whose head was hidden beneath a thick brown mask accurately shaped like the head of a Doberman Pinscher—complete with docked ears and tapered snout.

A series of chains held him in place and pinioned his arms to his chest. His legs were bent at the knee, as if he'd been ensnared while trying to crawl away.

A second man, dressed head to toe in latex, stood mute and imposing on the side of the stage. Three zippers had been opened over each of his eyes and his mouth, allowing him limited access to sight and air. After staring out into the audience for what seemed like eons, the latex robot stalked over to the metal contraption and laid his hand on a large wheel affixed to one of the vertical supports that stood between the naked man's legs.

The audience gasped in anticipation. Slowly, the wheel began to turn. As it did, an impossibly thick, twelve-inch studded pipe screwed to the pole began to creep closer to the naked man's open legs. With each turn of the wheel, the fervor among the guests seemed to grow like a nuclear chain reaction.

When the pipe first touched the bound man's buttocks, his body tensed, sparking a series of spon-taneous moans from the audience. As the pipe reached his anus, the man spasmed and pulled at his restraints. And as it continued to drive deeper into his rectum, his body began to buck and twist. His agonized screams were tamed into muffled cries by the macabre mask, as dark petals of blood blossomed from his buttocks.

The music finally ended, and the audience applauded wildly. Kate shifted away from the warmth of Fraye's body, trying to understand how this lesson had alternately sparked both a hot demanding pulse between her legs and a gut-wrenching nausea.

Chapter 9

January 30

IT WAS ALMOST ONE-THIRTY in the morning by the time Kate entered the Victorian building and jogged up the creaky staircase to her second-floor apartment. Located between Divisadero Street and Alamo Square Park, the affordable sublease had been an amazing find. The Western Addition neighborhood was close to the Hall of Justice and offered the casual, eclectic atmosphere Kate liked.

Year-round tourists flocked to the park, eager to explore its high, grassy knolls, and to capture their own pictures of the six Painted Ladies set against the downtown skyline. Along with the Golden Gate Bridge and the uniquely shaped Transamerica Pyramid, the series of shoulder-to-shoulder, ornate Victorian houses had become one of San Francisco's most iconic images.

Kate's building was nowhere near as ornate as any of the Ladies. A large iron fire escape dominated the cream-colored, three-story building's façade, an indicator of its late-nineteenth-century construction. On either side of the iron structure, the corners of the building blossomed outward, allowing for large bay windows in every corner apartment.

Kate crossed the lobby and shoved her key into

the antique lock. It had been an exhausting day at work followed by a strange, yet productive, evening with Fraye. Despite the late hour, her body seemed to hum with a nervous energy.

She opened the door, grateful to have reached the white-walled sanctuary of her sparsely furnished, one-bedroom apartment, whose high ceilings, crown moldings, and hardwood floors more than made up for its dated kitchen. Locking the door behind her, she dropped the red-velvet box Genevieve had given her onto the glass console table near the front door and hustled into her bedroom to change for a quick workout.

Twenty minutes later, Kate's muscles strained as she pushed her body to its limit. Spreading her legs a little wider and tightening her grip on her hand weights, she dropped into squat number twenty-five.

The bright-red color of Genevieve's box drew her eye across the room. After the things she'd seen that night, she could not imagine what the unusual hostess might have thought to distribute as appropriate party favors.

Clenching her teeth, she rose from the squat. Unanswered questions about the case swirled in her head. She glanced at the clock above the mantle—one of the few decorating concessions she'd made in the austere living space. It was almost two o'clock in the morning. She had to be back at work in a few hours, but there was no point going to bed—not until she tamed her tumultuous thoughts and emotions.

Preparing to drop for push-ups, the shrill ring of her cell phone stopped her cold. She scooped the phone off the glass coffee table, holding it a short distance from her sweaty face. "Barnes."

"Hey, Kate. Sorry to bother you so late, but I

want to run something by you."

Kate frowned, recognizing Detective Karinsky's voice. "It's fine. What's up?"

"You know how the special asshole's got me and the rest of the team working the tip lines for the Torturer case?"

Kate shook her head, silently condemning the detective's childish manipulation of Fraye's special agent title. "Have you got something?"

"Maybe. I got the call right before I left for home tonight." He paused.

Kate knew Karinsky's wife was undergoing cancer treatment and had seen the toll it had taken on the older man over the last few months.

"It was a cop with the SJPD. He told me about a missing person's report he took earlier in the day. See, the thing is, the woman hadn't even been gone a full twenty-four hours when her mother reported it, so I figured it might turn out to be nothing."

"And?"

"And, I told him to email me the report. Said I'd take a look in the morning. But there was something about it that bothered me. And with everything going on here at home, you know…" His voice shook briefly.

Kate waited quietly for him to continue. She began pacing the small area alongside the coffee table.

Finally, he continued in a much stronger tone. "It was the name of the missing woman. I was about to fall asleep a few minutes ago when it popped back into my head, and I remembered."

"Remembered what?"

"That you're the one that put away the boyfriend of Becky Hammonds."

Kate stopped in her tracks, recognition seizing

her heart. Her knees softening, she sat down on the coffee table, pressing the phone firmly against her ear.

"Kate? You still there?"

"Yes. I'm still here." Slamming a mental door on her memory vault and slipping back into cop mode, Kate continued. "What've they got?"

As if relieved at her response, Karinsky plowed ahead. "Hammonds dropped her kid off with the grandmother and left for school. She never came back for the kid, and the mother hasn't heard a word from her. I'll forward you the report from missing persons as soon as we get off the phone. You want me to report this to Special Asshole Fraye, or do you want to?"

"I'll talk to Fraye and Harding. Thanks, Karinsky."

Kate hung up and stared at the phone. Her first instinct was to call her partner, but their relationship had been so strained lately that she briefly considered calling Fraye instead. Respect for her partner won out. Harding answered on the second ring, sounding as if he still had one leg in the dream state.

Kate didn't waste time exchanging greetings. "Our guy's at it again."

"How do you know?" Harding was fully awake now.

"Remember Becky Hammonds?"

There was a brief pause. "The domestic violence case?"

"Yes. Her mother filed a missing person's report with the SJPD today." Kate exhaled loudly. "She's a college coed, and she knows me." The last words were barely audible.

"Fuck, Kate. I'm sorry. How long has she been missing?"

"By now? A little over twenty-four hours."

"Let's get an APB out on Becky and her car. Have

you told Fraye about it yet?"

"He's my next call."

"Good. Fed power should be able to light a fire under the SJPD. We'll get down to San Jose in the morning and interview the mother first thing."

"Right."

"And Kate…?"

"Yes?"

His commanding tone morphed into something softer and more intimate, reminding her of the night she'd spent at his place two months before. "This isn't your fault."

She was silent for a moment, fighting an overwhelming urge to invite him over—to disappear into the warmth of his strong arms. Finally, she managed to force out a response as pathetic as the tone in which she'd uttered it. "Yeah, thanks."

She hung up and began dialing Fraye, trying desperately to ignore the cacophony of voices in her head that relentlessly berated her for failing—yet again.

᚛ ᚛ ᚛

Harding parked in front of the small tan home belonging to Becky Hammonds's mother. The house's mission-inspired design deviated little from its neighbors. Other than variations in front-door location, paint color, and number of stories, there wasn't much to differentiate the houses on the quiet, tree-lined block.

Kate and Fraye emerged from the passenger side of the car into the cold morning air. Harding joined them on the sidewalk. All three investigators paused to scan the street before making their way to the door.

Kate pressed the doorbell. Hurried footsteps from within conveyed a frantic sense of urgency.

A fiftyish blonde woman with a thick midsection answered the door. Clad in jeans and an old sweatshirt, with her hair thrown into a hasty ponytail, she was clearly a mother laden with concern. Her eyes flew frantically from Harding to Fraye, then settled on Kate. Recognition flashed in her eyes, drawing her eyebrows together—teasing the light wrinkle at their center into a deep channel.

Harding held his badge up for her inspection. "Angela Hammonds? I'm Detective Harding with the San Francisco Police Department. We're here about Becky."

The worried mother stepped toward Harding, hope welling up in her features. "Have you found her yet?"

"No. But as I said on the phone, you can help us to do that by answering our questions. May we come in?"

"Yes, please!" Angela backed inside, waving them inward.

Closing the door behind them, she ushered them into a rectangular room with a dining area at one end and a modern kitchen at the other. Angela took a seat at the end of the large mahogany table. Kate and Fraye sat to her right, Harding to her left.

"Ms. Hammonds, this is Special Agent Fraye, and this is my partner, Detective Barnes."

She peered at Kate across the table. "Aren't you the officer who helped Becky when she lived in San Francisco?" Her voice trailed off at the mention of the city, as if its very name might be a catalyst for reigniting a painful chapter in her daughter's history.

"Yes, I am." Kate fixed the woman with a level stare.

Fraye filled the awkward silence. "We will do everything in our power to find Becky, Ms. Hammonds. Now, if you can please walk us through the events of the past two days. I know you went over this when you filed the report, but the slightest detail may prove helpful."

Angela dropped her hands into her lap and stared at the table's wood grain, as if the story she was about to tell was mysteriously woven within.

"Like I told the officer yesterday, she came here about half past six, night before last. She didn't want to be late for her history class because she had an exam and was late getting out of work. She's always in a hurry, running to work, running to school. But she's a wonderful mother to Hayden. She…" Tears threatened in the corners of Angela's eyes. She inhaled deeply, drawing on a reserve of inner strength.

A light buzzing sound drew everyone's attention to Fraye. Palming his cell phone awkwardly, he apologized to Angela and excused himself—walking back toward the front entry to take the call.

"Please continue, Ms. Hammonds." Kate leaned forward expectantly, her stylus poised above her iPad.

"She just never came home. At first I thought she was just running late. That her exam just took longer than usual, or maybe she had stopped to pick up a burrito or something on the way back. Becky's so busy all the time. I always have to remind her to take time to eat."

Fraye returned and silently took his seat.

Angela continued without skipping a beat. "I haven't heard from her at all. No calls, no texts, nothing. I checked her Facebook page. She hasn't posted anything since yesterday." Her eyes flew to Kate's. "You don't think Matt could have…"

Kate cut her off sympathetically. "Ms. Hammonds, we've already confirmed that Becky's ex-boyfriend is still safely behind bars."

The news seemed to help, but only momentarily. "Then where is she? I called all the hospitals, her friends, even her boss at the restaurant. She didn't just disappear. She..." A sharply inquisitive expression replaced the distraught one. "Wait a minute. You didn't drive all the way from San Francisco for a missing person's case. And the FBI wouldn't be involved either. You think it's more than that, don't you?"

She splayed her fingers on the table and leaned forward, coming out of her seat toward Kate. "Oh, God! You don't think this has to do with that other girl—the one that was all over the news?"

Kate winced.

Harding laid a gentle hand on Angela's shoulder. "Ms. Hammonds, we are trying to find your daughter, and we're following up on every possibility. Right now, you can help by giving us more background into Becky's life."

Angela settled back down into her seat as the detective slowly removed his hand.

"Has anyone been bothering her lately—any new friendships or love interests we should be aware of?"

Angela sniffed. "Becky has no time for new friendships, and she isn't dating anyone. She's a committed mother who's trying to get her life back on track. After what she's been through with Matt, she doesn't want to risk getting involved again. She's become very cautious. She even refused a Facebook friend request from one of her San Francisco friends last week."

"Why was that, Ms. Hammonds?"

"She wants to leave her memories of her time in

San Francisco behind her—'in the rearview,' as she always says. I think the guy wanted to be more than just friends, anyway."

"Did she tell you his name?"

Angela pursed her lips, trying to remember. "It reminded me of one of those boy bands…"

Kate flashed a quick look at Harding.

"I… I'm sorry. I can't remember."

A crash from the corner of the room drew all eyes to the kitchen, where an adorable little boy in denim overalls and a striped t-shirt looked guiltily at Angela through a tangle of blonde curls. On the floor next to him were the broken remnants of a glass baking dish. Scattered nearby were what appeared to be chunks of brownies.

Angela scrambled out of her seat and hurried to the little boy. Dropping to her knees, she grabbed the boy's arms. "Hayden, are you okay?"

The little eyes rolled upward in exasperation. "Yes, but I can't eat the brownies! They're too hot!"

"I told you, we have to wait for them to cool off, and I also told you never to climb up on the counters!"

He tilted his head toward the wreckage. "But I wanted brownies."

She grasped her grandson suddenly, hugging him with a wild desperation.

Kate rose silently from the table and joined Angela in the kitchen. Reaching under the sink, she retrieved a trash bin and began plucking the shards of glass from the floor. A small hand fell upon her arm. "Too bad you couldn't save the brownies."

Kate turned, finding herself almost nose to nose with Hayden.

"Thanks for helping clean up the brownies, lady.

Can you make me some more?"

"Um, no. But I'm sure your grandmother can."

"Hers aren't as gooey as the ones my mommy makes. Mommy went away for a little while. I miss her." His sweet expression clouded momentarily before brightening again. "Grandma says Mommy's coming back soon. Do you think she'll make me some brownies when she gets back?"

Kate's eyes dropped to the floor briefly before she dragged them back to the angelic face. "Yes, I'm sure she will."

"Yea! I'm gonna go play dinosaurs."

She watched his little form run down the hallway, feeling as broken and shattered as those pieces she'd just put in the trash.

▷▷▷

Thirty minutes later, Fraye and the detectives returned to the car. The two men filed into the front seat while Kate settled into the back.

As Harding eased the sedan away from the curb, Fraye turned to him. "We're not going back to San Francisco yet."

"Oh, really? Then where are we going?" Harding cast him an irritated glance.

"To San Jose State. That call I took at the house —it was from the SJPD. Becky Hammonds's Honda was found a few blocks away from campus. Security camera footage shows Becky walking off campus a little after eight-thirty. Our UNSUB probably abducted her on her way to the car." He shifted in his seat to look at Kate. "The boy is an interesting element, don't you think?"

Kate was about to ask what he meant, when her cell phone came to life. "Barnes."

"Kate? It's Kevin." Something in his tone set her nerves on edge. "Where are you right now?"

"In the car with Harding and Fraye. We just finished up with Becky's mother."

"I need you guys to pull over for a minute."

"Pull over?" Kate's brow furrowed.

"Yeah. Put me on speaker and get your iPad."

"Okay." She leaned forward. "Harding?"

"I'm on it." He engaged the turn signal and quickly pulled over in front of a small park while Kate pulled out her iPad.

As the car came to a stop, she placed her phone on the console between the two front seats and engaged the speaker function. "All right, Kevin. We're on the side of the road, and I've got you on speaker."

"Go into your email. I sent you a video file. Put your screen where everyone can see it, and turn up the volume. Let me know when you're ready, but wait to run it until I tell you."

Kate opened the email and passed the device to Fraye, who stood it up against the dashboard. "Okay, it's set up. What's going on?"

"This video was found by the Quantico guys. It was uploaded to YouTube within the hour. I thought you should see it right away. Go ahead and play it."

Fraye double tapped the file name. The screen went black for a moment, then a white lettered title block appeared. There was no sound, only letters.

HI, KATE.

Harding and Fraye glanced at Kate in unison, before returning their attention to the screen.

The words disappeared and blackness dominated

once again.

After a brief pause, the white letters returned.

IT'S ME, BECKY.

Kate grabbed hold of each of the front seats, forcing her head between them to get closer to the iPad.

A close-up of a pair of bloodshot, watery, blue eyes replaced the darkness. They trembled with a primitive fear.

The darkness returned, followed by more white letters.

YOU SAVED ME ONCE.

The words remained on the screen.

Fifteen seconds passed before the words disappeared. The eyes were back, but this time the camera had been pulled back far enough to reveal the head and shoulders of the woman to whom they belonged.

Greasy blonde hair hung limply about the bare neck and shoulders, which were discolored by a variety of bruises. A tight black gag hid her mouth.

"Oh, Becky." The words came out in a breathy whisper, prompting another quick glance from Harding and Fraye.

Becky's image disappeared, replaced once again by the black nothing. Moments later the white lettering returned.

CAN YOU DO IT AGAIN?

Becky reappeared, her eyes silently pleading. Slowly, the camera panned down between Becky's small, bare breasts. Kate inhaled sharply.

The skin between Becky's breasts was painfully red and swollen. The now familiar shape of the Norse thorn stood out in stark relief on her flesh. The camera zoomed in on the brand, fixing on the symbol for another full minute before the screen went black again.

No words appeared, only a protracted darkness. Kate checked the tracker at the bottom of the video. It was only three quarters of the way across the screen —the show wasn't over yet.

Thirty seconds later, Becky returned. Her head bobbed up and down manically, sheer terror evident in her eyes. Now free of her gag, she spoke for the first time. Her voice filled the car, the terror in it seeming to penetrate every corner of the sedan.

"P-p-please, Kate."

She paused, inhaling deeply.

"Please, Kate. Please help me!" Her voice rose into a high keening sound as she uttered the final words. The screen went black again as Becky's plea played over and over and over again before the video finally ended.

"You guys still there?" Kevin's voice sounded small and unsure.

"Yeah, we are." The words fell from Harding's lips like air from a deflating balloon.

"The good news is that the feds already notified YouTube. They pulled it before it got any views."

"YouTube?" Fraye inquired.

"Uh-huh. The freak posted it under the title, *For Kate, from Becky in the Tower*. The Quantico guys have been monitoring social media for any keyword hits— a bigger project than it should be, thanks to all the hype created by that jogger who uploaded the pic of Maggie's corpse. Luckily, they caught this the moment it was uploaded."

Harding jumped in, tabling his own feelings about the federal government's controversial methods. "If it was posted to YouTube, the guy had to have an account. Anything there?"

"Nothing. Fake account set up under a fake ID, uploaded through an untraceable IP. This guy knows what he's doing."

Kate sat back into her seat, looking dazed. Harding recognized the shell-shocked expression—he'd seen similar responses during his time in the military. Emotional overload—his partner was tuning out on them.

"Kevin, can you…"

"Scrub the audio and video and try to find anything that'll give us a clue as to where he's got her? Already on it. And, um…" He inhaled sharply. "I'm sorry about all this, Kate. I'll let you know what we find ASAP."

Kate reached forward and ended the call.

Fraye regarded Kate as she stared blankly at the phone, his expression softer than anything Harding had thought he might ever find on the stoic agent's features.

He restarted the engine and turned to Fraye. "I'm guessing we'll still hit San Jose State before going back to the Hall."

The agent tore his eyes from Kate and fixed them on Harding, who suddenly became immersed in the act of driving. Fraye continued to stare at the detective's profile. Finally, he dropped his eyes and turned to gaze out the window.

"Yes. I want to get a sense of the place where

Becky disappeared."

To no one in particular, he announced, "Believe it or not, this is a good thing. Our UNSUB wants to communicate with Detective Barnes. It may be our first real step forward, but we're going to have to hurry if we want to save that little boy's mother."

Chapter 10

THE DARK-GRAY tile and dim lighting seemed more fitting for a funeral parlor than a restroom. Beset by budget concerns, the San Francisco Police Department had better things to worry about than the appearance of the women's bathroom.

Leaning over the chipped sink, Kate stared at her reflection, hating what she saw. The woman in the mirror appeared shaken and weak. Her furrowed brow and anxious, tightly drawn lips were not those of the hardened, capable detective she'd worked so hard to become.

The visage before her suddenly disappeared, replaced by that of a panic stricken version of her fourteen-year-old self. Her pulse throbbed in her veins. The floor seemed to roll and pitch beneath her feet. Her inner voice morphed into her mother's cruelly mocking tone. Age-old taunts began to echo through her head. *"Look what you've done, Kate. You've ruined everything! It's all your fault, because you're so stupid and lazy!"*

Like a rock climber whose safety anchors had just torn loose, Kate reached out, clutching the edges of the sink with both hands. Squeezing her eyes shut, she shook her head in the juvenile hope that the motion might dislodge the awful jeering voice.

The door to the restroom swung open. A middle-aged female janitor entered. Pushing a large bin laden with cleaning supplies, she made her way to the bank of stalls on the far wall. Kate opened her eyes, the sudden interruption shocking her back to reality. It also reminded her there wasn't time to dawdle.

Fraye and Harding were waiting for her in the conference room, where they were going to debrief Captain Singh on the latest developments. She'd promised to meet them after stopping in the ladies' room first, not because she needed the facilities, but because she needed some space.

The drive back from San Jose had been exhausting. They hadn't finished at SJSU until around four o'clock in the afternoon, which had resulted in a grueling rush hour trek up the 101 Freeway. The drive, which should have been one hour, had stretched into a little over two.

Glancing back at the mirror, Kate fought to regain her steely determination. Reaching behind her head, she pulled the ponytail holder from her hair. With a few brisk movements, she rebound her tresses more severely than before.

Pain screamed along the nerve endings connected to her hair follicles. The sensation was nothing compared to the raw torrent of emotions inside of her, but it felt cathartic nonetheless.

Standing straight and raising her chin slightly, she nodded curtly toward her reflection, then exited the gloomy chamber. Walking down the hall, she trampled the emotions that had been welling up inside her all day.

As she approached the conference room, she could hear her partner's voice. When she arrived in the doorway, Harding, who stood near the head of the table, stopped speaking abruptly and stared at her.

Sitting at the table across from Captain Singh, Fraye glanced briefly toward her. Ignoring the sympathy in her partner's eyes, she took a seat next to her boss.

"We were going to show the video to the captain, Kate. I don't know if…" his voice trailed off uncomfortably.

Setting her shoulders, she met his eyes. "That's fine. Don't let me slow things down."

Fraye handed his iPad across the table to Singh. "Just hit the play button."

The captain did as instructed. Kate observed her boss while he watched. His impassive expression gave nothing away.

When it was over, he slid the tablet back across the table to Fraye and eyed him critically. "What's your take on this?"

"Detective Barnes engaged this UNSUB on a personal basis. He's telling us he intends to stay around for more than just one dance."

Singh swiveled his chair toward Kate, who held his gaze without a trace of the emotion she'd battled in the restroom. The captain sighed loudly and turned back to Fraye. "How many more?"

"That we don't know. But we can say the victim facilitation rate for any college coeds who know Detective Barnes is off the charts."

Harding piped up. "We know there'll be at least seven."

Like a provoked viper, Fraye abruptly spun his head toward the detective. Eyes blazing, he demanded, "And you know this because… ?"

Seemingly undeterred by the powerful scrutiny, Harding settled down on the credenza behind him. He crossed his arms casually, staring at the FBI agent.

"Because the Tower Torturer killed seven women on the East Coast."

Fraye's eyes narrowed with something close to disdain. "That's a flawed assumption."

"Flawed?" Harding tilted his head to the side, challenging the agent to repeat himself.

Fraye turned toward Captain Singh. "The role of Detective Barnes is key. During the East Coast killings, the Tower Torturer chose victims for their own intrinsic value. In this instance, victims are chosen specifically because they know Detective Barnes."

He inclined his head toward Kate briefly before continuing. "Thus, those who would have been primary targets in the past have become secondary targets in the present."

"Yeah, you've mentioned it before." The note of annoyance was clear in Harding's tone.

"Correct. And I've also said such a material change in victimology may be an indicator of a copycat."

Harding rolled his eyes in a perfect imitation of a prepubescent girl, and reclined against the wall. Addressing the ceiling rather than the special agent, he lamented, "Not this again!"

"Harding." The warning growl issued from deep inside the captain's throat.

Shooting upright, the detective fixed his eyes on his boss. "Come on, Captain! Are we supposed to believe somebody just happened to come up with the same MO? Our guy's even telling us his name. He titled the YouTube video 'from the tower' to taunt us!"

Singh paused, evaluating Harding's words, then fixed his eyes on Fraye—the unanswered question evident in his stare.

Unruffled by Harding's impassioned argument,

Fraye met Singh's eyes evenly. "My profile is not yet complete. His points have merit, but they are not bulletproof."

Harding opened his mouth to respond, but Fraye continued. "Originally, I considered the copycat option based on Detective Barnes's involvement alone—it being a sufficient deviation in victimology." He peered at Kate again. "But, given today's developments with respect to our newest victim, it has become far more likely."

"What—the YouTube video? So he's living in the twenty-first century where serial killers don't send taunting notes to the newspapers—they just post videos." Harding rolled his eyes skyward again. They dropped in surprise when the response he intended to hear from Fraye actually came from his partner.

"No, it's not the video." All eyes turned toward Kate. "It's Hayden." She looked to Fraye for confirmation.

Approval flashed in his eyes. "Correct. The child represents another pivotal change in behavior."

Kate stared at her partner, trying to will him to make the connection she had. When he didn't, she explained. "None of the prior victims had children."

"I know. But why does it matter?"

The special agent's cadence slowed dramatically as if he were offering the explanation to a child. "Because the allure of a fresh young college coed isn't the same as it is for a mother."

Captain Singh joined in. "Would our guy have known Becky had a child?"

Fraye retrieved his iPad from the table and began tapping the screen. "Take a look at her Facebook page." He passed the tablet back to Singh, who swiped his finger across the device several times before returning it.

"There are quite a few pictures of the boy."

"True." Harding uncrossed his arms and sat up a little straighter. "But, I checked out her page this morning before we left. It doesn't specifically say the boy is her son. For all anyone knows, he could be her little brother, or a nephew!"

Captain Singh turned back to Fraye. "Ever since that jogger, Warren Benthe, posted the picture of Maggie's corpse, the press has been breathing down our necks. A second victim is only going to add fuel to the fire. Are you ready to go to the press yet?"

"No. I want to spend some more time analyzing the video before I finalize the profile. Meanwhile, our UNSUB is communicating directly with Kate. There is no strategic gain in engaging the press at this point—all it will do is feed the maelstrom."

"What about our new victim? Any good leads?"

Kate spoke up, addressing her words to the table rather than any of the men in the room. "I heard Becky became active in a victim support group after moving to San Jose. Maggie was doing research for a paper on victim psychology."

Turning her head, Kate regarded each of them in turn. "I called Becky and asked her if she would be interested in talking to Maggie. She agreed, so I gave Maggie her number."

Harding thrust a hand through his hair and stared at the floor.

Fraye ignored the gesture, focusing on Kate. "When was that?"

"About a week ago."

"Do you know if they ever met or talked?"

"No."

Harding jumped in. "We're pulling Becky's phone

records; it will be easy enough to find out."

Fraye glowered at Kate intensely. "It might have been nice to know about this before…" He checked his watch. "Six fourteen at night."

"I'm sorry." Kate's weak response drew Singh's attention.

The captain peered at her sharply before turning to Fraye. "Let's question the members of the support group—see if anyone knows anything about a meeting between the victims. And keep me apprised of any further developments. The mayor wants this thing put to bed immediately."

Turning back to Kate, he stood. "Barnes, I'd like to see you in my office. Now."

Kate shot a quick glance at Harding, then stood and followed the captain out of the room and down the hall to his office. He held the door open for her and closed it while she took a seat.

"Captain, I…"

He held up a hand, commanding her immediate silence as he settled into his chair. "Kate, I'm worried this whole thing is spinning out of control for you.

She leaned forward. "Captain, just because I waited to mention the link between Maggie and Becky…"

The hand returned. "Listen, Kate."

Her right hand tightened reflexively at his use of her given name.

"You're one of the best cops I've ever worked with. You're tough, and you can handle almost any-thing." He observed her steadily. "Almost."

He watched as her jaw slid a bit to the left. Leaning forward, he placed both elbows on his desk. "I'm seriously considering pulling you from this case."

Kate shot out of her chair and placed both hands on her boss's desk, bringing her face within a foot of his. "You can't do that, Captain! This guy is communicating with *me*—he's choosing his victims because of *me*!"

"That's why I'm concerned." He sat back into his chair, waiting until Kate settled back into hers. Exhaling mightily, he continued. "I'm not just concerned about your objectivity, Kate. I'm concerned about your safety."

Kate parroted the juvenile eye roll Singh had witnessed from her partner in the conference room.

"You saw the video. He wants your personal attention, Kate. We saw what he did to Maggie... Hell, the FBI can't even tell us what his end game is."

Something in Kate's features seemed to soften. She gazed down at the floor.

When her eyes found his again, they were intense and focused. "Captain, I truly appreciate the concern. But you need me on this case. For whatever reason, this freak has fixated on me, and I'm going to have to be the one to stop him."

"A team will stop him, Kate. Not one individual."

"I understand, but I need to be a part of it."

He watched her silently for a few minutes, taking her measure. "All right. But, there's going to be a black and white outside your house. And I want you sticking to Harding and Fraye like glue."

Disappointment clouded her expression.

Singh continued before she could protest. "Those are the conditions. No debate. Accept them, or get off the case."

Inhaling deeply, Kate grabbed both arms of her chair and propelled herself upward. "Thanks, Captain. I'll accept it."

"Good. Now get back to work."

▷▷▷

The small bar was tucked into the ground-floor corner of the two-story, 1930s-era building. Windowless, its only decoration was a kitschy and faded old sign dominated by a comically styled martini glass. The marker glowed weakly in the night, its appearance further obscured by soft tendrils of icy fog.

To those driving by on the busy, narrow street, it resembled the typical sort of dive cops found themselves ducking into on their way home at night. A place where memories made toiling in the dark side of human behavior could be put on a shelf—to sit there, safe from home and family, until they must be reclaimed the next day.

A few feet from the door, Kate paused and regarded Harding wearily. "Why don't we just pass tonight? It's been a long day and…"

Laying a firm hand on her right shoulder, Harding propelled her forward. "It's not an option, Kate. We're going inside and getting you a good stiff drink."

After seeing Becky's video and fighting with the captain to retain her spot on the team, Kate didn't have much energy left to protest. Harding had picked her up early that morning for the drive to San Jose. He was supposed to be dropping her at home now, but had insisted on stopping at the bar first. One drink, then she'd be out of there.

Pulling his hand from her back, Harding took a few quick steps ahead and opened the weathered wooden door. Kate stepped inside and was pleasantly surprised.

The interior of the space bore no resemblance to the shoddy exterior. Decorated in bold hues of royal blue and jet black, with sleek lines and sumptuous finishes, the place was beautiful.

A long black bar dominated the right side of the room. Behind it, backlit pewter shelves, bedecked with bottles of alcohol, climbed toward the ceiling. A row of pewter barstools with blue velvet cushions ran the length of the bar. Demand exceeded supply—men and women stood pressed up against the barstools, chatting excitedly in groups of three to five.

Small black tables were lined up in a row on the left side of the room. Along the back wall, two booths were wedged together beneath a stunning canopy of dark-blue satin curtains. An old Duke Ellington jazz number played in the background.

"Not what you were expecting?"

Kate turned to find Harding smiling at her. "No. Not from the outside."

"Good. Now why don't you go grab the empty booth in back while I order us some drinks?"

Kate nodded and began making her way back to the booth. Given the narrowness of the place and the throngs of patrons, progress could only be made through a combination of sidestepping and dance-style maneuvers.

Sliding into the comfort of the padded booth, Kate pulled her phone out and began typing a message to Kevin. She was about to press send when Harding arrived with an incredibly dark beer and a lowball glass filled almost to the rim with a brown liquid.

Glancing up from the screen, Kate eyed the glass warily. "That beer had better be for me."

"No." Harding settled into the seat across from her, pushing the small glass across the table. "This is yours."

"What is it?"

"Bourbon, straight."

"Bourbon? Are you kidding me? The stuff will rot my stomach!" Kate turned her head away in disgust.

Harding didn't know much about Kate's past, but he did know his partner had had a hard time as a kid—something about an absentee father and an addict mother. He wondered idly whether her concern over ingesting the hard liquor might have deeper roots.

It didn't matter. Kate was wound too tight. She needed a break from the intensity. One drink wouldn't fix anything, but it certainly could take the edge off a bit.

Leveling her with his most authoritative glare, he leaned forward across the narrow table. "Drink it, Barnes. Now."

"But I don't…"

"I said drink it. Don't make me come over there." His commanding tone didn't leave room for argument.

Glaring back at him, Kate cocked her head to the side, lifted the glass, and took a sip. He watched with amusement as she tried to keep her face expressionless —knowing the liquid was burning a wicked trail down her throat.

"Good girl."

"If only." Dropping her chin, Kate's gaze turned inward.

"Kate, don't let that shit Fraye said today upset you."

Stoically, she fixed her eyes on his. "He was right. I should have told you guys about putting Maggie and Becky together from the beginning. There's no excuse for it."

"Oh, I don't know. Having a psycho kill the college kid you're mentoring, then kidnap another one you've helped in the past—either one of those could throw anyone off their game. Even the mighty Fraye."

"Well, I'd better send this before I screw up again." She glanced down at her phone meaningfully.

"What is it?"

"An email to Kevin, asking him to check out Becky's Facebook page—see if he can tell us whose friend request Becky declined."

Harding pulled his beer from his lips before taking a sip. "Don't worry about it. I already asked Kevin to check it out."

Kate deleted the email and stuffed the phone in her purse. "Thank God one of us is doing their job." To his surprise she took a voluntary sip of the molten fire.

He took a long drink of his beer. Placing the glass down on the table, he slumped back into the booth. "You're not alone in this, Kate."

"Really? Because it looks like I'm the only one this guy is after—and women are getting hurt because of me."

A strange expression flashed across his features. His hands clenched into tight fists. Aware Kate was watching him, he relaxed his hands and took a deep breath.

"You're not the only one who carries a burden, Kate." He took another long sip.

Kate pressed her lips together and dropped her hands into her lap. "I'm sorry. Sometimes I forget you've had your own share of tragedy." Harding's status as a widower was rumored about on the force, but he had never discussed it with Kate.

"Yeah. Well everyone does, right?"

"You've never told me much about your wife." The words spilled from Kate's lips before she could impose a filter.

A pained expression clouded his features. She was about to change the subject when he gazed deeply into his glass and began speaking.

"You already know I did a tour with the Army before college."

Kate nodded.

"Thought it'd be a good way to pay for school and get to see the world. As it turned out, they didn't end up paying much of my tuition, and the only part of the world I ever saw was a hot, dusty hell where the hostiles wanted to kill us, and the local citizens hoped they would.

"When I got back, I enrolled at Boston U, where I met Denise. We both grabbed for the last copy of a required statistics text at the same time." His lips twisted into a sad smile. "Denise was beautiful, smart, and she didn't take shit from anyone."

"Sounds like the perfect match for you."

"Yeah, she was perfect for me. Too bad I wasn't so good for her."

Kate cupped her hands around her glass. Harding had never revealed so much about himself before. "You had to have been pretty good. She married you, right?"

"That came later. First, we both finished our undergrad degrees. Then, I went on to the academy and she went on to grad school."

"Grad school?"

"Yeah, we were going to be the law and order team. I became a cop, and she became an attorney."

"Wow."

He took another sip. "Yeah, wow. Denise got into corporate law, and we got married a few years later. I worked my way up to detective. She took a job with a firm downtown. Everything seemed to be going great. Sure, she was making a hell of a lot more than me, but it was never really an issue—not for either of us, anyway. And she worked so many hours at her job, she didn't mind all the time I was away from home for mine."

"Sounds like you were happy."

Harding glanced away, pain tugging at his features. "We were. Until I fucked it up."

"You?"

"Yeah, I got too involved in the Torturer case—a case that consumed me. I was away from home even more than normal. One weekend I flew to South Carolina to follow up on a lead. Denise was home alone." His grip tightened on the glass—the whites of his knuckles appearing to be on a mission to escape the confines of his skin.

"What happened?"

"B&E. Some fucked-up meth head broke into our garage. Denise heard the noise and assumed I'd come home early. She went to the garage and… that's where they found her."

He sat upright, assuming a mask of calm detachment. "She'd been bludgeoned to death with one of the leftover bricks from the path I'd laid in the backyard the year before."

Knowing words were useless, Kate reached out and took one of his hands in hers.

"I got the call when I landed at Logan. After that, I wasn't much use to anyone. The all-important case didn't seem to matter anymore. Nothing really did. I took a leave and eventually left Boston to come here and work with you."

Kate tightened her grip on his hand. "Well, I'm glad you did. I wouldn't trade you for anything, partner."

"I'm glad too. It has been a while, but it's finally stopped hurting so bad."

He laid his other hand on top of hers. "Kate, about what happened between us that night…"

She pulled her hand away. "We agreed not to talk about it again. I think we need to leave it that way." Tossing back the last of the bourbon as if it were water, she eyed him steadily. "If we're all paid up, I need to get home and get some sleep."

"Yeah, we're all paid up. Let's go." He stood up and started for the door.

Kate followed him outside. Harding's car was parked a few blocks away. They walked in silence for the first block. As they crossed to the second, Kate spoke again.

"Singh wanted me off the case. It's what he wanted to talk to me about after our meeting with Fraye."

"I suspected as much."

"You knew? What did he say to you?"

"No, I didn't know. But I assumed he'd be worried about your safety."

"And my objectivity."

They arrived at the car. Neither of them made an attempt to climb inside. "What did you tell him?"

"That I'm fine. That I can handle it. But he made me agree to some very unpleasant terms, including having a black and white camped outside my apartment."

"Great idea."

"What?" Kate stared at him, mouth agape. "I can take care of myself."

"Of course you can. But this guy's different. He evaded capture the first time; we're damn lucky to be getting a second crack at him."

"If you believe it's the same guy."

"Don't start with Fraye's copycat shit again."

Uninterested in rehashing the debate, Kate stood in front of the passenger side door, waiting silently for Harding to unlock the car. To her surprise, he came around and opened the door for her. She climbed inside and had just finished buckling her seat belt when she noticed her partner was still standing in the open doorway.

He squatted down next to her, staring at her intently. "Now, let's talk about what happened that other night."

Kate looked away. "Nothing happened."

"Yes, it did. We had sex, Kate. Amazing, mind-numbing sex. And I haven't been able to stop thinking about it since."

"So, humans do that sometimes. And some of them shouldn't—like partners. It was a mistake, and we just need to move past it."

"Really?" He leaned inside. "Really, Kate? Are you going to tell me you didn't enjoy it?"

Kate shrank away from him. "Let's just go, okay?"

"No, it's not okay. Are you really telling me you don't want to do it again, Kate? Because if I remember correctly, you asked me to do it again and again that night. As I recall, there were at least four separate occasions, not including the shower, where you…"

"Okay! Okay! So it was amazing. So, I'd love to do it again! But…"

The pressure of his lips silenced her. Before she knew what she was doing, her mouth opened into his kiss, and her fingers were in his hair, pulling him in greedily.

A soft growl rolled low in his throat as his fingertips plunged into the open space beneath the buttons of her blouse. The sensation of his fingertips brushing against the top of her breast set her senses on fire, and her mind on alert. Tearing her mouth away, she placed both hands firmly on his shoulders and pushed him out of the car.

Smiling, he closed her door, then hurried around and climbed into the driver's seat. Feeling smug and frustrated at the same time, he drove to her apartment. Singh had been good to his word. A black-and-white patrol car was parked conspicuously across the street from the front door of the building.

Harding double-parked alongside the SFPD vehicle. Kate exploded from the car, slamming the door firmly before stalking toward the sidewalk.

Waving in recognition to the familiar officer in the patrol car, Harding called out to Kate with genuine joy in his voice. "To be continued, Barnes!"

Chapter 11

January 31

KEVIN WAS RELIEVED to find Kate sitting at her desk. He'd missed the daily, mandatory task force briefing this morning because of his project. Now, an hour after the meeting had ended, he was ready to share the results of his labors. Tapping his laptop anxiously against his thigh, he waited for Kate to finish her phone call.

"You got something for us?" Harding called out from his desk near the window. Kevin glanced back at Kate, who held up one finger, then inclined her head toward her partner.

Nodding, Kevin walked over to Harding's desk. "I found some things I want you guys to see."

The right side of the detective's mouth quirked upward in amusement. "You'd better had. Fraye was pissed you didn't show up to the meeting this morning."

"I texted him before the meeting and told him I was in the middle of something."

"In the middle of what?" Kate had finished her call and came to stand next to Kevin. A thick application of makeup only partially hid the dark circles under her eyes.

"Come on, I'll show you." He turned and headed for the conference room. The two detectives hurried along behind him.

Fraye was pacing the far end of the large room with his cell phone to his ear. Pausing in the doorway, Kevin rapped his knuckles loudly against the door. The agent turned and waved them inside.

Fraye eyed Kevin as he sat down beside Harding. Kate settled in across the table from him as the FBI agent ended the call.

"What have you found?" Fraye took a chair by Kate, watching Kevin intently.

Irritation honed the edges of the innocuous words into deadly weapons. Kevin sighed internally. He didn't really give a shit whether the agent was pissed with him. Getting what he had waiting on his laptop was more important than sitting in a meeting rehashing stuff he already knew.

Kevin opened his computer, wirelessly taking control of the large screen at the back of the room. Immersed in the contents of the display, he explained. "Harding asked me to find the person Becky shot down on Facebook."

"Shot down?"

The IT director peered over the computer at Fraye. "I mean the friend request she denied."

"And?"

Kevin looked toward the screen, where a Facebook page appeared. The profile photo featured a man in his late thirties, failing miserably in an attempt at a high-fashion-style pose. The plain brown eyes matched the shade of his seriously thinning brown hair.

Kate and Harding exchanged a meaningful glance across the table. Catching the interaction, Fraye

130

remarked, "I take it you two know Mr...." He turned back to the screen briefly before turning back toward Kate. "Mr. Jonas Riley."

"We met him the other day when we interviewed one of Maggie's professors at San Francisco State. He's a teaching assistant."

Kevin jumped in. "Profile says he's also a grad student."

Harding stood and walked closer to the screen. "So how would Jonas, who was a TA for one of Maggie's classes, know our second victim?"

"Becky went to SFSU when she lived here; maybe he was a TA for one of her classes too. Or maybe they just met on campus."

Harding squinted at the screen and began reading aloud. "Interests: chess, archaic civilizations, and mountain biking. Really? Who the hell lists archaic civilizations as an interest?" Harding turned around, incredulity painted across his features.

"I read through his posts; he's a pretty cerebral guy."

Fraye turned to Kevin. "Was Riley listed as one of Maggie's contacts?"

"No, but it's interesting you mention contacts. In addition to finding this guy, I've also found something else I think you'll be interested in." Kevin typed quickly. The Facebook page of a forty-three-year-old African American car mechanic named Daniel Fermel replaced Jonas Riley's page. The camera had caught Fermel in the act of downing what appeared to be a tequila shot.

"Who's he?" Harding inquired.

Kevin settled back into his chair, stretching his arms out over the arm rests. "I cross-referenced the two victims by degrees of separation. The only point

131

of commonality I could find between the two women was Fermel."

"How many degrees?" Fraye's eyes devoured the image of the man on the screen.

"On Maggie's end, he works with her boyfriend, Troy. On Becky's end, he knows a bartender named Carrie whose sister, Jenna Moysore, is a friend of Becky Hammonds."

Harding read from the screen. "Interests: boating, off-roading, and chicks. Just the opposite of the nerd, Riley."

"He also lives in San Francisco, and…" Kevin sat up and swiped his finger over the mouse pad. The Facebook page scrolled downward, stopping on a picture of a knife-wielding Fermel wearing blood-soaked camouflage fatigues. A deer carcass hung from a tree branch in the background. Lying in the tailgate of a green truck was an assault rifle.

"And he's a hunter." Fraye finished flatly. "I appreciate your time, Kevin, but this person has nothing to do with our investigation."

Disappointment flashed across Kevin's features.

Harding turned from the screen, leveling the agent with a dead stare. "We haven't even checked him out yet. How do you know he has nothing to do with it?"

"May I see your laptop, Kevin?"

"Sure." He slid it across the table to Fraye.

"Daniel Fermel is not involved for the following reasons." On the screen, the profile section reappeared. "One: Daniel Fermel is African American."

"So?"

Kate attempted to break up the flow of testosterone. "Our victims have been blonde-haired, blue-eyed Caucasians. Statistically, serial killers don't tend to venture outside of their race."

The agent nodded while Harding grunted loudly in disapproval. "But it can happen."

Ignoring the detective, Fraye continued. "Two, his interests, while masculine and aggressive in nature, reflect a boorish and showy nature. Three…" A close-up of Fermel and the deer replaced the profile page. "He took out a deer with an assault rifle—demonstrating a lack of restraint and finesse."

Fraye's gaze slid from the computer screen to Harding. "Based on the choice of dump site and the condition of Maggie's corpse, we know our UNSUB is efficient, methodical, highly organized, and well educated. Mr. Fermel is a stereotypical alpha male who lacks the intelligence, control, and sophistication required to commit these crimes."

Harding was about to respond when Kate shot him a warning glare, punctuated with a raised eyebrow.

"Jonas Riley, on the other hand…" Riley's Facebook page reappeared on the screen. Fraye stood and joined Harding, staring at the profile photo intently. "As a graduate student, he certainly would have the intellect. He's physically fit, and studies of archaic culture may have familiarized him with rune symbols such as the Norse thorn. And, it says here that his hometown is Boston."

Turning abruptly from the screen, he fixed his eyes back on Kate. "Let's arrange to talk to Mr. Riley as soon as possible."

ᚦᚦᚦ

The house on Thirty-Third Avenue was not much different from any other in the Sunset District. Viewed from the street, the residences appeared to be nothing more than double-decker boxes. A large window that

sat atop a garage on the first floor uniformly dominated the second story of each of the small domiciles.
Most of the homes had stairs that led to front
entrances on the second story, positioned either to
the right or the left of the window.

In typical San Francisco fashion, there was no
space between the structures, making it appear as if
they were merely rows of townhouses on either side
of the street. Charming architectural details such as
tiled roofs, arched doorways, or variations in window
design broke up the visual monotony.

With the space between the walkway and driveway consisting of only a foot or two, most residents
had chosen to forgo a spot of landscaping in favor of
utilitarian concrete slabs. A few stalwart nature enthu-
siasts bucked the trend, having installed small planters
here or there, serving as petite beacons of life in the
sea of concrete and stucco.

The foggy sky above was visible through an intricate and sloppy network of telephone lines, which
had been strung in a seemingly haphazard crisscross
pattern across the street, creating an almost claustro-
phobic feel. Kate and Harding paused, scanning the
front of the light green house.

According to the Department of Motor Vehicles,
Riley owned a blue 2002 minivan. There was no sign
of it anywhere.

Kate turned to her partner. "Main entrance is the
one on the ground floor. Riley's apartment is probably a garage conversion." Harding nodded and
started toward the door, which was actually a dull-
gray metal security gate. As they approached, a set of
stairs became visible on the other side of the gate.
The stairs climbed upward sharply, disappearing to
the right. Between the gate and the stairs, another

door led into the garage.

Exchanging a quick glance with Kate, Harding pressed the doorbell. After thirty seconds, he rang again. Movement at the large window above drew Kate's eye. The drapes, which had been closed when they had arrived, now swayed softly.

"Somebody's home."

Harding pressed the doorbell once more, holding it much longer than necessary. A door opened some-where above, and a female voice with a distinct Asian accent called out.

"Okay, okay! I hear you!"

The sound of leather slapping against the tile stairs heralded the arrival of a tiny old woman wearing a faded-blue housecoat. Holding on tightly to the iron railing, she plodded slowly down the stairs. Pausing a few feet from the gate, she peered at them through the metalwork. Shrewd dark brown eyes flitted about, inspecting them thoroughly.

"Good afternoon, ma'am. We're here to see Jonas Riley."

Tilting her head, she eyed them skeptically. "Jonas not home. You come back." She turned and began making her way back up the stairs when Harding called out to her.

"Please, ma'am. We are police officers. May we come in and talk to you?" Harding retrieved his badge and held it up to the gate. She paused and turned around.

"Police officers?"

"Yes."

Muttering something indistinguishable in her native tongue, she made her way back to the gate and studied Harding's badge. "What you want?"

Kate stepped closer. "We want to talk to Jonas.

135

We went to the university, but we were told he called in sick for work today."

Narrowing her eyes, the woman waved a withered hand dismissively in Kate's direction. "Maybe sick, but not here. You go now."

Kate could feel Harding's frustration levels rising. She laid a steadying hand on his sleeve and tried again. "Please, ma'am. Could we come in and talk to you? We are trying to save the life of an innocent young woman."

The wrinkled brow lifted slightly before she turned again and started back up the stairs.

"Fuck." Harding breathed the word, surprised to discover that the older woman's ears had not declined with age.

Holding on to the railing, she turned and shot him a warning look. "I go buzz you in, but no swear! You swear, I don't help!"

"Yes, ma'am. I apologize."

"Good." She continued up the stairs, leather slippers slapping the tile as she ascended.

Kate could not suppress the smile that blossomed on her mouth. Harding watched her reaction, and couldn't help but smile himself.

A loud buzzing noise echoed in the small foyer, indicating the gate had been unlocked. Harding pushed and the metal aperture opened inward. They went upstairs, where the owner of the house was holding the front door open. She ushered them in quickly, then led them into a meticulously clean living room, and gestured for them to take a seat on the couch near the window.

Something spicy and delicious was cooking in the kitchen to her right, reminding Kate she hadn't eaten anything since the bowl of cereal late last night.

Ignoring the rumbling in her stomach, she thanked their hostess for letting them in.

The older woman settled into one of the two antique-style armchairs across from them. Her gray hair fell in a straight curtain, its tips brushing lightly against her slightly stooped shoulders as she moved. A few short, more unruly strands stood up rebelliously on the top of her head.

"What your name?" The dark eyes bored into Kate's.

"I'm Detective Barnes; this is Detective Harding. And you are?' The question was perfunctory. On the way over, Kate had called Fraye to tell him they'd come up empty at Riley's place of employment. Fraye had Kevin run Riley's address and learned that he lived in a house owned by Tina Fung.

"I Tina Fung. I live here fifteen years. Fifteen years and no trouble from police. You think Jonas hurt young woman?"

"We are hoping Jonas might know something that can help us."

Keen intelligence flashed in her eyes, a wisdom amassed from decades of living. "Jonas hard working. He live here two years. No problems for two years. He live in apartment downstairs, no problems."

"That's good. Can you tell us if Jonas ever has any visitors?"

"No, he hard working—no time for play. He go to school for work and study, very hard working. He help with yard, work all the time. Even with tools."

"Tools?" Harding inquired.

Her eyes shifted to his. "Yes. He make own tools for studies."

"Where does he make these tools?"

"In shed."

The word resonated soundly with both detectives. Kate jumped in. "Ms. Fung, may we see the shed? It may be very important."

Raising her shoulders, Tina glared at Kate. "Jonas do nothing bad—only work hard. No trouble with woman from Jonas."

"I understand, Ms. Fung. But this is very important." Kate reached into her purse and retrieved her iPad. Pulling up a photo, she held out the screen toward the elderly woman.

Tina leaned forward and stared at the screen, her eyes pouring over the features of Becky's pretty, smiling face. "This woman has a little boy. We need to do whatever we can to help her."

The aged visage shifted from Kate to Harding and back again. With the spry movement of someone decades younger, she hopped out of the armchair and hurried toward the back of the house. "Come, I show you. You see Jonas good man."

Kate and Harding sprang from the couch and followed her down a hall. Tina opened a door onto a small wooden deck that overlooked a tiny yard. A stretch of grass occupied three quarters of the area. Perfectly manicured shrubs rose up from planters sprinkled throughout. Large juniper trees lined the back perimeter. Sitting in the northwestern corner was an aluminum shed about the size of a delivery truck.

Tina stamped her feet loudly. "You hurry now—very cold. Go see shed." Having issued her edict, she retreated into the house, letting the door slam shut behind her.

Kate and Harding hurried down the steep wooden stairs, pausing to look back at the house. "Trees provide privacy from back neighbors, but those to the right and left have full view," Harding observed.

Nodding in agreement, Kate continued across the dewy grass to the shed. Prefabricated in a royal-blue sheet metal, the small structure had double doors in the front. Harding reached for one of the handles and pulled. They peered inside, then exchanged a long glance.

Kate retrieved her phone and began dialing while Harding stepped inside.

A female voice answered. "Eileen Reddick."

"Professor Reddick, this is Detective Kate Barnes."

"Oh, yes. How are you doing, Detective? Have you made any progress with the investigation?"

"I believe so, Professor." Kate stepped into the doorway, glancing briefly at the table saw and other fabrication tools. "We are trying to get a hold of your assistant, Jonas Riley. Do you know where he might be today?"

Concern weighed heavily in the professor's tone. "I heard he's out sick. I assume he's at home."

"He's not. Any other thoughts where we might find him?"

"Detective, what is this about? Why would you be interested in Jonas?"

"We think he may be able to help in the investigation. Please, it's very important."

Harding made his way through the small space. Placing his hands on his hips, he turned and watched Kate, his demeanor transmitting a sense of controlled urgency.

Kate broke eye contact with her partner, turning to examine one of the wooden-handled instruments hanging from the ceiling. Kate didn't know what to call it, other than a vicious-looking type of scimitar. Like the rest of the tools in the shed, it was a recent reproduction of ancient tools of war—tools designed to kill and maim.

"I'm sorry, Detective. I don't know where Jonas is. Maybe he went out to get something at the store."

"Professor, you said Jonas is a graduate student."

"Yes, he's working on his thesis—an analysis of how weaponry in emerging civilizations reflected changes in social consciousness."

Kate repeated the statement out loud. Harding's eyes widened. Thanking Eileen, Kate hung up and glanced around the storehouse again. Holding up her phone, she began taking pictures.

"I'll snap a few more and send these to Fraye."

"Good. Tell him to ask the DA for a warrant so we can get into that apartment ASAP. I doubt Ms. Fung is going to give us access without it."

Kate nodded, already in the process of calling Fraye. She hoped her partner didn't notice the slight tremor in her hand as she held the phone to her ear. Never having been a religious person, Kate silently prayed they could save Becky in time.

Chapter 12

February 1

JOGGING UP MORAGA between Seventeenth and Sixteenth Avenues was easy. It was the following block that was the killer. Keeping her eyes on the ground ahead, seventeen-year-old Samantha Fulton plodded up the street, dreading what was to come. Hot sweat trickled down her neck from the short brown hair she'd hastily tucked into a San Francisco Giants baseball cap—its heat evaporating in the early morning cold.

Huge Monterey cypresses, a novelty in the tightly packed neighborhood, dominated the concrete planter to her left, dividing the one lane of eastbound traffic with the lane for the west. On either side of the road, two-story homes crowded together, appearing to huddle for warmth in the January chill.

The neighborhood was deserted. Except for the occasional passing car, Samantha seemed to be the only one around.

Raising her left wrist, she glanced at her watch. It was only five forty-three. There was plenty of time to finish her run and get back home to shower and change before school.

Despite the super-lame uniform and the fact that the student body was all girls, Samantha loved her private Catholic high school—mostly because of the awesome way everyone treated her. The other girls, and even the teachers, fawned over her like some kind of basketball god.

She'd earned their respect by leading the league in scoring for the past two consecutive years. As much as it sucked, staying at the top of her game meant adhering religiously to her conditioning routine.

It wasn't just the way people treated her that was on the line. Her parents had invested a small fortune in her education. If she could get a college scholarship, her parents could stop talking about crazy things— like cashing out their retirement funds to cover tuition.

She arrived at the intersection where Moraga deadended into Sixteenth Avenue. This was the part of her route she dreaded the most.

There was nowhere to go now but up. Of the one hundred and sixty-three steps that scaled the hill leading to Grand View Park, only the first span was visible in the thick morning fog.

Crossing the street, she arrived at the foot of the stairs where a streetlamp on her left struggled to cast a milky-orange glow. Lush landscape rose up alongside the staircase, setting the concrete structure apart from the neighboring houses. The concentration of greenery was a welcome relief from the jumble of structures that dominated the Inner Sunset District.

This morning the creamy conditions had swallowed the nearby structures perched along the hillside. Only a few feet of landscape remained visible on either side of the stairs.

Samantha plunged ahead, oblivious to the weather. Breezing across the sidewalk, she hopped onto the first stair. With the vivid imagination of one who has not yet embraced the ennui of adulthood, she imagined herself magically transported to another place. It was a world of whimsy and creativity, alive with nature's beauty and abundance.

The stairs themselves served as the portal to this magic dimension. Each of the risers was adorned with ceramic tiles that illustrated the fantastical realm with incredible artistry. Inspired by the vibrant colors of the famed Escadaria Selaron in Rio de Janeiro, the beautifully painted tiles had been fitted together to form an amazing mosaic that rose up the hill in an incredible tribute to the skill and talent of its creators. The neighborhood art project offered a unique and inspiring accompaniment to the arduous climb.

As visitors ascended, the images evolved from an underwater scene replete with all manner of sea creatures, through a fantastical garden. The garden transformed into a serene mountain valley that opened to the heavens above. Stars and a luminous quarter-phase moon nestled securely beneath the brilliance of the life-giving rays of the golden sun. A series of inter-connecting spirals swirled upward from the depths of the ocean to the mountain valley above, exuding a sense of movement and energy throughout the piece.

Channeling the vitality of the art below her feet, Samantha bounded up the first twenty steps with relative ease. Reaching the first small landing, she continued upward without pausing. Around the fiftieth step, her protesting hamstrings pulled her thoughts abruptly back to reality.

By the time she'd scaled another twenty steps, an annoying cramp had taken root in her side. Battling a somnambulant whisper tempting her to give up and go back to bed, she clenched her fists tightly. She pumped her arms harder, endeavoring to telegraph their strength into her protesting leg muscles.

Digging deep, she stared at each individual stair as she ascended, telling herself all she had to do was keep stepping. The words became a mantra in her head. That was all she had to do to be successful. *Just keep stepping.*

And then, Samantha stopped dead in her tracks.

She had just arrived at another small landing when she noticed something blocking her path. Sprawled across the next full expanse of steps, it had been affixed to the railings on either side with thick black ropes.

Gasping for air, she put her hands on her hips and studied the odd shape. It took a full extra minute for the image to register in Samantha's young mind. Though she considered herself to be a tough, disciplined person, when her mind finally comprehended the horror displayed before her, Samantha came apart at the seams—screaming like an inmate trapped within the darkest corners of bedlam.

▷▷▷

The uniformed police officers waved Kate through the barricades. Despite the early hour, a large crowd had assembled. Hastily parking in the middle of the closed intersection, she got out of her car and carefully scanned the area.

Plastic barricades and a handful of patrol cars effectively closed off traffic along Sixteenth Avenue and kept the crowd pinned back as much as one quarter of the way down Moraga. A thick fog enveloped much of the surrounding neighborhood, creating a seemingly impenetrable low ceiling overhead.

Fraye had called that morning to inform her that a body had been discovered on the Sixteenth Avenue steps, and that it was probably Becky Hammonds.

The FBI agent had obtained the necessary warrant to search Jonas Riley's apartment the night before. The apartment itself hadn't contained much other than textbooks and a few porn magazines. But the wicked weapons they'd found in the shed, along with a few pictures of Maggie, clearly taken without the subject's knowledge, had finally convinced Harding that Riley might be their guy.

The teaching assistant had never returned to his apartment. The APB hadn't yielded anything, and they had no leads on Riley's current whereabouts.

Kate hurried over to the sidewalk where Harding and Fraye stood talking at the base of the stairs. Instead of waiting for them to finish, she interrupted. "Is it Becky?"

Both men turned to look at her. Minor annoyance flashed across Fraye's features.

Harding's held a mixture of concern and sympathy. "We haven't gone up yet, but it sounds like this one is way worse than Maggie. A local teenager found the body. The girl's screams were loud enough to wake most of the neighbors."

He inclined his head toward the crowd. "The girl was so freaked out that she ran home to her parents, who called 911. They live over on Noriega. I called and told them we'd be over to question her after we finish up here. Crime scene techs are up there now; there's only so much room on the stairs. So we've been waiting for them to…"

"You can come up now!" The disembodied voice floated down from somewhere behind the wall of moisture above.

Fraye placed a foot on the first step. "Shall we?"

Kate started up alongside him, leaving Harding to trail behind them.

"Unusual stairs," Fraye murmured as they ascended.

"I wouldn't have wanted the job of painting all these little tiles." Harding's breathing was a bit labored from the climb. "I think they…"

He collided with Kate, who had stopped abruptly in front of him. Fraye halted too. About twenty stairs above them, the fog had thinned enough to reveal a large pink object lying on the stairs. Tentatively scaling another five feet, Kate stopped again and peered at the object through the murky precipitation.

Swaying slightly, Kate reached for the railing with her left hand. Recalling crime scene protocols, she snatched her hand away before making contact.

On the stairs above them was the bare body of a woman. The arms and legs were spread out in the shape of the letter X—having been secured to the railing supports at the wrists and ankles by thick black ropes.

The pink color was due to the fact that not only had the corpse's clothes been removed, but its skin had been removed as well—at least most of it. Appearing like a matching set of vivid white accessories, the remaining scraps covering the face, hands, and feet stood out in stark relief to the mass of muscles and connective tissue visible on the rest of the body. Long hair, blonde at the crown, trailed down in a sickly, bloody mess over the chest.

The soft shade of the cadaver contrasted sharply against the vibrant hues of the mosaic it was laid upon, creating a grotesque tableau that was at once revolting and strangely beautiful.

"Holy fuck!" Harding had issued the words, despite their severity, in the barest of whispers.

Camera flashes popped to the left. The two crime scene techs had ventured off the stairs, into the landscaping. One of them, a mustached man in his early fifties, lowered his camera and caught Fraye's eye. "This is one sick motherfucker, man."

"Apparently. Is it okay for us to get a closer look?"

"Sure. We just finished. But don't go above the body. We haven't made it up to the top yet. Oh, and watch out for that wet patch on the right of the stairs. The responding officer lost his Egg McMuffin all over the place."

Fraye nodded curtly, then started up the stairs, stopping a step below the body. Kate and Harding hurried up behind him.

Peering forward, Kate tried to study the face of the corpse, but the angle of the head was problematic. It rested upon one of the steps as if sleeping on a pillow, tilting the features skyward, making identification impossible. Setting her jaw, Kate climbed upward, delicately stepping between the ropes and outstretched limbs as if playing an intricate, yet gruesome, game of cat's cradle.

Standing on the step next to the cadaver's waist, she hunched down and peered at the face. An earthy and meaty smell—that bore no resemblance to any type of protein she'd ever eaten—rose from the body.

Fraye picked his way up and stopped across from Kate. "Strongly resembles our missing victim. What do you think?"

A slight shiver rocked Kate's shoulders as she gazed at the lifeless face. When it passed, she closed her eyes as if lost in prayer.

"Detective Barnes?"

Grasping the tops of her thighs tightly, Kate propelled herself upward. Still staring at the unnaturally white skin, Kate spoke as if the words themselves were slowly eviscerating her. "It's Becky."

"And this is our UNSUB's handiwork." Fraye gestured to the inside of Becky's left thigh, where the Norse thorn had been branded deeply into the muscle, giving it the appearance of a charred steak. "There was a brand on her chest in the YouTube video, but in removing his canvas, he lost his artwork."

"Why the hell did he bring her all the way up here?" Harding spun around and glanced down at the stairs, which had disappeared into the gently swirling mist below.

"He's creating a scene again. And he's doing it at the dead end of another long stretch of road. A long stretch anchored by a park at one end and a body of water on the other." Recalling the crime scene techs had already finished, Kate grabbed the railing, then turned and stared into the fog. "He left Maggie where Sunset deadends at Lake Merced Boulevard. It runs from the lake northward, all the way to Golden Gate Park." She patted the railing lightly. "These stairs lead up to Grand View Park. If we were here on a sunny day, we could see all the way westward down Moraga to the Pacific."

Fraye regarded Kate with the quiet pleasure of a teacher whose pupil has mastered an advanced lesson. "North to south with Maggie. Now east to west for Becky. The dead ends might have a special significance for him. Based on the amount of staging required to display the bodies, it may not just be about him. It may be about you."

Kate opened her mouth, but no sounds emerged. Swinging away from the lost look in her eyes, he focused on her partner. "He may be trying to taunt Kate. Serial killers tend to be extremely narcissistic. They want someone to notice what they are doing, and seek to prove their superiority to law enforcement.

"In that video Maggie posted, Kate appeared to be confident and strong. She was also identified as an SVU detective. He may be trying to deflate Kate's confidence, prove she's not as smart as she thinks—that all she will find is dead ends."

Harding glanced at the hillside. "There are houses built all along here. If not for the fog, all the residents would have a clear view of this area. At least we don't have to worry about any idiots snapping pictures from their living room windows."

Fraye nodded. "Like the De Anza statue, he chose another highly public place to display his victim, but was able to work in relative obscurity under the shroud of the weather. He was probably hoping the body wouldn't be discovered until the fog burned off so he would have a bigger audience."

Scrutinizing the stairs above them and then those below, Kate commented in a dull tone. "There's supposed to be more than one hundred and fifty stairs here. We haven't climbed that far, so we're closer to the bottom than the top. He must have parked at the sidewalk and carried her here."

"It certainly would be easier to carry her upward than to make it down these stairs with the awkward weight of a body throwing off your balance. Given the… condition of the corpse, he must have wrapped her in some sort of plastic for transportation."

Harding looked from Fraye to the corpse and back again. "Both these steps and the De Anza statue are within three miles of Jonas Riley's home. I wish we'd bagged that guy when we first met him." Noting the way Kate blanched at his words, he shifted his weight uncomfortably from one foot to the other.

"There was no reason to suspect Riley at the time." An uncharacteristically supportive tone laced the agent's words. "Now, however, it appears very likely that he may be our UNSUB."

Fraye turned and squatted down next to the corpse. His keen eyes seemed to catalog every length of sinew and tissue. "The one piece we're missing is where Riley would have kept Becky all this time. There was no trace of blood or other evidence in either his apartment or the shed out back."

"If something was going down at his place, the old lady would have known about it."

Fraye rose. "He must have another location where he took the women. It's got to be someplace he feels safe—he kept Becky for a few days. And this…" He gestured to the body, a deep frown creasing his brow. "This took some time."

Harding beheld Becky's mutilated form. "She reminds me of the deer."

Noting the blank looks on the faces of his companions, he elaborated. "You know, that other guy Kevin mentioned—Daniel Fermel. There was a skinned deer hanging in that photo he had on Facebook, remember?"

"Do you think that being a hunter makes one capable of doing this to a human being?"

"Of course not; I'm just saying that it reminded me …"

The sound of a car approaching below drew their attention.

Harding glanced at Kate. "That's probably Chau. If he's going to retrieve the body, he and his guys are going to need to get up here."

Stiffening, Kate swiveled around and started back down the stairs. "Let's give the man room to work."

The two men stood silently, watching her descend. Finally, Harding twisted toward Fraye and bowed grandiosely. "After you."

Something flashed in the special agent's eyes as he gazed at Harding, but it came and went before the detective could identify it. With one final, long look at the remains of Becky Hammonds, Harding spun around and followed his team members downward.

ᚦᚦᚦ

An hour and a half later, Kate and Harding thanked Samantha Fulton's parents and headed out of the well-kept, two-story home on Noriega Street. They had left their cars at the crime scene, opting to walk the two blocks to the girl's house.

The poor teen would likely suffer from nightmares for months. She had been unable to speak in coherent sentences and had broken down in fits of hysterics throughout the interview, extending the process far longer than they had planned.

Fraye had headed over to SFSU, where he was serving a warrant for the teaching assistant's records. As Kate stepped onto the sidewalk, her cell phone rang. It was the FBI agent.

He didn't waste time exchanging pleasantries. "Are you two finished with the witness?"

Kate glanced back at the house. "Yes. She wasn't able to add anything new."

"That's fine. I have the records. Riley's emergency contact is his landlady. No family members or significant others are listed. That's consistent with what Kevin turned up—parents deceased and no close next of kin. Apparently Riley's been an exceptional student and has never been in any trouble. All tuition payments current—funded by student loans."

"Sounds like a squeaky clean guy. Too bad he takes pictures of his students without their consent."

A wry tone slipped into the agent's voice. "Don't feel too sorry for her, Detective. Maggie took video of you without your consent, remember?"

Kate clamped her mouth shut, stifling an angry retort.

"I'm headed back to the precinct now. Chau's been told to finish the autopsy today, and Singh called asking for an emergency meeting with the chief of police. This new body is going to send the press into a feeding frenzy."

"That's just what we don't need."

"At this point, I think it is. I want to call a press conference—give them our profile and release Riley's information. No soft pitching as a person of interest. We'll announce he is a suspect and ask for the public's help in finding him."

Kate nodded vigorously. "Good. We need whatever help we can get. Harding and I are on our way back to the Hall. We'll see you there."

She ended the call and studied the ground, wondering how long she could keep going in a game she could not win.

"Kate?"

Pulled from her morose reveries, Kate focused on Harding, filling him in on the details of the call as they returned to the crime scene. The weather had cleared a bit, granting greater visibility.

Standing on the sidewalk, Kate considered the staircase, now able to see almost to the very top. Chau and his team had removed Becky's body, but she could somehow still feel its presence.

A warm hand wrapped around her upper arm. She turned to find Harding regarding her with a pained expression. "Kate, are you okay? Don't give me the pat answer; I want an honest one."

The emotions she'd been holding at bay welled up, threatening to spill over into a hysterical display rivaling the one she'd just witnessed from Samantha. Breaking eye contact, she shook her head dismissively. "Let's not get into this right now, okay? We've got a lot of work to do today. If you want the honest truth, I'm doing my best to remain professional. I don't need to start dipping into the 'woe is me' well."

He smiled slightly at her attempted quip. "All right, partner. We'll table it until tonight. I'll head over to your place with some takeout and a bottle of wine. How does that sound?"

It sounded lovely, but after what she'd seen today, she didn't trust herself not to fall to pieces the minute she entered the front door. Somehow, after seeing the horror that had befallen Becky, she'd sucked up all the guilt and recrimination and barricaded it behind a robotic shell. That shell had kept her functioning so far, but she couldn't hold it in place forever.

At some point she'd have to address it. She just didn't know if she was capable of combating such an awesome leviathan.

It was going to take all her strength to keep going through the rest of the day. She didn't have the energy to argue with her partner. Knowing she would cancel on him later, Kate manipulated her facial muscles into a faint facsimile of a smile. Lying blithely, she accepted the offer and rushed back to the Hall of Justice.

Chapter 13

BECKY HAMMONDS'S CORPSE lay on the table, appearing both abominable and pathetic in the harsh fluorescent light. A large white plastic sheet had been pulled up to her chest. Despite the quality of the lab's venting system, the stench from the corpse fouled the air.

Fraye stood nearby, seemingly immune to the odor. He flashed Kate an impatient glance as she and Harding entered the medical examiner's lab. They were late getting back from San Jose, where they'd gone to notify Angela Hammonds that her daughter had been murdered. Harding had argued that the SJPD could take care of the notification, but Kate had felt it was her duty to endure the pain of the mother's loss.

"This just keeps getting worse and worse, doesn't it?" Kate turned to find Chau regarding her wearily. Fraye had worked his magic again, ensuring the medical examiner rearranged his schedule to accommodate a same-day turnaround on Becky's autopsy.

"Yes, Tim. It does."

Harding stepped closer to the table, an odd expression clouding his features as he examined Becky's head and neck. "Is her face not quite…?"

"Not quite on right?" Chau offered. "You are correct." He walked to the table and stood a few feet from Becky's head. "Usually, I can cover up the intrusiveness of my work in the skull. But this victim had so little skin remaining that it was difficult to reposition it." He gestured to the plastic sheet. "Without skin, I was unable to close up the rest of the entry areas. The sheet is for you three. What's underneath is a lot to take in visually."

Kate scrutinized Becky's features, noting how her nose, lips, and scalp all seemed a little off. She tore her eyes away from the disturbing visage, leveling them squarely on Chau. "What did you find out?"

"Like our first victim, she was drugged with scopolamine. Of course, the causes of death were markedly different."

Looking past the medical examiner, Kate focused on a large black microscope sitting on the counter behind him. In a quiet tone, she asked the question that had been eating away at her since she'd first laid eyes on the defiled corpse early that morning. "Was she alive when this was done to her?"

Shifting uncomfortably, Chau took a deep breath. "Probably not for all of it. But definitely for a good portion."

In a voice as cold as the nearby cadaver drawers, Fraye responded. "It's consistent with the torture pattern. Flaying was another common method used during the middle ages. The torturer started with the face and slowly worked downward. According to the historical records, the victim usually died by the time they reached the waist."

Chau gestured to Becky's head. "In this instance, he didn't touch the face at all. He also left the dermis on the hands and wrists as well as the feet and ankles."

Fraye stepped closer to the table. "He wanted the victim to be identified easily. By leaving the skin, he's demanding that those viewing the body see more than just a mass of bones and muscle." His eyes settled on Kate, who remained stalwart in her observation of the microscope. "This way it's more personal."

"That may be true about the face, but I believe the skin on the extremities remained for another, more rudimentary, reason."

Fraye raised an eyebrow, waiting for the doctor to elaborate.

"This procedure was performed when the victim was tied up in a position similar to the one she was found in on the stairs. She would have to remain restrained during the process, so he removed everything up to the point of the ropes."

Fraye crossed his arms over his chest. "So, some of this was about convenience."

"I think so. I also think he didn't have much experience with human anatomy, but he does learn quickly."

Harding spoke up suddenly. "How do you know?"

Chau turned and retrieved a pair of blue latex gloves from a cardboard box on the counter near Fraye. Donning them with brisk efficiency, he eyed Harding. "Because of the condition of the right wrist."

Chau walked around the table and stood between Kate and Harding. Lifting the sheet, he grasped Becky's forearm and pulled it out. He laid the limb on top of the pale shroud, palm up.

The pink color of the muscles had faded to a light gray, reminding Kate of something out of a cheesy zombie movie. The skin over the hand looked like a macabre glove. It terminated in an oddly uneven edge, which encircled the remaining tendons, muscles, and bones in the arm.

"Here." Blue finger extended, Chau pointed to a series of severed, whitish cords just below the skin line. "In his first attempt, he cut too deeply into the wrist—severing everything from the flexor carpi ulnaris through the palmaris longus and the median nerve to the flexor carpi radialis."

"In English, please." Harding looked at Chau beseechingly.

"Sorry. I was referring to the tendons that connect the muscles of the forearm with the fingers. They allow us the ability to flex our digits." Chau held up his right hand, demonstrating by making a quick fist. "If she hadn't been tied up at the time and likely hyperextending her wrists to struggle with her bonds, he may have severed her radial artery and spared the poor girl any more pain." Something unpleasant seized the medical examiner's features. He shook his head sadly.

Bending over Becky's wrist, he continued, "You can see where parts of the tendon sheaths were torn off completely when he tried to pull away the skin." He pointed to the severed ends of the whitish tubes that hung unnaturally from the bone.

"The killer took much greater care with the left wrist and the neck—going so far as to change instruments. The damage to the right wrist was probably caused with a hunting knife. After that failure, it appears he moved to something more precise for the rest of the work—probably a scalpel. Of course, there would have been a great deal of blood when he severed all of the surface veins, but she would have remained alive and conscious for a while. Eventually, he pulled the skin down to the legs and made the final cuts around the ankles so he could remove the mainstay of the dermis."

"Anything else?" Fraye regarded the medical examiner shrewdly.

"We found those little bits of rust again in the remaining subcutaneous tissue inside the wrist."

"Were you able to identify them this time?"

"No. As I told you before, all we can say about rust is that it is oxidized iron. No testing procedure can tell you anything more than that. But I can tell you that she was probably killed a few hours before she was found on those stairs. And the brand—it was applied post mortem. At least he spared her something."

Fraye started toward the door. "Thanks. This has been very helpful." Kate and Harding followed the special agent to the exit. Saying good-bye to Chau, they headed down the hall and out into the reception area.

Fraye stopped, regarding both of the detectives in turn. "I was in a meeting with the captain and the police chief before Chau called. The press conference is set for tomorrow at noon. We prepared a few words for you to say. I'll email it to you when I get back upstairs." The last two sentences were directed at Kate.

After an extended pause, Kate lifted her chin slightly. "No."

The simple response was met with a stern frown. "It's not an option."

"And it's not appropriate for me to…"

"It's not your place to question this decision, Detective."

Harding looked about ready to blow. "Really? I thought we were a team. Or does that bit of crap fall to the wayside when it's convenient?"

Fraye reached for the door to the lobby. Pulling it open, he evaluated each of them. "This decision was made at the highest levels and deemed best for the investigation. Detective Barnes's statement will be limited to a few words. The purpose is to re-engage the UNSUB, and perhaps stop him from abducting another victim."

In a tone laced with disgust, he fired a parting shot before stalking out of the medical examiner's domain. "Stopping this killer from murdering another innocent victim should be the priority around here. Not engaging in pissing contests and ego wars."

Kate watched the door close behind him, dreading her role in tomorrow's press conference.

"That guy's such a dick! He just wants to put you out there to be a pawn in what he thinks is a fucking game of wits between him and Riley. He's playing with fucking fire! How do we know Riley's going to just pick up the phone and say, 'Hi, Kate. Want to talk about why I've been killing these girls?' For all we know, seeing you on TV might just push this guy to take another victim!"

Kate's mouth hung open as if she were expecting to vomit. Raking a hand back through his hair, Harding stared at the floor and dropped another expletive.

Sighing loudly, he glanced at his watch. "Come on. It's been a long day. Let's go upstairs and wrap things up. Then I'll go pick up some dinner and that bottle of wine I promised you."

The horror of Harding's forecast suddenly morphed Kate's emotions into an irrational anger. Her nerve endings began to hum with the desire to punch her partner squarely in the face. *What the hell was the matter with him? He didn't really care about supporting her. Like a typical male, he smugly envisioned following dinner with another ill-fated romp in the sheets.*

Despite the horrible events of the day and the irrational amount of guilt she felt over Becky's death, a small portion of Kate's mind remained rooted in rationality. It sagely whispered for her to rein in the power of the emotional volcano that was more likely attributable to epic levels of stress rather than to her perceptions about her partner's sexual interests.

Spinning away from Harding, she concentrated on the simple act of breathing. When the compulsion to strike out had passed, she turned back to him. "Thanks anyway, partner. But I'm going to be busy tonight preparing for the press conference."

Disappointment contorted Harding's features. "But he said you only have…"

Kate tilted her head at an angle, leveling him with a look that would brook no argument. "It's not an option. Maybe some other time."

He stared at her for a full fifteen seconds, as a variety of unreadable emotions flashed across his eyes. Nodding slowly as if unconvinced of the truth of her words, he reached for the door. "Yeah. Some other time."

ᚦᚦᚦ

February 2

Another frigid morning dawned with a desolate bleakness in Kate's quiet apartment. As it had since the investigation started, sleep had remained elusive.

When Kate had arrived home the previous night, she'd opened up the email Fraye had sent with her prepared statement for the press conference. Its contents confirmed Harding's suspicions—the wording was simple yet provocative. Fraye and the brass wanted to entice Riley to reach out to Kate, and the language they'd crafted was certain to achieve their aim.

The thought of standing in front of the cameras, where Maggie's and Becky's families could see her failure, where the whole world could see what she had done and failed to do…was debilitating. The weight of the guilt for dragging Maggie and Becky into this mess was becoming too much to bear. Images of the two corpses seemed burned into her corneas, super-imposing themselves over everything Kate saw—the same way a glimpse of the sun resulted in a bright little orb, superimposing itself on everything the eye beheld for minutes after the glowing star was seen.

And the thoughts of poor little Hayden. How was Angela supposed to tell her grandson that his mommy would never come home?

It was all too much to bear. In the wee hours of the night, Kate had longed for somewhere to go—somewhere she might feel safe from her failure and hide away from the guilt. But, as the night had yielded to day, she had been taken over by a sense of melancholy that bordered on fatalism.

Laconically, she rose from her bed, showered, and dressed for work in the somber black pantsuit she'd picked out the night before. Standing in front of her dresser, she opened the lid of the tiny plain brown box that held the meager amount of jewelry she owned. She retrieved a simple pair of silver stud earrings, pausing to stare at the little velvet pouch tucked into the front compartment of the box. Her hand hovered over the petite sack.

Raising her gaze, Kate looked into the wood-framed mirror hanging over the dresser. Without breaking eye contact, she reached for her Glock, which lay near the edge of the dresser. She lifted the weapon even with her face, with the muzzle facing skyward.

Her eyes shifted in the mirror, training on the gun. Tilting her head against it as if it were the sympathetic shoulder of a good friend, Kate closed her eyes, enjoying the press of cold steel against her temple.

Opening them, she laid the weapon back on the dresser. Plucking the pouch from the cubby it had occupied for more than fifteen years, she placed it on top of the Glock. Turning away, she finished getting ready with a single-minded determination.

When she arrived at the precinct an hour later, she went directly to the conference room for the daily team meeting. After it ended, she pulled Harding aside and told him she needed to head out for a quick errand.

"Okay. Let me return one phone call, and I'll go with you."

"No. I just need you to cover me for about an hour. I'll be right back."

His eyes narrowed suspiciously. "Where are you going?"

"Just cover for me. I'll be back well before the press conference."

"I don't know, Kate. The captain wants me to…"

"The captain?" She tilted her head slightly in a gesture laced with accusation. "Did he tell you to watch out for me?"

Harding looked away, confirming Kate's hunch.

"You know better than anyone that I can take care of myself. Besides, it's not like I'm going off anywhere dangerous. Please, Tyler."

Using his given name scored the direct hit she'd been hoping for. It was something she had only done during their one night of intimacy. Now it was used as a manipulative ploy, but she didn't have much choice.

His eyes softened. "All right, Kate. But hurry up about it!"

"Thanks."

She hurried down to the ground floor and out to

her car. Fifteen minutes later, she left the San Francisco city limits and drove along the 101 Freeway southward toward Colma.

A modern necropolis, the small town of Colma consisted of roughly two square miles, which are pinned between Daly City to the north and west, the beautiful and undeveloped San Bruno Mountain to the east, and the city of South San Francisco to the south. Famed for its deceased population, which out-numbered the living at a ratio of more than a thousand to one, the town was dominated by cemeteries.

As San Francisco's wealth and prosperity con-tinued to flourish after the gold rush, its forward-thinking politicians had decided that a city with such a small geographic range should not squander prime real estate on anything so wasteful as resting places for the dead. In 1912, the city had passed an ordinance banning cemeteries within the city limits.

Colma had grown up almost overnight. Its living residents, finding humor in the town's claim to fame, eventually adopted the motto, "It's great to be alive in Colma."

Among the famous people interred in the town's numerous cemeteries were Wyatt Earp, survivor of the famous O.K. Corral gunfight; newspaper magnate, William Randolph Hearst; and denim king, Levi Strauss. Bank of America founder A.P. Giannini and baseball legend, Joe DiMaggio, had become permanent neighbors at Holy Cross, a Catholic cemetery in Colma, and Kate's ultimate destination.

Keeping one eye on her GPS, she exited the freeway and made her way to Mission Road. The device promised she was only about half a block away. Scanning the street ahead, Kate noted the large monument sign and the ornate iron gates.

She pulled inside and followed the winding drive up a sloping green hill to the right. Parking in the deserted lot, she reached for the map she had printed before leaving her apartment. Glancing at it quickly to get her bearings, she paused to stare at the area she had circled in blue ink before grabbing her long black coat from the backseat.

Climbing out of the car, she quickly donned the warm garment, then set off in search of a place she'd never been. The skies above were gray, enhancing the vivid green color of the trees and rolling lawns. Hurrying along, Kate was careful to remain on the path. Though the dead had no capacity to care whether she tromped across their graves, the act still seemed somehow disrespectful.

She arrived at a massive redwood tree, whose base had been encircled in an iron bench. Checking the map, she decided it was time to venture off the path. Picking her way between the rows of headstones, she came upon a large mausoleum. Planted in the lawn to the right was the marker she sought. Gazing upon the headstone, Kate was immediately transported back in time.

She was fourteen years old again. Lying in bed on a summer's night, she was struggling with the anger and resentment that had been her constant companion since she could remember. Her friends had gone to the movies, and she hadn't been able to go—even though her dad had promised that this time she could.

Her father. The handsome, yet haggard, businessman who was barely ever home. Every day he left for work before she awakened. Most nights he didn't return until it was almost time for bed.

Like everything else in Kate's life, bedtime was self-enforced. Her mother wasn't capable of it—not when she was under the thrall of her "medicine" every night.

    Chloe Barnes's "medicine" came from little plastic containers with childproof lids. She had started abusing pain pills two years after Kate's younger sister was born. With single-minded determination, Chloe had been able to keep her illicit affair with drugs limited to the afternoon and evening hours. While Kate was at school, her mother was able to cling to sobriety long enough to tend to her younger daughter, Candace.

    At ten years old, Candace was both the joy of Kate's life and the bane of her existence. Bedridden by a severe joint disorder, Candace was a sweet, loving girl whose condition made her a prisoner in her own body.

    As soon as Kate returned from school each day, she was expected to take over the role of nursemaid and companion, while her mother retreated to her bedroom for another bout of medicine. The grueling schedule continued virtually year round. Summer was the exception.

    Chloe considered the summer season to be her vacation time, choosing to cede twenty-four-hour responsibility for Candace's care to her older daughter. Over the years, Kate had begged her father to help—but he was a man of empty promises whose only reliable contribution to the lives of his daughters was the paycheck he deposited every two weeks.

    In her heart, Kate knew Candace wasn't to blame. If anything, Candace's ready smile in the face of her hopeless condition more than made up for the bedpans and sponge baths. Besides, she was Kate's only compatriot—the only other person in the world who understood the horror of having their "medicated" mother stumble to her bedroom doorway in all manner of dishabille—not knowing if they'd be met with smiles and slurred praises or dark frowns and debasing accusations.

    Occasionally, Chloe mixed things up with a devastating violent outburst. Despite the combined efforts of the girls to keep their mother happy, Chloe's drug-addled mind was susceptible to an endless supply of triggers.

Unable to prohibit any such outburst completely, Kate had become adept at inserting herself between her mother and Candace —ensuring her sister was spared the worst of it. Whether it was happy Chloe or angry Chloe, both girls looked forward to the day when she would never darken their doors again.

On that particular night, searing tears, heated by frustration and indignation, had burned wide trails down Kate's cheeks. Her father had promised to come home early that night to take care of Candace, so Kate could actually go out like a normal teenager. When the phone had rung around six-thirty, she'd known he was calling to cancel.

Ever the dutiful sister, she'd prepared fish sticks and french fries for Candace and for Chloe, whose portion lay untouched in the oven. She'd fed her sister, bathed her, and cleaned her bedpan—all the while stifling a burning rage in her heart. Sitting in the uncomfortable wooden chair beside Candace's hospital bed, she'd watched two full-length, animated movies with her sister, before tucking her into bed.

As Kate sat on her bed in the gloomy darkness, she heard Candace call out from her bedroom down the hall. Years of pain and frustration set her nerve endings on fire. Rage boiled up—so powerful and consuming that she was taken aback by its ferocity. Unable to lash out against her parents, Kate's fury turned against the easy target.

And so, Kate had done that which she had never done before. For the first time ever, she ignored her sister's call. Reasoning that she wasn't responsible for catering to the little brat's every whim, Kate snatched her headphones off her nightstand, pulled them down over her ears, and blasted the uninspired lyrics of her favorite pop band into her head.

Eventually, Kate had cried herself to sleep. It wasn't until her mother shook her awake hours later that she realized the price of her actions. Fingernails boring into Kate's arms, Chloe had dragged her to the floor in a jumble of sheets, shrieking about how Kate had ruined everything.

After a bit of wrangling, Kate was able to free herself from her mother's clutches and run out into the hallway. Her father stood stiffly in the doorway to Candace's room.

Shouting to be heard above the roar of Chloe's wailing, Kate had asked her father what was wrong. He'd stared straight ahead as if unaware of her presence and deaf to his wife's caterwauling. Cautiously approaching her sister's room, Kate peeked inside the doorway.

Candace was still in bed. Vomit had soiled the sheets around her face and chest. The smell of spoiled fish sticks and french fries fouled the air. Candace's skin had turned the oddest shade of blue. His eyes still glued to Candace's wretched form, her father had asked Kate why she hadn't taken care of her sister.

It was a question that still plagued Kate to this day. Staring at her sister's headstone for the first time, she noted the final indignation her younger sister had been forced to bear from their parents. Etched into the face of the simple grave marker were Candace's birth date, date of death and the phrase *Beloved Daughter*. Kate stared at the words in amazement, wondering how her parents had had the audacity to use them.

Kate shook her head slowly, allowing the age-old pain to swallow her from the inside out. It was a pain she had learned to live with. And life had certainly been hard after Candace died. Her father had moved out a week later and filed for divorce. She'd never seen nor heard from him since.

Chloe, free of the obligation to limit her hours of pill popping, had embraced her addiction with gusto. Kate didn't know if her mother had ever learned to kick the habit; she hadn't had any real contact with Chloe since she'd moved out at eighteen.

Staring at her sister's headstone, she absently fingered the silver-plated cross hanging around her neck. It had belonged to Candace. The inexpensive piece of jewelry was the one memento Kate had kept from her childhood because it represented the one person who had ever returned her love during those dark years.

Joining the police department was something Kate had done as much for herself as for her sister. She'd never found a way to assuage the horrible guilt she felt over what she'd done that night, but had secretly hoped that serving in law enforcement might help her balance the scales.

Logically, she knew you couldn't blame a child for seeking a brief respite from the unfair demands of a home turned asunder by addiction and a tragic childhood illness. But there was a stronger voice (one whose slurred, cruel tones sounded a lot like Chloe's), which questioned whether Kate had really wanted Candace to die and free her from the never-ending responsibility—earning her a reservation for a special place in hell.

That voice had grown stronger with Maggie's death and even more so with Becky's. Becky had called out to Kate with the YouTube video, and Kate had failed her the same way she had failed Candace.

"Candace Barnes. A relative?"

Kate jumped at the sound of Fraye's voice, as if the devil himself had popped up from a nearby grave —ready to check Kate into a reserved private suite.

Watching her reaction, he stepped back awkwardly. "I'm sorry. I shouldn't have intruded."

Recovering quickly, she regarded him with tightly narrowed eyes. "What are you doing here?"

Unruffled by her direct inquiry, he responded in his typical professional, yet brusque, tone. "You're a lead detective who has somehow engaged the unnatural interest of a serial killer. *And* you are supposed to be attending a press conference in about two hours.

Let's just say I was curious when I saw you rush out of the Hall after that little tête-à-tête with Harding."

"I didn't notice you tailing me."

"That's because I'm good at what I do."

She cast one more rueful glance in his direction before turning back to the small headstone. Lifting the silver cross to her mouth, she pressed it briefly to her lips before letting it drop back to her chest. Sighing wearily, she turned and stalked back to the path.

Fraye walked beside her in silence as they traversed the sloping green hills.

Staring straight ahead, Kate spoke matter-of-factly. "I wasn't screwing around or setting off on some self-guided investigation of my own. I work more hours than the department could ever possibly compensate me for. I do that because it's my job and it's important to me. So I really don't think it should be such a big deal if one day I take one hour and…"

The touch of Fraye's hand on her elbow stopped her cold. Turning her gently to face him, Fraye looked so deeply into her eyes that she felt as if he were seeing directly through to her soul. "My apology was sincere. I am truly sorry. I was just looking out for you and this investigation."

There was something vulnerable in his tone and an almost pleading look in his eyes that not only convinced her of his sincerity, but caused something to stir deep inside her. It was a feeling she wasn't quite prepared for.

Averting her eyes, she murmured. "We've got to get back to the Hall." Then she sped off toward the lot, practically jogging to her car.

Chapter 14

HARDING WAS IN THE HALLWAY talking to the captain when Kate emerged from the elevator. Shoulders square, back rigid, she looked to Harding like one royally pissed off woman as she strode down the corridor. She was going to be even angrier when he told her about the email he'd received from Fraye.

When he finished up with the captain a few minutes later, Harding headed directly to Kate's desk. He was curious to find out where his partner had gone on her mystery errand, but in her current state, it was best that he approach with caution.

Kate sat at her desk, scowling at her computer screen. Dropping casually into the guest chair across from her, Harding sat quietly and waited until she acknowledged him. Finally, she dragged her eyes from the screen to his face. Relying on his military training, he remained silent, knowing any false move could set off a devastating explosion.

Leaning forward onto her elbows, she fixed him with a demanding glare. "Well?"

He smiled and raised his hands disarmingly, but remained mute.

Brows knotting into a frown, she bobbed her head angrily and turned away. When she looked at him again, there was a sea change in her demeanor. She settled back into her seat and smiled at him weakly.

"Sorry. I owe you for covering for me—although you didn't do such a good job."

His jaw jerked backward as if he'd been struck. "Yes, I did! The captain came looking for you a few minutes ago, so I ran interference. I was still talking to him in the hall when you came back in."

"Thanks. Too bad you couldn't keep everyone occupied."

Harding's eyes narrowed. "What do you mean?"

Tilting her head slightly to the left, she waited for him to reason it out for himself.

"Not that asshole, Fraye!"

"The one and only."

"Shit! How'd he find out?"

Kate shook her head. "Just forget about it. He's not worth it, and technically I shouldn't have left anyway. I've got more than enough to keep me occupied here." She reached up and fingered the little silver cross hanging from her neck.

Harding stared at the necklace, unable to recall having seen it before. Kate and religion—it didn't seem to be a natural match. Then again, maybe it had nothing to do with belief—maybe she just liked the look of it.

"So where'd you go anyway?"

Kate's gaze wandered back to her screen. "We'd better get downstairs. Fraye sent an email—he wants to brief us for the press conference. Did you see it?"

Harding stood. "Yeah, I did." He gestured for his partner to walk ahead of him, wondering how she was going to respond to the other email Fraye had sent.

▷▷▷

Fraye conducted the briefing in a small room downstairs. Robert Evers, the bald, nearly retired police

171

chief, whose massive girth was barely contained within the confines of his dress blues, was there along with Captain Singh. Evers announced that they were now unsure whether Kate should speak to the press at all.

The announcement sent Harding's eyes darting toward Kate. He noted her shoulders drop a half an inch with relief. The special agent quickly refuted the concept, insisting the detective would say the words he had prepared—warning she must stick to the script verbatim. When the briefing was over, they all filed into the large adjoining room where the media sharks were ready and waiting.

Space at the Hall of Justice was a valued commodity, necessitating many rooms to serve double duty. Today, the large modern chamber for public hearings had been converted into a pressroom.

Without acknowledging the presence of the eager assemblage, Fraye walked resolutely to the stage at the front of the room. He took his position at the podium, whose top was blooming with a multitude of microphones bearing the brightly colored logos of at least fifteen different networks.

Fraye waited patiently while the captain and the chief took up standing positions behind him. Kate and Harding stood to either side, serving as bookends for the powerful men.

"Ladies and Gentlemen, I am Special Agent Fraye from the Behavioral Analysis Unit of the Federal Bureau of Investigation. I am leading the investigation into the murders of both Maggie Stevenson and Becky Hammonds." He promptly rattled off a brief introduction of those assembled on the stage behind him.

"We do have a primary suspect in these murders and would like to ask for the public's help in finding this individual." The large screen to the right of the stage suddenly came to life with a four-foot-high image of Jonas Riley. The periodic stream of camera flashes erupted into an unending flood.

"Mr. Riley is a graduate student at San Francisco State University, where he also works as a teaching assistant. We have set up a hotline for the public to contact us as well as a special email address, and ask that anyone with knowledge of Mr. Riley's whereabouts contact us immediately." A phone number and email address appeared at the bottom of the screen, superimposed over Riley's photo.

The image whipped the journalists into a frenzy. Questions were shouted from virtually every corner of the room. Fraye waited in silence through the next three minutes until only a few persistent young voices remained.

"We only have time for a few questions." The room filled once again with the din of demanding calls.

Regarding the crowd shrewdly, the special agent's gaze settled upon a man in his mid-forties. He gestured to the man abruptly.

"Kevin Hubbert, ABC news. The picture of the first victim that circulated briefly on the Internet showed she'd undergone excessive torture. Do you believe Jonas Riley is the notorious Tower Torturer?"

"Mr. Riley is a suspect in the two homicides I mentioned. We are pursuing all potential leads—including possible links to other similar crimes."

Ignoring Hubbert's follow-up question, Fraye pointed to a Filipino man in his late twenties, wearing frameless glasses.

"Frank Estes, NBC news. Agent Fraye, can you confirm whether both bodies were branded with the Norse thorn?"

"Because this is an open investigation, we are not

at liberty to discuss any particular details of the case." He thrust a finger toward a striking dark-haired beauty who looked to be around Kate's age.

"Maria Torres, CBS news. Detective Kate Barnes is with you on the dais. Maggie Stevenson's Facebook page indicates she had a special relationship with Detective Barnes prior to her death. Did the video she posted of Detective Barnes have anything…"

"Detective Barnes?" Fraye turned and posed the question to Kate. Swallowing deeply, she stepped up to the podium.

She stared blankly out at the crowd, picturing the Arial font of the words from the email in her head. "The murders of Maggie Stevenson and Becky Hammonds are of paramount personal importance to me. Mr. Riley is considered a suspect because of information I've unearthed, and I ask him to contact me immediately."

Maria Torres tried to ask what exactly Kate had discovered, but her words were lost in the resulting crash of media voices demanding similar explanations.

Fraye nudged Kate aside, taking back control. "As I said, this is an open investigation. We cannot discuss any particular details that may compromise our ability to see justice served in this case. I'm sorry, but we are out of time and must conclude this conference. Thank you all for coming."

Spinning on his heel, Fraye turned and walked off the stage. The audience had turned into a disorganized mob, firing question after question at the retreating agent.

Minutes later, Fraye, Harding, and Kate filed into the elevator to return to the fourth floor, the tension in the small space palpable. Had the elevator not been crammed with other passengers, Harding would have brought up the special agent's recent email. But the tight space was not the appropriate venue.

The second the doors opened onto the fourth floor, Harding rushed out. He spun around, confronting Fraye and Kate as they stepped off the elevator.

"So, why don't we go into the conference room and discuss how my partner and I will execute your new directive."

The federal agent's eyes shifted away. "It was a simple enough request. I'm sure the two of you can carry it out without my help."

Kate glanced back and forth between the two men in confusion.

Enjoying Fraye's discomfort, Harding pressed further. "I don't know about that. I mean, shouldn't you help direct Kate in this process? You're the profiler. You know what will trigger this guy better than any of us, right?"

Refusing to remain in the dark any longer, Kate took a step toward Harding. "What are you talking about?"

"Fraye sent me an email, advising you to set up a Facebook page."

"A Facebook page?"

Harding looked to the special agent for explanation. Kate followed his gaze to Fraye, whose air of discomfort had been replaced by one of indifference.

"Maria Torres is right. All of this started when the first victim posted that video of you on Facebook. Now, Riley's gone silent on us. We have no leads on his whereabouts, and no idea when or where he may strike again. At this point, you're our only link to him. In case that invitation you just extended isn't enough, I want you to open a Facebook account and see if you can engage him."

Kate stared at Fraye, a mixture of fury and frustration in her eyes.

The agent regarded her steadily. "All you have to do is create the account, and then post to Maggie's page."

"But I can't post anything to Maggie's page unless she accepts me as a friend." Kate glanced at Harding, her voice dropping notably. "That's not possible."

"I'm not referring to the victim's personal page. Kevin apprised me that Maggie's friends and family set up a tribute page for her where people can go and mourn her publicly. According to Kevin, the boyfriend set up the account and administers it as a public page. All we need you to do is set up your own account and post."

"Post what? An invitation for Riley to come and make Kate the next victim in his fucked-up horror show?" Harding's outburst drew the stares of two other detectives as they walked by.

Fraye exhaled loudly. "No. She needs to post something as wildly arrogant and inflammatory as what she said in that first video. The intent is to engage him again before he decides on another victim."

The words struck Kate like a shot to the stomach. "So I should say something about how I'm sure we'll catch the guy, and how confident I am that he will pay for what he's done."

Fraye nodded. "And loosen up a few buttons on that blouse for your profile photo. A little cleavage can go a long way."

Kate's eyes widened, then narrowed angrily. Turning on her heel, she stalked back to her desk.

Harding stood there, wondering just how far Fraye thought he could push Kate Barnes, before she pushed back. Scratching his jaw absently, he contemplated whether the highly acclaimed FBI guru knew just how dangerous his partner could become.

▷▷▷

Kate stood in front of the vending machine in the lunchroom, unable to decide which of the sodium-infused, chemically-processed items she had the strength to ingest. Since receiving the order to post to Maggie's memorial page, her stomach had been in knots. She hadn't eaten breakfast, and it was well past time to feed her digestive system.

"None of those items are a smart choice."

Kate could see Fraye standing behind her in the reflection of the machine's glass window. Without turning around, she responded in a monotone. "Since I used my lunch hour for a personal errand this morning, I don't have time to pursue other options."

"Well, I do, and you're coming with me."

Spinning on her heel, she leveled him with a seething glare. "Thanks, but no. I tolerated enough of your unwanted presence this morning. I don't care to indulge in any more of the brilliant special agent routine than I have to."

Her words seemed to crash through his profes-sional veneer. He dropped into one of the worn plastic chairs nearby as if no longer able to bear up under the crushing weight of responsibility.

Kate took a cleansing breath and tried to swallow her anger. Fraye was doing his job—as irritating as it might be for her. The truth was that she was an emotional wreck, far off her normal game and out of her depth. Even his remark about the buttons on her shirt—it had been a legitimate strategy for engaging Riley. Yet, with her emotions riding high, she'd immediately taken it as an attempt to demean her.

She flashed a glance at the doorway to the empty lunchroom, then looked back at her team leader, who was rubbing a weary hand across his eyes. Pulling out a chair across the crumb-covered table from Fraye, she sat down heavily.

"Hey, I'm sorry. It's been a long day and it's only…" She peered at her watch, "two-thirty in the afternoon."

Shaking his head as if casting off unseen demons, he lifted his eyes and forced the semblance of a smile. "No need to apologize, Detective. You're right to be pissed at me. I overstepped this morning at the cemetery, and I probably deserve a lot worse than a bitchy retort."

Kate raised an eyebrow in mock horror. "Bitchy? Me?"

His smile broadened into a boyish grin. "Yes, you. I don't know how you keep from lacerating your mouth with that sharp tongue."

The image of knives and laceration wrenched Kate's thoughts back to Maggie and Becky. Visions of their defiled bodies swam before her.

Noting the sudden change in her demeanor, Fraye's smile vanished. "I checked Maggie's memorial site before I came in here." He reached into his jacket pocket, pulled out his phone, and began reading aloud. "Posted from Kate Barnes ten minutes ago, 'Maggie will be forever missed, but her killer will not go unpunished. I will personally see justice served. There will be no place for him to hide—not in heaven or hell.'"

Dropping his phone back in his pocket, he met Kate's eyes again. "Passionate and egocentrically confident—it's perfect. So was your profile photo."

Kate's hand momentarily flew to her hair, where

she plucked absently at the little black piece of elastic securing her ponytail. The success of the photo was due mainly to her partner. In addition to taking off her blazer and undoing quite a few buttons on her white blouse, Harding had also convinced her to let her hair loose for the photo. He'd then snapped a variety of shots until she'd been able to strike a pose that conveyed ultimate confidence mingled with a taste of sensuality.

She dropped her hand, reassured by the restoration of her familiar façade.

"You are doing a good job, Kate. I know I ride you pretty hard sometimes, but you're doing well."

Swallowing the impulse to correct him, she decided to pursue a different track—one that had been bothering her ever since she'd walked out of the elevator. "Why didn't you just ask me about the Facebook page? Why make Harding tell me?"

"Honestly?"

She crossed her arms tightly over her chest. "No, why don't you lie to me? That will be a much better use of our time."

His smile was laced with bitterness. "There's that bitchiness again. The truth is, I knew it would be a hard thing for you to do. Despite what you think of me, I felt bad about piling more on your plate. Since you're so close to your partner, I figured it might be easier if it came from him. Unfortunately, he chose to use it as another petty opportunity to spar with me."

Kate wasn't sure how to process the fact that he'd been worried about how she felt, so she decided to table it. "Something's been bothering me about Riley. Hearing all those journalists yelling about the East Coast murders today made me wonder about it."

Fraye sat up, snapping back into professional agent

mode. "About what?"

"Why Riley started killing again."

"We know why. The YouTube video put any speculation to rest. It's about you, Kate. He chose his victims because of their relationship to you."

"True, but I had nothing to do with the women he killed in Massachusetts. He went after them for a reason; now he feels compelled to go after people that I know. It feels like there's something else I'm missing. I just wish I understood more about his motivation for the original killings."

"Why?" His eyes narrowed.

"Because then I could understand why Riley started killing in the first place, and why he's so interested in me."

The agent's eyes flew open wide in appreciation. "My dear Katharine, there may just be a place for you at Quantico!"

"Thanks, but I think I've got my hands full right here."

"So do I." He stared at her for a moment longer, something unnamable moving in the depths of his dark eyes. "I know you've reviewed the case files, but would you like a crack at my personal files?"

"Your personal files?"

"Yes. As you may guess, unsolved cases don't sit well with me. For the last six years, I've continued to work the case on my own time." He glanced away ruefully. "I never seem to have as much time as I'd like to myself anymore."

His features brightened suddenly. "Listen, tomorrow's Saturday. Why don't you come to my place and look over what I've got. Maybe you can find something that will help you understand Riley's fascination better."

An unfamiliar sensation welled up inside Kate— one of hope. Since Becky's death, things had seemed so dire. Perhaps if she could get a look at Fraye's files, she might learn something that could help. Moreover, she might even find a way to make a real contribution to this case.

Eyes bright, she leaned forward in her seat. "That would be great. Just tell me where and when."

"The department put me up at a hotel here in town, but I prefer to spend the weekends at the place I inherited from my grandmother. It's my West Coast retreat, and I don't get there nearly often enough. I've got duplicates of all my original files there. If you want to come, and you don't mind driving, it would be easier if you just meet me there. That way I don't have to lug everything back and forth."

"Of course. Where is it?"

"Napa. Do you know how to get there from here?"

"Yes. You go over the bridge and stop when you run into the vineyards."

"Funny. My place is just outside of town on the east side. Get there in the morning around eleven." He snatched an unused napkin off the table and pulled a pen from his pocket. His hand flew over the paper in a series of quick strokes. "There's the address. Call me if you have any difficulties finding it."

He slid the napkin toward her, then stood and walked over to the vending machine. Feeding a dollar bill into the unit, he retrieved a plastic cup filled with instant spiced noodles from its bowels. Pulling back the paper lid, he ran some steaming water into the cup.

He paused in the doorway before exiting the lunchroom. Lifting the cup in Kate's direction, he stared at it pointedly before regarding her with a wry smile. "Aren't you glad you didn't take me up on that lunch offer?"

ᛈᛈᛈ

Bright-green letters stood out in the dark night, identifying the small, one-story building as the home of the Green Things grocery store. Known for its organic and locally produced foods, it was a favorite of many San Franciscans, including Kate Barnes.

With only thirty minutes until closing time, the day's rush was just about over. Kate pulled into the lot, forgoing many of the empty spots near the entrance for one tucked into the far corner.

Six hours earlier, in a state of desperation, she'd followed Fraye's lead and retrieved a dehydrated soup from the vending machine in the lunchroom. Now, Kate was starving. Knowing nothing but bare cupboards awaited back at her apartment, she'd headed to the store after leaving work, stomach set on the purchase of a loaf of whole-wheat bread and some organic sliced turkey.

Excited by the prospect of traveling to Napa to review Fraye's case files, Kate was eager to get home and work out so that she might actually be able to get some sleep tonight. But, there was something else she had to attend to first—something that had come up when she had left the Hall a few minutes before.

She'd felt like a fool this morning when Fraye had surprised her at the cemetery. Even allowing for her distracted state, she should have caught on that he was tailing her.

Studying the driver's side mirror, she adjusted it slightly and watched as the red sports coupe crawled into the lot and slipped into a spot near the entrance.

She had noticed the flashy vehicle following her within a block of the precinct. The candy-apple color and hot-rod-style body made it an odd choice for surveillance. But then, the driver didn't seem to be too hip to the rules of undercover work.

With a few easy maneuvers, Kate had tricked the coupe into pulling right up behind her at a stoplight, where she'd been able to read its plates in the rearview mirror as it approached.

Curious, Kate had called one of the beat cops from Central Station who worked the night shift. He'd answered on the second ring and had been extremely accommodating when she'd asked him to run the plates.

Kate watched as the car's lights went out, a slight smile tugging at the left side of her mouth. She pulled her iPad out of her purse and began re-reading some of the day's email correspondence. About four minutes passed before she heard a loud clicking sound, reminding her of the heavy tread of the mighty Clydesdales metal shoes as they tromped down Market Street during the St. Patrick's Day parade.

Laying her tablet on the passenger seat, she glanced back at the side-view mirror. Maria Torres, the local TV news reporter who had brought up Kate's relationship with Maggie at the press conference, and owner of the red coupe (according to the DMV), was striding toward Kate's car. Looking like something off the cover of a fashion magazine, the journalist was wrapped in a fitted, cream-colored trench coat—its belt tightly cinched around her tiny waist. The long hem of the garment reached just below her knees where an expensive pair of leather, stiletto-heeled suede boots encased her shapely calves.

A mane of impeccable ebony waves flowed from

the top of her head to the bottom of her ribs. The volume of the hair, its length, and impossible level of perfection suggested hair extensions as well as the professional assistance of the television station's hair department. Maria's artfully decorated and flawless Latina features hinted at serious time spent with the station's makeup department as well.

Dealing with a journalist was the last thing Kate wanted to do right now, but she did find it interesting that the woman was trying such clandestine, albeit pathetic, methods to reach her.

Fighting the urge to check her appearance in the mirror first, Kate grabbed her purse and her recycled Green Things shopping bag. Climbing out of her car, she started toward the entrance to the market. Torres hurried up alongside her.

"Detective Barnes?"

Turning toward the woman, Kate leveled her with her most stern expression. "No comment."

"Please, Detective. I'm not looking for an interview. I just want to talk."

"No comment."

"But I…"

"No comment." Kate strode ahead and hurried into the market, leaving Maria Torres standing out in the cold night air.

Inside the market, Kate completed shopping and paid for her items. Hoping the journalist had left, she headed out the automatic doors into the lot. To her relief, the red coupe was gone.

Kate scanned the lot, surprised the woman had given up so easily. But, there was no sign of the coupe or the news anchor anywhere. Relieved, she hurried to her car. Dropping her purse and purchases into the passenger seat, Kate started the engine. She had just taken her foot off the brake to begin backing up when she looked in her rearview mirror and glimpsed Maria Torres standing resolutely behind her trunk.

Slamming the brake to the floor, Kate shifted the car back into park. Temper flaring, she waited for the woman to move. A full minute ticked by—each second further fueling Kate's anger. After the second minute, Kate rolled down her window and shouted, "I am trying to back up; can you please move?"

Calling out from her position behind the trunk, Maria made her position clear. "Not until you talk to me."

"Either you move, or I will call for backup and have you escorted safely out of the way."

"Please, Detective. You don't understand; I'm just trying to help."

Something in the woman's tone, combined with the points Kate had to begrudgingly award her for guts and strategy, softened Kate's resolve. With a deep sigh, she cut her engine and waited while Torres scurried around to the driver's side window.

To Kate's surprise, the woman didn't speak. She merely thrust a small photograph through the window. In the photo, Maria had her arms around a pretty young woman in a sisterly embrace. Kate recognized the blonde right away. It was Gayle Nivens, one of the victims of the original Tower Torturer slayings.

Voice thick with emotion, Maria plunged ahead, stunning Kate into silence. "I dated Gayle's father for eight years—wasted some of the best years of my life on a guy who was over fifteen years older than me. But the one thing I don't regret was the relationship I had with Gayle. She was like a younger sister to me, and she didn't deserve what was done to her."

Kate met the woman's eyes, finding a sincere

mixture of iron determination and soulful heartbreak in their depths. "I'm sorry for your loss, but I cannot help you."

Shaking her head in exasperation, as if Kate's skull were as dense as the asphalt below her feet, Maria continued. "You don't understand. I'm not asking for your help. I'm offering my help to you."

Kate eyed her skeptically.

"I transferred here thirteen months ago. Prior to that I worked for WCVB in Boston, where I investigated the original murders. I have so much information. I can help you, I can..."

"Ms. Torres, as we stated in the press conference today, we already have a suspect. His name is Jonas Riley. If you have any information to share about him, you can contact us through our hotline. Now, I really must go."

Tucking the photo away in the safety of her shiny black purse, the newswoman retrieved another item and thrust it through Kate's window. Kate glanced down at the business card, upon which a personal cell phone number had been scrawled in blue ink.

"I'm sorry, I..."

"Detective, I know in my heart that the Tower Torturer is killing these women. I can't say how just yet, but deep down I just know."

Dropping the card into Kate's lap, Maria Torres turned and stalked off into the night.

Chapter 15

THE RAIN HAD ACCOMPANIED Kate throughout the entire drive to Napa. As she had headed
northward along Highway 29, Kate's thoughts had
remained riveted on her hopes for Fraye's personal
files. Her focus had been so intense that neither the
majesty of the Mayacamas Mountains rising up outside
her window, nor the serene beauty of the acres of
sprawling vineyards crawling out across the valley could
lure her thoughts from the case.

Renown for its premier wines, the region boasted
some of the world's most gorgeous scenery, set in an
idyllic location. Considered part of the Greater Bay
Area, the Napa Valley lay at the northernmost edge of
the San Francisco Bay and attracted tourists from every
corner of the globe. Despite its proximity to San
Francisco, Oakland, and San Jose, the locale retained
the relaxed pace and tranquility of its bucolic roots.

Having exited the freeway, she had traveled down
a series of rolling, two-lane country roads, then turned
onto a private drive. The narrow lane had led through
a thick stand of trees before opening into a small
meadow. Huddled at the back of the clearing, against
the base of the hills, she'd discovered a charming two-
story farmhouse. Built in the 1920s, it came complete

with a wraparound porch and weather vane. Fraye had met her on the front steps and led her inside, where the home was a mismatch of rundown finishes and newly remodeled elegance. He'd brought her to his office, which had been redone in the latter style, then had unlocked the drawers to his desk and left her to her studies.

She'd burned through the entire afternoon searching the files for answers. She had just finished when Fraye came in and asked her to join him in the living room.

Returning his files to the drawers, she made her way across the worn floorboards of the country-style hallway to the ultra-modern living room. The agent entered carrying a tray and a bottle of wine.

"Sit." Fraye nodded his head toward a comfortable-looking suede couch. Two glasses stood on an antique trunk, which had been positioned between the couch and the fireplace, serving as a coffee table.

Kate did as instructed, enjoying the warmth from the fire as Fraye placed the tray down in front of her. She had not realized how hungry she was until she beheld the medley of cheeses and meats assembled before her.

"Go ahead and dig in." Fraye sat on the striped armchair to her right, then passed her a napkin and filled her glass with red wine.

Popping a cube of white cheese into her mouth, Kate closed her eyes, savoring its smoky flavor and silky texture. "That's delicious."

"It should be. It's from one of the local dairies. The wine is local too—a great blend of varietals."

Fraye was right; the wine slid sumptuously down her throat, leaving a trail of fruity aromas, followed by a brief aftertaste of chocolate.

He watched with a bemused expression while she devoured almost half of the tray's contents. "So, you were in there for hours. What did you learn by going through my files?"

Kate paused, wine glass in hand, then took a long sip and settled back against the couch. "I learned you don't miss much. Your analysis of each victim—the way you seem to understand their innermost thoughts and motivations—is almost eerie."

"It's more analytical than magical. Humans are not as mysterious as some people would like to think. Did it help to answer your questions about our killer?"

Resting her elbow against the back of the couch, Kate rubbed her temple wearily. "I can't figure it out. I read your notes; I understand what elements about each of the East Coast victims made them suitable victims." She sighed heavily. "But I think I might have wasted your time coming up here. The more I think about it, this isn't really about the victims."

"How so?"

"Well, he's a psychopath, so he's not doing this because of some sort of mommy complex like the Coed Killer."

Fraye raised an eyebrow in question.

"You know, Ed Kemper—the Coed Killer. He murdered young women near UC Santa Cruz, to express his rage at his mother. She was a counselor at UCSC who was adored by the students because of her compassion and patience. But she wasn't so compassionate with her son. She displaced her anger at his father onto him, falsely accusing him of trying to hook up with his own sister, and locking him nightly in the basement to keep the girl safe. He kept killing women as stand-ins for his mother. And eventually he killed her too. Then he stopped and turned himself in."

He smirked. "Yes, I know who he is. I'm just glad to know you've been keeping up with your research."

Kate stared at the fire. "Our killer is doing this because he wants to, not because a phobia, a fixation, or a PTSD issue compels him to. I get that. What I still don't get is why I have taken center stage in his sick game."

Fraye slid off the chair and settled comfortably onto the floor. Using the chair as a backrest, he picked up his glass and took a long sip. "Let's see how well you really have kept up on your research. Tell me what a psychopath is."

Kate folded her arms over her chest, remembering how she'd started all of this misery by posing a similar question to Maggie. "Someone without a conscience—with no concept of empathy, guilt, or remorse. They are not capable of forming healthy relationships with other human beings because they don't understand social structure or respect its rules. They're emotionally handicapped." Her last words were punctuated with a shrug.

Fraye shook his head and gazed at the floor.

"What? I read the Robert Hare book like you told me to. Those are the main qualities he lists—along with being egocentric, deceitful, manipulative, and craving excitement."

"True, but in referring to them as handicapped, you imply there is something deficient in them—you are passing judgment."

Kate sat up abruptly. "But I'm right! They are incapable of…"

"Please, Kate. I, of all people, don't need a lecture on the topic. You need to stop sitting in judgment on the killer. It's the same lesson I tried to teach you by taking you to Genevieve's party. But your damn ego keeps getting in the way."

She paused in the process of refilling her wine glass. "My ego?"

"Yes. In addition to recommending research into serial killers and psychopaths, I should have also recommended some study into self-awareness."

"I saw the video. I know I came off like an uptight bitch, but…"

"It's not just the video, Kate."

She stared at him openmouthed.

"Most serial killers have some form of cop fixation—to appease it, they often try to become members of law enforcement themselves, or try to hang out in cop bars, drive similar vehicles, et cetera."

"I know."

"Then tell me why they have such a fixation."

Kate sat in glum silence.

"It's born from the desire for manipulation and control," Fraye answered for her. "Police officers exercise power over the citizenry and hold respected public positions—two things these killers crave. The law says you cannot speed, no matter what your excuse, but cops do it all the time. The law says you cannot double park in front of a coffee shop, but cops do it all the time. On a more fundamental level, the law says you cannot assault another individual or kill them—even accidentally. But cops are allowed to kill. To most psychopathic serial killers, police officers are kindred spirits who wield their power with as little respect for society's rules as they have."

"It's not the same! Sure, some cops misuse their power, but…"

"But what? You have more in common with this guy than you think. I'm not saying you would want to go around killing women, but you can understand him if you make the effort."

Biting her bottom lip, Kate looked away briefly. "Fine. Let's say I'm a psychopathic serial killer who has murdered all these women and feels no remorse for it."

"All right. Why would you do it?"

"Because I enjoy it—I crave the excitement. To me, it's no different than Genevieve's party."

"And?"

"And I don't see other people as valuable beings —just resources for my amusement."

"Right. Why choose college girls?"

The firelight reflected in Kate's eyes as she stared into the dancing flames. "Because they are a greater prize than prostitutes. I might have started with strippers or hookers because they are easier to come by, and no one really cares about what happens to them. But eventually I'd want something better."

"Good. And why would you have stopped killing?"

"I wouldn't, unless I really wanted to." She reached for the wine bottle again and refilled her glass.

"What if the police were getting too close?"

"I wouldn't stop. I just might change things up a bit. I would be killing for pleasure, not compulsion. That leaves me open to changing my MO in any way to throw the cops off my trail."

"And what about the video of Kate Barnes? What would you think of her?"

She paused for a full minute, considering his question. A dark expression clouded her features. "I would see elements in her—the egocentrism, the…"

"What?"

She turned and looked at him—her expression a mix of sudden awareness and intense torment. "In that video I said all psychopaths should be exterminated.

You said he is highly intelligent, and likely came from a good home. He knows he's not like others; he knows society would label him as a psychopath. But if what they say about psychopaths is true—that they are born, not made like Kemper—it sounded as if I have no empathy."

Fraye nodded slowly. "If someone without conscience behaves as if they don't have one, should we really be surprised? You don't have to accept the crimes they committed, but if someone is deaf, can you really fault them for not hearing?"

"The lack of empathy, the egocentrism—you don't think he believes I'm like him, do you?"

He paused and took another sip of wine. Setting the glass back down on the table, he studied her intently. "I think he sees something in you—something he feels he can relate to."

Kate shook her head adamantly. "That doesn't make sense. By definition a psychopath cannot relate to anyone. He is…"

The special agent held up a hand, silencing her immediately. "They cannot relate to others in terms of compassion and empathy. That doesn't mean they cannot understand people in other ways—it's one of the reasons they are so skilled at manipulation. Oddly enough, while you can't figure them out, at least one of them seems to understand aspects of you—and you're the one accusing them of being emotionally handicapped."

Fury flashed briefly in Kate's eyes. Then something seemed to break deep inside. Exhaling, she regarded her host wearily. "You're right."

Aware of the uncharacteristic tremor in her voice, Fraye glanced awkwardly at the floor. "I'm sorry, Kate. It sounds like I've struck a nerve."

She turned away, absently swiping her eyes. "We're discussing the case, not me."

He continued in a much softer tone. "I'm guessing this has something to do with the grave you visited yesterday?"

"No." The lie did not sound credible even to Kate. She reached for the silver cross hanging from her neck and began rubbing it absently with her left hand.

They sat in silence for a few moments longer, before Fraye spoke again. "He's using it, you know—the fact that you are so locked up in your own head. He's punishing these women, making you feel guilty about them. The more you focus on yourself, your own feelings and perceptions, the more you stay locked up in your own head—thus ensuring you'll stay out of his."

Closing her eyes, she let her head fall backward onto the top of the sofa cushion.

"Did you know guilt is not real?"

Her eyes opened, and she addressed the ceiling. "What do you mean?"

"It does not occur naturally in the human psyche. It is a tool society developed over time as a way of keeping people in line."

"That's not true. Everybody feels guilty when they do something wrong—it's innate."

"No, it is a societal construct. Guilt is something we teach children to perceive. We're not born with it. Think about children of drug addicts—emotionally, and often physically, abused by parents. Society conditions children to believe that everyone must respect their parents and have meaningful, lifelong relationships with them. Though it is completely against their own interest, the guilty children assume responsibility for the dysfunctional relationship, prompting them to hover around abusive parents, subjecting themselves to repeated pain. It's not about what is right or fair. It's about fear of failing to uphold society's expectation and having been conditioned to feel bad about it."

"If that's true, it's cruelly ironic," Kate replied.

"How so?"

"The psychiatrists say that a key trait in psychopaths is being manipulative. Yet, when it comes to guilt, society itself is the big manipulator. Maybe the psychopaths are the only ones lucky enough to be impervious to the game."

"I wouldn't say I agree entirely with that statement. Perhaps one might argue—in a vacuum, of course— that psychopaths are merely another step in evolution. They say the shark hasn't changed much since prehistoric times because it has already evolved to be the perfect predator—completely suited to excel in its environment. Perhaps humans have become too dependent upon social structures. Overcoming a societal construct like guilt might be an evolutionary step toward individual growth."

She lifted her head, allowing her gaze to drift back to the flames. "In an odd way, I think I envy them."

Fraye studied her silently.

"I mean, to live without guilt. It must be so liberating—for that horrible weight to be lifted off your chest." Sincerity and a quiet desperation burned in her eyes. "You could finally breathe."

Cocking his head to the side, Fraye listened, then stood abruptly. "Sounds like the rain has stopped." He held his hand out to her. "Come on."

"Where are we going?"

"I want to show you something before you leave."

Kate took his hand, allowing him to help her off the couch and lead her back to his office. Her first few steps were a little unsteady, owing to the warm embrace of the wine (of which she'd consumed more than she'd intended) and limited sleep. Concentrating, she quickly recovered her footing.

Fraye walked over to a credenza with a glass top, which stood between the front windows. He flipped a switch on the side of the unit, illuminating its contents. Displayed beneath the glass was a collection of gleaming handcuffs. Little placards had been placed beside each of the six sets of restraints, stating era of manufacture and country of origin.

He swept a hand across the top of the case. "I've been collecting these since I was a kid." He pointed to a pair set off on their own to the right side of the display. "Those were the first, given to me by my dad —he was a beat cop." Pride and nostalgia were woven thickly between his words.

"Kate, the fight between good and evil has been going on a long time. Ever since man started organizing into real societies, there have been those who want to steal, cheat, rape, and kill. But there have also been those who tried to protect the innocent."

He stepped closer, shrinking the distance between them. Powerful emotions burned inside his dark eyes.

"I know the loss of those girls has been hard on you, and I've been hard on you. But what we do matters, Kate. And no matter what the outcome of this case, you have to be content knowing you're doing your best to help."

"And if my best isn't good enough?"

"You can't save the world, Kate. No one can— not even Special Asshole Fraye."

Her eyes opened wide.

"Come on, you think I don't know what your team calls me behind by back? I'm an investigator—

uncovering facts is my specialty. Although I'm not sure what is so special about my asshole, or why your team is so concerned with that particular aspect of my body."

Despite herself, Kate started to giggle.

"I do have some other parts that are quite exceptional, if I do say so myself."

Kate's giggles escalated into all-out laughter, prompting a smile from Fraye.

"I like seeing you laugh." Something in the intensity of his stare caused a flutter in her stomach. Reaching out, he tucked a few stray hairs back behind her ear. "You have some pretty exceptional parts yourself, detective."

The laughter dissipated. Kate studied his features in the dim light of the display case—struck by a sudden desire for the man who had caused her so much grief and consternation since they'd first met.

She stared at the thin scar that cut through his left eyebrow. For all the anger and frustration Fraye had made her feel, there was something about him—a mix of confidence and raw power that was almost intoxicating. Or maybe it was the fact that her sex life was really just a pattern of infrequent one-night stands that had relegated her to the role of a wanton woman after one good bottle of wine.

Her eyes found his, and in their depths she recognized a desire equal to her own. Rational thinking instructed her to walk away—to increase the space between them. She was about to step aside when Fraye leaned in and kissed her.

The SFPD detective in her mind screamed out, demanding she get the hell out of there. But her emotions roiled tumultuously in a sea of alcohol-fueled lust, anchoring her firmly in place.

She opened her mouth readily. The kiss, which had started out tentatively, morphed into a fervent passion as they explored each other's mouths.

Pulling his lips from hers, Fraye began working his mouth down her throat. Between kisses, he murmured the same words that she'd been fighting to banish from her head. "We shouldn't be doing this … it may complicate things…"

His mouth and tongue were performing miracles against the right side of her neck. Gasping for air, she replied haltingly. "You're… right…"

"Do you want to stop?"

"No."

"Neither do I."

He tore off her top and paused, gazing lustily at the dark nipples straining against the thin fabric of her pink lace bra. Mumbling something unintelligible, he spun her around, enveloping her in a close hug. Her breath caught in her throat as she felt the full extent of his need.

Reaching inside her bra, he cupped each breast roughly before sliding his hands down between her legs. She arched her hips against the pressure of his hands. In response, he growled a simple directive. "Upstairs."

They progressed slowly, stopping briefly on the stairs, where he pushed her against the wall—desperately trying to devour her on the spot. The wooden wainscoting dug cruelly into Kate's back. Rather than demurring from the pain, she gloried in it.

Fraye broke away and started fumbling with her jeans. The movement caused him to rock unsteadily on the narrow, old steps. He grabbed for the railing, regaining his balance. "We'd better keep moving." He looked down at the wooden staircase pointedly. "This could get dangerous."

Kate felt as if she were speeding toward a sheer cliff, and all she could think of was stepping on the accelerator. Lips parted, she looked up at him, her voice husky with desire. "I hope it does."

He grabbed her waist, twisted her sideways, and pushed her up the stairs ahead of him. As they walked down the hallway to the set of double doors at the far end, he began tracing seductive patterns down her back. She tried to turn around, but he prodded her forward. "Not until we get inside."

She opened one of the doors into a huge master bedroom that had been exquisitely remodeled. A modern, ebony poster bed dominated the chamber, which was decorated in simple hues of black and white.

They fell to the bed and flew at each other—shedding clothes, nipping, sucking, and tasting with abandon.

"I've wanted to do this to you ever since that night at Genevieve's." The words rushed from Fraye's lips.

Brief images from the S&M party flashed in Kate's mind—leather, lace, clamps, restraints. "Too bad you didn't. It might have been fun." A small smile played on her lips before she knelt and flitted her tongue gently across the tip of his penis. Fraye gasped loudly. Aroused by his response, she opened her mouth wide, slipping every inch of the engorged surface into the silky warmth of her mouth.

He threw his head backward, lost in the sensation. Groaning softly, he began pumping his hips in rhythm with her enthusiastic maneuvers. Suddenly, his eyes snapped open. He pulled away reluctantly. Taking her chin in his hand, he raised her eyes to his and kissed her softly. "Would you have liked it that way—like what you saw at Genevieve's?"

The seductive smile returned. "Maybe."

"Hold on." Fraye scrambled from the bed, leaving Kate kneeling alone with a demanding pulse beneath the thin fabric of her panties.

Assuming he was going for a condom, she watched lasciviously as he walked to the closet and retrieved a small red-and-black velvet box. It was one of the parting gifts Genevieve had handed out to her guests as they departed.

A dark curiosity intensified the heat between her legs. "Do you know what it is?"

He smiled and laid the box on the bed next to her. "No. I haven't opened it yet. Go ahead—take a peek."

Kate slid her index finger under the black ribbon, then quickly tugged on it. Placing both hands on the lid, she tilted it open so its contents were revealed to her alone.

Fraye leaned forward expectantly. "Well? What is it? Do you want to try it?"

Still staring into the box, Kate tilted her head to one side. He watched as an internal struggle seemed to play out across her features. Finally, she looked up at him slowly. A wicked smile spread across her features. "Oh yes. I want to try it."

ᛈ ᛈ ᛈ

February 4

It was well past midnight when Kate drove across the Golden Gate Bridge on her way home from Napa. The intensity of the bright-red paint adorning the span's steel towers was diluted into a dark blush by the fog.

A similar hue burned in Kate's cheeks. The heat fueling it had continued to simmer since she'd left Fraye's house. It was a heat fueled by shame and regret. At least those were the two emotions she was willing to acknowledge.

Satisfaction and lust also contributed to the mix, but there was no point indulging either feeling. To do so would only complicate things, and she had certainly done enough of that tonight.

Sleeping with Fraye had not been something she had planned on doing. It had been all that talk about guilt and the wine and… She shook her head, warding off the excuses.

So they'd had sex. So she had let him strap her to the bed and violate her in various and sundry ways. This case would end, and Fraye would leave. There was no future for them, and that was okay. Neither of them wanted one anyway. It had just been one night. One glorious and raunchy night that had left every orifice in her body with a barely tolerable soreness. Her bra had been hastily shoved into her purse—its thin fabric proving too painful for her much-abused nipples.

Leather restraints and clamps not withstanding, they were both professionals. They could go on as if it hadn't happened—she was confident of that. It wasn't like what she'd done with Harding. That mistake had been far messier than this one.

What Kate was more reticent to think about was the depth of emotion she'd experienced when talking to Fraye about guilt. Changing lanes, she suddenly remembered his explanation about the behavior of children of addicts. Recalling his words, another memory she had thought long buried sprang to the surface.

One fall day during her junior year of college, a knock at Kate's apartment door had prompted a reason to believe things might be different with her mother. Not having spoken to Chloe since she walked out at eighteen, Kate was shocked to find her mother standing on her doorstep.

Abandoned dreams leapt unbidden from her heart in rapid-fire succession. Yet, as she noted the second-hand clothes and the emaciated form beneath them, reality barged back in, sucking every ounce of hope from her chest.

With uncharacteristic humility, Chloe greeted her daughter and asked to be invited in. Zeroing in on the trembling hands and the familiar look of desperation, Kate had demanded to know what her mother wanted.

The humility abruptly disappeared, replaced by a haughty disdain. Chloe shifted to attack mode, blaming her daughter for her sad state and insisting Kate give her money to rectify the situation.

Kate's temper flared with each spiteful word from her mother's lips. Finally, she demanded, "You actually think I owe you anything?"

"Of course you do. I'm your mother!"

Memories of the sight of Candace's lifeless body and the smell of vomit flashed through Kate's mind. Their color was immediately washed away in a sea of red. "You crazy bitch! Look at you, you're a pathetic junkie! You've no idea what it means to be a mother! You destroy everything you touch. First your marriage, then Candace. You tried to destroy me, too, but you couldn't. Because I'm not weak like my poor sister was. You should have died that day—you, not Candace!"

Kate paused to inhale. In that moment she realized that not only had her mother stopped arguing, but Chloe seemed to shrivel inwardly during her daughter's tirade. Her eyes had filled with tears and her lower lip was trembling.

Rather than prompting remorse, her mother's response had only fueled Kate's fury. She could not count the times Chloe had *pulled crocodile tears from her expansive quiver of manipulation weapons.*

Fearing she was about to lose physical control, Kate balled her hands into tight fists and screamed, "Get out of here! The only time I ever want to hear about you again is when I hear you're dead!"

Chloe's gaze dropped like a dried up piece of fruit falling from a branch. Watching her mother shuffle down the street, Kate had fought the urge to hurry after her. Bitterness and an overall lack of faith had won the day.

In the intervening years, Kate had thought about that retreating form more times than she'd cared to remember. Despite everything Chloe had done to their family, and everything she knew about addiction and addicts, Kate's heart remained bound in guilt for whatever ill fate had since befallen her mother. Whether she'd become a homeless wretch, strung out in a doorway in the Tenderloin, or whether she had already succumbed to an ignominious death, Kate felt it was entirely her fault.

She should have stopped her mother that day and tried to get her help. Moreover, if she could have gotten through to Chloe when she was younger, their whole family might never have been torn apart.

Without realizing it, she had allowed Chloe to join her sister Candace as links in the unbreakable chain of guilt, which bound the darkest part of Kate's heart. And for what? As Fraye had said, guilt itself was just another weapon of manipulation. There was no reason she should feel sorry for her mother—no reason in the world.

Approaching the toll plaza, she pulled into a FasTrak lane and was startled from her reveries by the ring of her cell phone. Her pulse quickened—she prayed it wasn't Fraye.

Glancing at the phone, she recognized the name of her partner. She pursed her lips and sped through the tollgate. Talking to Harding wouldn't be as unpleasant as talking to the special agent. But because of their history, and Harding's feelings toward Fraye, it felt strange nonetheless.

Placing a lid on her emotions, she tapped the speaker button and answered the call.

"Hey, Kate. You're never going to guess who just walked into the Hall of Justice and asked to speak with you."

Kate's eyes flashed to the dashboard clock. "Are you still there at this hour on a Saturday night?"

"Technically, it's Sunday morning, and no, I'm not there yet, but I'm on my way. Seriously, partner, you're never going to guess."

Kate wasn't in the mood for games—she'd already indulged in far too many tonight. "Who is it?"

He paused, taken aback by the irritation in her voice. "It's our suspect—Jonas Riley."

Kate felt as if she'd just been sucker punched. Gripping the steering wheel, she did her best not to lose control as she plunged into the darkness of the Funston Avenue Tunnel.

"You've got to be kidding!"

"The guys at the front desk just called me. Apparently, he walked in off the street and said he wanted to speak with you. The best part is that he's alone—no lawyer."

"Does Fraye know?"

"Not yet; I'll call him as soon as I hang up with you. Meet me there as soon as you can."

"I'm on my way, but we won't be able to question Riley for a while."

"Why not?"

"Because it will take Fraye at least an hour or so to get there, and I know he'll want to be there when we start."

"An hour? Where is he?"

Her mind raced as she searched for a simple explanation. "I thought I heard him say he was going to be in Napa tonight."

"Are you kidding me? He's dicking around in the wine country in the middle of an investigation! Fuck, that guy is…I'll call him right now." He hung up without saying good-bye.

As Kate emerged from the far side of the tunnel, all thoughts about the awkwardness of seeing Fraye again dissipated. She drove across town with a single-minded focus—to get her hands on Riley.

Chapter 16

JONAS RILEY SAT PERFECTLY STILL in the empty interrogation room. His pale complexion appeared sickly in the glare of the overhead lights. Wearing frameless glasses, a simple long-sleeve gray sweater, and jeans, he did not look like the type who would wind up in a police station.

A large mirror occupied the opposite wall. His eyes were fixed on the reflective surface, where they had remained since the desk sergeant had first brought him there. That had been over an hour ago.

The officer had returned four times, offering water and promising Kate would arrive soon. In truth, the detective had arrived—thirty minutes earlier.

She'd gone directly to the small observation room. After speaking briefly with Harding, Kate had taken a standing position in front of the two-way mirror. She was still there—staring at the motionless suspect in the next room. Harding sat at a nearby table, watching his partner as intently as she observed the suspect.

The hallway door jerked open suddenly, stirring both detectives from their ruminations. Fraye strode into the room, immaculately clad in one of his designer suits. No one would have guessed what he'd been up to earlier in the evening.

Walking to the mirror, the agent stood alongside Kate and watched Riley. Abruptly, he turned to

Harding. "How's he been?"

"Just like what you see now."

"And he's been in here for over an hour?"

"Yeah. Only speaks when spoken to, and hasn't moved much."

Fraye nodded. "You wait here. Detective Barnes and I will go in together."

Harding shot from his seat. "Hold on. I've been waiting here this entire time, while you…"

"He asked to speak with me. I'll go in by myself." Both men turned to look at Kate, whose determined expression appeared to be carved from granite.

Fraye studied her for a moment before glancing back through the glass. His gaze flashed briefly in Harding's direction before returning to Kate. Seeming to have made up his mind, he took a seat at the table. "Okay. You break the ice. I'll join you when I feel it's appropriate." His unyielding tone indicated there would be no further discussion.

She picked up a pen and notepad from the table and started toward the door.

"Wait." She stopped abruptly at the sound of Fraye's voice. "If he is our killer, he will be extremely egocentric. He'll employ a variety of techniques to gain the upper hand. Don't be surprised if he answers your questions with questions of his own—or if he tries to make inflammatory statements to rattle you."

"I can handle it." A steely glint shimmered in her eyes before the door closed behind her.

Seconds later, Kate entered the interrogation room. Taking a seat in the chair across from Riley, she stared at him for a full minute before speaking.

"Mr. Riley, thank you for coming in."

His brown eyes regarded her shrewdly. "Before we start, I want you to understand that I chose to come

207

here without my lawyer because I am innocent." Despite his fit physique, the nasal inflection in his voice made him seem weak and geeky.

"You left us no other alternative."

"There are always alternatives." He slumped back in his seat, looking sullen. "You didn't have to go on TV and call me a suspect."

"Mr. Riley, we are interested in what you know about the recent deaths of Maggie Stevenson and Becky Hammonds—two young women with whom you were acquainted."

His lips pursed as if he were sucking on a lemon.

Kate leaned forward slightly. "You haven't been to your apartment in days, and you haven't shown up for work. Where have you been, Mr. Riley?"

His hands began to move in his lap—the fingers of his right hand idly picking at the cuticles of those on his left.

"Look, Detective, I came here to tell you I had nothing to do with this." His voice broke awkwardly around the last words. Taking a deep breath, he glanced around the room before continuing. "I was notified about an important event at the last minute. I can promise you it had nothing to do with the disappearance of either of these women."

"So where were you?"

Rising up regally in his chair, he looked down his nose at her. After a long pause, he reached into his back pocket and retrieved a laminated card. He laid it on the table with a flourish, then slowly slid it toward Kate.

About four inches wide by nine inches long, the card was forest green. At its center, were elaborately scripted capital letters—LOTR. Below the letters were a series of dates, flanked by what appeared to be Celtic symbols.

Nonplussed, Kate raised her eyes from the laminated paper to Riley's face. "And this is?"

Riley's eyes went wide. "My alibi, of course."

Kate nodded her head slowly. The gesture sharply contrasted with the look of disbelief on her face. She picked up the card and flipped it over. The backside was a mirror image of the front.

"So what is LOTR?"

He jerked backward, staring at her with incredulity. "You must be joking, right?"

Kate's lips compressed into a thin line. "Two women have been brutally murdered, Mr. Riley. This is not a joking matter. So I'll ask again. What is LOTR?"

His eyes sparkled with a barely suppressed energy. "LOTR is the acronym for the *Lord of the Rings*."

"As in the Tolkien stories?"

"Yes. This was my pass for the *Lord of the Rings* fan fiction conference, which was just held in Fresno. The badge clearly indicates that I was there from the…" his gaze dropped to the card in her hand. His features twisted into a horrified grimace. "You're bending it!"

Lunging across the table, he snatched the small rectangle from her grasp. Placing it reverently on the table in front of him, Riley ran his right hand over it—methodically smoothing out imperfections that were apparent only to him.

When he was satisfied with the appearance of the badge, he looked up at Kate petulantly. "Now that you know I was simply out of town for the last few days, I expect you'll be issuing a public statement saying you no longer consider me a suspect in this case."

"We will need to verify you actually were in Fresno the entire time." She pulled the cap off her pen and held the tip to her notepad. "What was the name of the hotel you stayed in?"

"I didn't stay in a hotel. I stayed at my friend's place."

Kate tilted her head to the right. "Really, Mr. Riley? We've been digging into your life for days, and it doesn't seem like you have many friends."

The accusation flipped an inner switch. Riley's body went rigid. A dark rage smoldered just beneath the surface of his eyes.

"I do have friends," he growled.

Kate crossed her arms and raised an eyebrow.

"I do!" He looked away briefly. "Most of them don't live around here. I meet them online."

"I find that hard to believe, Mr. Riley. We've questioned your landlord, neighbors, and the people you work with. No one remembers hearing about or meeting any of your *friends*. You only have ten contacts on Facebook. With the exception of one of the victims, they are all faculty members you have worked with at SFSU."

He shook his head. "Who cares about Facebook? It's crappy old technology anyway. With my studies and my work at the university, I don't have time to waste on that. Besides, there are a variety of other ways to socialize on the net."

"We'll need the name, address, and phone number for your friend in Fresno."

Riley blinked twice, then glanced away. "It won't help. He lives in a trailer on a farm outside of town. He's traveling abroad right now, but he gave me the key and said I could use his place anytime."

"He's out of the country—that's very convenient."

"Look, you can check with the convention center. They know I was there." He brightened suddenly.

"And you can call that trilobite, Zach Wellerby, who owns Mighty Hero Comics."

"Is Mr. Wellerby one of your friends?"

"No. He's the Neanderthal who had me escorted from his booth at the show." His eyes narrowed. "Wellerby was trying to pass off a reproduction of Anduril. It was an obvious fake, but he was trying to pawn it off on some guy for five thousand bucks! He was claiming it was the real one used in the movie version of *Return of the King*. I outed him and he called security."

"Anduril?"

He raised his eyes toward the ceiling and sighed. "Anduril is the name of Aragorn's sword—the one he uses to defeat Sauron. It was forged from the broken pieces of Narsil, which, of course, was split into only two pieces in the book version, but six in the movie version."

"You like swords and old weapons, don't you, Mr. Riley?"

"Yes, I do. Ancient weaponry is the center point of my doctoral dissertation."

"I saw your collection."

Irritation sparked in his eyes, charging the room with energy. "I do not appreciate the fact that you went through my things. And quite frankly, I do not appreciate being considered a suspect."

The words had no impact. "Just what exactly was your relationship with the two women?"

He rolled his eyes dramatically. "Please do not waste my time. I have already spent over an hour waiting for you. And I just proved to you that I wasn't even in town the last few days." He tilted his head to the right, daring her to continue.

Kate went on without missing a beat. "You served

as a teaching assistant in classes both of the women had attended at San Francisco State."

His hand shot into the air before he could retract it back into his lap. Struggling to regain control, he inhaled deeply. "That is *not* correct."

"Mr. Riley, we know you work as a teaching assistant…"

"Correct. I *work* as a teaching assistant. I do not *serve*."

Unflustered, Kate pressed ahead. "The photos, was it hard to take them?"

Something flashed in his eyes.

"Maggie obviously didn't know you were taking them. Was it hard to photograph her without her knowing what you were doing?"

The tension in his lips broke into an easy smile. "Is that what all this is about? The public appeal, the use of the word *suspect*? All this drama over some photos?"

The door opened and Fraye walked in. He took a seat at the head of the table between Kate and Riley. "Yes, Mr. Riley. It's all about photos." He tossed the file folder he'd been holding onto the table in front of Jonas. "Photos like those."

Riley held his stare, seemingly oblivious to the item that lay only inches away.

"Those photos are a little more interesting than the ones you took, Mr. Riley."

Kate reached for the folder, drawing Riley's eye. She opened it and began thumbing through the glossy pages.

Glancing at Riley, she gestured toward the pictures. "It must have taken a great deal of planning to pull this off."

"Let me guess. Those are the crime scene photos?"

His gaze bounced back and forth between Fraye and Kate. "Is this the part where I'm supposed to look at them and salivate? Shall I start foaming at the mouth with my eyes rolling in my head like some sort of rabid dog—admitting that I killed these women because of some sick sort of fetish?"

At the mention of the word fetish, Kate shot a quick glance at Fraye. Noting the exchange, Riley smiled lasciviously. "Did that strike a note, Detective Barnes?"

She turned back to Riley, as if unfazed by the remark, but the false pretense was shoddy at best.

Fraye stepped in before Riley could probe further. "Mr. Riley, you have offered a potential alibi for the murder of Becky Hammonds. We also want to know where you were at the time of the disappearance and murder of Maggie Stevenson."

Riley studied Fraye for a moment. "You're the FBI agent, right? The one who failed to apprehend the Tower Torturer years ago? If you had been capable of doing your job back then, we wouldn't be sitting here today—would we?"

Ignoring the question, Kate pounced again. "We understand you were attending UMass at the time of those murders—murders of college coeds, just like we have here." She waved a hand across the photos. "The killings stopped not long after you relocated to the Bay Area. Why do you suppose that is, Mr. Riley?"

"What is wrong with you people? I am a graduate student and I work as a TA for a state university. I am not a crazed killer! Perhaps you should pursue some higher learning yourself, Detective Barnes. At most what do you have, a bachelor's degree?" Derision dripped from his voice. "And here you are trying to piece together a flimsy case against me. Based on the fact that I knew both victims and happened to have a few photos of one of them in my home." He shook his head in disgust.

"There is another reason we are interested in you."

Riley's eyes shifted in Fraye's direction. "You have certain interests…" The special agent reached into his jacket pocket and pulled out a small stack of four-by-six photographs. He laid one of the images down on the table midway between himself and the suspect. "If I'm not mistaken, it is a Sumerian sickle sword. Correct?"

Straightening in his chair imperiously, Riley snorted. "You are acquainted with ancient forms of weaponry?"

Fraye shrugged. "I have a casual interest."

Kate sat silently, aware that Fraye's "casual interest" was solely attributable to the discovery of Riley's weapons in the shed behind Ms. Fung's house.

Riley studied Fraye carefully, trying to determine whether the agent was dissembling. Making up his mind, he leaned forward and picked up the picture. "You are correct; it is one of my better reproductions."

"And the cuneiform inscription?"

Riley proudly examined the photo, admiring the angular script he'd engraved into the blade's hilt. A genuine smile brightened his features. Then something in the room seemed to shift and his demeanor changed completely. He tossed the four-by-six in Kate's direction.

"Good try, Special Agent. You're trying to appeal to my interests. To build a rapport. And look, you happen to be sitting the exact same way I have been —with your hands in your lap. Really, Agent Fraye, I have undergraduate and master's degrees in criminal justice, and I'm working on my doctoral dissertation.

I am well versed on interrogation techniques such as mirroring.

"And now you suppose that because I fabricate ancient forms of weaponry, I must be the Tower Torturer. Let me educate the both of you. The era I am interested in is antiquity—an era that gave rise to weapons such as the sickle sword in that photo. It was invented around the third millennium BCE. According to the media, this killer you're searching for is torturing women with methods commonly used during the Middle Ages—a period that started around the fifth century CE. You may think old stuff is old stuff, but I can assure you there is very little commonality between the two eras in human history."

Fraye leaned back casually in his chair. "The torturers of the Middle Ages did not exist in a bubble, Mr. Riley. In most instances, they took what others had used before them and merely adapted it based on the technology and resources they had available at the time. Take torture by the brazen bull, for example. Roasting a person alive was a relatively common practice in the Middle Ages. Yet, it was the ancient Greeks who came up with the idea of cooking a human alive in a metal oven shaped like a bull. One that would dance around and entertain the audience as the victim writhed in torment within its belly."

He crossed one ankle casually across the opposite knee. "And you happen to have some very fine reproductions of ancient Greek weaponry in your collection. Speaking of collections, I understand you're a fan of *Lord of the Rings*. Interesting how Tolkien created an entire writing system based on ancient Anglo Saxon and Scandinavian runes, wouldn't you say?"

Riley stared at Fraye for a full minute before exhaling loudly. "If neither of you have any relevant questions for me, I think it's time for me to go."

"Look at these fucking photos!" Kate's voice boomed in the small chamber. Shooting out of her seat, she flipped each of the four pages face up on the table in front of Riley, as if dealing a game of high-stakes blackjack.

Taken aback by her sudden outburst, the suspect did as instructed. His air of supremacy dissipated as he studied the first two pictures of Maggie. Turning his attention to the photos of Becky, he swallowed awkwardly and began to drum the fingers of his right hand against his thigh.

"Why did you take those photos of Maggie, and where were you when she was murdered?"

Riley smirked at her defiantly. "The truth is that the photos were just a mistake; I was trying to take pictures of her laptop. One day after class, she waited and wanted to show me something she was working on. I guess I snapped a few pictures of her by mistake. I'm not the best when it comes to taking pictures with my phone."

"It was a mistake? A mistake you took the time to print out and hang on the wall of your bedroom?"

The smirk grew into a beaming smile. "Men hang pictures of women on their bedroom walls all the time."

Kate glared at him with a dark intensity. "Not of dead women."

"How about Marilyn Monroe? She's dead, but men still enjoy looking at pictures of her." He waved a hand in the direction of the crime scene photos. "Everybody dies sometime. Some of us just get to do it with a bit larger fanfare than others."

Kate's entire body went rigid and her left hand began to tremble, drawing Fraye's attention.

"Detective." It was a command, not a warning. Chagrined, Kate dropped back into her seat.

Riley watched the interchange, a childish glee sparkling in his eyes. "Really, Detective Barnes, I had nothing to do with these murders. I've tried to be as helpful as I can by coming here voluntarily and speaking with you."

He spun back to Fraye. "You clearly have no other evidence—no DNA, no witnesses putting me at the crime scene, no proof I was anywhere near the women at the time of their abductions. In other words, you have nothing that will hold up in court. I doubt the DA will want to arrest me with so little evidence."

Kate opened her mouth, but Riley steamrolled ahead. "I spoke with my attorney before coming here. He tried to convince me not to come without him, but I felt confident you would realize your mistake and end this. Unfortunately, you do not want to be reasonable. I will not say one more word without my attorney present." He settled back into his chair and crossed his arms primly.

"That's fine, Mr. Riley. Please be aware that you are being placed under arrest for the murders of Maggie Stevenson and Becky…" The words marched slowly and determinedly from Kate's lips—obliterating the smug expression on Riley's face.

▷▷▷

Kate stared blankly at Harding's legs, which hung limply over the side of the credenza in Kevin Nguyen's office. It had been a long night, and both detectives were exhausted.

"Okay, I'm in." Kevin's announcement drew Kate's gaze back to Jonas Riley's laptop, which had taken center stage on the IT director's desk.

Riley's attorney had arrived shortly after they'd finished booking him. They'd had to wait while the suspect conferred with his counsel before they could continue the interrogation. As expected, the barrister had stonewalled, allowing Riley to answer only a handful of questions before insisting his client be released. Fraye had refused, and Riley remained in custody.

After Riley's attorney had left, Harding found his van parked two blocks away from the Hall. The warrant they'd obtained to search Riley's apartment had also included his vehicle. In the van, they turned up the lost treasure that had been missing from Riley's apartment—his computer.

After a call from Kate, Kevin Nguyen had hurried in. Arriving two hours earlier than usual, the IT director had set to work immediately, trying to bypass the device's security protocols.

"I'll hand it to the guy, he's got a pretty sophisticated firewall setup. Let's see what we've got." Kevin's fingers flew over the keyboard as the desktop materialized on the screen.

He regarded Kate dryly over his shoulder. "A *Lord of the Rings* fan?"

Kate frowned. "How do you know?"

Kevin nodded toward the screen, where a series of icons were displayed against a rugged landscape with a craggy mountain range rising up in the background. An impressive citadel sat in the center, climbing heavenward amid ragged peaks, its strong fortifications balanced by the breathtaking splendor of its architecture.

"It's Minas Tirith, the white city. This picture is from *Return of the King*—the third movie in the *Lord of the Rings* trilogy."

"You know about this stuff?"

"Yeah. Why?"

Kate looked to Harding for help. Hopping off the credenza, the detective sauntered over and stood beside Kevin. "Because you're a pretty normal guy and most of those fantasy and sci-fi fans are total losers."

Kevin turned back to the computer. "I know what you mean. There are a lot of dorks out there. Either of you ever been to WonderCon?"

Harding groaned loudly. "You mean that convention they hold at Moscone Center? The one where all the weirdos on the Western Seaboard dress up as their favorite *Star Wars* character, hoping to find an exclusive action figure in mint packaging? Don't tell me you've gone to that circus."

A wry smile tugged at the corner of Kevin's mouth while he scanned the variety of prompts appearing on the screen. "That's the one. And yes, I may have gone a time or two. But it's not just *Star Wars*. It's *Star Trek*, *Dungeons and Dragons*, comic book characters, video games... And not everyone who goes to WonderCon is a weirdo."

Kate shot Harding a warning glance over the IT director's head. "Ignore my partner, Kevin. I happen to know that he has a collection of vintage Superman comics. He probably sits in his car, parked outside the doors of WonderCon, wondering should I or shouldn't I—like a heroin addict huddling outside a methadone clinic."

Eyes still glued to the screen, Kevin erupted into a quick fit of giggles.

"Anyway, Riley claims he was at a fan fiction convention in Fresno when Becky was murdered."

"You guys think it's a legit alibi?"

Karinsky is on his way down there to check it out.

But Fresno is about three hours away by car. Depending on how long he stayed at the conference each day, Riley could have come back and killed Becky, then dumped her body before…"

Kate's voice trailed off as Fraye marched into the office. Earlier, he had called the district attorney and roused her from bed. She'd come directly to the Hall to meet with Fraye and review the interrogation footage. If the smoldering expression on Fraye's face was any indication, the meeting hadn't gone well.

Walking around the desk, the special agent stood next to Harding and nodded toward the laptop. "Have you gotten in yet?"

Kevin nodded without looking up from the screen. "I just did. Riley is getting his money's worth out of this machine—the hard drive is almost filled to capacity. For a guy who took such care with security protocols, he's got mega cookie action and his web history is… Let's just say it's going to take some time to review it all."

"Start with video files and Internet activity. Reach out to Quantico for help, if you need it."

"Will do."

"Good." He appraised each of the detectives with gravity. "We've got less than a day and a half to find what we need."

Harding glanced briefly at Kate before turning to Fraye. "Isn't the DA going to charge Riley?"

"That's going to depend upon what Kevin and the crime lab team can tell us. This is a high-profile case, and she wants to leave no room for error. As it stands, she doesn't think we have enough to charge him. She has agreed to hold Riley for up to thirty-six hours. If we don't come up with something else by then, we have to release him."

Swearing softly, Harding drove a hand back through his hair. "Riley was right."

"How so?" The question was laced with acid.

"He said we didn't have enough to hold him, and he was right."

"Perhaps. But Riley was wrong about the fact that we would not arrest him. Because of that arrest, we now have his car and his computer. The evidence is there. Even if he was able to dispose of the bodies without leaving any traces of hair, fluids, or fibers in his vehicle, his computer should provide all the evidence we need."

Chapter 17

February 5

AT SIX O'CLOCK in the morning, the line at the Starbucks on Divisadero Street was mercifully short. Two businessmen were all that stood between Kate and her morning caffeine fix. She inhaled deeply, settling for the tantalizing aroma of espresso until she could get her hands on the liquid version.

Her need partially sated, Kate pulled out her phone and checked her email. There were no new messages. Last night she had learned that the lab could not match any of the hairs or fibers found in Riley's car to either of the victims. Everything was riding on Kevin now. He had to find something hidden on Riley's computer today, or they would be forced to release him.

Disappointed, she dropped the phone back into her purse and waited impatiently for her turn to order. When the businessmen finished their transaction, Kate hurried forward.

"Same as usual, Kate?" The inquiry came from the jubilant blonde cashier named Trudy. She was in her early twenties, and her straight, shoulder-length hair had been streaked with vibrant hues of pink and blue. The colored portions had been pulled up into high ponytails. With her impish features and fanciful hair, Trudy's look was very Japanese anime.

"As always."

Trudy grabbed a paper cup and a Sharpie, then made the necessary marks for a grande nonfat latte, before passing it to the barista. Pulling a banana from a nearby basket, she laid it on the counter before Kate. A mountain bike had been inked into Trudy's hand between her thumb and forefinger.

"New tattoo?" Kate asked.

"Yeah. Totally cool, right?" Trudy thrust her hand outward for inspection.

Kate nodded and smiled.

"Oh, and your total's three seventy-five. So, did you have a good weekend?"

Kate thought about it for a moment as she passed her bank card to Trudy. While their ability to keep Riley detained was uncertain, at least he was in custody. It was a far cry from where they'd been Friday.

"I think so."

Trudy's eyebrows leapt toward her scalp. She leaned across the counter and dropped her voice. "Hook up with any hotties?" She winked at Kate mischievously—the movement exaggerated by Trudy's impossibly long false eyelashes.

Images of Saturday night's experimental tryst with Fraye popped into Kate's mind, bringing an unexpected flush to her cheeks.

"Kate, you're blushing!" Trudy swiped the card through the register's scanner, then handed it back. "So what happened?"

Stowing her card back in her wallet, Kate picked up the banana and dropped it into her purse. The upside of coming to this Starbucks every morning was that she'd become familiar with the staff, who always did their best to push her through the line quickly.

The downside was that the ever-perky, yet quirky, Trudy had become a bit too familiar with her.

"Wouldn't you like to know…" Kate smiled enigmatically and proceeded to the far end of the bar to await her drink.

Undeterred, Trudy called out to her. "Hey, that's not fair!"

"Being cruel to the cashier? That's a new low, Kate." The words were issued in a deep baritone, but lightened by a trace of humor.

Turning, Kate found herself face to face with her partner. "Trudy's just kidding around—like she does every morning. What are you doing here?"

"I wanted to talk to you—privately."

"Okay. But how'd you know I'd be here?" While she was relieved he hadn't shown up at her apartment, she felt a bit irritated by this intrusion into the privacy of her morning ritual.

"You show up every morning with a Starbucks cup." He cast a brief glance around the coffee shop. "This one's around the block from your apartment building. It didn't take a genius to figure it out." Hitching a thumb over his shoulder, he pointed in the direction of a table. Upon its surface, a white paper cup stood among the ruins of what might have once been a pastry. "I've got that table over by the window."

Kate stared at the table for a moment, consternation furrowing her brow. She should have seen Harding when she walked inside, but she'd been too lost in her own thoughts—not a good trait for a Special Victims Unit detective.

"I'll get my drink and…" Kate paused as her name suddenly echoed through the shop. "Never mind; sounds like it's ready." She retrieved her latte, thanking Kurt, the forty-something barista whose arms were a collage of intricately detailed tattoos.

Making her way between two other small tables, she sat down across from Harding, where she dubiously eyed the ragged landscape of coffee cake crumbs. "What was so important that it couldn't wait until I got to the Hall?"

Harding took a quick sip of his coffee. "I want your take on Riley."

"Riley?" Suspicion drew Kate's brows together. "Why?"

Harding watched her for a moment as if trying to foresee her reaction to his words. "What's your take on the *Lord of the Rings* angle?"

Kate shrugged noncommittally. "I think it appeals to his interest in archaic weaponry. I saw one of those movies. It was one long, boring battle scene after another."

His eyes narrowed. "Fraye said virtually the same thing about the weaponry."

"Because it's true." Brushing aside a small section of detritus, Kate made room for her cup. "Look, it's early in the morning, and we're under the gun to find evidence on Riley. I don't feel like playing twenty questions. Just tell me what's bothering you."

"I was up all night thinking about it. The more I go over Riley's responses, the less I feel like he's our guy. It was what Kevin said about…" His words trailed off while he watched her raise the coffee cup to her lips.

Remembering Harding's outlandish kiss the other night, Kate turned her head to the side and took an angry sip. Swallowing thoughtfully, she glanced back at him, urging him to continue.

"It's this whole fan fiction thing. I mean, it is one thing to think the books or movies are cool. But going to those conventions and getting that excited over hobbits and elves—that's just plain weird."

"A lot of criminals are weird."

"I get that. But Fraye said our guy was a true psychopath, right? Someone who kills because he wants to, not because he has to. A master gamesman —a true badass."

"Right. So?"

"So, Riley is no calculating badass. He's more of the Columbine High School type—who would kill to get back at society for seeing him as an outcast. Maybe both of the girls rejected him, and he lashed out at you during the interview because you're another strong female that he could never have."

Kate considered his words carefully—replaying the interrogation in her mind. "Okay. I guess you could read his behavior that way. But so what? Even if you're right, then Riley is still our guy."

"The point is that if I'm considering this angle, why hasn't Fraye?"

Kate placed her cup back on the table. "Because Fraye sees two sides to Riley. There is the geeky unsure side that we saw in the first half of the interview. Then once cornered with evidence, the geeky veneer disappeared and he became combative and smug. The guy is smart, egocentric, and manipulative—he fits the profile."

"I know. Fraye made it clear he thinks Riley's dorky side is a ruse."

"Or at least an exaggeration."

She could tell from his expression that he still was not convinced. "Let's put it this way. If Riley really were the Lord of the Rings super geek you suspect him to be, why wouldn't his apartment be crammed full of action figures, posters, and character statuettes?

Have you really ever seen the home of a die-hard fan? It's like entering the bedroom of a ten-year-old."

Harding sat back in his seat. "I guess I just don't like the way this investigation is going."

"Is it that, or is it that you don't like the man leading it?'

"A little of both. But this isn't about my feelings toward Fraye, or the fact that he's a total dick. It's about the fact that we've been working this case—a case that is costing you a hell of a lot—and I'm not feeling like the guy sitting in lockup is our perp."

Harding leaned his elbows on the table, heedlessly flattening the debris beneath the sleeves of his sport coat. Kate thought about saying something, but decided to let it go. Harding had never been overly concerned about his appearance. In that way, and so many others, he was very different from Fraye. It wasn't surprising that the two men saw things so differently.

"Kate, do you know who the Green River Killer was?"

"I didn't before this case, but I do now—Gary Ridgway. He murdered women and teenage girls up in Washington during the eighties and nineties. He'd kill them, dump the bodies, then go back and have sex with them later. If I remember correctly, he was convicted of killing forty-eight victims, but confessed to a much larger number."

"Right. But did you also know that Ridgway would have been caught much earlier if the FBI profiler on the case hadn't fucked up royally?"

"What do you mean?"

"About halfway through Ridgway's killing spree, he sent an anonymous letter to a newspaper. The FBI profiler saw the letter but dismissed it, saying the author didn't fit the profile. Do you realize how many more people died because of that mistake?"

Harding watched as his partner paled visibly at his words. "All I'm saying is that these guys aren't infallible. Riley's attorney is bitching about how this investigation has tunnel vision because we're not considering any other suspects."

"We don't have any other suspects!"

His gaze flickered briefly to the floor and then back. When his eyes found hers again, there was something far more complex hidden in their depths. "Kate, seeing what this case is doing to you is killing me. I know you like to act like no one can get through that tough Barnes' exterior, but..."

Standing abruptly, Kate snatched her cup off the table and stared pointedly at her partner. "Time is ticking off the clock. We have a job to do. That is why we spend time together—because of our job. So let's go to work."

She hurried out of the shop through the double doors and into the driving rain. He watched her disappear around the corner without ever turning back.

Lost in thought, he didn't even feel the scalding heat as his right hand contracted into a fist, destroying the cup and spilling the hot contents all over his hand.

▷▷▷

Kate stood in the doorway of the conference room, observing Fraye as he sat in the shadows, steadily typing on his laptop. At this late hour of the night, the department was just about deserted. There were only two weak light sources in the cavernous chamber—the single emergency fixture, which hung at the front of the room, and the light from Fraye's computer.

Even after a long day of disappointment, the special agent still managed to look as if he'd just walked out of a GQ photo shoot. Gradually, his fingers stopped moving. He leaned back in his seat and closed his eyes.

"Long day, huh?"

He sat up, a weak smile tugging at the corners of his mouth as he spotted Kate. "Something like that."

"I checked with central processing. Riley was released ten minutes ago."

He nodded pragmatically. "Well, we were tasked with finding new evidence, and we failed. If only Kevin had found something on that laptop, or if Karinsky hadn't been able to verify that Riley had attended the conference in Fresno."

Kate folded her arms across her chest. "But Karinsky couldn't verify Riley's nighttime activities in Fresno—he still could have come back and killed Becky. And Kevin did find that photo of Riley astride the De Anza statue. It was taken three months ago, and Riley's pose mimicked that of Maggie's corpse."

"All circumstantial."

"So, where do we go from here?"

"Massachusetts."

"Digging deeper into Riley's past?"

"Yes. I'm going tomorrow. I'll be here for a few hours early tomorrow morning, then I'll fly out in the afternoon. I think the local law enforcement officers may have missed something when they were interviewing Riley's former associates."

He followed Kate's gaze as it dropped to the floor. "You don't agree?" he asked pointedly.

Glancing back at him, she tucked a lock of hair that had escaped her ponytail back behind her ear. "Of course I agree. It's a good idea."

Fraye closed his laptop and walked over to join Kate. His voice matched the soft expression in his eyes. "Don't tell me you're losing hope already. This is only a momentary setback."

"I know that. I just…"

He leaned back against the doorframe. "Is this about Napa?" His voice held a note of apprehension.

Kate looked wounded. "No, not at all."

"I'm sorry if you expected more, Kate. But I thought we were of a like mind on that issue. You have to understand, my career is…"

Kate laid a hand on his chest, silencing him. "Let's be clear. I did not expect, nor do I want to get involved with anyone right now."

"Then what is bothering you?"

She glanced around awkwardly as if unsure how to proceed. "It's about Riley."

"I told you, we'll redouble our efforts and…"

"No!" The word came out louder than she'd anticipated. Frustrated, she walked into the room and collapsed into one of the chairs. Swiveling the chair around to face him, she raised her chin defiantly. "Do you ever question whether Riley really is our guy?"

Suspicion clouded his features. "Where is this coming from?"

Kate looked away guiltily.

"I have already provided you and the entire team with my take on Riley. You concurred with my findings yesterday. Why are you questioning me now? I thought we finally resolved your trust issues in Napa."

"It's not me. It's just that this morning, Harding…"

"Harding! So that's it. Your wayward partner is undermining me again." Fraye strode back into the room and sat down across from Kate, leveling her with an unwavering stare.

"He's not undermining you."

"Really? If he has concerns about my profiles or my analyses of suspects, then why doesn't he come to me directly? Why not bring it up during the meeting this morning?"

Kate had no response for the legitimate questions.

"He's doing the same thing he did when we investigated the Torturer back in Boston." Fraye stared off into the distance. "It's almost as if he's purposely…"

"Purposely what?"

Fraye stared at Kate for a long moment, before a smile broke the tension in his features. "Never mind." He reached for his laptop and began typing again. "I'm sending you a copy of Robert Hare's *Psychopathy Checklist.*"

"That's not necessary."

"Clearly it is. You analyze Riley for yourself. If I can't convince you, perhaps running the checklist yourself will."

"I don't need to. I respect your opinion."

"You may, but you are also questioning it. Right now we need to stay focused on Riley. Hopefully, after running the checklist you can show the results to Harding and bring him back on board."

Standing, he closed his laptop and started toward the door. "I'm convinced Riley is the Tower Torturer. Don't let Harding or anyone else fool you, Kate. Jonas Riley is a cold-blooded psychopath. It's been five days since the last murder. His cool-down period is almost over. He'll be ready to kill again soon. We have to get him back behind bars before he chooses another victim."

He walked out of the room leaving Kate alone in the shadows, struggling with the weight of his words and the knowledge of just how high the price for failure would be.

▷▷▷

February 6

The bay waters surged against the shore. Overhead, the early afternoon sun shone brightly in the clear-blue sky. The rainstorm the day before had whisked away any traces of the ominous, brown pollution that had become an all too regular presence on the horizon.

Growing annually in density, the haze was created by the millions of people who lived, worked, and played along the shores of the San Francisco Bay. While still regarded as one of the most beautiful areas of the world, the region was no longer the lush watershed it had once been. Prior to the arrival of the white man, the Bay Area had been pristine. A vibrant ecosystem, it had teemed with innumerable species of the land, water, and air. In those days, the human population was a mere afterthought, comprised of a handful of Native American tribes dotting the landscape.

But with the European intrusion came a population boom, which forced the retreat of so many indigenous species of plants and animals—some to the point of obliteration. The bay wetlands were hold-ing on by a very weak thread.

Only a small number of such areas remained, having been reduced to a few tiny pockets of protected life—huddling anxiously under the hungry eyes of developers. Developers like those who had built the two modern office buildings at the base of the San Mateo Bridge. Knowing only that this stretch of bay front shoreline in Foster City led to a tidal marsh touted as an ideal route for bikers, Trudy pulled her yellow Volkswagen bug into a parking spot toward the back of the lot.

Exiting the car, she hurried to the trunk and began dismounting her mountain bike from the rack. It had been a bit of a drive down from San Francisco, but the moment she'd pulled into the lot, she'd known it was going to be worth it.

From this spot she could see all the way from the Bay Bridge in San Francisco, down to the Dumbarton Bridge in Menlo Park. Across the blue expanse of water, the cities of the East Bay crept from the shore-front up along the distant mountains.

She locked her car and shoved her keys into the little black zippered pouch strapped under the bike's seat. Straddling the bike, she pulled her brightly colored helmet on.

When the strap was properly fastened, she popped her earbuds into her ears. An old punk tune from the eighties roared in her head. Clad in neon pink spandex from head to toe, she pedaled eagerly out of the lot and onto the bay front trail.

In less than a minute, she had disappeared into the shade under the bridge. She stared up at the network of steel and concrete supporting the mass of cars whizzing by overhead. With a few more rotations of her pedals, the bright sunlight returned.

To her left, the trail dropped away in a cascade of large boulders. The pathway ran along the top of the levy, which the US Army Corps of Engineers had constructed in the 1960s to keep the bay waters from flooding one of the region's most substantial landfill projects, Foster City.

To her right, the trail dropped away in a rush of green vegetation toward the wide expanse of asphalt that constituted Beach Park Boulevard. On the other side of the boulevard, a row of immaculate 1960s-era houses stretched along the roadway. All of the residences were two stories, maximizing some of the most beautiful waterfront views in the region.

Trudy picked up the pace, relishing the fresh, briny breeze. It was only one-thirty in the afternoon. Since most kids were still in school and most adults were still at work, she had the trail virtually to herself. Occasionally, a passing shadow prompted her to glance skyward, where she was delighted to spot the passing seagull or brown pelican.

She couldn't remember which of her hundreds of Facebook contacts had recommended this trail, but she silently vowed to thank whoever it was the minute she had her phone back in her hands. For now, the device was safely tucked away in the pouch with her car keys.

A short while later, her muscles pleasantly warm, she approached a large curve in the trail. Here the bay waters formed a barrier, dividing Foster City and its neighbor, Redwood Shores. The area between the two cities was a tidal marsh, the very spot she'd been looking forward to finding.

Her Facebook contact had promised that the most enjoyable ride could be found by venturing off the levy and continuing southward into the wetlands themselves. Ahead, she could see a thin bike path cutting its way through the short grasses. In the distance, the trail disappeared into a stand of extremely tall grasses, where she lost sight of it completely. One word drowned out the punk tones screeching in her head—adventure.

Preparing the muscles in her arms and legs to serve as added shock absorbers, Trudy rode off the levy. For a heart-soaring moment, she hung, gloriously suspended in midair, before gravity claimed its due. She bounced down over the uneven surface to the large expanse of dirt and shore grass.

Oblivious to the damage the thick tread of her tires caused as they chewed up the frail ecosystem, Trudy plunged gleefully down the unsanctioned trail. Within moments, she'd disappeared into the depths of the tallest grasses.

Standing well over seven feet tall, the dried yellow husks enveloped her as she whizzed by, transporting her to a surreal world in which all that existed was Trudy and the roughly hewn, narrow path before her.

The sensation reminded her of a scene in a movie she'd seen years before. Some kid had run into a cornfield and had become lost in the high stalks. Eventually, the kid had started to freak out and began running frantically through the corn. It had been really high-tension stuff.

The odd sense of solitude did not bother Trudy—rather, she reveled in it. It may have been different if she had heard the eerie sound the wind made as it whispered through the vegetation. But the punk riot blaring through her earbuds drowned out everything else.

Up ahead the trail rose over a small hill. Pedaling faster, Trudy jumped the hill, thrilled at the amount of air she achieved before dropping back to the ground. The terrain beyond remained level for a few yards before disappearing around a tight turn.

Suddenly, a violent jolt turned Trudy's elation into panic. Doing her best to keep from going over the handlebars, she allowed her body to absorb the shock, then hopped off and engaged the kickstand. Crouching down beside her bike, a sight worse than she'd anticipated confronted her. Not only was the front tire flat, but the rear was as well.

Swearing loudly, she straightened and grabbed for the handlebars. It would be a long walk back to her car.

She was about to turn the bike around when a gloved hand abruptly snaked around her from behind, clamping firmly over her mouth. A split second later, something stung painfully at her throat. Terror overwhelmed her senses, rendering her momentarily immobile. Her survival instincts ensured it was only a brief moment.

She screamed wildly into the oppressive grip, which effectively destroyed any chance that anyone might hear her. Releasing the bike, she reached for the gloved hand, trying to pry it loose. As the pain in her neck faded, her energy began to wane. Not just in varying degrees, but in its entirety.

Seconds later, her feet were knocked out from under her, and she fell to the ground. The sudden impact jarred her earbuds loose. They spilled onto the ground, their once deafening volume now as meek as an insect's buzz.

Struggling to her knees, Trudy tried to scream but was foiled by a thick piece of duct tape that now clung firmly to her lips. Traitorously, the last of her energy faded and she collapsed back onto the ground.

Unable to move, she watched as a pair of legs walked back along the path down which she'd just ridden. A gloved hand came into view, carefully sweeping away some dirt and dried grass from the corner of the trail. Trudy blinked slowly, fighting back the exhaustion that threatened to drown her in unconsciousness.

Something was being lifted out of the ground, casting off more debris as it rose. Trudy stared at the item—a large wooden board whose center portion was clustered with three-inch metal spikes.

An insidious cold overtook the hot terror that had thundered in her veins, as she realized just what the wooden implement meant. Whoever had attacked her had been lying in wait—the thought sparked a thousand questions. But the darkness was descending quickly. With no more strength to fight, she slipped from consciousness—her final moment of awareness plagued by hopelessness and fear.

Six minutes later, a tall man emerged from the same spot where Trudy had first entered the marsh. Wearing a cap and coveralls, he looked like one of the county workers charged with keeping mosquito populations under control in the marshes.

Before him, he pushed a large black wheelbarrow. A dirty piece of burlap covered the cart's bulky contents. On its right side, the handle of what appeared to be a rake was wedged between the material and the metal surface.

Making his way to the levy, the man followed it to a service ramp about twenty yards to the west. Pushing his burden up the ramp, he negotiated his way across the levy and down the ramp on the opposite side. Stepping onto Beach Park Boulevard, he pushed the cart a few more feet to a large, white commercial van.

He opened the two doors at the rear of the van, then pushed the wheelbarrow close to the bumper. To anyone watching from the houses on the other side of the street, he and the cart were all but obscured behind the large doors.

Extracting the long wooden tool, he tossed it into the back of the van. Careful not to disturb the burlap, he hefted the rest of the contents out and laid them in the van. He was about to reach for the doors when he noticed a bright-pink object sticking out from under the coarse material. Tucking the item back under the cover, he slammed the doors shut—plunging the inside of the van into darkness.

Chapter 18

KATE ESCORTED TROY out of the conference room and down the hall to the elevator. Maggie's boyfriend had shown up around four-thirty that afternoon, demanding to see the detective. The moment she had arrived in the conference room, the young man had erupted into a firestorm of expletives, demanding to know why Riley had been released.

Kate sat through the justified tirade like a devout monk engaged in a whip-wielding bout of corporal penance. When Troy had finally wound down, he'd collapsed into a chair, allowing her a chance to speak. She had calmly explained the district attorney's position and assured him the department was doing everything in its power to get the evidence they needed to convict Riley.

Pushing the call button for the elevator, Kate laid a hand on Troy's forearm. He glanced at her, the pain in his eyes rending her heart far more severely than anything he'd spat out earlier.

"We'll get Riley, Troy. I promise."

The elevator doors opened, and Troy entered without a word of reply. Kate turned away and headed back to her desk, battling the nagging worry that time might prove her to be a liar.

Lost in a maelstrom of guilt and self-doubt, she did not notice Detective Karinsky until they practically collided in the hall.

"I think we've got another one." There was no need to ask what he was referring to. Everyone in the department was dreading the same news—another victim.

The room began to spin. Digging deep inside, Kate searched for whatever strength remained in reserve. She could not give in to the desire to drop onto the floor and curl into a ball, so she concentrated on Karinsky's weathered visage instead.

"Tell me."

"I just got a call from the Foster City Police Department. They've got a young woman down there who claims her friend was just kidnapped."

He glanced down at the black notebook in his hand and began to read aloud. "Alleged victim is a twenty-three-year-old Caucasian female, five foot seven, one hundred and fifteen pounds, blonde hair, blue eyes. Her name is Trudy Morris and she…"

"She works at the Starbucks on Divisadero."

A mixture of surprise and sympathy dominated the older man's expression. "You know her?"

"Unfortunately for Trudy, I do. What else did they tell you?"

"She was going for a bike ride on a waterfront trail at around one-thirty this afternoon. Apparently she announced her plans on Facebook. The friend had the afternoon off. She saw the posting and decided to surprise the victim and join her out there. She found Trudy's bike abandoned in the wetlands a couple of miles from where she'd parked her car. The car's still in the lot, and there's no sign of Trudy. The friend freaked out and went to the FCPD."

Kate turned and headed for the elevator. She called back over her shoulder to Karinsky. "Harding is out on follow-up interviews. Get hold of him, and tell him to call me."

"Where are you going?"

Kate glanced back just before stepping into the elevator. "To pay a visit to Jonas Riley."

ᚦ ᚦ ᚦ

It was dark when Kate slammed her car door and walked across the street to Tina Fung's house. Her partner was waiting for her in the driveway. Harding had called her as soon as he'd heard from Karinsky, warning her to wait for him before talking to Riley. Her response had been simple—she had hung up the phone.

"What are you doing here?" Kate demanded.

"I told you I wanted to be here when you talk to him. Listen, Kate, we've had eyes on this place the whole time. I called our guys on the way here. They say Riley hasn't left the house since he was released. There's no way he could have abducted that girl this afternoon."

Kate turned away, striding toward the front gate. Harding joined her just before she began jabbing at the doorbell. Thrusting his hands into the pockets of his slacks, her partner shifted uncomfortably back and forth while they waited for a response.

The door above opened and a light brightened the entryway on the other side of the gate. Clad in a floral dress and a cardigan sweater, Tina Fung made her way steadily down the stairs. As she reached the ground level and proceeded toward the gate, she stopped short. Recognition flashed across her features, followed by irritation.

"I no talk to you. You already arrest Jonas for no reason." She pointed an accusing finger in their direction. "You get new job; you no good at police work!"

Kate grabbed hold of the gate handle. "Ms. Fung, you need to open this door. We have to talk to Mr. Riley right now."

"I no need to do anything. I go to Mahjongg tournament tonight. You make me late." She waved a dismissive hand toward the detectives and began to turn, when Kate's voice stopped her.

"Ms. Fung, another woman has gone missing. We still have an open warrant to access this property. If you do not let us in immediately, you will be under arrest for obstruction of justice."

Shuffling toward the gate, Tina Fung gazed up at Kate through the bars, weighing the veracity of the detective's threat. After a protracted silence, she shuffled back toward the stairs, calling out over her shoulder, "I go unlock, but you waste your time."

Harding could feel the pent-up energy swirling inside Kate as she stood anxiously at the gate. The moment the buzzing sound echoed in the small chamber, Kate pushed the gate open and rushed toward the door to Riley's apartment.

She pounded on the door, far louder and longer than was customary. When Kate's fist stilled, the landlord's voice rang out from above.

"Jonas no talk to you. He good man. You leave now!"

Kate resumed her pounding, the noise reaching an almost intolerable level as the sound echoed and amplified in the small entryway. "Open up, Mr. Riley! It's Detective Barnes and Detective Harding from the SFPD!"

After a protracted silence, Tina Fung spoke again. This time, her voice emanated from a short distance behind them, rather than from above.

"No break door. I let you in." She pushed between Kate and Harding, driving a key into the lock and pushing the door open. The light from the entryway spilled into the apartment, only making it a few feet before yielding to absolute darkness.

Aware Kate had made enough racket to raise the dead, the partners exchanged a quick glance and reached for their weapons, while carefully edging Tina back out into the entryway. Harding made a quick motion to the elderly woman, instructing her to keep quiet and go back upstairs.

They sidled up against either side of the doorway. Kate reached inside and began carefully groping for the light switch she'd recalled seeing during their previous search of the apartment.

Extending her arm further, she came upon a smooth piece of plastic. An inch or so more to the left, she felt the familiar shape of the switch. Locking eyes with her partner, she nodded slightly, then flipped the switch. As an overhead fixture filled the small room with bright light, Kate swung around and entered the apartment, sweeping her gun before her.

From her prior visit, she knew the unit consisted of only three rooms. The chamber Kate had just stepped into housed a well-used, oversized suede couch across from a metal-and-glass entertainment center, as well as a small kitchen against the far wall. In seconds, she confirmed the room was clear and began to move slowly toward the partially open bedroom door to her left.

Sidestepping along the wall, Kate reached the doorframe, aware that Harding had come in beside her. The light was off in the bedroom, allowing it to harbor as many secrets as it liked.

Glancing quickly at her partner again, Kate reached

around for the bedroom light, repeating the same nerve-wracking process she'd just completed at the front door. Finding the switch, she turned on the light and charged inside.

Like the kitchen and living area, the bedroom was sparsely furnished. A double bed sat in the middle of the room, with a lone nightstand at its right side. Undeterred, Kate proceeded to the bathroom, where she was soon as disappointed as she'd been with the apartment's other two rooms.

Exiting the bathroom, she exchanged a look of displeasure with her partner, who promptly shoved his gun into its holster. Kate was just in the process of holstering her gun when a figure suddenly charged into the bedroom.

Drawing her weapon on the sudden movement, Kate relaxed her finger a fraction of a second before she could actually squeeze the trigger.

Surprise and anger contorted Tina Fung's features. She hurried over to Kate and poked a wrinkled finger at the detective's solar plexus.

"You crazy lady! Why you point gun at me?"

Harding reached out and laid his hands gently on the older woman's shoulders. He began cajoling the irate landlord, carefully backing her away from Kate, who shut her eyes and took a deep breath. Hands trembling slightly, Kate reengaged the safety on her weapon and tucked it under her blazer.

From behind Harding's large frame, Tina dodged back and forth, hurling angry words at Kate as if she were a grenadier. Reverting to her native tongue, she fired a string of what was most likely Chinese profanity.

Swallowing deeply, Kate tuned out Tina's diatribe, letting her partner walk the landlord back out to the living area. When the Mandarin cacophony died down, Harding returned to the bedroom, expecting to find his partner shaken up by how close she'd come to injuring the innocent elderly woman.

Instead, he discovered a seething dragon that paced the area in front of Riley's bed like a caged lion.

"Kate?"

She shot past him and out of the apartment. In the foyer, she practically knocked Tina Fung down as she sprinted past her up the stairs.

Ignoring the slew of protests from the old woman, she shot through the open doorway into Tina's house and proceeded to search the entire home. Harding joined her. Within a few minutes, they had completed the search and were headed down the wooden staircase to the backyard. The yard and the shed were as empty as the house had been.

Slamming the door to the shed shut, Kate whirled on her partner. "How the hell did he get out of here without us knowing? Just before we came in here, you told me our guys have been watching the house. You said there was no way he could have gotten out and taken another victim."

He rested his hands on his hips and shook his head. "Okay, so I was wrong about him being in this house, but…"

Kate spun around, peering at the fencing that encircled the yard. "He must have jumped the fence."

"But we've got two sets of eyes here." He hitched a thumb back over his shoulder toward the front of the house. "One on Thirty-Third Avenue…" He paused and pointed forward. "And another on Thirty-Fourth. Even if he jumped the fence, they would have seen him trying to get away."

Kate pulled out her cell phone and started back

toward the stairs.

Harding hurried along behind her. "Who are you calling?"

"The captain. He needs to know what's going on."

"What about Fraye?"

"I left him a voice mail earlier. He's still in the air. His plane doesn't land at Logan until ten-thirty tonight."

Harding reached for Kate's arm, stopping her as she began to climb the stairs ahead of him. "Riley may be hiding in any one of the houses on this block. I know you think he's taken another victim, but…"

"I'm calling the captain to let him know we want to search every one of these houses. But I don't think we'll find him here. As Fraye said, he holds his victims somewhere else—somewhere he knows he won't be interrupted. We're still going to search this block— just in case." She turned and started up the stairs, then paused and looked back at her partner.

A bright light mounted just below the roof backlit Kate's body, outlining her with its brilliance, evoking the image of an avenging angel in her partner's mind. "I know how to do my job, and I don't let my beliefs or opinions get in the way. Maybe you should try to do the same thing."

"What the hell does that mean?"

She punched a button on her phone and held it to her ear. "It means you are so dead set on proving Fraye is wrong about Riley that you're letting it get in the way of what is right in front of your nose."

ᚦᚦᚦ

Kate hung up the phone, and leaned back into her chair. Fraye had called from the airport in Boston the moment his plane had landed. The call had gone just as she'd expected. He'd been as pissed as she was about the fact that Riley had escaped their surveillance.

And Riley had indeed escaped. They'd already spent hours searching every house on the block. As Kate had expected, Riley was nowhere to be found. They suspected he had fled in a delivery van parked at one of the houses on the backside of the block.

The surveillance team had become accustomed to the movement of the van, which was owned by a Chinese laundry owner—who also happened to be a good personal friend of Tina Fung.

When Tina had converted her downstairs into an apartment, she had sealed over the access way that connected the backyard to the garage. The narrow hall was a standard feature in the neighborhood homes—including the one owned by the laundryman.

Kate and Harding believed Riley had jumped over the back fence and made his way to the laundryman's yard at the far end of the block. There was no sign of forced entry at the backdoor to the accessway.

They believed the house's owner had opened the door for Riley, then escorted him through the passage to the garage where the van was parked in the drive-way. With the back doors of the van opened, it would have been virtually impossible for the detective across the street to see Riley sneak into the vehicle.

Confirming Kate's suspicions, Detective Felts, who had been stationed in front of the laundryman's house, reported seeing the van arrive at quarter past eleven in the morning—giving Riley plenty of time to get down to Foster City and kidnap Trudy around one-thirty.

With another victim in the Torturer's hands, Fraye had promised to take the first plane back. He'd just flown over five hours across the country. Kate had wanted to tell him it wasn't necessary to fly back right away, but she didn't. The truth was that she needed him here; they all did.

A sudden movement drew her eye. Kevin was jogging toward her with an unreadable expression on his face. He pulled up alongside Kate's desk. Dropping down onto one knee, he pulled her keyboard toward him and began typing.

"Kevin?" Kate rolled her chair backward to create more space between them. But when she looked at the prompts appearing on her monitor, she inched closer to get a better view.

The IT director called out to her partner, who was at his desk. "Harding, you're going to want to see this too." He glanced briefly at Kate. "Has Fraye landed yet?"

"Yes, I just got off the phone with him."

"Call him back and get him on speaker."

Kate hit the speaker button on her phone, then the redial button. Fraye answered on the first ring.

"Hey, it's Kate again. I've got Kevin here and he…"

"Kevin, I just opened the email. Is this what I think it is?" There was an uncharacteristic note of dread in the special agent's tone.

"Uh-huh. I'm going to run it here for Kate and Harding. You ready to launch it on your end?"

"Yes."

Kevin reached across Kate and tapped her mouse on the file that bore the familiar title, *For Kate*.

The video file began to run, filling Kate's screen with a black background. Fifteen seconds later, Kate glanced at Kevin. She was about to ask whether the file was working properly when white block letters appeared on the screen.

I LOVE YOUR FRIENDS.

As the potential meaning of the words swirled in Kate's head, what appeared to be a narrow dirt trail winding between thick, dry grasses filled the screen. Recalling the wetland location where Trudy's abandoned bike had been discovered prompted an upwelling of corrosive bile into Kate's mouth.

Moments later, a female cyclist bedecked in bright-pink spandex rode slowly into view. A thin wall of grass stood between the cyclist and the camera, partially obscuring her. The perspective reminded Kate of that which a lion might have as it sat in the tall grasses watching its prey.

The woman applied the brakes and climbed off the bicycle, leaving her back to the camera. The screen went black again. Ten seconds later, the white letters returned.

CAN'T WAIT TO SHOW HER A GOOD TIME.

A still image of an unconscious woman replaced the words. She was lying on her right side—her features visible only in profile. The bright-pink spandex clinging to her shoulders confirmed it was the cyclist from the video clip. Her helmet had been removed, revealing shoulder-length blonde hair streaked with pink and blue.

Another photo replaced the image—a headshot that provided a more detailed view of both her face and her right hand, which lay inches from her mouth. Kate didn't need to see the newly inked bicycle tattoo to confirm the woman's identity. The creative splashes of color in the blonde hair had been enough.

"It's Trudy." Kate spoke in the barest whisper, drawing awkward glances from Harding and Kevin.

As if the video's creator was unsure whether the rest of the viewers would rely on Kate's word alone, a close-up of Trudy's driver's license replaced the image on the screen.

The screen faded to black once more. Eventually, the letters returned.

THANKS, KATE.

Kevin clicked the mouse and the video disappeared. "That's it. Same setup as the last one. It was posted to YouTube and is totally untraceable. Since it had the same title as the last one, we discovered it the minute it was posted. Don't worry—it's already been pulled from YouTube."

"Good." Fraye's tone belied his simple retort.

A sudden buzzing sound echoed from Kevin's backside. He reached into his back pocket and retrieved his cell. His brows knotted into a tight frown as he stared at the small screen.

"What is it?" Harding asked warily.

"I've been monitoring Maggie's memorial page on Facebook. You need to see this." He reached for Kate's keyboard again.

Seconds later, the Facebook page appeared. Kevin reached across the desk and pressed his finger to the monitor, indicating the latest post.

It was a simple question, typed in all capitals.

CAN YOU DO IT AGAIN?

"Holy shit!" Harding slammed a fist against the table.

Fraye's voice rang out from Kate's phone, flush with irritation. "What is it?"

Harding looked to Kate, who stared at the screen as if mesmerized. He addressed Kate's phone, as if doing so would somehow improve their connection with the special agent. "There's a new post on the memorial page. It reads, 'Can you do it again?' and it was just posted by…"

Harding checked the screen again to make sure he hadn't been mistaken. The name of the sender was highlighted in blue font next to a miniature photo. There was no mistake. "Jonas Riley."

The special agent didn't miss a beat. "Those are the same words he used in Becky's video."

Kate's eyes flashed from the screen to her partner. "No one can think that bastard is innocent now."

Harding broke eye contact, unable to accept all the emotion streaming through his partner's gaze.

Unaware of the intense exchange between the two detectives, Fraye spoke in a voice firm with resolve. "Kevin, find out what server Riley used to post this message. Maybe we can pinpoint his location."

"Given the level of sophistication he's demonstrated to this point, I doubt we'll find anything, but I'll check anyway. I'll let you guys know the minute I find anything." With one last sympathetic look at Kate, Kevin hurried off to his office.

Fraye continued, undeterred by the IT director's lack of hope. "Riley holds his victims for days before killing them. He took Trudy this afternoon. We have time, but the clock is ticking. Let's go back to SFSU. Riley spends his most of his time there. Perhaps there is a place either on campus grounds, or affiliated with

251

it, where he's taking his victims. You two need to meet with the head of the Facilities department first thing tomorrow morning."

He paused and added one final thought, which Kate clung to like an alcoholic to her sobriety calendar. "I don't care what it takes. We are not going to let Trudy die like the others."

Chapter 19

JONAS RILEY CHECKED the luminous dials on his watch. Frowning slightly, he continued making his way down the dark corridor. A bright circle of blue light shone from the metal pendant attached to his keys, providing ample illumination for the late-night sojourn.

He had already become accustomed to the faint aroma of chemical and biological fluids that clung in the air. A familiar attribute of medical buildings, the acrid scent was muted by a pervasive mustiness.

Up ahead, the passageway dead-ended at a set of well-worn, oak, double doors. Small windows were inlaid in each of the portals, designed to provide a limited view of the chamber beyond. Flicking his wrist, Riley flashed the light briefly toward the windows. A thick layer of dust, built up during years of neglect, sealed off the room beyond as effectively as if it were comprised of steel. To the left of the doors, a cracked, plastic sign hung precariously by a single screw, indicating a laboratory lay ahead.

Deep gouges and other indications of severe wear marred the beige linoleum floor. Given the age of the building, the material was likely full of cancer-causing asbestos fibers. Riley hurried forward, uninterested in the potential carcinogenic nature of the materials around him. The person he was about to see was far more important than any health risks presented by being in the building.

Besides, there were greater risks. The police had been watching him like a hawk ever since his attorney had gotten him out of jail. Thanks to Tina, he'd been able to slip out from underneath their noses earlier today. But he could feel them out there—hunting him down with the single-minded determination of a pack of yapping bloodhounds.

Just the thought of the SFPD set his teeth on edge. Those pathetic idiots thought they had everything figured out. They were so fucking arrogant that they had actually believed they could hold him without any real evidence!

And then there was the issue of Detective Katharine Barnes—the woman who had called out to him on national television. His hand tightened reflexively around his keys, causing the irregularly shaped pieces of metal to dig painfully into his hand. A confluence of emotions effectively muted his pain receptors.

He had never been one for brunettes, but something about Kate had drawn him in from the first time he'd seen her. Detective Barnes possessed a keen power of observation and a fiery passion for her career.

Then again, she was far too self-assured and confident about things she would never fully comprehend. That hubris was a dangerous trait—one that required firm correction. But, there was something else about the detective. It was something shadowy and complex—a dark enigma that lurked just behind her eyes.

Arriving at the doors, Riley pressed firmly against the smooth metal push plate that served in place of a handle. The door opened inward into the next room, heralded by a high-pitched metal whine. Riley strode through the opening, confident that his evening was about to take a decided turn for the better.

He swept the small beam of light to the left and right of the large tiled room. Eventually, it settled on an object in the far corner of the chamber. Seated uncomfortably on a beat-up old chair was the individual he had risked so much for today. Smiling, he walked across the tile floor—his eyes soaking up every feature of the figure before him. His blood surged, fueled by anticipation and curiosity.

A little while later, the door to the hallway was opened once more. When it closed, only one of the two people remained in the room—and that one happened to be dead.

ᚦᚦᚦ

February 7

Kate arrived home at a little past one-thirty in the morning. She waved curtly to the patrolman parked outside her building before ducking inside.

Wearily climbing the stairs to the second floor, her thoughts turned decidedly morose. Swirling images of pretty young blondes crowded her mind fighting for space with that of her younger sister. In seconds, the lovely countenances transformed into nightmarish horrors. Guilt clawed at her heart, prompting a tight constriction in her chest.

Soundly shaking off the ghoulish images, Kate jogged up the stairs and back toward her unit. She was about to fit her key into the lock when her phone vibrated to life inside her purse. An unfamiliar number appeared on the display.

Driving the key home, she answered the phone, tucking it between her left ear and shoulder.

"Barnes here."

"Hello, Detective Barnes. I hope I'm not waking you."

Kate slipped inside, closing and locking the door behind her. Her brow furrowed as she tried to place the feminine voice.

"Who is this?" Kate demanded.

Ignoring the question, the caller continued. "I didn't want to wait until morning. I found out something today, and…"

There was something slightly off about the way the woman spoke. Subtle and almost undetectable, it had to do with the pronunciation of the letter "R." Kate was reminded of her partner and his Bostonian accent. It was as if someone had started with Harding's thick accent and had made a studious attempt at erasing it.

Kate's eyes flew open wide. She tossed her purse angrily onto the kitchen counter. "Ms. Torres, I told you I have nothing to share with you about this case. I don't know how you got my cell phone number, but…"

"Please, Detective. Just give me a minute. I told you, this isn't about a story for my network."

There was a note of quiet desperation in the newswoman's voice that kept Kate from ending the call. Closing her mouth, she allowed the woman to continue.

"I've got a lead for you. Last month, I did a story on a string of gang-related rapes in the San Jose area. A woman who volunteers at the crisis center called me earlier today. She is worried her sixteen-year-old nephew may have been involved in the disappearance of Becky Hammonds."

Kate rolled her eyes skyward. "Ms. Torres, there is no evidence to suggest that the recent murders could have been committed by a teenager. Thank you for trying to help…"

"She didn't say her nephew killed Becky—just that he was involved in her disappearance. She over-heard him talking about the night Becky went missing. He and a friend had been hanging out in front of an abandoned house near San Jose State. A pretty young blonde started down the street, and they went over to try to mess with her. An older Caucasian man stopped them before they got very far—driving them off at gunpoint."

"Ms. Torres, I…"

"The story is true, Detective. I sent Gracia a photo of Becky Hammonds, and she showed it to her nephew. He confirmed Becky was the girl he'd been hassling. Unfortunately, the young man has had quite a few brushes with the cops. He refuses to talk to the police. But Gracia convinced him to speak with me."

Who knew how reliable the young man's information was, or how useful it could be. Dancing with a rattlesnake was more prudent than trusting a news reporter. Just this phone call alone could be enough to have Internal Affairs breathing down her neck. Kate sighed heavily.

"I know you don't trust me because I'm a journalist, but you need me."

"Do not flatter yourself, Ms. Torres."

The reporter paused for a few seconds. "Look, I'm trying to help you. Swallow the bitchy cop routine and just listen!"

Kate glanced skyward once again, gathering her patience. "Go ahead."

"The nephew shared something else with Gracia —an observation about the man who rescued Becky. He said the guy stuck out like a sore thumb in the rough neighborhood. Though he didn't fit in at all, he didn't seem uncomfortable, and he certainly knew his way around a gun."

Kate's ears perked up. As far as they knew, Riley had sold the only gun he'd owned to a shop in a Boston suburb in 2008. According to the records, he had never applied for a license in the state of California.

Unfortunately, the fact that Riley didn't have a license meant nothing at all—there were innumerable ways to acquire firearms outside of legal channels. If the story was true and Riley had come to Becky's rescue, Maria may have scared up a legitimate lead after all.

"Did the kid get a good look at the man?"

"Gracia seems to think so."

"Good. I'll need the contact information for Gracia as well as the nephew and his friend."

"Hold on! Gracia is my contact. I already told you, there is no way the kid is going to talk to the police. He's had a pretty rough upbringing and doesn't particularly trust authority figures. Talking to the police would hurt his street credibility."

"If he is withholding information about a murder case, the last thing he'll have to worry about is his street credibility. Another woman is missing, Ms. Torres. If this is a viable lead, we don't have time to waste!"

There was a sharp intake of breath on the other end on the phone. "Oh, God! Who is she, and when was she taken?"

Kate kicked herself mentally. The media hadn't caught wind of Trudy's disappearance yet. "That is not your concern. Just give me the kid's name."

"Detective Barnes, I found this young man, and I've come to you in good faith. I'm driving down there to meet with them at eleven o'clock this morning. Just give me a few more hours. If there really is something here—and I believe there is—I'll convince the kid to meet with you. It's the only way you'll get him to cooperate."

Kate felt her judgment slipping toward a dangerous precipice. Her first inclination was to threaten the reporter and force her to give up the information. In the end, common sense won out. Riley had Trudy, and as Fraye had said, the clock was ticking. Like it or not, Maria Torres was her only viable lead.

"You can meet with him first, but I will drive down to San Jose as well. If this kid really has something, you call me immediately and tell me where to meet you."

There was a long pause. "You've got a deal—on one condition."

Kate braced herself, preparing to shoot it down.

"I want you to investigate this—on your own. No other SFPD or FBI, okay?"

"That is not possible. I am a member of a team. The more people we have working a lead, the more likely we are to…"

"No!" The word was issued with much more vehemence than Kate had expected.

"Do you mind telling me why?"

"Since Gayle died, I learned that trust is something best meted out in small quantities. At this point, my gut says I can trust you. So, will you respect my one condition?"

Gritting her teeth, Kate reluctantly agreed. "Okay, I'll keep it quiet. But I can't promise to do so for long.

At any point, if I feel that it is in the best interest of this investigation, I will share it with my team."

"That's fair enough. And please remember, I only want to stop this bastard. For me, this isn't about getting a story. You can trust me."

With a click, Maria Torres was gone. Kate stared at her phone—weighing the woman's words. She laid the device on the counter, realizing that ever since this case had started, she had developed a growing difficulty trusting herself, let alone anyone else.

▷▷▷

Harding was tired of waiting. He glanced at his partner, who stared pointedly at her watch. They had arrived at the drab, single-story offices of the SFSU facilities department just before seven o'clock that morning. But they had spent the last twenty-three minutes standing anxiously at the window in the waiting area. Apparently, the university's director of facilities was not an early riser.

Frustrated, Harding slammed his hand down on the counter, causing the dim-looking, obese coed on the other side of the window to jump in her seat.

Her placid blue eyes slid from her computer screen to the source of the noise. "Is there a problem, sir?"

"I need you to get off your ass, call your boss, and find out when he is going to get here!"

Her thick lips, coated in a sickly shade of peach, fell open like those of an immense grouper. As she tried to frame a response, a door opened in the office area behind her. A gray-haired man in black slacks and a black polo shirt stepped into view.

Swiveling her rotund head, the clueless coed smiled in relief at her boss. "Director, these cops want to talk to you." She cast a haughty glance in Harding's direction. "Just to warn you—they are not very nice!" Hefting her girth from the poor stool upon which she had balanced her layers of unwieldy fat, she stalked away from the window.

Clean-shaven, short and incredibly fit, the fifty-seven-year-old facilities director hurried over and opened the door to the reception area. Intelligent brown eyes assessed each of them in turn. "I'm Matt Virance. How can I help you?"

Bristling at the duration and manner in which the man had appraised his partner, Harding thrust his badge forward. "I'm Detective Harding and this is Detective Barnes of the SFPD. We're investigating a string of recent high-profile killings."

Gray eyebrows shot skyward. "You mean the Tower Torturer murders? I heard one of the victims was a student here, and that she was found right over at Lake Merced."

Kate stepped forward. "Do you have somewhere we could talk?"

"Oh, yes. I'm sorry. Come on back to my office."

They followed him through the door and over to a large office that reminded Harding of a poor man's version of a NASA control room. Virance took a seat at his desk, behind which a large aerial map of the surrounding area had been hung. A thick purple line outlined the boundaries of the campus—numbers had been printed on each building within its confines.

"So, how can I help you?"

"Our primary suspect is a teaching assistant here."

"Yes, I heard. Jonas Riley. From what I understand, he's been put on administrative leave."

"That is correct."

Kate interjected. "Mr. Virance, we're looking for

the place where these women are being held and killed." She stared up at the map. "It would have to be somewhere outside of the bounds of campus security. Somewhere out of the view of security cameras—an area without much foot traffic, where he can come and go without fear of detection."

The director's lips compressed into a tight line, and he shook his head slowly. "I'm sorry, detectives, but we have a student body of over twenty-five thousand on this campus. It is a densely populated area, bordered by a major shopping center and major transportation arteries. There really aren't any completely isolated areas like that around here."

Kate stood and walked over to the map. "What is this?"

Reaching upward, she pointed to a section of buildings on the north end of the campus. They stood alone from the main circular body of the campus, and had been outlined with shiny red tape. Unlike the rest of the campus buildings, they did not have numeric designations.

Turning in his seat, Virance gazed up at the map. "That's the expansion."

Harding stood and joined Kate. "Expansion?"

"Yes. We needed more dormitories, so the university purchased those vacant, old medical buildings behind the mall. They're in horrible condition. With all the lead paint, asbestos, and structural problems, it's cheaper to just tear them down and rebuild rather than try to remodel. They're scheduled for demolition next month. Trust me—no one would want to hang out for long there."

Kate glanced at Harding. "Is there any way Jonas Riley would have known about the buildings?"

"Everyone on campus knows. This is going to

solve a lot of housing problems. It's a pain in the ass for me, but it's a huge deal for the school."

"Take us there, *now*."

ᚦ ᚦ ᚦ

Kate watched Fraye stride down the corridor of the building where Matt Virance had admitted them forty-five minutes earlier. He joined her at the entrance to the lab. The crime scene technicians had propped open its double doors. They had also erected standing, battery-powered lights that brightly illuminated the long room beyond.

"Is Chau here yet?" He peered into the tiled space, his eyes cataloging every detail of the room.

"No, but cause of death isn't too difficult to figure out." The disappointment in her tone was palpable.

He followed her inside, where the two crime scene technicians stood awkwardly near a row of cabinets along the left wall.

Glancing back at Fraye, Kate noticed his stride didn't seem to have quite the same air of confidence she was used to. Looking toward her partner, who stood forlornly on the other side of the room with his hands shoved deep in his pockets, Kate detected a similar sense of dejection. The discovery of this victim had been like an explosive device dropped into the middle of the investigation. All team members were reeling from its concussive effects.

All in all, it seemed that both men had stomached the information far better than Kate had. What she and Harding had found in this room had made her feel as if she were coming apart at the seams.

Fraye walked over to the corpse, which had been secured by rope to a large but badly worn-out leather chair. Although the facilities director had assured them there was no plan to try to remodel the structure, someone had recently applied a fresh splash of color to the far wall.

A few feet from the ground, about even with the victim's head, dried blood had liberally splattered the beige tile. Small masses stood out here and there, where bits of bone and tissue clung to the wall.

Fraye bent over the body of Jonas Riley. His face closed to within inches of the dead man's head, which lay unnaturally on his right shoulder. A neat, black hole had been driven into the left temple of the skull. Leaking downward from the opening onto Riley's cheekbone was a thin trail of blood. Despite the seemingly neat appearance of the bullet's entry site, the copious amount of splatter on the far wall hinted at a far greater catastrophe on the other side of the skull.

Without turning toward any of the room's live occupants, Fraye spoke aloud. "There is gunshot powder and stippling around the wound—obviously a contact shot. The shot was precise and lethal. It was performed execution-style, allowing the killer to intimately experience the moment of Riley's death."

He stood and walked slowly around the chair. "It was a perforating wound, and the exit damage is severe. There seems to be no other visible signs of a struggle. That implies Riley was brought here willingly. He either knew his assailant or had reason to trust them."

"How do you know?" Harding's tone was hollow —as if the question came from habit rather than actual interest.

"The only other likely explanation is that Riley has been using this place to keep his victims and his killer caught him unaware. But we know that didn't happen." Fraye straightened and gazed pointedly at

Harding. "I talked to the university's facilities director outside. After you and Detective Barnes searched this building and the two others in this complex, he conducted his own search. He is confident no other areas have been disturbed since he toured with the demolition experts yesterday morning. Before that, crews had been in and out of these buildings for days on end. Riley did not hold his victims here."

Kate crossed her arms. "But we still have no idea where Trudy is."

"Or whether she's still alive." Harding's words seemed to linger in the stale air.

Finally, the special agent broke the silence. "She should be. According to Riley's pattern, he would have held her a few more days before killing her."

Harding gestured to the corpse. "Hopefully, whoever did this found out where Trudy is before killing Riley. God knows we made our suspicions about Riley public enough. And his release sure pissed off a lot of people. Someone must have found a way to lure Riley here."

Fraye pondered Harding's words, then peered at Kate. "What do you think?"

Kate looked briefly in the direction of the crime scene techs, who were now busy preparing the inclinometer and laser to measure the bullet's trajectory. Before she could answer, Fraye's phone buzzed to life inside his suit pocket.

Retrieving the device, he checked the screen before answering. "Hi, Kevin." As he listened, his stance grew rigid. Tightening his grip on the device, he began to pace. "What do you mean?" He listened intently, then stopped and stood rooted to the tile floor. "We're on our way."

Ending the call, Fraye glanced quickly at Harding

and Kate before hurrying from the room. "We've got to meet with Kevin right away."

The detectives exchanged a worried glance and fell into step behind him.

"What's up?" Harding asked.

Without turning back, Fraye spoke words so disturbing that Kate stumbled over her own feet. She would have gone face-first onto the grubby floor had her partner not reached out and steadied her at the last minute.

As they hurried out under the misty veil of morning fog, Fraye's words continued to echo in her head. "We've got another YouTube video."

Chapter 20

KEVIN WATCHED AS Fraye, Harding, and Kate filed into the conference room. If he'd had his way, they would all be down in his office, but it hadn't been up to him.

As the new arrivals dropped into their seats, Kevin cast a sidelong glance at Captain Singh, who sat rigidly to his left. Like Kevin, he had already viewed the latest YouTube video. Unlike Kevin, his purpose in attending this meeting went beyond the desire to inform. Singh was here because everything about this case had started to unravel, and he meant to find out what the hell was going on.

When the rest of the team was settled and all eyes had turned to Kevin, he cleared his throat self-consciously. "The video I'm about to show you was posted at six-fifteen this morning."

"Six fifteen?" Fraye sounded incredulous. "Why are we just finding out about it now?"

"Because it was hard to spot. It didn't contain any of the keywords that were used in the previous videos. There was no reference to Kate or the victims. The title was short and simple, but not one that would raise any flags. He called it *Big Disappointment*. We didn't even know it had been uploaded until someone viewed it and flagged it for removal. As soon as the YouTube monitoring team watched the video, they pulled it and contacted us."

"How many times had it been viewed by the time they pulled it?" Fraye appeared shades paler than when he had first sat down.

"Luckily, it was just the one time."

"US or international user?

"I don't know.

"Find out. We'll want to speak with that person."

Kevin knew the directive would likely prove fruitless, but he agreed anyway. Turning his attention back to the keyboard, he launched the video. All eyes were immediately drawn to the large screen at the front of the room.

White capital letters, which had by now become all too familiar to the investigators, appeared on a black background.

NOT SO SMART, KATE. THIS ONE IS ON YOU TOO.

The letters faded away. Seconds later, a balding man in his late thirties appeared. He was seated in a chair in a dark room. A bright circle of light illuminated the man's head and torso.

As the camera moved closer, they could see the restraints binding the man's arms to his sides. He struggled with his bonds, trying vainly to turn in his seat toward whoever was behind the camera.

"Shit!" The expletive had come from Harding, who looked pointedly at his partner for a long second before turning back to the screen.

Without moving his eyes from the video, Fraye confirmed the facts that had prompted Harding's outburst. "It's Jonas Riley. We just came from that lab room."

On screen, the camera appeared to be drawing nearer and nearer. Eventually, Riley's balding pate dominated the screen. It lingered there for a moment before swinging around to the left side of the teaching assistant's head.

Riley's movements ceased immediately, as the shiny muzzle of a handgun was thrust against his temple. Up to that point, the video had run like a silent movie. Without warning, Riley's panicked voice filled the conference room. His words spilled out in an indistinguishable stream as he pleaded for his life. Just as suddenly, a deafening blast cut short the entreaties.

On screen, blood and gore erupted onto the tiled wall behind Riley. His head slumped over awkwardly onto his right shoulder, and the screen went black again. Another title block appeared moments later.

AND JUST TO BE CLEAR . . .

When the letters faded, a close-up photo of an unconscious young blonde woman whose hair had been streaked with pink and blue dye replaced them. Neatly displayed around her head were ten driver's licenses.

DON'T YOU EVEN WANT TO TRY TO SAVE THIS ONE?

The screen went black. Kevin tapped gently on his laptop's mouse pad, shutting down the feed to the main screen. He was about to open his mouth to speak, when the captain cut him off.

"Any guesses as to whose driver's licenses those were?"

Fraye shot from his chair with an uncharacteristic show of frustration. "I'm assuming they belonged to the victims."

The captain leaned forward in his seat, glaring at Fraye. "Yes. Three of them belonged to the San Francisco victims. The rest belonged to the East Coast victims. Sherrie Jamison, Michelle Steere... They are all there."

Fraye's eyes shifted briefly to Kate's before settling back on Singh. "Obviously, we were wrong about Riley."

"Two women have been murdered, another abducted, and our lead suspect—make that our only suspect—is dead. An innocent man was killed just to prove a point to us. Is that all you have to say?"

Fraye sighed deeply. "Profiling is not an exact science."

"Exact? We weren't even in the ballpark."

"I understand and share your frustration, Captain."

"Whether you understand me or not is irrelevant. You're here to understand the killer. So, what does this tell you?" He gestured toward the blank screen.

Fraye walked slowly around the table and stared at Kate, who raised her chin in a halfhearted attempt at bravado. "I think we have as good a shot as ever of catching him."

"Really?" the captain asked. "Because from where I'm sitting, we're right back at square one."

"We're not back at square one," Harding corrected. "We never moved beyond it. Riley was never our guy—we should have paid better attention to the signs when we interviewed him."

Fraye stared up at the ceiling, avoiding the detective's gaze. "Ah, yes. You saw the signs, but instead of voicing your concerns to the team, you merely grumbled about it behind my back. We can see how helpful that strategy was."

Harding's face contorted, preparing for war. A quick glance at his partner's pained expression softened his features. Taking a deep breath, he proffered a wayward truce instead. "Sometimes people see only what they want to see."

Other than a slight tick in his jaw, there was no sign the special agent had even heard Harding's response. Still staring at Kate, Fraye continued. "From the outset, the killer has been fixated on Detective Barnes. She influences his choice of victims. He creates these videos specifically to affect her. She remains our closest link to the killer and our best chance for catching him."

Planting her hands awkwardly on her armrests, Kate stood. "Captain, I…" She closed her eyes and started again. "I am concerned that we've reached a point where my involvement has become a liability."

Harding spun in his seat, staring upward at his partner in surprise.

Kate held the captain's gaze, the gentle tremor in her voice undermining her determination. "Fraye is right. Maggie, Becky, Trudy—it's all my fault. Not only were they individually at risk because of their connection to me, but I also put them in contact with one another. Maggie came with me one day when I stopped by the Starbucks where Trudy worked. The two girls seemed to hit it off and spent a good deal of time talking while I took a call outside."

"Did they continue a relationship from that point?" Fraye inquired.

"I don't know." Kate glanced away miserably.

Kevin piped up from behind his laptop. "They may have talked at a coffee shop, but I don't think Maggie and Trudy ever communicated beyond that. The two women were big-time Facebook users, but they never became Facebook friends. I've already gone through the laptop you guys picked up from Trudy's apartment last night, and there was no evidence of email correspondence or other social media communication between the two women. There was nothing in the phone records either."

Fraye took a step, then paused and spun around to face the captain. "There is no reason for Detective Barnes to quit this investigation. In fact, it would be exceedingly detrimental for her to step away at this point. As I said, she remains our best link to the killer. We need a cohesive team to solve this case. Recriminations, second-guessing and…" He glanced pointedly at Kate. "… overdramatizing will only impede the investigation."

Singh nodded. "Agreed." He glanced at his watch and turned to the two detectives. "We need to finish interviewing Trudy's friends and coworkers ASAP. Mobilize Karinsky and Wallace. Find out everything you can about Trudy Morris."

Harding rose from his seat. "We're on it." He nudged his partner, who had been glaring at the special agent with a mixture of surprise and angst. "Let's go, Kate."

Following Kate out of the room, he paused briefly to cast an appraising glance at Fraye. The special agent stood silently staring at the empty computer screen, looking like a young soldier after his first defeat in battle.

ᐳᐳᐳ

The trunk of the car was uncomfortable and cold. With nothing to do but wait, Kate had spent the last nine minutes leaning against her vehicle in the empty parking lot of a vacant, single-story, manufacturing building in San Jose.

Placing both hands behind her, Kate pushed away from the vehicle and checked her watch again. She had lied to her partner about where she was going. After viewing the video earlier, they'd met with Karinsky and Wallace, then headed out to conduct interviews.

Kate had stopped Harding before they'd left the Hall, informing him she wasn't going to accompany him on the interviews. Instead, she had said she wanted to revisit the crime scenes to see if there hadn't been something she'd missed about the killer's dump sites—something the killer may have left for her alone to figure out. The idea itself was a bit of a stretch, and certainly not the best use of her time, so it was not surprising when Harding had tried to talk her out of it. Anxious to be free of her partner, she had reverted to the tactic that had proven useful in the past—emotional manipulation.

All it had taken was a short sentence about how hard it had been to watch the video, punctuated by a pronounced crack in her voice, to earn the sympathetic look from her partner. Unfortunately, sympathy was not all that had occupied his expression. Doubt had staked a claim in Harding's hazel eyes—he was no longer sure whether Kate could handle the job.

It had been a hard thing to see—then again, watching the video had been far more difficult. By the time the image of Trudy had faded from the screen, Kate had felt as if she had plunged into a deep ocean trench, where the pressure threatened to rupture every cell in her body.

She had meant it when she had said she was ready to resign from the case. It had been an impulsive offer, and Kate had been glad when the captain declined it. The impotence and overwhelming guilt she'd felt after viewing the video had evaporated in the fire of indignation sparked by Fraye's accusation that she had overdramatized the situation.

As quickly as the fire had ignited, it flared out—dampened by the all-encompassing desire to save Trudy. The best way to do that was to meet with Maria Torres, and the small lie she'd told to Harding had been enough to free her up for the drive to San Jose.

Kate had just crossed the San Jose city limits when Maria Torres had called and confirmed that the kid's information was indeed legitimate. The reporter had instructed her to wait in this parking lot.

Movement at the entrance to the lot drew Kate's eye. Maria Torres's red convertible purred into the spot next to her.

The engine died and Kate walked to the passenger window, which rolled down as she approached.

Maria Torres waved to her anxiously from the driver's seat. "Get inside!"

Kate paused, taken aback by the drastic change in the journalist's appearance. Dressed in a faded Boston U hoodie and jeans, face scrubbed free of makeup, and hair pulled into a low ponytail, this version of Maria Torres bore little resemblance to the glamazon Kate had previously encountered.

Recovering from the surprise, Kate responded in a controlled tone. "I'm not getting in your car, Ms. Torres. On the phone you said you had arranged for me to meet a witness to a murder investigation. Tell me where the witness is and I will…"

"Either get in the car, or forget about the meeting. Like I said, this kid is the real deal, but he's spooked about talking to the cops. It was all I could do to get him to agree to meet you. And by the way, you're another reporter working for my network, so keep the badge and gun out of sight. Now hurry up; we don't have much time!"

Pursing her lips against the spillage of irretrievable comments, Kate pulled the door open, and dropped into the low leather seat.

Fourteen minutes later, the coupe pulled into the cracked driveway of a small, two-story apartment building, which was desperately in need of a fresh coat of paint. Dilapidated, rusty air conditioning units hung tiredly from most of the windows—enjoying their winter respite from the region's hot summer months.

Maria parked in a spot near the badly splintered staircase. Shooting Kate a quick glance, the reporter climbed out of the car and headed up the stairs. Following less than a step behind, Kate glanced back down at the lot as she ascended, noting that the sports coupe was as incongruous with its surroundings as a bull in a china shop.

At the top of the stairs, Maria turned, heading for the door on the right. A small clay pot sat nestled between the door and the wall—the cheeriness of its bright yellow flowers as out of place as the reporter's car below.

Maria rapped on the door. As if waiting expressly for the sound, a petite Hispanic woman in her late twenties opened the door. Based on the brief overview Maria had provided in the car, Kate guessed she was meeting Gracia Hernandez, the aunt of the teen she was here to see.

Greeting Maria in Spanish, she eyed Kate cautiously. The reporter issued a quick introduction. Kate extended her hand. After a hesitant glance at Maria, the woman consented to a quick shake, then stepped backward, beckoning her guests to follow.

Inside, it appeared as if a devastating winter storm had struck the living area, raining down every manner of children's toys over the furniture and the floor. The carpet itself was a collage of stains and small holes.

A large television dominated the living area. Brightly colored, animated dinosaurs romped across an idyllic green field on the screen, their mindless banter inaudible. Though the program's audio had been muted, the silly conversation was scrolling along the bottom of the screen in closed captioning.

Kate stared at the white block letters set against the black background, recalling the video she had watched less than two hours earlier. Fixated on the scroll, she seemed not to notice as their host made a quick gesture to Maria before disappearing through a doorway at the far end of the room.

A cacophony of rapid-fire Spanish erupted from the next room, drawing Kate's attention from the screen. She cast a quick glance at the reporter, who rolled her eyes dispassionately.

Kate was suddenly struck in the back of the leg with a force so great that her knee buckled under the impact. Fighting to regain her balance, she automatically reached for her gun.

"No!" The warning had barely escaped the reporter's lips before she lunged forward and laid a calming hand on Kate's shoulder. The detective was about to wrest her arm from Maria's grasp when a high-pitched giggle filled the air.

Turning back down toward the point of impact,

Kate discovered an impossibly pudgy toddler with curly black hair and huge round eyes preparing for a second run at her leg. Clad only in a sagging diaper, the child waddled toward her on its fat feet.

Kate swiveled around. Just as the porcine babe was about to ram her again, she snatched her from the floor and propped the girl onto her hip.

No sooner had the little troublemaker settled in, than she promptly leaned forward and bit the detective on the shoulder. Miniature teeth clamped down with the strength of a ravenous wolf. Kate yelped in surprise, wrenching the child away from her body and depositing it soundly onto the carpet.

Gracia rushed in from the back room, scooping the child into her arms. Her various attempts to soothe the little cretin were unsuccessful. It was not until she sat the child down on the sofa and pried open the lid of a gigantic plastic canister of red licorice that the wailing began to cease. Casting one last contemptuous glance at Kate, the child turned her attention to the screen and began gnawing thoughtfully on the twisted candy.

"Allie does not like you, lady." Kate glanced in the direction of the unfamiliar male voice. Leaning against the doorframe through which Gracia had just emerged was a young man wearing a baseball cap.

His eyes flickered to Maria Torres. "So this is your friend, huh?" He glanced back at Kate and leered at her suggestively. "I'm glad you brought her by. I bet we could all have a good time together."

Though Maria had informed Kate that Gracia spoke very little English, the woman obviously understood enough of her nephew's meaning to swat him on the side of the head, then shoo him into a seat at the rickety oak dining table.

Kate and Maria took seats opposite the young man, while Gracia settled in on the couch next to her child.

"Emilio, why don't you tell Kate about what happened the night Becky Hammonds disappeared."

"No." He sat back into the chair and glared at her churlishly.

"Emilio." There was a note of warning in the reporter's voice that caught Kate off guard.

"Screw it, *chica*. I already told you once. You want her to hear it—you tell her about it."

Maria relaxed into her seat, crossing her legs casually. "Fine. You want to play that way, that's how we'll do it. I just thought you'd rather not go to jail, but…"

The young face pulled into a mask of rage. "Jail? What the hell, bitch? I told you…"

Maria leaned forward. "And I told you not to fuck with me. Now either you tell my friend your story, or the cops are going to hear all about your little stunt at the fairgrounds last month."

Shock penetrated the rage. Gazing at the reporter warily, the hardened veneer dropped. "How did you find out about that?"

"Don't worry about how I found out, Emilio. Just know that I've got enough on you to send you away for so long that you're going to spend the rest of your life taking it up the ass from guys that are bigger and much badder than you. So just tell my friend the story."

Grabbing the bill of his cap, the frustrated teen tugged on it several times before exhaling loudly. Slouching back in his seat, he struggled to resume an air of nonchalance as he recounted the details of his interactions with Becky on the night of her abduction.

Kate listened attentively, interrupting at random intervals. When Emilio was done, he stood and held his hands out at his sides expansively. "I told you what you wanted to hear. Now you two bitches can get out of my auntie's house."

Gracia sat up from the couch and issued a warning in Spanish. Emilio stared at her angrily for a few moments, before finally rolling his eyes and dropping back down into his seat.

Kate eyed the boy for a few moments longer. "Tell me the rest."

"There's nothing more to tell," he grumbled and glanced away.

Maria frowned as she studied the young man's body language. "Is there something else, Emilio? Something you didn't tell me about?"

Anger flashed in his dark eyes. "It's no big deal!"

"We'll decide that for ourselves."

"Whatever. That guy was a real pussy. He never would have messed with us if he didn't have a gun."

Kate connected the dots. "So you went to get a gun of your own."

"So? We went to a friend's house nearby. It only took a minute or two. When we drove back to settle up with that motherfucker, we passed a white SUV on the street. There was a girl passed out in the front seat. She looked like the same bitch."

Maria leaned forward expectantly. "Did you get the plates?"

A cruel smile appeared. "Get the plates? Who do you think we are, the fuckin' cops?"

"Did you notice anything else?" Kate's tone erased the smile.

"The guy who was driving—he wasn't the same guy that had started shit with us before."

"Are you sure?"

"Yeah. Me and my friend both saw them."

"Was there any sign of the man who had drawn the gun on you?"

"No, just this new dark-haired guy and the *chica*. Now will you get the hell out of here and leave me alone?"

Kate eyed the boy for a few moments longer before leaning forward and placing her elbows on the table. "How much?"

Emilio's dark eyes found hers in a heartbeat. "What d'you mean?"

"I want something more from you, and I'm prepared to pay for it. So how much?"

The young man nodded sagely, believing he'd regained control once again. "Depends on what you want."

Kate told him exactly what she wanted. The teen jumped from his seat and waved her off, simultaneously issuing a slew of insults. He was just about to disappear into the back room when Maria's voice stopped him.

"One thousand dollars—cash."

He stood there for a moment before turning around and ambling back to the table. "If you got a thousand, you probably got two thousand."

"I told you not to fuck with me, Emilio. That's the offer. Either take it and do as my friend asks, or we're getting the hell out of here. I don't know why we're even wasting our time dealing with a kid."

Cupping his reproductive organs, the young man glared at her. "Come to the bedroom, and I'll show you who's a kid, bitch."

Shaking her head, Maria stood from the table. "Let's go, Kate. This kid's not interested in easy money. He'd rather sit around and play with his nuts."

Kate stood as Maria called out to Gracia, thanking her for her time and hospitality. The detective had just reached for the door handle when a small voice called out.

"Wait. My auntie could really use that money."

Both women turned to find Emilio bareheaded, working his cap into a small lump between his hands.

Kate exchanged a quick glance with the reporter before pulling out her cell phone. "Give me your number. I'll call you when I have everything in place."

"Okay." He rattled off a series of digits. "So when can I get the money?"

"As soon as you've done what I want."

"Cash?"

Maria nodded. "Of course." She waved to Gracia and called out one more thank you before both women hurried out of the apartment.

When they were back inside the car, Kate turned to Maria. "You handled that kid pretty well. I'm impressed."

Maria started the car and pulled out of the parking lot, glancing sidelong at Kate. The hint of a smile played on her lips. "Think cops are the only ones who can be tough when they need to be?"

"No. It's just that you struck me as…"

"A prissy chick who only cares about looking good and owning pretty things?"

"Something like that."

"I work hard for the stories I get. Sometimes they take me into places I'd rather not go, but it's the only way to find out the truth."

Kate sat quietly pondering the weight of the words and the fact that they were as applicable to her career as to Maria's.

"By the way, where is the thousand coming from?"

Maria tightened her grip on the steering wheel. "Me. I make a good salary and…"

"Wait. I thought you were going to charge it to some network expense account."

Tearing her eyes from the road, the reporter looked at Kate. "When I told you I'm doing this for Gayle, I meant it. None of what we're doing here is for a story. That's not to say that I won't write about it down the road, but I won't do anything to jeopardize this investigation. I want this bastard caught whatever the cost…" Her words trailed off into an awkward laugh.

"Why are you laughing?"

"A thousand dollars may seem like a lot, but I think I'm getting off easier than you."

"How so?"

"You're going to have one hell of a hospital bill. I wouldn't be surprised if Gracia's little monster gave you rabies."

Buoyed by the knowledge that she was on the brink of a potential break in the case over which she'd felt so hopeless that she'd almost stepped down from it, Kate began to laugh. But the moment of levity was short-lived.

It was abruptly squashed when her thoughts drifted to another youngster she had met during this investigation—Becky's son. Hayden was a sweet little boy who would never again know the love of his mother, all because of Kate.

Chapter 21

SITTING ALONE IN THE DRIVER'S SEAT of her car, Kate waited for the uncomfortable silence to end. She glanced down at the phone's display, confirming the line was still active.

When Maria Torres had returned the detective to her car a few minutes earlier, Kate had hopped inside and called Fraye while the reporter went off to procure the money for Emilio. Her initial request had been for the special agent to conference in Harding. When both men were on the line, she had explained where she had been during the past few hours and what she'd learned.

Kate had included every detail, except those concerning Maria Torres's involvement. The revelations had been met with a protracted silence from both men.

Anxious to move past the shock factor, she jumped into the void. "I know you are both mad at me for keeping this from you, but it was a confidential lead and I wanted to vet it before dragging any more resources into it. This kid, Emilio, saw the man who drove off with Becky. We need to get him in front of a sketch artist immediately. He's agreed to do it. I told him I'd be back in two hours. I will call the SJPD and see if they can get us someone local."

Another long beat of silence followed before Fraye responded. "In the interest of time, I'll forgo my comments about withholding information from the team. Instead, I will contact the SJPD myself and make sure they give you one of their best people. You're still in San Jose, Detective Barnes?"

"Yes. When you talk to SJPD, tell them to have the artist call me on my cell. I'll pick him up and take him directly to Emilio. There is no way I can get that kid into a police station. Just the sight of a black and white anywhere near his aunt's place will be enough for him to take off running."

"Fine. Stay where you are. I will contact you when I have confirmed we have an artist on the way. And by the way, there will be repercussions for your actions today, Detective Barnes." With a click, the line went dead.

Kate was about to start the engine when her phone rang again. Tightening her abdominals, she answered on the second ring.

"Fuck, Kate! What the hell were you thinking?" Harding's voice boomed through the speaker.

"I was just…" Her response was cut off by a long slew of curses and admonitions. Lowering the volume on her phone, Kate slumped lower in her seat. When her partner's anger finally ebbed, she tried again.

"I get that you're pissed, but…"

"Damn it, Kate!" Harding paused and continued in a quieter tone. "You know better than to run off on your own like that. I'm your partner. There's one primary rule about being a cop that you obviously never learned, so I'll teach it to you now—you don't screw over your own damn partner."

Kate frowned, unsettled by the sound of Harding's voice. Something about it seemed oddly threatening, but she was not about to be intimidated. "Confidentiality was a condition for this informant. You know I would never intentionally cut you out, but I didn't have a choice. Besides, it's the only viable lead we have right now—you should be happy I've been working it."

She could hear his car grumbling to life in the background. Hoping to change the direction of the conversation, she asked, "Where are you anyway?"

"I was just interviewing Trudy's boss at Starbucks. I'm going to follow up on a quick lead before heading down."

"Down where?"

"To meet you."

"Don't bother. I've got everything under control here."

She only caught bits and pieces of the ensuing string of obscenities before her partner stopped himself and requested her location. When she objected, the caustic tone slipped back into his voice.

"Just tell me where the fuck you are, Kate. I'm done playing games."

Shaking her head for no one's benefit but her own, Kate gave in and told him where she was.

"I'll be there in about an hour and a half. Don't start without me.

▷▷▷

The room was dark, just the way Emilio liked it. His auntie preferred having all the drapes in the apartment open during the day—even those in the bedroom he used when he wasn't crashing with his buddies.

She said it was good for the baby to have as much natural sunlight as possible. But video gaming and sunlight didn't go together well. With the drapes open, he could barely see the action on the shitty, old, twenty-five inch television that sat on cinder blocks in the corner of the room.

Sitting on the floor with his back to the unmade

bed, Emilio tried to lose himself in the bloodshed and mayhem he was creating on screen. Using his thumbs, he tapped out a complicated choreography on the buttons of the plastic game controller, guiding his commando character through a futuristic metropolis overrun by zombies.

An odd crashing sound from the direction of the living area momentarily drew his attention back to the real world. Eyes still glued to the action, he called out to his aunt in Spanish.

It wasn't until he'd eradicated a full cadre of bloodthirsty undead that he paused the game and called out to his aunt again. As he sat there in the quiet, he vaguely recalled his aunt standing in the doorway earlier, saying she was taking Allie to the park. That must have been thirty minutes ago.

Scrambling to his feet, he wondered whether his aunt had remembered to shut the front door properly before she left. Something had been wrong with the lock for over a month, but getting the damn landlord to fix anything around there was like trying to make peace between the crews—it would be nice if it could happen, but it never would.

Smiling at his own joke, he headed toward the living area. If his auntie had left the door open, that hot newspaper lady may have made the noise. She was supposed to be coming back with some dude—maybe they had already let themselves in. He couldn't wait to get his hands on that one thousand bucks. It would be the easiest money he'd ever made, and his auntie could definitely use it.

All he had to do was describe the guy he saw driving away in that white SUV. The truth was that he'd only caught a glimpse of the guy that night—enough to tell it wasn't the same dick that had hassled them earlier—but not enough to actually identify the guy. Still, if the lady wanted to pay so much, who was he to argue?

Crossing the threshold into the living area, he stopped walking and stood absolutely still. What he beheld made his fingers itch for the pistol he kept in the box on the top shelf of his closet.

Keeping the gun hidden away in the apartment was really important because little Allie seemed to find her way into everything. He'd bought the used Glock off a crackhead near the downtown for a little less than two bills. Since then, it had been very useful during a couple of retaliation robberies, but he had never actually shot anyone with it.

Barely breathing, he raised his arms in supplication. The muzzle of a gun pressed against his forehead, demanding both his attention and his compliance. A harsh voice instructed him to drop to his knees.

Finding yourself on the wrong end of a gun was an occupational hazard when you decided to run with a crew. It was something he had often envisioned but had never really prepared for.

Fighting a sudden and compelling urge to curl up and cry, Emilio dropped his head and knelt slowly. Lips trembling, he blinked back the tears. As he opened his mouth to try to reason with his captor, he heard a loud noise. Before another thought could form in his mind, everything went dark with the same suddenness and lack of fanfare involved in turning off a TV set.

▷▷▷

Harding opened the door and dropped into the passenger seat of Kate's car. Turning to face his partner, he was overrun by an avalanche of irritation.

287

Kate glanced pointedly at her watch. "I thought you said you'd be here in an hour and a half. You're over forty minutes late."

Harding stared at her for a full twenty seconds before responding. "You know where I've been. I told you I had to follow up on a quick lead. It took a little longer than I thought."

"Longer than you thought? Do you realize…"

"Yes, I do realize. In case you've forgotten, I happen to be a police detective who takes his job very seriously. It may not be as glamorous as being a special agent for the FBI, but it also means I don't have to be as big an asshole either."

Sighing loudly, Kate turned to stare out the window. "You're right. And I'm sorry for jumping on you. I guess I'm just getting overly anxious. I can't believe we haven't heard from the sketch artist by now."

"Let's call Fraye and…" The ring of her cell interrupted Harding.

Kate picked up the phone. After a brief exchange, she hung up and started the car. "That was our artist. We'll pick him up at the local precinct, then head to Emilio's."

Her partner watched as she reached into the backseat and retrieved a thick white envelope, which she deposited carefully on the console between their seats. "What's that?"

"Nothing."

Waiting until both of her hands were engaged in negotiating a left-hand turn onto the street, he snatched the envelope away. The ploy earned him a seething glare.

One glance inside, and his eyes flew open wide. Nestled in the envelope was a stack of fifty-dollar bills. "What the fuck? Please do not tell me we are paying for his cooperation!"

"*We* are not paying for anything."

"Don't tell me this is your money."

"I won't, because it's not."

"Then where did it come from?"

Kate stared silently at the road ahead.

"Do I have to remind you that we're partners?"

"No, you don't. But if you want to be included in this process, just keep your mouth shut and play along."

Despite himself, Harding began to smile. Turning his eyes back to the road, he nodded slowly. "All right, partner. We'll play it your way—for now."

They continued in silence to the precinct where a poorly-shaven, chubby man in his early forties stood awkwardly on the sidewalk, clutching a much-abused leather satchel. Kate pulled up alongside the curb. After a brief introduction, he climbed into the back-seat and they sped off to meet with Emilio.

They arrived at the apartment eleven minutes later. Kate instructed both men to wait in the car while she went in and talked to Emilio. The kid was expecting Kate to bring one extra person, not two, and she didn't want to spook him.

Tucking the envelope inside her jacket pocket, she jogged up the stairs. At the landing, she stopped suddenly, staring at the door to Gracia's apartment, which now stood ajar. Knowing it was too cold for anyone in her right mind to leave their front door open, let alone a single mother trying to keep control of her heating expense and her young child, Kate reached for her gun.

Pausing to lean over the railing, she nodded her head toward Harding, who was already climbing out of the car, weapon in hand. Kate moved alongside the door and waited while her partner made his way quickly up the stairs.

When Harding was in position on the other side of the threshold, Kate called out. "Gracia? It's Kate. I'm back to see Emilio…"

Her words were met with a high-pitched squeal that emanated from the sidewalk at the base of the stairs. Glancing down, Kate saw Allie trying to wrest her arm from her mother's tight grasp. Kate held up a hand, warning Gracia to stay where she was.

As Gracia started up the stairs, the sketch artist popped out of the car and came to her side, speaking gently to her in Spanish and coaxing her back out into the parking lot.

Locking eyes with her partner, Kate nodded, then pushed the door fully open with the side of her foot. Leaning forward, she hazarded a quick glance into the unit, before dropping back into position and nodding at her partner.

Leading with his gun, Harding entered the unit. Kate followed closely behind. Though she had only entered the apartment once before, she recognized immediately that during her absence, a lot had changed.

The place had been tossed. The wall separating the kitchen from the living area was now decorated with purple spray paint that bore the stylistic hallmark of a graffiti artist's tag. In front of the wall, Emilio's body lay crumpled in a pool of blood.

The detectives quickly swept the rest of the space to ensure Emilio's visitor was no longer on the premises. Holstering their weapons, they hurried back out into the living room.

Kneeling beside Emilio, Harding felt for a pulse. The young man lay face down, arms extended forward. The middle finger of each hand had been removed.

Blood and tissue littered the carpet in front of the body, as well as the couch. Based on the amount of debris and its position, Kate guessed the coroner would find a bullet-entry wound hidden somewhere in the thick, dark hair on the back of Emilio's head.

Rising from the floor, Harding looked up at Kate wryly. "I guess we won't be getting that sketch after all." He turned to study the single word scrawled on the wall. "It's a Locos tag. Based on that and the manicure, it's clear your little gangbanger and his crew pissed off the wrong guys."

Kate nodded at the mention of the Locos, who had grown to become one of the most powerful gangs in the South Bay over the last few years. Disappointment raw on her features, she pulled out her phone and dialed Fraye.

He had just answered when she heard a commotion in the doorway. Turning, she found Gracia staring openmouthed at her nephew. In the next second, the woman fell to her knees and began to howl as if she were being eviscerated.

Harding rushed to the woman's side. He issued words of consolation in his limited Spanish, while ushering her out of the crime scene.

Kate apologized to Fraye for the uproar.

"What was that noise?"

"Emilio's aunt."

"Why is she screeching like that?"

"Because Emilio's dead."

The line went silent. Kate waited as the seconds ticked by. Finally, the special agent inhaled deeply. When he spoke again, his voice was so weary that it seemed as if a centenarian were on the other end of the phone.

"I assume you didn't get the sketch?"

"There was no time. I just got here with the artist from the SJPD. The front door of the apartment was ajar. Looks like a single bullet to the back of the skull. The killer tagged the wall behind the body, and took both middle fingers. Harding said it's likely a hit from the Locos."

Fraye made a noise that was part laugh and part groan. "A gang hit? Are you fucking kidding me?" He paused again, swearing softly. "Did I hear you say Detective Harding is there?"

Something in the agent's tone triggered Kate's instinct to lie. Ignoring the irrational emotion, she answered honestly. "Yes."

"Isn't he supposed to be conducting interviews here in San Francisco?"

"He came down to assist me." Kate didn't know why she felt the need to defend her partner.

"Did you need his assistance?"

Not in the mood to play monkey in the middle, she ignored the question, choosing to focus on the current state of events. "With Emilio gone, we're going to have to work harder to identify the guy who drove off with Becky in that SUV."

"You don't think this is a dead end?" Hope sluiced through the phone.

"I hope not. Emilio was there with a friend that night. He said his friend didn't see the guy because he was busy driving. Maybe Emilio was wrong. Maybe the friend remembers something. At this point, I'll take whatever he can give us."

"Get in contact with the head of the SJPD gang unit. Track this friend down right away. And tell your partner to get his ass back up here so he can finish interviewing Trudy's family and friends. If this other kid can't give us any more leads, we've got to start generating some new ones."

The line went dead, leaving Kate alone with the dead kid, and only Gracia's muffled cries to keep her company. Blocking out the sound, she placed another call.

"Did you get it? Will it help?" Maria Torres's anticipation was so intense it was almost palpable.

"No, we didn't. We never got the chance."

"What do you mean?"

"I'm at Gracia's right now. Emilio's dead. Looks like a gang hit."

"Please tell me you're kidding."

"I wish I were. My next call will be to the SJPD. Hopefully they can get me a lead on Emilio's friend, but it may take time and we don't have the luxury. That kid is the last possible witness to Becky's abduction. You said you wanted to help with this investigation, so I'm asking now. Do you happen to know where I can find him?"

"I don't have any idea. But I might be able to find out. By the way, are Gracia and Allie okay?"

"Yes. They were out when the hit went down."

"Thank God. Does Gracia know yet?"

"She does, and she's not taking it well."

"That poor woman. Life has not been kind to her."

Kate raised an eyebrow, surprised by the reporter's compassion.

"I'll head over right now and see if there is anything I can do to help."

"Don't come—at least not now. My partner is here. There will be hell to pay if he recognizes you."

Maria dropped her voice. "So, our relationship is still a dirty little secret?"

"And it's going to stay that way. Like I said, we

don't have much time. I need whatever information you can get on that friend, and I need it now."

"I'll put out the word to my other contacts down here. We've got to be able to find this other kid."

"And we've got to do it soon. Trudy's life depends on it." Kate ended the call and marched out of the apartment where death had staked its claim.

Chapter 22

KATE CASUALLY PLACED the paper cup and the brown bag on her partner's cluttered desk. Even though it was already seven o'clock in the morning, Harding was nowhere to be seen.

Her eyes darted to the computer monitor. Neither the sleep mode indicator, nor the power indicator lights were illuminated. Perhaps he had a late start this morning. Hopefully, the large coffee and blueberry scone would help get his day on track.

She'd brought breakfast as a peace offering, feeling she needed to do something to smooth over the sting of her recent solo activities concerning Emilio. Since Maggie's death, Kate's normally even-keel relationship with her partner had turned turbulent, and that needed to change.

When she had walked outside Gracia's apartment the day before and delivered Fraye's directive for Harding to return to San Francisco, he'd called a cab to take him to his car and had disappeared without another word. Kate had been left to work the crime scene with the SJPD. Later, she'd headed over to the local precinct and met with the head of the gang unit, who said they knew of Emilio's friend, Juan, and promised to track him down ASAP.

By the time Kate had finally climbed into bed that night, she'd found herself unable to sleep. Instead, she had lain awake staring at her bedroom ceiling, trying to purge the memory of Gracia's tortured cries from her mind. It had occurred to her that while the relationship between aunt and nephew certainly did not fit the Brady Bunch paradigm, there was no denying that it was rooted in a strong sense of familial affection and loyalty.

In those quiet hours, Kate's thoughts had eventually turned morose. She'd wondered who might mourn her passing, and whether it mattered if anyone did. After years of adamantly avoiding anything that vaguely resembled intimacy, Harding was the closest thing Kate had to family or a real friend. The items cooling on his desk were evidence of her desire to hold on to that bond, in whatever way she could.

She was about to turn back toward her desk when a memo scrawled on a post-it note near Harding's monitor prompted her to hesitate. It was an email address that seemed vaguely familiar, but her partner's cramped handwriting made it hard to make out. She had just bent closer to better decipher the cryptic scrawl when the unexpected sound of Harding's voice made her jump.

"What's this?" He gestured to the basic breakfast, a frown creasing his brow.

Her eyes opened wide. "I just wanted to do something nice for my partner. Is that such a bad thing?"

The beginnings of a smile tugged at the corners of his lips before dropping into a flat line. "No, it's not. Thanks. I'll see you in the meeting." He snatched the items up and headed off down the hall.

It hadn't been the reconciliation she'd hoped for, but Harding would thaw in time. Dropping into her seat, Kate returned another in the unending series of calls from Becky's mother. The poor woman sobbed on the phone, begging Kate to say her daughter's killer had been found.

Twenty minutes later, Kate delicately ended the call and hurried to the conference room for the daily meeting. She paused in the doorway, noting that she was the last one to arrive and that, for the first time, her partner had not saved her a seat.

He sat between Fraye and Captain Singh. Heads together, the three men exchanged a series of hushed whispers. Kate took the empty seat next to Kevin, who offered her a soft smile.

Noting Kate's arrival, Fraye offered a final word to the captain, then opened the meeting, asking Kate to provide an overview of what had transpired in San Jose the day before. When she was done, Harding gave a brief update on the interviews of Trudy's friends and family, which had turned up nothing new.

Carefully observing the dejected faces of the room's occupants, Fraye stood and waited until all eyes were riveted in his direction. "As some of you may know, I met with the FBI's special agent in charge (SAC) of the San Francisco office last night. They are extremely short-staffed right now and need some assistance on another case. There are no other BAU agents available to help them, so I've drawn the short stick.

"This case will remain my priority, but I will not have as much time to dedicate to it as I have to this point. I will remain the lead on this investigation, but Captain Singh and I have agreed that Detective Harding will step up his role to cover the shortfall. From now on, Detective Harding will be the main point of contact for requests and decisions related to this case."

With that he dropped back into his seat and asked Kevin for an update on the investigation into the YouTube video. The IT director reported the same disappointing results as the two detectives who had spoken before him. Kate listened passively as Fraye concluded the meeting, but did not move from her seat until her partner stood and headed for the door.

As if as one, Harding, Captain Singh and Agent Fraye moved together down the hallway and into the captain's office. The door closed firmly behind them when she was but steps from the threshold.

"That bit about Harding stepping up was quite a bomb, huh?"

Kate turned to find Karinsky staring meaningfully at her. She took a few steps back down the hall, carefully drawing the older detective away from the door before responding quietly. "You could say that."

"What do you think it's all about?"

"It sounds like it's about a lack of resources."

"You know it was coming?"

"I had no idea," Kate responded icily.

"You ask me, I'd say something's up. Fraye's stuck on himself. There's no way he'd make Harding his number one general unless he was forced to."

▷▷▷

The late-afternoon sun shone weakly through the gray sky above. Kate pulled her coat tighter as she stepped up onto the sidewalk. To her left, the western supports of the Bay Bridge rose up from the earth, supporting the thousands of motorists racing back and forth across the breathtaking expanse of steel and concrete above.

Straight ahead, perched along the waterfront, was a squat, aging building about the size of a small cottage.

Wincing slightly, Kate strode inside the doorway, where the aroma of fried food overwhelmed the briny smell of the bay.

A handful of male diners sat at one of two picnic tables that appeared as old and weathered as the little shack itself. As she passed, one of the men, who wore the telltale uniform of a BART maintenance worker, offered something that might have passed as a pickup line. She ignored it, heading straight for the counter.

"Hey, what can I get for ya?" The smile on the buxom woman behind the counter looked as tired as the décor. Ballpoint pen held at the ready, she stared at Kate dully.

"I'm supposed to meet a friend here."

"That's great, honey. But what can I get ya?"

Kate was about to decline, when her stomach rumbled emphatically. She glanced up at the menu posted above the counter and ordered the first item she saw. "A burger and a coke."

That'll be six twenty-five." The woman turned and yelled the order in the general direction of a disheveled cook who was dourly flipping some sort of meat substance above a grill so thick with grease that Kate felt the urge to cancel the order. Figuring it was too late to turn back, she handed over cash in exchange for a metal stanchion upon which a plastic number had been mounted.

"Your friend's waiting around back. I'll bring your food when it's ready." The woman pointed to a narrow doorway in the wall to her left.

"Thanks."

Kate walked down the narrow hall and through a back door that opened onto a small patio. A mismatched collection of plastic tables and chairs had been set up around an improvised barbeque pit from which bright orange flames leapt into the cold afternoon air.

Seated at one of the tables closest to the pit was the area's sole occupant, Maria Torres. Placing her number on the table, Kate dropped into the frigid seat across from the reporter. The plain-Jane look Maria had adopted in San Jose was a thing of the past; she had transformed back into an impeccably groomed beauty.

"Outdoor dining… in January?"

The reporter smiled mischievously. "Come on, we're enjoying bayfront seating here. Besides, I figured you didn't want anyone seeing us together. No one's crazy enough to hang out here in this weather."

"Good point. So tell me what was so important that we had to meet in person. I already heard back from my contact with the SJPD. They've questioned Emilio's friend. The kid didn't see our perp. Emilio was the only one who saw the killer, and he's dead."

"Emilio's death is the reason I'm here. I heard from a couple of very reliable sources that his death wasn't a gang hit."

"What?"

"From what I understand, the evidence at the scene made it look like the Locos were responsible."

Kate's eyes narrowed suspiciously. "How do you know that?"

The reporter shrugged. "I told you before—I have my sources. And those include some pretty powerful players within the Locos. They said taking out a small-timer like Emilio would be a waste of their time. And the more I thought about it, the more I realized they were right. Someone else killed Emilio, and tried to pin it on them."

"Another gang?" Kate asked.

Maria opened her mouth, but closed it again as the buxom woman sidled out of the back door and deposited food and drinks on the table. When the woman retreated back inside the restaurant and the door had shut behind her, Maria continued. "I don't think so. I asked around and heard the same thing over and over again. Emilio was too small-time to really get on anybody's radar. He wasn't even formally acknowledged in the crew he claimed to be running with."

"What are you saying?"

"I'm saying that somebody wanted Emilio dead, and they took great pains to lead the police in the wrong direction."

"But who?"

Maria stared at her long and hard before reaching into the red plastic basket and retrieving a fish sandwich. She took a bite, regarding Kate thoughtfully while she chewed. "I'm a reporter. I dig up the information. You're the detective—you make sense of it."

▷▷▷

When Kate returned to the Hall, her partner was still notably absent from his desk. She sat down, staring at the vacant seat across the aisle from her.

"Detective Barnes?"

She turned to find Fraye standing in front of her desk. "Yes?"

"Do you have a quick minute? There are some things I would like to discuss with you."

When she made no effort to move, he glanced around and practically whispered, "In private."

"Okay."

Kate stood and followed him down to his office, taking a seat while he shut the door.

301

He started without preamble. "I know you have something to say, and I want to hear it."

She watched in silence as he took his seat behind the desk.

"Well?"

"I'm still trying to figure out what opinion you're asking for."

He tilted his head to the side, regarding her dryly. "Don't play games. I made an announcement at this morning's meeting. It concerned your partner and you had not been apprised in advance."

Kate stared at him for a moment. "Fine. I was surprised. I wouldn't have pegged you as one of Harding's biggest fans."

"Are you upset I didn't give the opportunity to you?"

"No. Harding has more experience than me, and he started this case with you back in Boston."

"But you are upset in general."

"Is that relevant?"

"Yes."

"Why?"

"Because I do not want frustration to hinder your judgment."

"You don't need to worry about that. Irrespective of my feelings on any given subject, this case remains my number-one priority. There is nothing else that matters."

A pained expression flashed across his features. Leaning back in his chair, he glanced toward the window, then found her eyes once more. "I know this case hasn't been easy for you. Who knows? Maybe it's because of you that..."

"That what?"

"Never mind. I just wanted to let you know that I

wasn't entirely forthcoming in explaining Harding's elevated role this morning."

"The FBI doesn't need your help on other cases?"

"They do, but it's not as time-consuming as I made it out to be. I could still dedicate my full attention to this case. But the truth is that I've made some inexcusable mistakes already. We can't afford any more. Harding's instincts, on the other hand, have been spot on."

"I wouldn't say spot on, he…"

"He was right about Riley, and I wouldn't listen. Somehow I became so myopic that I couldn't see what was right in front of my face. Once Harding saw how Riley reacted during our interrogation, he immediately knew Riley didn't fit the profile. I should have seen that, and I didn't."

"Well, I made the same mistake."

"Forgive me for saying so, Kate, but it's not quite the same. I am one of the foremost profilers in the country, and you…"

"I'm barely learning, and because of that, there is a trail of dead girls piling up behind me."

"That's not what I meant—at least not exactly."

The clarification earned him a weak smile.

"The point is, I've lost perspective in this case. I need to step back and let Harding run with things for a while. I hope that by taking a bit of a backseat, I can see things more clearly."

"But…"

He waved a hand dismissively. "It's not just perspective that I've lost. It's also control. You've decided to run your own rogue investigation with no respect for the team or for me as its leader. Then Harding abandons his interview assignments to chase your hotter lead in San Jose."

Fraye looked down at the desk, countenance forlorn. "Control and perspective—two of the most basic things I teach scores of aspiring profilers every year." He shook his head adamantly. "And I lost them both."

"Do you think it would be better if you just asked to be transferred off the case?"

"And give it to another agent? No." Anxiety flashed in his eyes. "Is that what you want?"

She broke eye contact under the weight of his stare, focusing on the corner of his desk instead. "No. I think you are the right man for this case. No one knows the facts as well as you do. I've already learned so much from you. I can't really imagine going on with someone else."

When she found his eyes again, there was no trace of the commanding confidence that normally lay within. For as frustrating as Kate had found the special agent's arrogance, its absence seemed to alter the effects of gravity, making her head spin and her stomach cartwheel.

This was not the bigger-than-life hero to whom she had so eagerly submitted herself that night in Napa. With stunning clarity, she realized that the man before her was indeed that—just a man.

ᚦᚦᚦ

A collage of bright-orange shapes and pain—that was Trudy's only reality until she fully emerged from unconsciousness. With each beat of her heart, she became aware of a different pain in her body. It seemed as if every one of her joints was screaming out in aching agony. Just as she was about ready to open her eyes, a new awareness was added—it was difficult to breathe.

Frowning as she battled through the last tendrils

of oblivion, Trudy finally opened her eyes only to clamp them firmly shut again. It was impossibly bright—as if a thousand suns burned on the other side of her lids.

Instinctively, she tried to jerk her head downward away from the source of the blaring light, but found she could barely move it more than an inch in any direction. Confused, she reached her hands toward her head, but they moved less than a few inches from their starting position.

Panicking, Trudy opened her eyes wide. But the brightness was relentless, forcing her to retreat from the sighted world once again. She kicked outward with her legs reflexively, but they fared no better than her arms and head.

Desperate, she risked peeking out under the limited protection of her lashes. It took a moment or two for her eyes to acclimate, moments during which she fought to repress the horrible pain in her lower back and throat, as well as the myriad aches through her joints.

The sound of a door opening ripped through the silence, followed by the sound of footsteps drawing near.

"Wake up, sleepyhead." The voice was male, congenial, and oddly familiar. Trudy cried out for help, but the plea was indistinguishable and muffled.

"I'm guessing you're having trouble making sense of everything. Let's see here…" There was a shuffling movement nearby. "This should help. Just give me a minute to get it lined up properly."

Something reflective popped into view. Trudy risked opening her eyes a bit wider. The item was a black-framed mirror mounted on a pole. It bobbed back and forth in the air before her.

"I think if I just angle it a bit more... there you go!"

The mirror stopped moving. Peering into the large rectangle, Trudy could see that it had been trained on another mirror, a long one by the looks of it, on a nearby wall. What was reflected there was nothing short of hell.

A large steel wheel had been erected in the middle of a white-tiled room. It looked like a smaller version of a carnival Ferris wheel, except this wheel only had one passenger—a naked woman. Her body had been bent backward, arms extended beyond her head into the shape of the letter "C." Tight black restraints bound her head, arms, and legs to the arc of the wheel. Blonde hair, streaked with pink and blue, nestled between her upper arms. Now the pain, the difficulty breathing—everything made sense.

Trudy's eyes flew open wide, offering up her corneas as sacrificial lambs to the powerful fluorescent lights mounted in the ceiling just feet from her head. She thrashed madly against her restraints, howling into the duct tape stuck firmly to her mouth.

"Oh, come now. It isn't all that bad—at least not yet. Here, let's get your little ride started. Maybe that will put you in a better mood."

The wheel jerked suddenly, the fluorescent bulbs above seemed to be moving. It wasn't until the world began to turn upside down that Trudy realized that it was the wheel itself that was moving. Raw terror consumed her as the wheel continued to turn, drawing her headfirst toward the floor. She fought with every ounce of strength to free herself, but it was no use.

She was certain she was going to lose her mind, but that was before she saw what had been mounted to the ground below. The mirror had only afforded her a glimpse of the base of the wheel, not what lurked beneath it.

As the wheel continued its painstakingly slow revolution, Trudy's head began to inch under the bottom. Her eyes bulged painfully, engorged by the pressure of blood rushing into her head.

What she saw in the next moment made her wish her eyes had just popped from their sockets, sparing her from ever beholding the impossibly twisted sight before her. Terror held full court over her consciousness, enthroned by the shining metal serpents below. Stretching end over end like freewheeling yoyos along the ground over which she was about to pass were coils and coils of razor wire.

Chapter 23

JUST OUTSIDE THE SOUTHERN confines of the city of San Francisco, squatting on a tiny peninsula between Bayview Hill and the frigid waters of the bay, was the final resting place of a concrete monstrosity. To those old enough to recall the days before the names of sports arenas were bought and sold by corporate sponsors, the open-air coliseum had been known simply as the "Stick."

Constructed in the late 1950s as a baseball stadium for the recently relocated New York Giants, Candlestick Park was later retrofitted to serve dual use as a football stadium for the San Francisco 49ers. But the stadium had been ill-conceived and poorly designed. Situated on a small peninsula with no natural barriers to the relentlessly biting bay winds, the venue had become the bane of both players and fans alike—its retrofitted design catching the wind and swirling it round and round like a centrifuge.

Eventually, the Giants had abandoned the Stick in favor of a new downtown ballpark, and the 49ers had struck a deal to move south to Santa Clara. Despite two fatalities, the construction of the new stadium was completed, and in the grandest style of American capitalism, the old stadium (which had been the site

308

of the last Beatles concert) had been demolished to make way for a new shopping center, office park, and housing.

Left to preside over the remains was a skeleton security crew. One of those crew members was twenty-six-year-old Rob Genty, who really didn't care about the ballpark's history or its future.

Especially not right now. He ignored the shrinking image of the security shack in the rear-view mirror as he drove across the parking lot—the bright lights of the security pickup cutting a limited path through the early morning darkness.

His graveyard shift was supposed to end in fifteen minutes, but instead of relaxing in the comfort of the security office at the main gate, he'd been ordered to get out into the shitty pickup, which couldn't so much as cough out a puff of warm air into its stale, cigarette-scented interior.

According to his boss, one of the security cameras had picked up something odd out by the northeast perimeter gate. Just what qualified as odd to Rob's boss was anyone's guess, but it had become his friggin' mystery to solve.

Clenching his teeth firmly against the icy air, he peered out into the murky fog. Frustration mounting, he stepped on the gas. The pickup lurched forward, churning up pieces of crumbling asphalt as it sped through the gloom.

Ghostly orbs materialized above, indicating he had reached the perimeter fence whose tall, inter-mittently-spaced lights provided an eerie illumination. Without slowing, Rob wrenched the wheel to the right. Seconds later, he yanked the wheel back to the left, setting a course parallel to the fence. Speed-ing along the barricade, the young man bemoaned the unfairness of the late assignment and life in general.

He had progressed about one hundred yards when he suddenly stood on the brakes, bringing the pickup to a stomach-lurching stop. Something was piled up along the outside of the fence. He'd briefly glimpsed it as he had whizzed past, but had not gotten a good enough look to determine what it was. All he did know was that the clock was counting down on his shift, and he wanted the hell out of there.

It was likely that the object was just some type of old junk. Besides chasing off drug dealers and prostitutes, the security team's time was dedicated to cleaning up after illegal dumping. The perpetrators were often members of the construction trade who juiced additional profits out of their projects by avoiding disposal costs. Over the last year, Rob had discovered everything from piles of drywall rubble to entire air conditioning units, which had been carefully stripped of any copper parts before being abandoned beside the fence.

Throwing the engine into reverse, he carefully eased the truck backward until he'd drawn up alongside the mysterious object. Maneuvering the vehicle perpendicular to the barricade, he studied the relatively large item, which stood out starkly in the pickup's headlights.

Rob's head flipped side to side like a marionette as he studied the pale-skinned creature before him. It lay face down with its legs tucked beneath it. Its shoulders and hips appeared vaguely human—feminine in fact. But the pose was so unnatural that Rob convinced himself it must be a dummy. Maybe it had broken in the storeroom of some clothing store and the owner decided to save on the cost of an extra trash pickup.

Whatever it was, the thing was in pretty rough

shape—especially the head, which lay strangely pinned between its shoulder and the fence. Though the face was hidden from view, the tangle of multi-colored hair gave the thing a sad, broken-down air.

Rob had just reached for his radio, pleased to report a simple dumping incident so that he could finish this damned shift, when the object began to move. Shock drained the strength from his fingers. The radio clattered loudly to the floor, bouncing off the steel-reinforced toe of his right boot.

The fate of the device was irrelevant to Rob, who watched as first one and then another blood-streaked hand reached out and clawed at the fence. As the two dark crimson talons found purchase between the links of metal, the figure drew itself slowly upward, revealing the macerated, wet remains of what had once been a human chest.

Horrified, Rob stared transfixed at the poor wretch fighting to right itself on the other side of the barrier. He reached into the foot well, groping desperately for the radio. Finally, cold plastic registered beneath his fingers.

Pressing the device painfully against his lips, Rob chocked out a brief cry for help before painting the dirty windshield in a bright wash of vomit.

▷▷▷

Kate rushed through the sliding doors into the harsh lights of San Francisco General's emergency room. She hurried across the cavernous waiting area, ignoring the throngs of dour-faced patients awaiting treatment.

Halting in front of the admitting desk, Kate pulled out her badge and flashed it in the direction of a young Filipino nurse, who clutched the clipboard she was holding a little tighter to her chest before smiling weakly and offering assistance.

"Trudy Morris was admitted here within the last half hour. Where can I find her?"

"And you are?"

"Detective Kate Barnes, SFPD."

The younger woman consulted her clipboard and then nodded. Glancing around briefly to ensure no one was within earshot, she turned back to Kate. "Ms. Morris has been transferred to a private room in the ICU. Down the corridor on your right to the elevators, and up to the second floor."

Kate murmured a quick thank you over her shoulder as she made her way to the elevator. Emerging on the second floor, she proceeded directly to the nurse's station. A few feet from her goal, she glanced down the corridor to her right where she spied Harding and Fraye conferring with a gray-haired doctor. Without breaking stride, she changed course for the corridor, pausing to show her badge to one of the two uniformed policeman standing guard at the entrance.

Harding glanced over at her as she approached, his expression full of warning that she was about to receive unpleasant news. Holding up a hand, he silenced the older gentleman, then gestured toward Kate. "Doctor Simms, this is my partner, Detective Barnes."

The doctor nodded politely. "I was just telling Detective Harding and Agent Fraye that I cannot allow anyone to question Ms. Morris. She has lost a lot of blood and is suffering from severe dehydration as well as exposure. When she was delivered to us, she was in a near catatonic state. Not long after we started the transfusion and IV, she regained full consciousness and became so highly agitated that she required sedation."

Fraye crossed his arms over his chest. "I don't think you appreciate the magnitude of the situation, Doctor. This woman is a crucial witness in a high-profile investigation. We need to speak with her right away."

Regarding the special agent from beneath hooded lids, the doctor responded. "Quite frankly, I don't care whether this patient is a witness or whether she's the president of the United States. Her condition is critical. She needs rest, and she will have it. I will call you as soon as she is well enough to speak with you."

Fraye held the man's gaze, assessing the determination behind his words. Nodding slightly, he looked at each of the detectives in turn. "Fine. We'll give her time. Meanwhile, the officers will remain in place at the entrances to this corridor as well as the entrance to her room." He punctuated the last words with a glance over his left shoulder, where Kate spotted two more uniformed officers flanking a door.

"Whatever you think is necessary." The doctor turned and disappeared into a nearby room.

Kate's eyes flew from Harding to Fraye. "Were either of you able to see her before she was sedated?"

"No." Fraye turned on his heel and began walking toward Trudy's room. The two detectives fell in step behind him.

"How bad is she?" Kate's voice sounded frantic and a bit too loud in the empty corridor. Her partner cast her a sympathetic sidelong glance, but did not comment.

Arriving outside of Trudy's room, Fraye nodded curtly to the officers, then positioned himself in front of the long, narrow window just to the left of the door. After a moment or two, he stood aside and gestured for Kate to take his place. "See for yourself."

On the other side of the glass, Trudy lay in her bed, tethered to a vast array of machines and tubes. Little of her features were visible beneath the patchwork quilt of thick bandages affixed to her face.

Kate's gaze dropped to Trudy's chest, which had been wrapped as soundly as that of an ancient Egyptian mummy. She blanched at the unnaturally flat appearance, recalling the damage Harding had described when he'd phoned earlier. The skin between the young woman's shoulders and the base of her pelvis had been sliced to shreds. As the doctors had tried to repair the damage in the operating room, they'd realized the cuts had gone as deep as the rib cage—many of the bones, as well as the sternum, bearing the scars of a depraved mind's savagery.

Swallowing tightly, Kate turned away from the window. "Well, she's in the best place she can be right now. Did the guy who found her…"

Fraye's dark grimace sucked the air from her lungs. Glaring pointedly at the officers, he spun around and headed toward the elevator. Stabbing at the call button, the special agent addressed her acerbically. "There is no need to divulge confidential information in front of the security detail. The last thing we need is a leak to the press."

Harding stepped in before Kate could offer a response. "We all know that. Kate didn't reveal anything important, so let it go." Despite the detective's relaxed stance, there was a distinct note of warning in his tone.

The special agent frowned, opened his mouth to respond, then paused and slumped back against the wall. "You're right. I'm just so anxious to question Trudy that I can barely see straight."

Harding placed his hands on his hips. "We're all

anxious. But at this point we've just got to be glad we've got a victim to question." He turned back to his partner. "God only knows how Trudy escaped."

The elevator chimed and the doors slid open. Harding entered first, the words he spoke echoing the sentiment in Kate's heart. "I'm just really glad she did."

ᚦᚦᚦ

According to Kate's watch, it was nine thirty-five. The exact time was a confirmation of what she already knew—the morning was dragging by at an agonizing pace. It had been only a little over three hours since she'd rushed to the hospital, but it felt like it had been days.

Checking her watch every five seconds definitely was not helping time pass any quicker.

Neither was checking her phone like an obsessive-compulsive, but she could not help herself —there was too much riding on Trudy and what she might tell them.

After they'd left the hospital, Harding and Fraye had agreed that when the doctor allowed them to see Trudy, it would be best if Kate were the one to question her. Given the severe trauma the woman had endured, Kate's familiar female face was likely to coax more from Trudy than either of the men could hope to glean.

Kate did not begrudge Trudy the rest. The woman had suffered horribly. The last thing Kate wanted to do was make her relive the terror she'd endured. But that same sense of responsibility she felt for Trudy's misfortunes extended to Becky and Maggie. If they didn't stop this guy immediately, more young women would share their fate. It was a future she could not bear to consider.

She shifted her gaze back to her computer monitor. Although she was itching to join Karinsky, Felts, and Wallace in searching the neighborhood near the old ballpark, Fraye wanted her to remain here so she'd be ready the moment Trudy was ready to talk. Until then, the best way to pass the time was to pursue all other potential leads. Clicking her mouse, she brought up a series of photos.

The previous day at lunch, Maria Torres had been convinced Emilio's death hadn't been a gang hit. Kate was determined to answer the very question she had posed to the reporter—if a rival gang had not murdered the young man, then who had?

The photos were from case files she had obtained on known hits carried out by the Locos in the Bay Area. She'd gone through twenty different files this morning. In each instance, the crime scenes looked just like what she and Harding had found in Gracia's apartment.

"Gang hits?"

Kate turned to find her partner peering quizzically over her shoulder at the screen. Since the information about the Locos's disavowal of the hit on Emilio had come from Maria, Kate discretely clicked her mouse and minimized the screen. So far she had kept her relationship with the reporter a secret, and she meant for it to remain that way.

"Yeah. When I was talking to the guys at the San Jose gang detail, they offered to send me these so I might learn how to identify markers of hits made by different local gangs."

Harding frowned. "Well, I guess it's always good to learn new things, but unless you're planning to transfer to a gang unit, I don't see how it will really help you much. You should wait until this case is over before spending any more time on it. With Trudy, we finally have a good chance to catch this guy. Everyone needs to be one hundred percent focused on this case."

Kate nodded. "Of course. I was just checking to make sure they attached the right files before I filed them away for future reference. Besides, I'll never have any problems calling a gang hit with you around, right?"

"What do you mean?"

"When we found Emilio's body, you immediately pegged it as a gang hit."

"Sure. I spent some time working with gangs in Boston before I entered the SVU department. Didn't I tell you that before?"

"No, I don't think so."

"Ah, yes. The Boston days. Good times, right Harding?"

Kate and Harding looked up at the sound of Fraye's voice. Neither had noticed his arrival.

"I guess it depends on which times you choose to remember. I've got to check in with the captain."

Fraye watched Harding stalk away, before turning back to Kate. "What was that about?"

"I'm guessing there are some things about his time in Boston that Harding would rather forget. It can't be easy to lose a spouse, especially under such circumstances."

"True. It was stupid of me to bring it up. I'm so excited about finding Trudy that I…"

"Wasn't thinking? Why do I find it hard to believe that you have moments when you ever stop thinking?"

Fraye's eyes narrowed as they ran down the length of her body and back again. "Now, Detective Barnes, I think you know from experience that there are times when I'm rendered incapable of organized thought."

Kate crossed her legs and her arms, drawing attention from the wry smile that had formed on her lips. "I thought you had forgotten about that."

"You made certain I never could."

A pained expression flashed across Kate's face. Shaking her head slowly, her eyes fell to the floor. "Too bad I couldn't have been certain to keep Maggie, Becky, and Trudy safe."

Fraye dropped into the seat opposite Kate. "Look, we've been over this enough times. At some point you're going to need to let go of the guilt."

"I know. I've told you—I have no intention of letting it get in the way of the investigation."

"It's not just the investigation—you can't let it get in your own way. After this case is over, you're going to have to move on with your life. There are going to be other cases, other victims, and you can't feel responsible for all of them."

She sighed deeply. "I'll have to ask my partner how he does it."

"Does what?"

"Lives with guilt. I can't imagine how bad he felt about not being there to protect his wife when she was killed."

A frown drew the special agent's brow into a tight knot.

The expression became contagious. "What?"

He shook his head. "Nothing. I was just remembering how odd I thought their relationship was."

"You knew Harding's wife?"

"No, I never met her—which shouldn't surprise you. As you've gathered, your partner and I were never the best of friends."

"Then how could you form an opinion about their relationship?"

He smiled wryly. "The same way I have an opinion about anyone I've ever profiled."

Wariness edged into Kate's voice. "You profiled Harding?"

"No. I mean, not intentionally." Noting the turbulent emotions playing out on her face, he attempted to clarify. "It's not what you think. Just like you and everyone else on this planet, I form impressions of people based on their behavior. Harding never wore a wedding ring, and he never mentioned his wife. There was a picture on his desk, so everyone knew he had someone, but I worked with him for months, and marriage just never seemed like a real part of his life."

"He's a cop. You've got to be good at compartmentalizing to survive in this job."

"I'm well aware of that. Harding's marriage always struck me as different somehow—even for a cop. But he must have cared deeply for her. After all, he removed himself from the team, then picked up and moved out here after she was murdered."

"It must have been a big loss for your team when he quit."

Fraye turned and looked toward the line of windows along the far wall. When he gazed back at her, there was an unreadable expression in his eyes. "Believe it or not, I was glad to be rid of him. There were quite a few issues that had come to light with respect to Harding's performance on the team during that last month."

"Issues? Such as?"

"Nothing specific. More like an overall sense of sloppiness in his work. When you are trying to apprehend a highly evolved serial killer, the devil is in the details. We could not afford any mistakes, especially bonehead ones like forgetting to file interview reports, showing up late for meetings, et cetera. As it was, we never had to discuss it because he stepped down. And right after Harding's wife died, the Torturer went silent on us.

"The last victim had been discovered the week before Harding left. We had been so close to catching him, I could almost taste it. We had a witness who had seen someone hanging around the crime scene right before the body of Gayle Nivens was discovered. As you know, that witness disappeared and everything went quiet."

"Until Maggie."

"Until Maggie." His gaze dropped to the floor. "It is odd though."

"What?"

"That the Tower Torturer's spree ended right after Harding bowed out of the investigation. And when another victim finally surfaced, it was here in San Francisco—the same city Harding relocated to."

Thunderclouds threatened in Kate's countenance. "What are you trying to say?"

"Relax, Kate. I'm not accusing your partner of anything. I'm merely suggesting that there may be another angle I've overlooked before."

"Such as?"

"Perhaps you are not the first law enforcement official our UNSUB has become fixated on." Fraye pursed his lips, looking as if he'd just tasted something unpleasant. "But, you both represent different genders, and the UNSUB never tried to engage Harding personally as he has with you."

Shaking his head once again, he rose from his chair. "Never mind me. My brain is all over the place.

The only sensible thing I've done lately is to elevate your partner's role in this investigation. Whatever difficulties Harding had during that last month in Boston are long gone. He's doing a great job on this case. I'm lucky to have him. Just look at me sitting here and wasting time, scouring over old territory—hoping to find a hidden gem."

He winked at Kate. "The reality is that we've already got our hidden gem. We just need to wait a few more hours before the doctor will let us talk to her."

At the prompting of a buzzing sound from his coat pocket, Fraye reached for his phone and answered it. He turned and began to walk away, stopping abruptly after only a few steps. As Kate watched, the special agent's shoulders seemed to crumble around his frame. He ended the call, but remained rooted in place.

Standing up, Kate shuffled like a condemned man to Fraye's side. She did not utter a word, but merely waited until his eyes found hers.

"That was Dr. Simms. Trudy Morris took a sudden turn for the worse."

"We'd better get down there right away. I'll go get Harding and…"

"There is no need. Trudy is dead."

Chapter 24

KATE THANKED THE average-looking, middle-aged receptionist on her way out of the lobby of the single-story warehouse building that housed Bay Paint Supply, Ltd. Pushing through the heavy glass door, she emerged into the brisk afternoon air. Without pausing, she hurried down the walkway to the street.

After receiving the devastating news about Trudy, she and Harding had joined Karinsky, Wallace, and Felts—interviewing the business owners in the industrial neighborhood on the northeast side of the old Stick where Trudy had been discovered early that morning.

The security footage they'd received from the former ballpark's perimeter cameras had shown Trudy crawling into view on her hands and knees and collapsing against the fence about an hour before she was actually discovered. It appeared that she had been coming from Gillman Avenue—one of the roads that linked the coliseum to the Bayview-Hunters Point neighborhood.

Once known as Butchertown—a moniker attributable to the abundance of slaughterhouses crammed into the small region—the area was one of the most dangerous within the San Francisco city limits.

After the Japanese had bombed Pearl Harbor during World War II, it had transformed overnight into a flourishing naval shipyard. Lacking enough local labor to feed the burgeoning American war machine, the area had received a huge influx of African Americans, who flocked there as part of the Great Migration, hoping to make a better future for themselves and their families. When the war had ended, the US military's interest in the neighborhood had ebbed and then dissolved altogether.

The jobs dried up, leaving the recent immigrants with poor economic prospects. As a bonus, the area had become an environmental disaster zone, thanks to the numerous contaminants the military had left behind in the soil and groundwater. Almost seventy years later, the Bayview-Hunters Point neighborhood remained one of the poorest, most unhealthy, crime-ridden neighborhoods in the Bay Area.

Third Street, the main corridor linking the forgotten land to the rest of the city, had undergone a substantial attempt at re-gentrification over the past few years. But new streetlights and building facades had not been enough to overcome generations of disenfranchisement, high cancer rates, and the ever-climbing murder toll.

The southernmost section of the neighborhood, where Kate now stood, consisted of a couple of blocks of ramshackle, single-story industrial buildings, as well as a school, a park, and a fairly new low-income housing project. The small zone created a buffer between the old ballpark site and the worst the neighborhood could offer. Many of the buildings were vacant, solidifying the sense of hopelessness that had become the area's hallmark.

Despite Kate's best efforts, the sense of general malaise in the air penetrated her skin, burying itself deep within her marrow. Turning to her left, she peered southward. In the distance, Bayview Hill was visible. Early that morning, it would have been too dark for Trudy to see the hill where the old ballpark used to stand—she may have simply followed the streetlights looking for salvation.

Clenching her teeth, Kate resolved not to let the disappointment of Trudy's death defeat her. Despite incredible odds, Trudy had fought to escape her fate—the only victim of the Tower Torturer ever to do so. There was hope in that, and hope was what Kate needed—hope and some good old-fashioned detective work.

Given the severity of her injuries, Trudy had to have escaped from somewhere relatively nearby, though the inhabitants of the apartment complex adamantly denied having seen her. In this neighborhood, residents generally denied they had witnessed anything, evidence of a generations-old distrust of the police.

The team had not learned anything from the local business owners either, except Felts, who had obtained security footage from the mattress importer a block away. Their footage showed Trudy stumbling by their front door about fifteen minutes before the stadium's security cameras picked her up.

Across the street, the front door to the recycling warehouse opened. Harding emerged, jogging down the few steps to the sidewalk as she crossed to meet him.

"Any luck?" he inquired hopefully.

"No. Same story. They don't open until eight o'clock in the morning. No one was here early enough to have seen anything."

Kate turned and glanced back toward the ballpark property. "You'd think more of these people would have security cameras focused on the street."

Her partner gestured to the badly ruined sidewalk and the faded, dirty exterior of the building he'd just visited. "Come on. Look at this place. These companies are here because the rents are some of the cheapest around. These guys don't typically have a huge budget to spend on top-of-the-line security systems. They're just trying to scrape by."

"You're right."

"I should be. These are the only kind of tenants I can get."

"Tenants? You have tenants?"

Harding checked his watch. "Come on. Let's get over to the tractor-refurbishing company on the next block."

Kate laid a hand on his arm. "Wait a minute."

His hazel eyes fixed on her hand, then shifted to her face. What he saw there transformed his expression.

Dropping her hand, but refusing to drop the inquiry, Kate asked, "What do you mean your 'tenants'? Are you saying you own commercial real estate?"

Frustrated, Harding turned away and started down the block.

Without taking a step, Kate called out after her partner. "Oh, so now you won't even have the decency to respond to me when I ask you a question." Watching him continue down the sidewalk, she decided to press further. "I guess with your new elevated position on the team, you think you're above me now."

That was enough. He stopped in his tracks. When Kate came up alongside him, he responded without looking at her. "That's not fair, Kate. It's not like I was promoted or anything. Besides, it's no big deal. I have a part ownership in some small concrete tilt-ups."

"If it's no big deal, why haven't you ever mentioned it before?"

"One, it never really came up in conversation. Two, I could give a shit less about it. And three, I've never had the money to invest."

"So did the real estate fairy just put the deeds under your pillow one night?"

"Why are you so stuck on this?"

"I just want to know, that's all."

"All right. I've got partial interests in about twenty different properties on the West Coast."

"What?" The revelation brought Kate to a halt. Between Harding's lack of fashion sense and his general state of dishabille, he'd never struck her as the type of guy with any real money. She'd been to his place before—it was a Spartan nest, thinly lined by the meager wages of a cop's salary.

Rolling his eyes skyward, he stopped and spun around. "Look, it's no big deal, okay? I'm not Donald Trump. The property interests are leftovers from my marriage. My father-in-law was a textile guy who liked to play in the real estate markets, but only with really inexpensive stuff. He left the properties to his kids, and when Denise died, I inherited her share. It's only a twenty-five percent interest, and most of the stuff is really crappy shit in areas like this.

"Whatever isn't sitting vacant gets us the most pathetic rents you ever saw. The repair costs are usually so high that we never see a profit at the end of the year. Luckily, my brother-in-law handles everything. Every January he lets me know if I get to cash a skimpy check or whether I have to cut one of my own. Are you happy now? Or do you want to review my tax returns for the last five years?"

Glancing away guiltily, Kate quickened her pace.

"Sorry to pry. It was just such a surprise. Sometimes I think I know you so well; other times, I…"

"You do know me, Kate. In fact you know…" The ring of his phone interrupted Harding.

He answered it, listened intently for a few moments, then nodded and ended the call with something akin to a quick grunt. Spinning around, he began heading back in the opposite direction. As Kate struggled to keep up with his long stride, she inquired, "Now where are we going?"

"To get the car so we can get back to the Hall. That was Fraye. Chau's got preliminary autopsy results back on Trudy."

"Already?"

"Uh, huh. Call Karinsky. Tell him to cover the tractor company interview for us."

▷▷▷

Kate stared at the coroner as he spoke, her mind numb to the litany of Latin that slipped loquaciously from his mouth. She wished the numbness could extend to her heart, which was bleeding over the sickening photos of Trudy's chest displayed on the large computer screen on the back wall of the lab.

The photos had been taken with a high definition camera before Chau had made his first incisions into Trudy's torso. The mangled tissue stood out in stark evidence of the sadistic cruelty the UNSUB had wrought on the vibrant young woman.

When Chau had finished, he reverted to plain English. "She could not have made it very far in her condition. I'm guessing it was only a matter of a few blocks at the most."

"We gathered as much." Fraye confirmed dryly. "At this point, we do not know whether she escaped from a nearby building, or a vehicle. Do you have anything that can help us to narrow down our search?"

"I would say she was held nearby, on a property that had once been used as a pesticide storage facility."

Fraye's eyes flew open wide, then he shot a meaningful glance at Harding.

Watching the exchange, Chau called out to his assistant who was seated before a keyboard on the left side of the room. "Raisa, bring up the slide shots."

To Kate's relief, the images of Trudy's ravaged abdomen disappeared, replaced by a series of oddly shaped blotches.

Chau waited a moment for his audience to study the screen. When all three turned to him with quizzical expressions, he elaborated. "I found traces of dichlorodiphenyltrichloroethane in the dirt under her nails."

Kate looked down at the floor, mentally breaking the epic word down into more readily digestible bites. Her face brightened as recognition dawned. "DDT?"

Chau smiled at her like a proud parent. "Correct."

Harding frowned. "You mean that stuff they banned in the early seventies?"

Fraye responded in a clinically detached tone. "It was banned here in the US in the seventies, but it wasn't banned on an international scale until the Stockholm Convention in 2001. During the 1940s, it was heralded as the pesticide of the future, having had huge success in reducing the death toll from malaria by controlling mosquito populations."

"True," Chau interjected. "But the success came at a high price. DDT is a serious contaminant that was later discovered to pose considerable environmental risk. Banning it was one of the best things the government ever did. Studies have shown that children who were exposed to it have increased risk for numerous types of cancer."

"Hold on." All eyes turned toward Kate. "If this stuff was banned in the US almost forty years ago, how did Trudy get into it?"

Chau pulled a pencil from his pocket and tapped the eraser end on the screen. "See these samples? While I was able to identify them as DDT, they are extremely degraded. The typical half-life for DDT can range anywhere from less than one month up to thirty years. And, while its usage was banned in the US in the 1970s, we continued producing that poison through the 1980s, and exporting it for use in countries that were not as discerning about what they put into their soil and water sources. Based on the level of degradation, I'd say this sample is somewhere between twenty-five and thirty years old."

Fraye looked at Kate. "We need to run an immediate search on the buildings on the north edge of Candlestick. Shorten the list by excluding anything built within the last twenty years. With any luck, we'll be paying our UNSUB a visit before dinnertime."

ᚦᚦᚦ

Kate hung up the phone and slumped back into her chair. Harding watched her intently from his desk across the aisleway.

"Bad news?" he called out.

Kate brought her hands to her face, rubbing her eyes with her fingertips. "Not bad exactly." Dropping her hands, she rose to her feet and walked over to her partner's desk. "That was the county recorder's office. Up until 1989, they have no record of any pesticide companies doing business in that neighborhood."

"You had them searching business licenses, right?"

"Right."

"Maybe the company was there, and they just stopped paying their annual license fee. Or maybe they moved out prior to 1989. Have them go back further."

"I tried, but the older records are still on microfiche." Kate practically groaned the words.

"Sounds like you're headed for city hall."

"Want to come along?"

"To go root through microfiche? No, thank you. But I'll tell Fraye to call over there and make sure they don't dick you around when you get there."

"Thanks, partner!" Kate called out dryly as she headed for the elevator.

Fifteen minutes later, she walked into the city hall rotunda. Constructed in the French-inspired Beaux Arts style, with a sweeping staircase that would make Scarlett O'Hara swoon, the entry to the government seat for the City and County of San Francisco was impressive enough to rival that of a foreign nation. In terms of height alone, the building's classically styled dome held the distinction of being one of the largest in the world, its height even topping that of the US Capitol.

The building's majesty was irrelevant to Kate, who hurried across the opulent marble floor and down one of the side corridors to the county clerk's office. Fraye's call had worked its usual magic. The moment Kate flashed her badge to the pregnant Latino woman behind the long counter, she was escorted into a private back room and seated before an ancient microfiche machine. The woman offered a brief tutorial on how to use the device, then gave Kate access to a nearby computer before leaving her alone.

As the door shut firmly behind her, Kate pulled out her iPad and opened the note application. She had made it through four years of business license records, before finding what she sought. It was a license for a company called Pacific Ag Distributions. In the field titled "primary business activity" the firm had entered "pesticide exporting." According to the records, they had been operating out of a building located two blocks from the old ballpark. As she recalled, the building was vacant and sat next door to a dirt lot.

Kate typed the information into her iPad, then returned to the records to verify whether any other neighboring firms may have been involved in a similar enterprise. When she had searched back another twenty years with no result, she went back to the entry for Pacific Ag and verified that she had copied the address correctly.

Rolling her chair over to the computer, she pulled out a map of the neighborhood, which Kevin had printed for her when she'd returned from the coroner's office. Scanning the map, she found the appropriate address and the corresponding assessor's parcel number.

With a few keystrokes, the website for the San Francisco County Assessor's office appeared on screen. Kevin had explained that through this site, she could access the property tax records, which would provide the property owner's name. She hastily entered the parcel number into the required field, then watched as an hourglass appeared on screen.

As the icon rotated slowly before her, Kate pulled her phone from her coat pocket. The gravity of the discovery caused her hand to tremble slightly. Her thumb was poised above Fraye's speed dial number when something on the computer caught her eye. It was a word, one that reminded her of a night not long ago when she could not sleep and had decided to put a niggling curiosity to rest.

After Harding had opened up to her about his wife, Kate had become more curious about the woman who had captured her partner's heart and had left him under such tragic circumstances. On a whim, Kate had run a search on the Internet with the key-words, *Tyler Harding, marriage, Denise* and *Boston*.

The result had been a series of links to newspaper announcements about the couple's marriage, and then, of course, Denise's tragic death. Kate had read through each of the stories, feeling like a voyeur all the while. There had been one minor fact that she had held onto from that late-night foray into her partner's past.

The similarity of Denise's maiden name, Barnem, to Kate's last name, Barnes, had made it one of those odd, yet meaningless, points of connection that stuck in her head. The spelling of the name had also stuck out in Kate's mind, as it deviated from the more common spelling of the name made world famous by the circus and its wildly colorful creator, P.T. Barnum.

According to the records, the Barnem Family Trust, LLC, owned the property in question. Kate stared at the name for a moment longer before shifting her thumb over to the right and pressing the speed dial number for her partner.

He answered on the second ring.

Kate started without preamble or greeting. "Do you own property out there?"

There was a brief pause. "Kate? What are you talking about?"

"I just found out that you own properties today, and I want to know if you own property out there?"

"Out where?"

"South Bayview."

"I… I don't think so. But I really don't know. I told you, I don't pay much attention to that stuff. My brother-in-law handles everything."

Kate inhaled deeply.

"Why are you asking?" A note of discomfort crept into Harding's voice.

"What is the name of the trust that owns your properties?"

"It's in Denise's family name. Why? Kate, what the hell is going on here?"

"Just tell me. I need to know the exact name."

"Barnem Family Trust, LLC. Now, for God's sake, tell me what the hell is going on?"

"I found the address we're looking for."

"That's great, but why are you asking…"

"Because you own that building."

Chapter 25

IN THE DARKNESS, two lonely sodium lights mounted to either end of the roof shone over the glass, double-door entrance of the vacant building. No security cameras were visible on the exterior. The property's only adornment was the overgrown landscape and the real estate broker's sign.

As soon as the blue sedan came to a stop in front of the building, Kate, Harding, and Fraye shot from the car, clad in department-issued Kevlar vests. Less than twenty seconds later, four more patrol cars arrived at either end of the block, effectively closing off the street in either direction.

With a curt nod to the detectives, Fraye drew his weapon and started toward the front door. Harding followed, while Kate split off to the right, heading for the south side of the building.

Gun drawn and held securely down by her side, Kate picked her way through the landscape, pausing as she arrived at a six-foot-high row of escallonia. She hurried southward, passing four more towering shrubs before hurrying around the edge of the last one.

Crouched under the thick network of branches, she peered across the vacant dirt lot at the warehouse. By then, Fraye had opened the lockbox hanging from the front door handle and retrieved the key that had been left there by the vacant building's real estate broker.

On her side of the building there were no doors, only two rows of thick-paned windows. The first ran about three feet below the roofline. The second was oddly placed about a foot above the ground. Lighting on this side of the building was sparse. Two roof-mounted lights—one near the mid-span of the roof and the other at the far corner of the warehouse—provided the only source of illumination.

Kate scurried across the dirt lot to the structure. Once there, she hurried alongside the building. Slowing as the corner approached, she paused to listen. When she was satisfied that there were no sounds in the still night, she peered around the corner.

The backside of the building was better illuminated, with multiple lights shining on the loading dock area below. In the center, a set of metal stairs led up to a metal door. Flanking it were two large, roll-up doors designed for the offloading of trucks. Positioning her back against the corner of the building, she grasped her gun with both hands and waited while Fraye and Harding searched the interior.

Ten minutes later, Harding's voice sounded in her head. Kate placed a hand over the earpiece in her right ear as he spoke. "The building's clear. I'm coming out the back."

Kate holstered her weapon and started toward the stairs just as the metal door opened, squealing loudly on well-worn hinges. Seeing her partner, she broke into a jog, quickly joining him on the small landing.

"Nobody home?" The disappointment was raw in her voice. "No. But this is where Trudy was kept." He disappeared inside, leaving Kate to grasp for the door before it shut in her face.

The temperature inside the concrete structure was

no warmer than it had been outside. Pulling her flash-light from her pocket, Kate followed her partner across the cavernous warehouse. They had covered about half the distance when bright light suddenly flooded the space.

Squinting against the glare, Kate spotted Fraye standing near a light switch. Though his face betrayed no particular emotion, she could sense the tension coming off him in waves. Her partner, on the other hand, remained impassive.

"The lab team will be here in twenty minutes." Having made the announcement, the special agent turned, leading them through another door into a small open area flanked by perimeter offices. Paneled in wood that looked like it had been repurposed from a 1970s stage dressing, the room stunk like old carpet and sweaty sneakers.

Passing a series of offices, Fraye opened a badly scarred wooden door on the south side of the chamber. Kate followed both men down a narrow set of stairs. As they descended, the temperature seemed to drop ten to fifteen degrees.

The stairs ended in a room that shared the approximate dimensions as the one they'd just left. Four tracks of fluorescent lights provided illumination from above. Along the far wall, near the ceiling, was a row of windows—the same windows Kate had seen earlier. One of the apertures hung open on its hinges, a fact the shadows outside had hidden from view. Despite the open portal, an acrid sewer smell pervaded. Kate swallowed tightly, suppressing her gag reflex.

In the far corner was a metal cot with a thin, dirty blanket draped over the edge. Nearby a two-foot-high aluminum bucket lay on its side. The interior of the vessel matched the appearance of the dried waste on the floor near the opposite corner of the room.

Following Kate's gaze, Fraye nodded. "That must have been Trudy's toilet."

Snaking out from the corner leg of the cot, where it was affixed to the bed with a series of thick knots, was a length of black nylon rope whose end was jagged and irregular. Similar lengths of material were affixed to the other legs, the only difference being that they did not appear to have been similarly mutilated.

"How'd she do it?" Harding asked. "With the damage he did to her, she must have been in an incredible amount of pain."

"That's what he was counting on." Fraye offered. "He left her here to die. Clearly Trudy had other ideas." Walking along the length of the cot, the special agent squatted down, peering beneath it. He then straightened, leaned over the bed, and began to carefully inspect it.

Instead of peering over Fraye's shoulder like her partner, Kate took a few steps closer to the window. "Trudy found something to cut that rope. Then she untied the other ropes, dumped the contents of her toilet, and turned it over to use as a stool. She put it on top of the cot so she could reach the window. See how the bucket's knocked over? It must have fallen to the floor as she hauled herself up and out."

She pointed a finger upward. "There's blood all over the bottom of the frame. The vacant lot is right on the other side of this window. The opening is narrow even for someone slender like Trudy. To get out, she probably had to scramble through the dirt on the other side. That's how the soil contaminated with DDT got under her nails."

"Thanks for stating the obvious, Kate. What I

meant was how did she have the strength to do it?"

Kate whirled on Harding, fixing him with a seething glare.

Unfazed by the bickering, Fraye asked, "The ER doctor said he thought the wounds looked like they had been made with razor wire, right?"

The partners turned toward Fraye and answered in unison. "Yes."

Glancing up at them with something mildly resembling mirth in his expression, he continued. "There's a piece of razor wire wrapped in this blanket. That's how she cut the first rope."

"Razor wire? How did she get her hands on that?" Harding asked.

Kate folded her arms over her chest. "That's not the real question. What we should be asking is where did the rest of the razor wire go, and where is all the blood? You can't cause that type of damage to the human body and not make a mess."

Fraye looked at her approvingly. "Kate's right. We need to go over this place with a fine-tooth comb. There's got to be another room somewhere that we missed."

Twenty-five minutes later, they convened at the reception area near the building's entrance. A lab technician—one of four presently scouring the building —stood nearby running a thick brush over the handles to the front doors.

Harding raked a hand through his hair. "Shit. There's nothing else here."

Fraye gestured to the lab technician. "We don't know what's here. Not until the lab team finishes processing the scene. The large office in back reeks of bleach. He obviously tried to clean up after discovering Trudy had escaped."

"But if he was going to clean up that section, why not clean up the basement too?"

"He may have felt he was running out of time. For all he knows, Trudy was rescued and told the police about this place. He only took that which was most important to him. He's too smart to wait around for the police to show up. Now it's our job to keep the UNSUB on his toes."

"And how do you propose we do that?"

Fraye looked at Kate. "Let's get back to the Hall. I think Kate should do a little late night posting to Facebook."

ᚦᚦᚦ

Kate stared at the flashing cursor on her computer screen. Fraye and Harding had crammed into the small space on either side of her chair, flanking her like bookends. Hands poised above the keyboard, she struggled to find the appropriate words to type.

Her eyes searched the room, half hoping the words might be hiding behind another detective's chair or filing cabinet. It was half past ten, and the floor was deserted, which was probably a good thing. Kate did not want any witnesses for what she was about to do.

Noting his partner's hesitation, Harding turned to Fraye, ready to rehash the same argument that had dominated their drive back to the Hall. "I know you don't want to hear it, but this could blow up in our faces."

Fraye's gaze remained riveted to the screen. "This is the best option we have. We must move on it while we have the chance."

"But what if the UNSUB knows Trudy is dead?"

The special agent sighed deeply. "As we've discussed, when Trudy was discovered, we locked that hospital down tight. No one knows we had even found her, let alone that she died. It's time for the UNSUB to stop wondering what happened to his last victim."

"But Trudy's family still hasn't been notified. Everyone who monitors Maggie's memorial page is going to see Kate's post—including the press. If we get caught publicizing the fact that Trudy's alive when we know she's dead, we could fuck up the DA's chances of prosecuting this case. It's not enough to catch this guy, you know. We've got to win a conviction too."

"I am well aware of that. That's why I took it upon myself to notify her family this afternoon. They have been sworn to secrecy, and they've pledged to uphold that vow in the interest of catching the person who murdered their daughter."

Kate turned in her chair, craning her neck to look up at Fraye. "You did what?"

"I notified Trudy's parents while you were tracking down the address where she'd been held. Do you have an objection to that, Detective Barnes?"

"No, I just…"

"You just thought I should withhold such vital information from a worried family?"

"No, I… Never mind." She planted her hands on her desk, forcing her chair backward into the two men.

Grabbing the back of Kate's chair as she stood and began walking away, Harding demanded, "Where the hell do you think you're going?"

Kate turned and folded her arms squarely across her chest. "My Facebook page is open. It doesn't matter who types in the entry—it will appear as if I did. Either way, I'm going to take the heat for this, so go ahead and figure out whatever you two want in there and type it in yourselves. Last time I checked, secretarial duties were not included in my job description."

She expected to hear their voices calling her back as she stalked away, but silence reigned in her wake. Frustrated with herself and tired of feeling that way, Kate headed away from the elevators, opting for the lunchroom instead.

Crossing the threshold, she was momentarily enveloped in darkness. After a few steps, the motion sensor activated, filling the room with light. Without pausing, Kate headed directly for the coffee pot, which was empty.

Still fuming, she snatched the pot from the cold burner and thrust it under the faucet. Watching the receptacle fill with water, the irony of the task prompted her to chuckle mirthlessly.

"What's so funny?" Harding asked as he joined her at the sink.

"Just this." She gestured to the running water, the smile fading from her lips.

Responding to his blank stare, she explained. "I said I wouldn't type for you guys like a secretary, but here I am making coffee like one."

Harding nodded, leaning back against the counter while Kate replaced the pot and began adding coffee grounds to the machine.

"You didn't like covering the back tonight, did you? You wanted first crack at the UNSUB, and we didn't give you the chance."

"Whose decision was that?"

"Fraye made the final decision, but I recommended it."

"How could you do that to me? I have…"

"Because I wasn't sure how you were going to

handle it after losing another victim."

"We've lost victims before, and I've always kept my composure. What did you think I was going to do? Run in there like Rambo—shoot up the place like a vigilante?"

"Not necessarily, but you did run off on your own and investigate the Emilio lead."

"Come on. I have stuck my neck out so far for you that I probably won't have a head come morning. You just stood there and warned Fraye that he shouldn't engage in risky moves that might have long-term implications when this case goes to trial. Do you really think no one is going to take the time to find out who owns that building? If anyone should have been sidelined tonight it should have been…"

Harding took a sudden step toward Kate, grabbing her arm just as another voice called out.

"Who should have been sidelined? Detective Harding, perhaps?" Fraye entered and sat down at a nearby table, staring pointedly at the hold Harding had on his partner. "And why would you say that you stuck your neck out for him?"

Releasing Kate's arm as if it were suddenly a hot coal, Harding walked over to the special agent. "Did you finish the post?"

"It's done. Remember to keep your phone close tonight. Kevin set up all of our phones to receive feeds from Maggie's memorial page as well as Kate's Facebook account—even the private ones. You should already be able to see my post."

"When did Kevin do that?"

"I stopped by his office on my way to see Trudy's parents this afternoon."

"Oh." Harding pulled his phone from his pocket, tapping the screen a few times. "Okay, I see it. You really swung for the fences, didn't you? 'Our little free bird sang all day. Already found her cage. Now I'm coming for you.' If our perp is watching Facebook, this'll piss him off good. Call me if anything else comes up." He flashed one more heavy glance at Kate before leaving.

Kate turned back to her task, setting the machine to brew. She could hear Fraye get up and make his way over to the spot Harding had just vacated.

"I need to know. Are you still in this, Kate?"

"Of course I am. Why would you even ask that?"

"Because you continue to undermine this investigation at every turn."

She took a few steps back before responding, uncomfortable with the close proximity. "You have no right to say that. I am giving everything to this case."

Fraye closed the distance, coming so near she could feel the heat of his breath upon her mouth. "You went to the county recorder's office today, true?"

Still uncomfortable but not wanting to cede an inch of ground, Kate stared back at him. Her dark eyes flashed like steel. "Yes, I did."

"With the map Kevin gave you? The one that showed the assessor's parcel numbers for each of the addresses in that neighborhood. Do you expect me to believe you did not use that to find out who owned the property?"

"It's not owned by an individual—just some kind of trust." Her breath seemed to fade toward the end of the sentence, the last words issued in almost a whisper.

"You would lie to me—even now?"

"I'm not lying to you."

"No, you are simply omitting facts that are known

to you—material facts that affect this investigation."

The conversation had become far too intense. Kate no longer had the strength to feign bravado. Relenting, she walked over and sat down at the vacant table.

"So, you already know?"

"Yes. Harding called me the minute he got off the phone with you. At least one of you cares about this investigation enough to do the right thing."

Kate's shoulders sagged. "He should have told me that he was going to let you know about it. If I had known that, I never would have tried to keep it quiet."

"You never had to either way. What you had to do was tell me immediately, but you chose to omit the truth—to risk this investigation because of some kind of misguided loyalty to your partner."

"Harding went to you on his own—that should tell you what kind of character he has. He didn't try to hide away from it. He is a good man and a good partner. My loyalty to him has never been misguided."

Folding his arms across his chest, the special agent eyed her carefully. "What is the nature of your relationship with your partner, Kate? For you to jeopardize this case—one where you have been so personally tormented by the death of each victim—it must go well beyond the professional limit."

"Harding and I are partners—that is all. Now, if you're done with this fishing expedition, I'm going home for the night."

"What about the coffee?"

"I've swallowed enough bitterness tonight. I don't need anymore."

She paused in the doorway, turning back one last time. "If you knew Harding has an ownership stake in the building, you should have sidelined him tonight. Why didn't you?"

"Because I don't believe Detective Harding is our UNSUB. But I doubt it's a coincidence that the killer chose that particular building to keep his victims. Either way, I'd rather have your partner out in the field than sitting behind a desk."

"So you have loyalty to him, just like I do. And like me, you were willing to bend the rules for him."

"I guess we're more alike than we'd care to admit."

Kate thought about it for a moment, then nodded slowly before walking away.

ᚦᚦᚦ

February 10

The shrill cry of the cell phone woke Kate from the last in a series of tumultuous dreams. She groped for the phone through the tangle of sheets.

"Barnes here."

"Good Morning, Detective. Since you didn't bother to call in, I'm assuming you haven't been monitoring your Facebook account." Fraye's voice was the last thing she wanted to wake up to this morning, especially because of the prominent role he'd played in her nightmares.

Kate scrambled to sit upright in bed. A quick glance at the clock revealed it was only four twenty-five. She thought she had activated the notification ringer on her phone before going to sleep. Apparently, whatever she had done had not worked. Either that, or she had slept right through it. "Did we get a response?"

"Yes, we did. Although I must admit that it is not what I was hoping for."

"What do you mean?"

"Another video has been posted to YouTube."

"A video? He didn't respond to Facebook?"

"He did, but not by posting to it. He uploaded another *For Kate* video. The message he posted with the video confirms he read your post."

"But he has no victims. What did he post a video of?"

There was a long pause. When the special agent spoke again, the edge had eroded from his tone. "It was a video of Maggie being tortured. It is pretty brutal." His tone softened further, becoming down-right gentle. "Kate, I think it will be better if you never see it. You don't need those memories in your head."

Kate dropped backward into her pillows, taking a minute to compose herself before she spoke again. "No, I'll need to see it. What was the message?"

"Why don't we do this at the Hall?"

"Are you there now?"

"No, I'm just about to leave my hotel."

"I'm on my way as well. I'll be there in twenty minutes." Kate climbed out of bed and hurried to the closet, stripping off her shirt as she walked. "I know you think you're helping me, but I need to know what he said. I promise—I can handle whatever you tell me."

Another long pause. "Fine. It was a short message, just four lines: 'None of the little birds are special to me, Kate. Only you. I hope you come soon. I'll be waiting.'"

Chapter 26

KATE YANKED THE WOODEN CHAIR out from under the table. The sudden movement visibly surprised Maria Torres, who had been sitting alone at the back table in the funky little coffee shop, staring intently at her cell phone.

The reporter smiled thinly as her guest sat down. "Glad you could make it."

"You said it was important. Start talking. I don't have much time."

"Do you want any coffee?" Maria asked, gesturing to the thick mug on the table in front of her. "No offense, but I think you could use some. It looks like you've aged ten years since the last time I saw you."

"Thanks for the unsolicited opinion. I don't have time to waste on coffee. Just tell me whatever it is you have to say." Kate's eyes darted around the shop, whose tables and chairs had been painted every color of the rainbow. An eclectic mix of African masks, small Persian rugs, and British ceramic plates adorned the walls.

Under other circumstances she may have been charmed by the offbeat décor. This morning all she cared about was making sure that no one she knew was here to witness her meeting with Maria.

"I saw your Facebook post last night, and I must say I was a bit surprised." The reporter's gaze was laced with pique and curiosity.

"About?"

Maria's mouth pursed tight. "Level with me, Kate. You've had my trust and honesty from day one."

"And I've told you from day one that I will be as forthright as I can, but this is an open investigation, and I am limited by the rules of confidentiality."

"Admit it. You were using that post to try to bait the Tower Torturer, right?" She waited for a response. When none was forthcoming, the reporter continued. "Just tell me one thing. Do you have Trudy Morris? Is she alive?"

Kate's expression was glacial. "I cannot discuss details in a pending investigation…"

"Bullshit!" Maria hissed. "We have worked this case together, Barnes." She leaned back, struggling to regain her composure. "You know what I think? I think you are trying to make it look like you have Trudy, but you don't—not really." The reporter's eyes studied Kate's countenance as if trying to decode some sort of cipher.

"If you had Trudy, you would have gone public with it. After all, it would be your first real success in this case, and it would take some of the political and media pressure off. But you didn't do that. So what *is* going on?"

None of Maria's words had elicited the slightest thaw in her companion. Maria glanced away in frustration.

Five seconds later, the detective pushed her chair backward, preparing to leave. Maria turned back, her expression desperate. "How much do you trust those around you?"

The question halted Kate mid-movement. "Why do you ask?"

"Because I have been doing some more digging. Did you know the reason your partner dropped out of the original investigation was because his wife died?"

"Of course I do. What's your point?"

"At the time, Boston PD believed she was murdered by an addict who had broken into her house looking for money. But the suspect was never caught."

"Unfortunately, that happens sometimes. Look, I really have to get back to…"

"But why did Harding drop off the force and move to the West Coast? A cop who has a reputation for putting everything he has into his job? Why wouldn't he have taken it upon himself to bring the killer to justice?"

Kate shrugged. "Chances are his captain told him to steer clear of it—to keep the investigation clean."

Exasperated, Maria shook her head. "Do you know where Harding started out his career as a detective? In the Boston PD *narcotics* squad."

"I know."

"And did you know about the first case he solved in that division? It involved a junkie who had broken into a woman's house looking for money."

"That's fascinating, Maria. But you're out of your mind if you think Tyler Harding is involved in this."

The reporter sat back in her chair, regarding Kate with a look of sympathy mixed with disdain. "In that case, the junkie killed the woman by bashing her head in with a brick."

Kate's eyebrows knitted, and the color disappeared from her cheeks.

"Does that sound familiar? If you recall how Harding's wife died, it should. I guess the real question to ask is, how many people are murdered in Boston every year by a brick-wielding junkie?"

▷▷▷

Kate emerged from the warmth of the coffee shop into the icy morning air. With neither the inclination nor the time to walk the four blocks back to the Hall, she waved her arm briskly, hailing a cab. During the short ride, she stared vacantly out the window, her mind a jumble of images, facts, and emotions.

Fraye was probably right; she never should have insisted on watching the YouTube video. When she had arrived at the Hall earlier that morning, she'd gone directly to Kevin's office. The IT director had tried to talk her out of it, but Kate had insisted.

The memory of the chainsaw splitting through Maggie's vagina had been more than she could bear. Despite herself, she had looked away from the screen, too distraught to continue watching. Thankfully, Kevin had stopped the video, mercifully sparing Kate any further horror.

The video itself seemed to be another dead end. The UNSUB had shrewdly positioned the camera to ensure he could not be identified—only the saw and Maggie had been visible.

The memories of Maggie's torment churning up the acid in her stomach, Kate decided to focus on the unusual conversation she had just had with Maria Torres. Just then, the taxi arrived at her destination, denying her the chance to consider the topic further. Instructing the cab diver to pull over across the street from the Hall, she paid her fare, then hurried across to the main entrance.

As she stepped onto the sidewalk, she noticed Kevin pacing anxiously about twenty feet to her left, clutching his laptop firmly to his chest with his left hand. Without a jacket, he trembled violently in the morning air.

While the lack of outerwear was unusual, what was downright shocking was the fact that the IT director was smoking. It was widely known that Kevin had given up the disgusting habit after witnessing his father succumb to lung cancer after a painful and protracted battle.

Noting Kate's arrival, he jogged over to meet her. "Thank God, I'm so glad you're back! I need to talk to you right away."

"What's happened? Did you find something?"

Kevin nodded adamantly, taking a long drag on his cigarette. "Is it about the new video?"

He continued to nod as the end of the cigarette grew brighter and brighter.

"Why didn't anyone call me?"

Pulling the nicotine stick from his mouth, he tossed it to the ground and stomped on it angrily. Leaning in toward her, he whispered, "No one called because no one except for me knows about it."

"Let's get inside. We'll get Fraye and Harding, and…"

"No!" Seeing Kate frown at his adamant refusal, Kevin softened his tone.

"Please, Kate. I just need to talk to you first. You don't understand, it's… I… Please, can we just go somewhere so I can explain it to you?"

"You're right. I don't understand, Kevin. If you've found something, we need to share it with the team right away."

"Listen, I've done a lot of favors for you over the years, right? Can't you please just give me a chance to explain this to you my way? Can you come with me, so I can show you what I've found? It's just a short drive away."

The sincere misery spread across his features, mixed with the beseeching tone, prompted Kate to nod before better judgment could prevail. Relieved, Kevin led her to his car.

He drove along the city streets as if traffic laws were nothing but twisted fairytales—told to scare motorists into compliance. They crossed into the Outer Mission, parking across the street from a small cyber café.

Kevin jumped from the car with his laptop, imploring Kate to hurry before running heedlessly across traffic. Not wanting to further enrage the drivers who had been interrupted by Kevin's mad dash, Kate waited dutifully for traffic to subside before jaywalking to the café.

Although it was still early, the establishment was fairly full. Patrons of various ages sat at small tables and couches, immersed in their laptops and tablets. Toward the back, a long display case offered various pastries. A young Asian woman worked behind the counter, preparing espresso drinks.

Kate spotted Kevin sitting on a lumpy purple couch along the right wall, typing diligently on his laptop. As she sat down beside him, he snatched the top of the device, closing it firmly.

Without warning, Kevin started in on a lengthy diatribe about proxy servers, proxy hopping, and MAC address masquerading. Kate listed carefully, but he lost her somewhere after the third sentence.

She held up a hand, stopping him. "Kevin. You can go on all day like this, and it's not going to help. Give me the kindergarten version."

He tapped his hands nervously on his knees,

apologizing before taking a deep breath and starting again. "Remember how I told you we couldn't track down the person who posted those videos to YouTube because they were using untraceable IPs?"

"Yes."

"Okay, so every time you go on the Internet you can either access it through a direct Internet connection on your own computer, or you can go somewhere else and use their connection—either hardwire or Wi-Fi."

"That much I know."

"Good. So when you access the Internet, the servers you use along the way and the sites you visit can identify your individual computer and its unique IP address. That's what allows us to trace people's activity on the web—just like a trail of breadcrumbs."

"Okay."

"In this case, the UNSUB was using technology known as proxy servers to function as intermediaries. The proxy looks as if it is the one requesting the access, not the UNSUB."

"Got it."

"Our guy was very sophisticated. He was using a combination of proxy hopping techniques and customized software based on TOR design to hide his tracks."

"TOR?"

"It's a commercial software package originally developed for the US Navy."

"How do you get access to something like that?"

"Just go online and sign up. In today's world, privacy is highly prized—not just by law enforcement for conducting surveillance, but by journalists, rape victims, and people who suffer from certain types of illnesses. TOR routes your traffic through a series of random relays that change every ten minutes or so, making it virtually impossible to trace the activity back to the user.

"In addition, he was manipulating his IP address so that even if anyone was able to trace the point of origin, they'd have no idea who it actually was."

"So what did you find out about this video?"

"There are a variety of programs like ProxyButton that allow users to switch back and forth between their proxy setup and their direct Internet connection. I don't know how it happened—I can only guess he was so stressed about losing Trudy that he finally screwed up. The net result is that this time he forgot to switch back to the proxy. I was able to trace the origin of the last video posted to YouTube."

Kate glanced around the café with a critical eye. "And this is where he uploaded it?"

"Yes."

The word came out with a finality that caused a rash of goose bumps on Kate's arms. Regarding Kevin warily, she reflected on the uncharacteristic anxiety in his demeanor. A crucial break in this case was no reason for clandestine meetings—nor the conflict that the IT director was obviously experiencing.

Breaking eye contact with Kate, he continued. "As you can see, this is a small, independently owned café, and as I noticed when I drove over here an hour ago, there are no video cameras."

"Right."

"But there is that newer apartment building across the street. The manager gave me access to their security footage for the two hours before the video was uploaded."

He reached for the laptop, placing his hand on the lid. "As I told you, I found something, and I don't exactly know how to handle it. Shit! The truth is, I don't want to have to handle it. I don't want anything to do with it."

Opening the laptop, he positioned it directly in front of Kate. On the screen was a frozen image of a set of glass lobby doors looking out onto a street. Kevin reached over and tapped the mouse pad, thawing the frozen image.

A man in a suit appeared on the left side of the doors. A moment later he smiled pleasantly, then opened the door for a beautiful blonde.

"Oh, sorry. This is the view from inside the lobby over there." Kevin tapped the pad a few more times, engaging a zoom option that enlarged the view of the street outside the doors. The storefront of the café became visible. "Just wait a second more... There! Do you see?"

Kate watched as a man appeared on the left side of the screen. She immediately recognized the strong jaw and formidable build of her partner, Tyler Harding. He held a computer tablet in his right hand—one much smaller than the standard department issue.

Suddenly, Maria Torres' recent speculations sounded in her head, merging with snippets of conversations Kate had had with Fraye and Harding himself. The words descended upon Kate's reality, shredding it like a pack of hungry wolverines. On screen, each step her partner took toward the door of the café dragged her deeper and deeper toward the abyss.

Repressing an irrational desire to slam the laptop shut, Kate watched as Harding opened the door and walked inside. He took a place at a table near the window.

Kate's gaze flashed momentarily to the same spot where a young couple now sat, before fixing back on the screen. As Harding began typing on the tablet, Kevin spoke again—his words barely registering in Kate's mind.

"I checked it over a million times, Kate. The time on the security footage exactly matched YouTube's record for when the video was uploaded. You don't think Harding really could be the guy, do you?"

Kate stared at the screen feeling as if she were fourteen years old again, standing at the door to her dead sister's bedroom.

▷▷▷

The doorbell rang, waking Harding from a restless sleep. He got up from the recliner and turned off the TV. Glancing at his watch as he made his way over to the front door, he wondered who could possibly be visiting him at eleven-thirty at night.

"Who is it?" he called just before checking the peephole.

The voice that answered was as astonishing as the visage he glimpsed through the miniature window. Pulling the door open, he stared quizzically at his guest, waiting for an explanation.

Kate looked at him awkwardly. "I wanted to talk. Can I come in?"

"Of course." He opened the door wider.

"I'm sorry to come so late. I probably should have called first, but…"

Kate entered and began removing her coat as Harding closed the door behind her.

"No worries. I didn't see much of you today."

"I spent the majority of the day out at the building where Trudy had been kept. Even though the crime lab hasn't reported all their findings yet, I wanted to look it over for myself in the daylight."

"Can I get you something?" He stepped into the kitchen area and opened the refrigerator. "I don't have much—just a few beers and some orange juice."

Folding her coat over one of the barstools on the other side of the counter, Kate declined.

Heedless of her response, Harding pulled two longneck domestic beers out, removed the caps, and passed one to her. Emerging from the kitchen, he gestured for her to take a seat on the leather couch.

Kate took the proffered seat, settled back, and took a long sip from the bottle. Harding sat down on the edge of the badly scarred coffee table, facing her.

"What's going on, Kate?"

"I just don't know anymore, Tyler."

He pulled the bottle from his lips. "Don't know what?"

"Whether I can keep doing this."

"Kate, this case has been an ass-beater, but you have been making it a lot worse for yourself than it needs to be. For example, you insisted on watching that video of Maggie. Fraye told you not to, but you did it anyway. I'm sorry to say it, but some of this, you're bringing on yourself."

Something sparked in Kate's eyes, but quickly died. She took another sip, then crossed her legs. His eyes were drawn to the lithe limbs. Clad in skintight denim, they moved enticingly on the black leather. Drifting upward, his eyes fixed upon her bulky, white-knit sweater, which primly swallowed up the rest of her curves.

Glancing away, he tried again. "Look, Kate. I don't want to see you going through this. I guess part of it is my fault too."

"What do you mean?"

"Well, I knew you weren't really ready for a case

357

of this caliber. As soon as we found out about the UNSUB's interest in you, you should have stepped down. Now, you're really deep in the shit, and it feels like there's no way out. Doesn't it?"

Kate leaned forward, placing the beer on the table. "Is there a way out?"

"There's always a way out."

Her expression darkened. "That's true. Maybe if I was dead, this would all stop—no more dead young women, no more guilt…"

"Jesus, Kate!" He slammed his bottle on the table next to her and stood. "You don't have to die to end this."

She stood, the challenge clear in her eyes. "Really? Then what do I have to do to end this, Tyler? Because we both know it has to."

"You're right." Kate was so close he could smell the alcohol on her breath. "You've been playing a dangerous game—a game you weren't strong enough to win. The only question left is—how will it end?" He reached up, tracing the side of her jaw with the fingers of his right hand.

She flinched at his touch, then stilled, allowing him to run his fingers back through her hair. Working his way around the nape of her neck, he pulled her to him, crushing his lips down on hers. Salty tears poured down her face, diluting the kiss. He was about to pull away when she opened her mouth, greeting him with the warmth of her tongue.

Kate reached for his hand, stroking it as he held her securely to him. As her fingers interlaced with his, the tension in his hand relaxed.

In that split second, Kate spun around, twisting his arm behind his back and bending his wrist so painfully that he dropped to his knees. "What the hell are you doing?" he roared just before he recognized the sound of handcuffs fastening over his wrists.

Before he could speak again, Kate stood before him and lifted a black wire out from the neckline of her sweater. Regarding him with the air of a mortuary technician, she spoke three small words that sealed his fate.

"I've got him."

Chapter 27

KATE STOOD IN THE DARKNESS, watching her partner who sat quietly in the interrogation room on the other side of the two-way glass. He stared intently at the metal handcuffs she had placed around his wrists a little more than an hour before.

His attorney, Catherine Lygus, sat to his right. A trim brunette in her early forties, dressed in a slim-fitting black pantsuit, she was busy making notes on her iPad.

Glancing over her shoulder at Captain Singh, Kate flipped a switch mounted to the wall, allowing audio access to the room they were observing. The attorney whispered something to Harding, the sound barely audible over the speakers.

The conversation halted as the door opened and Fraye entered. He took a seat directly opposite the detective, placing a file folder in front of him. The two men had not spoken since the arrest, as Harding had exercised his right to counsel moments after Kate issued his Miranda warning.

Fraye regarded the woman critically before turning his attention to Harding. "When did you start torturing women, Detective Harding? Was it the first victim we found in Boston, or did you get started a long time before that?"

"I didn't torture anyone."

Leaning forward, the brunette eyed Fraye stoically. "My client maintains he is innocent of these crimes. He has a stellar service record with the SFPD, Boston PD, and the US military. I suggest you find another scapegoat, Agent Fraye."

"Your client was caught on camera—uploading a torture video to YouTube that featured the first victim. The café's Wi-Fi records corroborate that fact. Moreover, your client owns the building where the last victim was held. We are already going through his personal computer, electronic tablet, and phone. I recommend you advise him to start talking."

Straightening in her seat, the attorney glared back. "We will have our own experts verify the veracity of the security footage and the café records. As for the fact that Detective Harding owns a partial interest in the building you mentioned, that is pure coincidence, not an indicator of culpability."

Turning back to Harding, Fraye tried again. "You did this because of Kate. You chose every victim because of the impact it would have on her. Were you ultimately planning to kill her or…"

"Agent Fraye, I…" Her client cut Catherine off.

"Kate is my partner. I have taught her quite a few things, but I've also learned from her." Harding's gaze shifted to the two-way mirror, fixing so determinedly on its surface that it appeared he had the ability to peer right through it. "Ever since our first case together…"

"Let's forget about Kate for a moment, and talk about your dead wife instead." Fraye waited for the concussive effect of his words to dissipate.

Opening the file folder, he scanned the first

document before riveting his gaze back on the detective. "Just before you left the Boston PD, a junkie broke into your garage. Your wife went out to investigate. The junkie used a brick to bludgeon her to death. A sad ending for an intelligent woman with a bright future, but it is also almost a verbatim account of what happened during the first case you investigated in Boston.

"Perhaps your wife was becoming curious. Maybe you were worried she would figure out that you have a twisted proclivity for torturing young women. Either way, her death provided a convenient reason for you to leave Boston."

Catherine's gaze slid warily to her client.

Fire blazed momentarily behind Harding's eyes, but he remained silent.

"I've had a chance to observe your relationship with Kate firsthand. When exactly was it that you decided to make her your partner in all things? When you decided Kate would find each of your new victims for you?"

Harding's gaze shifted back to the federal agent, fiery hatred radiating from his glance. "I always thought you were a dumbass, but..."

The attorney stood abruptly. "Mr. Harding, I advise you not to answer any more of these questions. They are designed to entrap you, not derive the truth."

Fraye tried to smooth things over, but his efforts were useless. Catherine Lygus was not going to yield.

Kate and the captain exchanged a disheartened glance before she flipped the audio switch once again. They watched in silence as Fraye rose to leave. Moments later, the door to the observation room opened.

Appearing unscathed by his recent dismissal, Fraye entered. "No surprises there. His attorney is doing what she can—trying to posture." He nodded curtly in Kate's direction. "Good job, by the way."

When the detective failed to respond, he clarified. "Discovering that his wife's murder exactly mirrored the facts of the first case he ever worked as a detective. I remember hearing about how his wife was murdered at the time, but I never thought to dig any deeper."

Kate stared off, as if suddenly lost in thought.

"You okay?" Fraye prompted.

She paused for a moment, considering the question. "I'm not quite sure how to answer that." Leaning back against the wall, it appeared she was relying on it to keep her vertical.

Observing her exhaustion, Fraye recommended she head home for the weekend. "It looks like you've had enough. Why don't you finish your reports and get out of here?"

Before she could respond, Singh interjected. "Don't forget to be here by seven Monday morning. Because of your relationship to both the victims and to Harding, Internal Affairs is going to want to talk to you and…"

Deep lines of worry appeared at the corners of the detective's eyes. "I hadn't even thought that far."

Aware of the slight tremor in her voice as she spoke, the captain softened his tone. "Fraye's right. Take the weekend and get as much rest as you can."

Fraye nodded curtly. "According to the district attorney, Harding won't be arraigned until Monday afternoon at the earliest. She doubts that any judge will grant bail."

Singh frowned. "Between now and then, the

mayor's top aides will be scrambling to figure out how to break the news to the press that one of the most notorious serial killers of the modern era turned out to be one of our own SFPD detectives—and a senior ranking member of the investigation team at that. This is going to create a media maelstrom unlike anything we've seen so far. Any way you slice it, we're going to come out looking like complete incompetents."

Fraye sighed aloud. "Don't feel too badly, Captain. The FBI is not going to look much better. The SF bureau chief is shitting bricks right now too. After this fuck-up, I'll be lucky if they ever let me out of Quantico again.

"You've got to give it to Harding, though." The special agent's words drew quizzical looks from his companions. "He did a good job of covering his tracks—killing his own wife because she probably started asking too many questions, then killing Emilio before he could provide a sketch, and trying to throw us off by making it look like a gang hit.

"He played the game masterfully—with the exception of executing Riley. That was a move born of pure frustration. He had tried to convince Kate she was going down the wrong track with Riley, but she refused to listen. So he simply removed Riley from the equation.

"His real mistake was uploading that video directly to YouTube; otherwise Kevin never would have tracked down that café footage. Without that break, who knows how long this would have continued."

Singh stretched his neck from side to side, then shoved his hands deep into his trouser pockets. "Harding fooled all of us. But we have him now, and it's finally over. At least the families of the victims will have some closure. See you Monday, Barnes."

The words seemed to catch Kate unaware. She pondered them carefully before responding—as if unsure whether she ever wanted to come back to work again. Eventually, she forced a weak smile. "Sure, Captain. See you then."

Visibly relieved at her response, Singh left the room.

"Your department will have resources, you know." Fraye pulled out a chair and sat down at the table.

"Resources?" Kate regarded Fraye quizzically.

"Yes. Support groups, psychiatrists, et cetera. This whole situation is going to be with you for a long time, Kate. Hell, who am I kidding? It's going to be with all of us for a long time. There's going to be constant self-recriminations. Why didn't we see it? How could we have worked so closely with him and not known..."

She took a chair across from him. "Honestly, I'm not even there yet. I'm just kind of numb all over—like the world could end right now, and I just wouldn't care."

"That's to be expected, all things considered."

"The one thing I do wish is that I could have hung with him a little longer tonight before putting the cuffs on him."

"What do you mean, 'hung with him'?"

Placing her elbows on the table, she raised her hands to support her face as she slumped forward. "I should have gotten Harding to confess. But I just... came apart when he touched me. I thought about each of those young women and I..."

Fraye reached forward and rubbed her forearm. "It's okay, Kate. You're not Wonder Woman."

"But if I had been able to get a confession..."

"Obviously a confession would have been ideal.

365

But the truth is that you were in the hands of a brutal serial killer with whom you shared a close professional relationship for almost two years. Harding was playing this game with you, Kate. And it was one-on-one."

His demeanor shifted suddenly, suspicion clouding his features. "Did you and Harding ever sleep together?"

"What?" Kate practically choked on the word.

"I asked whether you had ever slept together. His fixation on you is quite deep. Perhaps you had engaged in a physical relationship and then changed your mind?" He studied her carefully. "Yes. I think that's exactly what happened. Your rejection triggered him. It was the precipitating event that caused him to start killing again after all this time."

Kate's arms crossed over her stomach, looking like someone battling a bad case of food poisoning.

"Do you realize what kind of danger you've been in?"

Incapable of responding, Kate gawked at him. Awkward moments passed until she dropped her arms and found her voice. "Whatever danger I was in is irrelevant; I should have gotten that confession. Now he's in there with his lawyer, and we'll never get anything out of him."

"We have all we need. Besides, Harding was able to fool me too. And as many convicted men will tell you, that is not an easy undertaking. He could not have pulled it off this long if he wasn't a master strategist. There is no way he was going to confess to you. Remember what I taught you. The Tower Torturer was not killing because he had to; he was killing because he wanted to. There was no psychosis behind it. No troubled childhood—just a pure psychopath working without the limitations of guilt or empathy."

"I know. I just don't understand why he had to bring up our first case together—and the implication that we're working together somehow... that I was helping him to choose those girls..."

"It was another little game. He knew you'd be on the other side of the glass. He's still trying to rattle you."

Kate frowned deeply, her thoughts turning inward once again.

Fraye glanced around the room, his expression growing as pained as Kate's. "Don't worry. The crime lab will go through the evidence they've collected from Harding's apartment, and Kevin will study the hardware that was collected. Harding is not going to get out of this."

"Uh-huh." The two syllables offered no indication of how she felt. Her brow remained deeply furrowed.

"There is something else I'd like to talk to you about. I want you to know that..." He looked down at the table, then closed his eyes tightly. "I want you to know that even though the case is ending..." His eyes opened, fixing on hers as if unsure how to finish the sentence. "You see, I'm not normally like this when I work a case. I don't screw up this bad." He chuckled softly. "But you and I, we seem to have formed a connection—one that, despite my best efforts to the contrary, has become very distracting."

"Distracting?" Kate's lips formed around the word as if it was part of an exotic foreign language.

"What I mean is that when everything settles down, if you're interested... That is, I'd like to see you again—personally, not professionally."

He plunged ahead before she could respond. "You don't have to say anything right now. I probably should not have even brought it up. I just wanted you to understand how much you matter to me. And if I can do anything to…" His eyes sparkled with hope. "I know what will help."

Reaching into his pocket, he retrieved a ring of keys. Freeing one, he placed it on the table before her. "That's the key to my house in Napa."

She backed away, shaking her head. "No. I don't need to run away."

"Kate, you're not running away. It's the weekend, and you need to get ready mentally. Singh is correct —this is all about to get infinitely more difficult. Napa is the right choice. If you want, you can have the whole place to yourself. Go relax for the weekend. Consider it my gift to you for being such a good student throughout this process."

Whether out of sincere interest or just because she didn't have the strength to argue anymore, Kate reached for the small piece of metal. "Okay." She stared at it for a moment, before tucking it into her pocket. "But I don't know that I feel like being alone."

"I understand. I have a couple of meetings planned with the SAC of the San Francisco office tomorrow morning, but I can meet you out there around two in the afternoon. Just promise me one thing. As hard as it will be, try not to think about any of this while you're there."

▷▷▷

It was just past noon when Kate arrived in Napa. Though it had not been included in the forecast, rain had fallen steadily from a thick blanket of soggy clouds, soaking the valley floor.

She had planned on arriving sooner, but the morning hours had been consumed with pondering questions for which she had no acceptable answers.

When she'd finally glanced at the clock, she realized how right Fraye had been about getting away for a while. If she had not made plans to go to Napa, it was likely the entire weekend would have been spent in the same pointless pursuit.

Parking in front of the federal agent's home, Kate cut the engine and stared at the picturesque farmhouse. Grabbing her overnight bag from the backseat, she took a moment to brace herself before climbing out of the car and making a mad dash for the front porch.

She retrieved the key from her back pocket and opened the door. Water coursed down her cheeks as she crossed the threshold. Absently, she brushed the moisture from her face, and locked the front door. Crossing the foyer, she started up the stairs to the guest bedroom. She knew Fraye wouldn't mind if she stayed in his room, but she wasn't comfortable with the level of intimacy it implied.

Unlike the master, the guest room had not been remodeled, but its worn oak floors and tarnished brass bed created an air of historic charm. She dropped her duffle on the bed and plopped down next to it, gazing out the large picture window that looked out over the backyard and the base of the surrounding mountains. The scene was enchanting, but its beauty was lost on Kate whose thoughts were still turned firmly inward.

Singh was right. Things were not going to get any easier from here on out. The question was whether she had the strength to do what was required to see this process through to the end. Courtroom visions appeared in her mind, complete with digital crime scene images, and pieces of grisly evidence. And through it all, the Tower Torturer, Tyler Harding, would sit and watch—internally preening over his handiwork.

An unbidden chill coursed through her body, followed by a swell of nausea. Rubbing the damp sleeves of her cardigan, she stood and walked into the adjoining bathroom. To Kate's surprise, the washroom had been remodeled with espresso-colored wood floors, stark white paneling, and pewter fixtures.

The room's centerpiece was a modern replica of a claw-foot, slipper-back tub, which faced the window, offering a panoramic view of the mountains. Without thinking too long about it, she turned on the faucet and poured in bubble bath, flooding the tub with hot soapy water.

A few minutes later, she stripped out of her damp clothes and piled them on the counter. Slipping beneath the warm bubbles, she eased against the back of the tub. Miraculously, the water seemed to leech away all thoughts of her maniacal partner. They were replaced by memories of Fraye, and yesterday's awkward attempt to ask if she would consider dating him in the future.

Shaking her head, she wondered how she could have read him so wrong when they'd first met. In those early days, she had been so intimidated and frustrated by Fraye, who had seemed to think she was worthless. Now she realized he had been mentoring her—the veteran teaching the rookie, but she had allowed her ego to get in the way.

Now it was also clear that Harding had set her up for that misread—building an odd air of suspense around Fraye's arrival and casting him in a bad light from day one.

As the water cooled around her, Kate reached for the silver cross hanging from her neck. Her fingers moved across the smooth metal, as her mind skipped ahead, deciding upon the next step in her attempt to unwind.

Plucking the stopper from the drain, she watched for a minute as a tiny whirlpool formed around it, sucking the water downward. She tried to envision all of the guilt and pain she'd suffered disappearing along with it. Tearing her gaze away, Kate climbed out of the tub, dried off, then dressed in a fresh pair of jeans and a sweatshirt.

Downstairs, she headed directly to the kitchen where she poured herself a healthy glass of chardonnay. Leaning back against the counter, she lifted the glass and drank deeply. The wine slipped inside her, warming her on its trek toward her stomach. As one sip followed another, the alcohol worked its magic. After weeks of obsessing on the case, the intense barrage of thoughts and emotions was finally waning.

During her last visit, she had noted that one whole bookshelf in Fraye's office was dedicated to classic literature. Taking her glass, she headed through the short hallway, crossed the small foyer, and entered the den. Along the way her mind wandered into what had always been a forbidden path—wondering what it would be like to share a house like this with a man who cared about her.

Toward the rear of the room, bookshelves lined all three walls surrounding the desk. Stopping just inside the door, she took a moment to examine the custom display case that housed Fraye's handcuff collection.

She'd been genuinely surprised when he had explained the exhibit, never expecting him to open up about his family history or what drove him to dedicate his life to helping others. Learning about that side of him had been a huge game changer in their relationship. Intense physical attraction notwithstanding, it had been one of the major reasons she'd felt comfortable having sex with him and venturing so far afield.

A warm blush worked its way up her neck, prompted by the recollection of the set of cuffs Fraye had used on her during her last visit. Smiling, she thought about recommending that he add the velvet-lined pair to the display. But that joke, along with any type of future with the handsome agent would have to wait until things settled down.

She closed her eyes, allowing some of the more poignant scenes from that amazing tryst to shove out the guilt and pain. A sudden craving for Jane Austen prompted her eyes to open wide. She was about to turn toward the bookshelves in hunt for her quarry, when something about the display caught her attention.

Inside, the handcuffs had been arranged on small wooden blocks, which were laid out in three columns. The first was comprised of three display items, the second column contained only two. The star attraction, the original pair of handcuffs upon which the collection had been started, sat atop the only block in the third column.

The bases were spaced evenly within each column, with each row equidistant to the others. Kate's head tilted to the right, as she tried to figure out what it was about the display that had caught her interest. She placed her glass on a nearby table, then gently lifted the lid of the case, and peered in to get a closer look.

Then it hit her. The cuffs were laid out in a pattern that had become all too familiar to her over the past few weeks. The first column created a vertical line. If two diagonal lines were drawn from the first column, through the second, and joined to the terminal point at the third, it created a perfect Norse thorn.

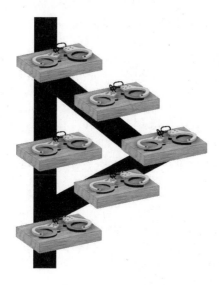

Wondering how long it might take before she stopped seeing that damn image everywhere, Kate shook her head ruefully and lowered the lid. It slipped from her hand as she lowered it, crashing down soundly. Luckily the impact had not damaged the glass. Kate leaned over to inspect the seam where the lid rested atop the case praying she had not damaged the prized possession.

The left and front sides looked fine, but when she examined the right side, she found a small piece of wood extruding just below the lip of the lid. It did not appear to be splintered or damaged in any way. The sides were smooth and even, as if they had been fabricated that way.

Whatever it was, it didn't appear to be anything she had caused. Glancing down, she realized that the odd little piece was positioned directly outside Fraye's most prized set of cuffs—the exact tip of the Norse thorn.

Spurred on by instinct, Kate bent over once again and pushed against the small extrusion. A narrow drawer shot forth from the front panel of the display case, revealing a far older pair of handcuffs, which had not fared well with the passage of time. Rust had accumulated in the joints and mottled every surface.

Lying next to the cuffs was a white plastic square with an inset black button. The little device reminded Kate of a garage door opener—an odd thing to find in a house without a garage.

She picked up the handcuffs, wincing at the coarse feel of the metal. Pursing her lips against the unpleasant sensation, she rubbed the metal between her thumb and forefinger. A few seconds later she stopped and examined her fingertips, which were now speckled with tiny flakes of rust.

Unbidden, the medical examiner's voice sounded in her head with the clarity of a digital recording—replaying every one of his prior statements about the traces of rust found in the wrists of each of the Torturer's victims.

Time seemed to stand still. It was as if every aspect of her life were grains of sand, which had been heated to form a huge wall of glass. Before her next breath, reality threw a hammer at the wall, shattering it into billions of infinitesimal particles.

It took a full fifteen seconds for the shock to wear off. Once it did, thoughts began flashing through her head like lighting, replaying the events of the last few weeks—making connections and recognizing misdirections. She grabbed the small plastic device and swiveled around the room, squeezing the button over and over again.

The moment she neared the doorway, she heard a soft hum coming from somewhere out in the house.

She ran into the hall just in time to watch a portion of the paneled wall under the staircase fall inward on hinges, moving like a door. The movement activated a sensor, which suddenly bathed the steeply descending staircase beyond in bright light.

Approaching the stairs she could see that they ended at a large metal door a full floor below.

"It's an exact replica of the room I had in Boston. Now you finally get the chance to see where Maggie, Becky, and Trudy had so much fun."

The voice pierced the silence just behind her. As she started to turn toward the sound, a sudden impact to the back of her skull made everything go dark.

Chapter 28

"KA-TE, OH KA-TE…" The melodic chant danced at the edge of Kate's consciousness.

A sudden deluge of icy water jolted her awake. Lips sputtering, she tried to shield her face from the liquid, an effort made all the more difficult by the rusty handcuffs now circling her wrists. Squinting through the cascade, she could see Fraye standing above her, holding a white plastic bucket.

"I'm glad you've decided to join us." The special agent deposited the empty receptacle on a nearby table. Just to its left was a thick branding iron, the end of which had been formed into the shape of the Norse thorn.

Kate shook like a dog, trying to rid herself of excess moisture. Recovering her senses, she sprang to her feet—or tried to. A two-and-a-half-foot length of black nylon rope had been affixed to the handcuffs, tethering her to a metal bracket mounted to the floor. She pulled at the restraint for a full minute before accepting that it would not yield.

Dropping onto her knees, she rapidly scanned the white tiled room. Her gaze settled on the chair in the center where a solitary figure sat—visible only in profile. Wrapped in a gray blanket, head completely concealed beneath a black hood, the unknown victim had been bound to the seat by thick, black nylon ropes. From the way the individual's head hung awkwardly to the side, the person was either dead or unconscious.

Tearing her gaze away, she looked past the figure to the back wall, which was covered floor to ceiling in a long row of cabinets. A video camera perched atop a tripod just in front of the woodwork. A green light shone from the top corner of the device.

To her right, two large planks of steel had been welded together in the shape of the letter "X" against the wall. The pieces had been affixed to both the tile floor and the wall with steel plates and bolts. Thick leather cuffs adorned each corner of the structure. A three-foot-tall toolbox stood to the left. A long-nosed meat saw lay on top of it. The toolbox and the structure were reflected in vivid detail in the long mirror that ran the length of the wall on her left.

Behind her was the metal door she had glimpsed from upstairs. The sight of it added a hopeless ambiance to the sterile chamber, made all the more insidious by the emerging chorus of ghost-like whispers in her mind. Memories of Becky's plaintive appeals for help played in a continuous loop, punctuated by imaginary screams from the other two victims who had been brought here because of her.

Fraye's eyes darted eagerly back and forth, visually devouring every aspect of his guest's face. "Come on! This is what you've been waiting for—to find the lair of the Tower Torturer. Don't you have anything to say?"

She turned toward him, the shock and horror rendering her mute.

When he spoke again, his voice took on an oddly hollow tone. "I've spent a long time planning this—ever since I first came across that video Maggie posted with your pathetic rant about serial killers. In that one little diatribe, you revealed almost everything I needed for a profile.

"Kate Barnes. Dedicated law officer, trying to cover up for her own inexperience. A jaded woman, harboring a borderline-compulsive desire for justice. One whose career makes her feel superior to the deviants she dragged off the streets, hiding the fact that she is no less deviant. And underneath it all? A severe guilt complex—an unhealthy belief that she is somehow responsible for making the world a better place, no matter how it has treated her. All stemming from the tragic death of her little sister and a decidedly unhealthy childhood."

"You don't know anything about me." The soft utterance lacked any real conviction.

"On the contrary, I know everything about you —including how your pussy tastes."

The debasing comment cut straight through the terror. Kate's hands tightened into fists. She leveled the special agent with a withering glare.

"Don't pretend I have offended your Victorian sensibilities. You really should thank me. I've been giving you what you need all along. And I have another present for you."

He walked toward the strange structure. "Like all of my toys, I made this myself. I've become quite the craftsman over the years, wouldn't you say?"

Gesturing with one of the few body parts that remained free from restraint, Kate inclined her head toward the hooded figure. "Who is that?" The forced bravado in her voice was not fooling anyone. Her hold on it—like that on her sanity—was tenuous at best.

"The woman who is going to give me the pleasure

of breaking you for good. After a while, I realized one might only go so far in torturing the human body, but the mind—that is a world of limitless possibilities." He glanced away, a look approaching regret etched in his face. "For a time, I had almost hoped that you could be reformed—that you might be capable of evolution."

"Evolution?"

Irritation flashed in his eyes. "Psychopaths, are merely the next stage in evolution—beings free of the limitations of primitive impulses programmed into us by society."

"Guilt, remorse and empathy are not limitations. They make us better human beings," Kate replied.

"Better? Feeling bad makes you better?"

Kate stared back at him silently for a long moment. "Just tell me who she is."

He closed the short distance between them with frightening speed. "Why so anxious to get started, Kate? Don't you want to savor the foreplay?" He reached down, fingering the metal cuffs. "I lied to you about the origins of the collection in my office. It really all started when I found these in my grandfather's barn as a little boy.

"They were manufactured in the 1880s—a marvel for their time. The designer was the first to invent the double lock system. Ironically his name was John Tower. Funny, isn't it? The nickname, Tower Torturer, suits me in more ways than one."

"Fraye, this is between you and me. Let her go."

"No. She will be an instrument, the harbinger of more pain than you could ever imagine. This time you won't just see the result of my work—you'll get to be here to experience it with me."

Returning to the chair, the special agent gently

laid his hand on the top of the woman's head and turned to look at Kate. "I can't tell you how entertaining it's been to watch you suffer. But this..." He stared pointedly at the hood beneath his fingers.

"Playing with you has been much more fun than anything I've ever done. Your anguish has been almost palpable at times. Especially last night—when you turned on poor Harding."

The detective flinched at the mention of her partner's name.

"I tried to tell you he was trustworthy, but you didn't want to listen. So now he is languishing in jail, waiting to be convicted for my crimes."

Kate squeezed her eyelids shut—a meager attempt to block out the reality of his words.

"It really is a shame you didn't trust him. He could have helped you. And we both know how much he cared about you. But you insist on keeping people at arm's length."

She opened her eyes, just in time to see the head beneath his hand begin to roll slowly upward.

"Are you sure you haven't figured out who is under here yet?"

Kate's lower lip trembled. Unable to speak, she shook her head.

"I really am disappointed. Especially after I went to the trouble of downloading a special app that made it look like the text I sent her came from your phone.

"And today... just for you, Kate... I'm going to do something I've never done before. You know, the Norse people were amazingly ingenious. Their runes and mythology have always captivated me—hence the nifty Norse thorn I use as my signature. In keeping with the theme, your friend will be given the blood eagle."

Recognition flashed in the detective's eyes, sparking another bout of wild thrashing. Heedless of the pain in her wrists, she begged, "No! God, no!! Fraye, please! Not that!"

His tone grew reverent. "The blood eagle is a form of torture that borders on an art form. The goal is to transform the victim into a bloody eagle by freeing its own set of wings for the world to see."

Striding purposefully to the steel construct, he proceeded to explain. "I will strap her in face-first, exposing her back. Using the saw, I will cut into her back next to the spine, carving through her ribs. Then I will pull them outward, reach into the opening, and pull out her lungs so that they can hang freely against her back. They will hang there like bloody eagle's wings—a rare and beautiful sight.

"The trick is to keep her from dying of shock before we're finished. I'll have to move fast because there will be a lot of blood, and we don't want her to bleed out before I've had a chance to pour salt on her lungs.

"And just to make sure we're ready..." Turning to the large toolbox, he lifted the saw, pausing to plug it into a nearby wall socket. He depressed the power button, and the device vibrated to life, issuing a high-pitched whine that echoed deafeningly throughout the room. The sound sparked a series of involuntary tremors that violently wracked Kate's body.

Fraye turned off the saw and placed it back on the box with brisk efficiency.

"And after she's dead?" Kate uttered between the tremors. "Then what?"

"Then you and I will have our own brand of fun."

She raised her chin. "They will come looking for me."

"And I will tell them that you were here and left. Your car will be found at the foot of the cliffs along Highway 1. The crash and ensuing fire will remove all evidence of our time together. A tragic, but under-standable, ending considering everything you've been through.

The hooded figure moved again, drawing Fraye's attention. He walked over and stood next to the chair, posing his hand a few inches above the woman's head. "I guess I can't prolong the suspense anymore. Too bad she's not a blonde, but I guess you can't always have a perfect set. Anyway, look who I brought all the way up here for you…"

He snatched off the hood, revealing a beautiful woman whose brown eyes squinted against the sudden brightness. Realizing she was bound, she pulled franti-cally at the ropes. The thick gag tied around her mouth dampened her hysterical screams to high-pitched whines.

Kate briefly observed Maria Torres struggling before turning her gaze toward the far wall.

"Please, Detective Barnes. Don't try to pretend this doesn't bother you. I've known about your little friendship with the reporter for quite a while now."

Maria's movements had slowed to a halt during the exchange. Fraye yanked the gag from her mouth, then paused and turned back toward the table. Pick-ing up a ten-inch, wickedly sharp blade, he gestured toward the reporter.

"Ms. Torres, you are about to join a very elite club of victims. But first you must be initiated with the Norse thorn."

Maria eyes flew open wide. She looked frantically from Kate to their captor and back again. In two strides he was at the reporter's side, grasping her chin with brutal force. Before Kate could protest, the knife flashed, carving a scarlet trench down the right side of Maria's face. A second of pregnant silence passed before the reporter's screams pealed through the room.

Horrified, Kate watched as Fraye deftly slashed a short diagonal line, which intersected with the first. Blood welled up from both wounds, flowing freely onto the gray blanket where it left a sickening stain upon the fabric. Maria's tortured screams echoed through the tiled chamber and continued for a full two minutes, during which time the special agent stood unperturbed—observing his victim.

Watching the savage scene play out before her, Kate's emotions rose and fell precipitously. With the first slice, she'd felt horror laced with a lethal dose of guilt. Yet as the special agent regarded his prey, an odd calmness had stolen over her. In the ensuing moment of clarity the question before her was clear— would she be a victim or a cop? There was no changing the fact that she had failed her sister, or that she had failed Fraye's other victims. But Maria wasn't dead yet; there was still a chance to help her.

Fraye turned toward Kate, raising his voice to be heard over the din. "What's the matter—feeling left out? Don't worry, you'll join the club, next. I just have one more cut to make."

Bound as she was, Kate could not rely on her hands or her legs. Her mind flew ahead looking for solutions to the seemingly impossible problem. The answer came from the most unlikely of places—a memory from her childhood. A saying she and her sister had clung to throughout the darkest days echoed in her mind—the times when things seem impossible, are the times when you need faith the most.

While Fraye completed his task, Kate dropped her neck to her chest. She pursed her lips, pressing the thin silver chain of her sister's necklace against her skin. Drawing her lips inward, she maneuvered her tongue against the cold, metallic strand, gathering as much of it as possible into her mouth.

As the piercing volume of the reporter's cries melted into a weak stream of gravely moans, Fraye approached Kate once again. The detective's gaze snapped upward. The only indication she was remotely aware of the severity of her friend's torment was the growing pool of tears nestled in the corners of her eyes.

Satisfaction blossomed across Fraye's features. He dropped slowly onto one knee before her. Reaching out with his left hand, he ran the tip of his index finger against the line of her jaw. "It's your turn to join the club."

Time slowed to a crawl. The iron laden scent of fresh blood filled Kate's senses. Her chest pounded as if her heart would erupt at any second.

Now! Kate dove forward, throwing her head back and slamming her chin upward toward his brow. Her pulse roared in her ears, as she bared her teeth. A pinpoint of light reflected off the tip of the object clenched firmly between them—her sister's silver cross.

The pendant's spiked end sunk deep, impaling Fraye's right eyeball. Blood and fluid erupted into Kate's mouth. Undeterred, she latched onto the damaged organ like a suckling pup.

Screeching, the special agent jerked backward. But most of his eye stayed behind. The knife fell from his hand, clattering against the floor.

Kate spat out the cross and its grisly ornament.

Yanking the pendant free from its chain, she threw it to the floor.

"You bitch! You fucking bitch! What did you do to me?" The wounded agent stumbled toward the mirror along the far wall, toppling the table on his way.

"Nothing you didn't deserve." She stomped her foot on the floor, squashing Fraye's oculus beneath it. Her eyes were already scanning the floor, fixing on the abandoned blade. It lay three feet beyond her reach. She searched the room. There had to be something...

Fraye surveyed the damage with his one good eye. Horrified by his gruesome visage, he roared, "Crazy, fucking whore! I'll tear your pussy apart with a barbed wire dildo!"

Threats were useless without a weapon. The knife—where had he dropped it? He wheeled around.

On the floor—mere feet away. And Kate?

She was sitting on her heels, frantically working on the handcuffs. The sullied cross was gripped between her trembling fingers, its point buried inside the rusty lock.

Fraye flew across the room and snatched up the blade. In another few steps he was beside her.

The lock wasn't budging. She'd run out of time.

Kneeling down, he grabbed a wad of Kate's hair. Yanking her head toward him, he growled, "Let's start with an eye for an eye!"

Fraye raised the knife above his head like an ancient Incan priest preparing for sacrifice. He was too slow.

The iron brand, freed from its hiding place between Kate's legs, swung through the air. The bludgeon slammed into the side of the agent's head.

He toppled over, sprawling unconscious across the floor.

Laying the brand down, Kate bent over and pulled the knife from his hand. Seconds later, she was free from the tether.

Hurrying to Maria's side, she cut through each of the four restraints. Maria rose unsteadily from the chair. Seemingly immune to the bloody deluge flowing from her face, she walked over to the fallen agent. Retrieving the brand from the floor she pulled it back over her head.

Kate caught the reporter's wrist in midair. "No! Not like this."

"I have to kill the bastard! For Gayle!" Maria's tone flirted with hysteria.

"No. Don't you see? That's exactly what he wants —a quick death."

"But he deserves it, don't you see? He…"

"I know, but if you kill him, you won't be able to come back from it." The truth of the warning was evident in the reporter's anguished expression. A moment later, one corner of Kate's mouth slowly crept upward. "But I have an idea…"

As Kate explained her vision, a disturbing smile crept across Maria's face.

Chapter 29

April 12

KATE FOLLOWED THE GUARD down the long corridor. Along the wall to her left were a series of small windows, which admitted weak rays of sunlight. The illumination did little to alleviate the harsh sterility of the passageway.

Arriving at the end of the hall, her escort paused and flashed a badge in front of the plastic white panel mounted near the door handle. Glancing up at the small black camera mounted above the door, he waved curtly.

A metallic click reverberated from somewhere inside the door. As if by magic, it began to swing outward on its hinges. The officer grabbed the handle, gesturing for Kate to precede him into the next room.

Having barely crossed the threshold, the detective spun on her heel and fixed the officer with a dry look. "I can take it from here."

"Sorry Detective Barnes, but I'm…"

"I'll knock on the door when I need you."

Kate waited until she heard the metal click before turning around to take in her new surroundings. The room was relatively large, allowing ample space around the single prison cell, which stood alone in its center.

This was the special cell—the one reserved for the hard cases who could not be included with the general population. And the cell's current occupant was as much of a special case as you could get. Not only would all the rest of the prison's inmates be chomping at the bit to get at an FBI agent, but there would be additional street cred for taking down the infamous Tower Torturer.

Benjamin Fraye lounged on the single bed, reading a book. He had not bothered to look up since her arrival. Despite the prison jumpsuit and mean conditions, he still exuded an air of confidence.

Kate's eyes narrowed as she regarded him. It had been two months since she had returned from the special agent's house of horrors. That first day had been dedicated to debriefing sessions. Captain Singh, the District Attorney, and the SAC of the San Francisco FBI Field Office had been waiting for her in the conference room.

The District Attorney had been focusing on smaller details which Kate herself had not yet considered—such as how Fraye had posted the first YouTube video when he had been with Kate and Harding interviewing Anna Hammonds at the time.

Her explanation had been simple enough. She had recalled having been interrupted by Fraye's cell phone and watching him step out to take the call. As to Jonas Riley having posted to Maggie's memorial page the night after Trudy's abduction, the Special Agent must have made the post, having seen the list of passwords Riley had kept in his laptop.

They were relevant questions, but minor details compared with the overwhelming evidence they'd uncovered at Fraye's house. In a safe concealed behind the cabinets in the basement, the crime scene technicians had found the driver's licenses of every one of the Tower Torturer's known victims. Unfortunately, they also uncovered twenty additional licenses belonging to other missing women.

In the same safe, they had uncovered an independent hard drive, which housed a variety of videos. Featuring the special agent, they captured the horror he had inflicted on his victims in disturbing detail—relegating his taped interrogation to the final punctuation on a treatise on atrocities.

They'd accepted much of her story, but had peppered her with a barrage of difficult questions about the nature of Fraye's injuries. The details explaining the damage to Fraye's eye were accepted without question, as had her explanation about knocking him out with the branding iron.

Though they hadn't said it, she felt they had been impressed when she'd explained how she had spied the iron on the floor where it had fallen after Fraye knocked the table over. She had slid it between her legs and sat down on her haunches to conceal it from him. Trying to open the handcuffs with the cross had been a simple ruse to draw him close.

The other damage was a bit hard to swallow—even for a room of hardened members of law enforcement. As the hours had dragged on, she had remained impassive, never allowing exhaustion or frustration to shake her. After all these weeks, she could almost feel Singh's eyes boring into hers as he'd demanded answers.

Internal Affairs had shown up the second day. The jaded, balding investigator seemed even less convinced than her previous audience, but she'd stuck to her story. On the third day, she'd been ordered to meet with the department's psychiatrist, Dr. Wissel.

Banishing the memories from her mind, Kate walked over to the left where a plastic chair stood against the wall. Carrying it to the cell, she positioned it directly across from Fraye. Wordlessly, she sat down and waited.

After a full minute, he sighed and looked up. The sunlight from a nearby window illuminated every feature of his face. Ignoring the discreet black patch over his right eye, Kate studied the other prominent addition to his appearance. The last time she had seen him, Maria's handiwork had been obscured by copious amounts of blood. Her breath caught in her throat as she realized that Maria's act of vengeance had been beautifully executed.

After explaining her vision, Kate had removed her handcuffs, then helped Maria secure Fraye to the chair. She had handed Maria the knife and gone upstairs in search of a phone. Before leaving the room, she'd been careful to close the door to ensure Fraye's screams would not be heard by the 911 dispatcher.

While Fraye had carved the Norse thorn into Maria's cheek, the reporter had chosen a much larger canvass upon which to reciprocate. The sunlight revealed every nuance in stark detail.

A thick vertical line of mottled purple and white scar tissue trailed from Fraye's hairline, down over his forehead, alongside his nose, through his lips to the end of his chin. A diagonal line intersected the first just above the bridge of his nose, and crossed his face, running down below the eye patch, and terminating just below his cheekbone. There, it intersected with a third line, which ran diagonally down through his upper lip, and connected with the main vertical line just below his lower lip.

He stared at her, as if the only thing marring his once handsome face was a small nick from shaving. "Katherine Barnes. You came here to my cell rather than meet me in an interview room, which would have been neutral territory. Do these metal bars give you an illusion of safety?"

Her left eyebrow rose skyward. "Still trying to profile me?"

"What can I say? It's a talent. Why are you here, Detective?"

Dropping her gaze to the floor, Kate considered the question. Her mind, slipped back to the mandatory psych sessions she'd been enduring for the past two months. She had done so reluctantly, tolerating the head shrink's intrusions into unwanted territory—dissecting her emotions concerning the victims, the nature of her physical relationship with Fraye, and even probing into her childhood.

It had been a painful process, but the doctor had only gone as far as Kate had allowed him to go. Meanwhile, Maria Torres had remained adamant about taking sole responsibility for torturing Fraye. While Singh and everyone else (including her partner) thought there was more to the story, the consensus was to let it go for the sake of media relations. Two weeks ago, Internal Affairs formally closed their investigation. Kate was officially the hero of the story. The FBI had even gone so far as to offer her a job.

Dr. Wissel had eventually cleared her for duty, with the caveat that she continue to see him once a week. There was no telling what the good doctor might have thought about Kate's decision to come here today.

She fixed her gaze back on Fraye. "I've been struggling with something for a while."

"Mmm, you struggling—it happens to be one of my favorite fantasies."

"I've been second-guessing my decision to keep you alive. I can't sleep at night because I wish I'd had the guts to end you in that room."

Rising from the bed with feline grace, Fraye took a step toward her then veered to the cell wall to her right. Leaning back against the bars, he observed her from the corner of his eye. When he spoke, there was a slight lilt in his tone—hinting the reins controlling his emotions might be pulled tighter than normal. "As I've said before, you and I are more alike than you wish to believe."

"You know what Ben?" She watched as his jaw tightened at the use of his given name before continuing. "I think you were right—about a lot of things."

Intrigued, he turned to face her. Glimpsing the sincerity in her eyes he drew closer, step-by-step, until he stood just a foot and a half from where she sat.

Fearlessly, she stood and moved toward the bars, bringing herself within easy reach of his hands.

"Really? I've told you that psychopaths are the next step in evolution. But you think of me as a flawed mutation. Is that what you are, Kate? A flawed mutation?" His eyes probed hers relentlessly.

"I believe you were right about a lot of things—but not everything."

A slight droop in his eyelid betrayed his disappointment. "So how are we alike then?" he challenged.

"You enjoy capturing and torturing people." She held his gaze for another moment before continuing. "But you only do it over a period of days, and you do it for your own personal amusement. Me, on the other hand, I want your pain to last a lot longer. I used to think the justice system was a sham because of all of the wasted time and politics, but now I realize it is the best possible system for what you deserve—because it is so agonizingly slow."

His mouth split into a wide grin. "Come now, Kate. You don't really think I will ever have to pay for this, do you? You know how the public feels about executing the mentally ill."

"You are a psychopath. You do not suffer from a mental illness. There are many people like you in the world and they don't choose to torture and murder."

"Every psychopath has different tastes. Some of us just want to climb the corporate ladder, to enjoy crushing all the little people they step on along the way. Others choose to be conartists, bilking the opposite sex out of their life savings and their will to live. Either way, the average civilian who sits on a jury is not going to understand the difference.

"They will hear psychopaths have no guilt or remorse, no ability to empathize," Fraye continued. "And do you know what their little minds will do? They will shut down—they will refuse to accept that such a creature exists. They will assume I must be mentally ill because I don't have the ability for any of those things—poor me."

"You are not ill. You have the choice about whether to commit acts of violence, just like everyone else."

"Just like you, Kate?"

"Yes, just like me. But after much soul searching, I finally realized that getting violent with you was never the answer. Like you said, physical torture is nowhere near as gratifying as mental torture. I started with that silly little symbol on your face and I'm going to enjoy the game from here on out Ben.

"Since you're not privy to the goings on in the

outside world, I'm happy to tell you that every TV station, social media site and lunchroom is ripping you to shreds. Since your arrest, tons of studies have come out exposing how effective psychopaths are at manipulating the mental health system. There isn't one credible professional who will be willing to risk looking like they are your pawn. You won't be able to plead mental defect no matter how hard you try."

"I sincerely doubt that to be true Kate. Besides, at the very least I will avoid the death penalty. Though it's still on the books in California and Massachusetts, both states have become too liberal to enforce it. Worst case, if by some odd fluke I get a life sentence, I intend to spend my days in more intellectual pursuits." He gestured toward the book lying on the bed. "The literary world is full of materials that suit my tastes."

"Oh, what a shame! I guess your lawyer hasn't told you yet." She opened her eyes wide with mock sympathy. "Emily Ravens. She was one of the girls we didn't know about—one of the ones we saw on your video collection. You remember her, right?" Kate posed the question as if she were referring to a long lost friend from high school.

Looking suddenly and entirely bored, Fraye turned away and walked back to the bed. Picking up his book, he carefully lowered himself and began to read.

Undeterred by the obvious attempt at dismissal, Kate pushed ahead. "She was from Mississippi. You were down there on assignment for four months in 2009. You abducted her while she was jogging and tortured her in an old barn on a property adjacent to one where you had conducted a sting operation three months before.

"I contacted your old partner and showed him the

video. He remembered the barn. We dug up almost every square inch of that property before we finally discovered Emily's body at the western edge. Funny thing about that property—the state line runs right through it. I guess you didn't realize that you actually murdered and buried her in Alabama."

Fraye's lips compressed tightly. He looked up from his book, staring blankly into the distance.

"California and Massachusetts may be blue states, but Alabama is very, very red. Did you know they hand down the death penalty more often there than any other state in the union? They even have a special judicial override allowing judges to overrule a life in prison sentence and change it to capital execution. Apparently it's something they do quite a lot down there. You might say that state is a veritable killing machine. And guess what? They still offer the electric chair. It would be a much better way for the Tower Torturer to go out than a measly lethal injection.

"The paperwork to extradite you to Alabama is already in the works." A genuine smile formed on her lips. "It will be a long road between the trial and the inevitable appeals. The best part is the certainty that you will be executed and you will know that I am the reason for it. Until then, every time you look in a mirror you'll remember that I won and you lost."

Fraye's grip on the book had tightened with each successive word. His knuckles strained against his skin and the paper puckered around his fingers. In all other respects, he remained unimpressed.

She went to the door, her fist poised to rap upon it. Pausing, she turned back to the ex-special agent. "Maybe Maggie was right to post that video of me after all. In hindsight, it was rather prophetic, don't you think?"

Without waiting for an answer, she knocked loudly upon the door. It opened instantly. Kate pushed past the guard as she exited.

Harding was waiting for her in the parking lot, seated on the hood of his car. "Feel better?"

She shook her head. "Maybe I'll feel better after he's executed, maybe not. Either way, I've had enough."

"You're quitting?"

"Call it an early retirement."

"Kate... What about the offer from the FBI?"

"I declined. My nerves are fried and I haven't had a peaceful night's sleep since all this started."

"So take some time off, get your head clear. But don't make a rash decision."

"The shrink equates this to post traumatic stress; he said I need to focus my energy on putting some things to rest. I'm not going to heal by accepting another tour of duty."

"What things? And what about us?"

She smiled back at him—something approaching regret pulled tightly at the corners of her mouth. Before he could press for an answer, she kissed him. "Good-bye, Tyler."

Turning on her heel, Kate strode to her car. Her suitcases were in the trunk, her plane ticket folded in her purse. The private detective she'd hired had given her the name of a small town in Washington state.

She'd be expected back for the trial, but for now she planned to make a home up north. She had been a victim of the past for too long—not anymore. Starting the car, she smiled to herself. For the first time in her life, she was going to start taking care of herself.

The Kate Barnes story
continues in

DARK OBSESSIONS

A special sneak peak starts
on the next page.

Kate Barnes returns in.. **DARK OBSESSIONS**

Intermittent rustling sounds accompanied the man as he trampled the broken branches, fallen leaves and other bits of detritus, which carpeted the forest floor. A thin blade of light sliced through the darkness as he swung his flashlight from left to right.

He hadn't planned on tracking tonight. Wearing jeans, a charcoal gray hoodie and a black baseball cap, he certainly wasn't dressed for it. Typically, he preferred to pursue his quarry during the daylight hours. Tonight he was after something much higher on the evolutionary ladder than deer.

Sweeping the light up and across the branches of a nearby tree, he searched intently for clues. After a moment, he cut the beam back across a lower branch whose edge hung at a forty-five degree angle. Within seconds he descended upon it, seizing hold of the fractured limb. He stroked his thumb over the moist yellowish pulp, which lay exposed beneath the bark. Satisfied the damage was fresh, he straightened and started off in the direction of the break.

He picked up his pace, confident that she was nearby. The certainty was undermined by a raging frustration, which had accompanied him since the start of the journey. Emotional control was paramount. He couldn't afford any distractions. The goal was to get the little bitch back in her cage as soon as possible.

Upon learning of her escape he hadn't bothered to change into hunting attire. He had figured she had about ten minutes on him, so he had only paused to grab the essentials. While her bare feet would likely slow her progress, he didn't have one second to spare.

A crunching sound off to his left brought him to a sudden halt. His nerves burned with anticipation. She was so close now that he could feel it.

With Zen-like patience he remained motionless for a full six minutes before his prey finally broke cover and fled frantically into the forest. Breaking into a sprint, he dashed into the darkness behind her. She made a glorious run of it—leaping over fallen logs and ducking under branches. Age and size gave her an advantage in the dense woods, but his flashlight made up for it in the end.

Just as he feared losing sight of her, she darted around a massive pine, then seemed to hang frozen in the air ahead of him. Suddenly she dropped out of view amid a cacophony of rustling and grunting.

Approaching her location, he slowed and flashed the light across the ground. The beam illuminated a steep, six-foot drop. Huddled face down and mewling at the base of the steep hill, his prey appeared to be stunned. He scrambled down next to her, the commotion compelling her to struggle to find her feet again.

"Oh, no you don't!"

The command didn't stop her, but his weapon did. A static crackle filled the air just as she fell into a paroxysm. When she hit the ground, he depressed the trigger once more on the Taser. A grin of satisfaction spread across his dark countenance as he watched her body seize once again.

Yanking the barbed electrodes from her skin, he thrust the gun securely back into the holster at his waist. He regarded her critically for a moment, noting the scantily clad, pale form covered in mud and bruises.

Reaching over, he gently brushed the dark hair from her deeply furrowed brow. Her delicate Asian features seemed permanently carved by excessive physical torment. On some abstract level it seemed a shame to him that one so young should have experienced such pain. But in the grand scheme of things, these shots from the Taser were the least of what the young teen had and would experience.

He bound her wrists and ankles with zip ties, then hefted her up and over his shoulder. As he made his way through the forest, he solidified his plans for her punishment. In the end, it would exceed any torment she had heretofore endured.

Marie Sutro is a native of the San Francisco Bay Area and a member of Sisters in Crime. A proponent of adult literacy, she volunteers with California Library Literacy Services, helping adults improve their reading and writing skills. Her great-grandfather, grandfather and father, all served in the San Francisco Police Department; collectively inspiring her debut novel. She currently resides in Northern California.

For more information about Marie, visit her website at www.mariesutro.com. She loves hearing from her readers and may be reached through via email at mariesutro@mariesutro.com, or through Twitter, Facebook or Instagram.